The Storm Girl

KATHLEEN MCGURL

HQ
An imprint of HarperCollins*Publishers* Ltd
1 London Bridge Street
London SE1 9GF

www.harpercollins.co.uk

HarperCollins*Publishers*
1st Floor, Watermarque Building, Ringsend Road
Dublin 4, Ireland

This paperback edition 2022

1
First published in Great Britain by
HQ, an imprint of HarperCollins*Publishers* Ltd 2022

Copyright © Kathleen McGurl 2022

Kathleen McGurl asserts the moral right to be
identified as the author of this work.
A catalogue record for this book is
available from the British Library.

ISBN: 9780008480868

MIX
Paper from
responsible sources
FSC™ C007454

For Juliet, Mick, Jan and Dave
– my Mudeford pals

Five and twenty ponies
Trotting through the dark
Brandy for the parson
'Baccy for the clerk
Them that asks no questions
Isn't told a lie
Watch the wall, my darling,
While the Gentlemen go by!

– 'A Smuggler's Song' by Rudyard Kipling

Prologue – 1784

He'd done what he'd promised – he'd warned them of an imminent raid by unfriendly Customs officers. He'd seen the Revenue men coming down the road from Christchurch with a band of militia, and had run to the pub to warn Esther. She would have time to hide everything that she needed to. He felt good. He cared so much for Esther – more than she knew, and all he wanted was for her to be safe.

He headed away from the inn, back towards Christchurch, taking the path that led around the edge of the marsh. Along the way he stopped to smoke a pipe, sitting on a fallen tree that was tucked out of sight just off the path. Rain was still falling, though easing off now. Even in this weather the marsh and harbour held a beauty of their own. It was a good place to live. It'd be better still when he was married to Esther.

And then he heard something that made his heart pound. The militia and Customs men had left the pub but had not gone far. They were on the path behind him.

'She's hiding something, I'm sure of it. Give her five minutes and we'll go back. She won't be expecting that, and she'll have let down her guard,' a gruff voice said.

'Ha! We'll have her. Thinking she can outwit us – she'll have to think again, eh?' Another man laughed cruelly.

He had to go back; he had to warn Esther the militia were returning. And he had to go back without them seeing him. Thankfully there was a way – the secret way, which only a handful of people knew about. He could get into the inn by that route and warn her. There was no time to spare. As quietly and quickly as he could, he made his way across the marsh to the secret entrance.

Chapter 1 – Present day

It all started, I suppose, when my cat had her kittens. How it escalated from there into a tale of smuggling, betrayal and murder is a long story.

I'd only recently moved in, to my dream house – or at least it would be my dream house, once I'd renovated it – when I realised Mir was pregnant. She's a lovely little cat – a tabby, petite and very friendly. At barely a year old she was young to be pregnant, but what can you do? Anyway, as her time grew near, I placed a few boxes lined with old towels around the house so she'd have a choice of labour wards and would hopefully spare my bed. It worked – she had her kittens in a box I'd put in the kitchen, near her food bowl. Just three in the litter – two were tabby and white, and the third slightly gingery in colouring. All healthy.

And then, when they were four days old, Mir decided to move her kittens. According to my book on caring for cats and kittens, this is quite common behaviour. The mother cat's instincts make her want to hide the kittens somewhere away from where they were born. I'd left the boxes around to give her some options, but she declined all those, and chose the most awkward place imaginable.

I had just discovered where she was, when the doorbell rang.

I ran to answer it, feeling flustered, not wanting to leave Mir and the kittens where they were but honestly not having much choice for the moment.

On the doorstep was a tall man perhaps a little older than me, in his thirties, with medium-brown hair and an attractive smile. He held out his hand to shake. 'Nick Marshall, from Marshall Construction. You must be Mrs Galton? You asked me to come and quote for some building work?'

I had forgotten I'd arranged for another builder to come round to look at the work I wanted doing. I'd already had one good quote, from Seaway Renovations, but it's always wise to get a few quotes and compare. Well, I hadn't totally forgotten – just the panic I'd been in that morning as I searched for Mir and the kittens had put it right out of my head.

'Yes, thanks. Call me Millie, though, please.' Since splitting up with Steve I found I didn't like being called Mrs Galton anymore. I was debating reverting to my maiden name of Sedgewick but I'd never much liked that surname and changing it once had been enough of a hassle. 'Come through. I'll show you what needs doing.'

He followed me through the small hallway and into the sitting room at the back of the house. I glanced over to the bricked-up chimney breast, and couldn't help myself from blurting it all out. 'I'm a bit distracted, Mr Marshall, sorry. My cat's taken her kittens through there. I can't reach them, and they can't stay there.'

'Where? And please, call me Nick.'

I bent down to show him. The fireplace had been closed up at some stage in the house's history, with a plastic grid embedded to provide some ventilation. The grid was broken, and Mir had somehow squeezed herself and her kittens in through it. Using my phone as a torch, I could see her curled up in the furthest corner with the kittens neatly in a row, suckling. It was a large fireplace and my arms were not long enough to reach them to pull them out. 'There. Can you see them?'

4

'Ha! Yes. My word, that is really not very convenient, is it?'

'It certainly isn't.'

'OK, so I have a few tools in the car. Not everything but I think I can fix this.' Without waiting for an answer Nick went out to his car, parked on Stanpit just in front of my house. He was back in a moment carrying a blue canvas tool bag, which he dumped down in front of the chimney breast. Pulling out a large screwdriver he began trying to take out the rusted screws that held the grid in place.

I wished I'd thought of that. Somewhere in the garage I had a box of tools. Not many – Steve had kept most of our joint tool collection. But he'd sorted me out a 'starter kit' as he'd called it. 'So you can do the basics,' he'd said, with a sad smile.

Nick grunted. 'Arrgh. Screws are so rusted. And this one's lost its slot – as though someone's tried to remove it before and the screwdriver's slipped. I can crowbar the grid off, but it might mean some of the surrounding plaster breaks away.'

'That's OK. I'm thinking of opening up that fireplace anyway.'

Nick nodded. 'OK, then.' He pulled out a crowbar and rammed it behind the grid, levering it outwards. As he'd predicted, some plasterwork around the edge of the hole crumbled away, sending a cloud of dust into the air. With the grid off, there was more space to reach into the fireplace.

'Thank you, I think I can get them now. Can you shine the torch while I reach in …' I crouched down and put my whole arm and shoulder into the hole, and could just reach the animals. Should I grab Mir first or the kittens? The kittens, I thought. If I got them out, she'd follow.

With Nick leaning over me angling the phone's light inside, I got one kitten out, transferred it to my other hand and picked up the second, which Nick took from me. As I grabbed the third Mir decided to assert her authority. I was holding the kitten around its tummy, and she grabbed it by the scruff of its neck. A tug of war ensued. 'Bugger!' I exclaimed.

5

'What's wrong?' There was not enough space for Nick to see what was going on.

'We're having a bit of a tussle over the third kitten.' I let go, extracted my arm and took the two kittens we'd retrieved, placing them into one of the prepared boxes. Mir then, as I'd hoped, came out from the fireplace to see where they were, and I was able to quickly reach in and remove the third kitten. 'Come on, girl. Here they are, look. All safe and sound and believe me, this is a much better place for them.' I put the third kitten with the other two and watched while Mir sniffed and licked them, checking all was well, and then with a glare at me settled down in the box to feed them.

Nick was standing, hands in pockets, grinning. 'The things you do in this job. I've never before had to rescue kittens from a fireplace.'

'Thanks so much,' I said, grinning back at him.

He knelt down again and switched his phone torch on once more, inspecting the inside of the fireplace. 'So you want to open this up? It's huge – almost an inglenook. It'll make a real feature in this room.'

'Wonder why someone closed it off?'

'Maybe too draughty. It's probably too large to work well as a fireplace. Hmm, that's interesting.'

'What?'

'It looks like … hold on …' He reached in, as I had done, his whole arm and shoulder. It looked as though he was groping around at the back. 'No, can't quite reach. Well, I guess when we knock this brickwork out we'll be able to see.'

I suppressed a smile at the way he'd said 'we'. I hadn't even talked through what I wanted done on the house yet, nor had he quoted. And I was fairly certain I'd use Seaway Renovations, as their quote had been very reasonable. Yet I liked Nick, already, and not just because he'd helped out with Mir and the kittens. 'So tell me – what did you spot in there?'

He shrugged. 'Not sure. Looks like there's some sort of metal backplate to the fireplace. Which is odd. Anyway, as I said, we'll see.' As though realising the assumption he was making that I was going to employ him, he blushed a little. 'I mean, when you open up the fireplace, whoever does it, you'll see then.'

I smiled. 'Right, I should talk you through all the work, I guess. Come on, let me give you a tour. I only moved in a couple of weeks ago, and this place looks as though it hasn't been updated since the Seventies. But I fell in love with it as soon as I saw it.'

'It certainly has potential. Right then, lead the way.'

I'd first seen the house four months earlier. I'd not been in the best state at the time. Steve and I had decided to separate – actually we'd been drifting apart for a long time, but somehow we hadn't wanted to admit it was over. Besides, neither of us could afford to move out and pay rent.

But then Mum died. That brought it home to me that I needed to move on. You only get one life to live, after all. We had a long, tearful conversation and agreed to call it a day. Mum had left me a big wodge of money, and it meant that I could afford to start looking for my own house. We put our marital home on the market too, and Mum's money plus my share of that meant I had a reasonably large deposit. Just as well, as my salary wouldn't allow for too big a mortgage.

I can't remember how many houses I looked at online, or even how many I trudged round in the company of an estate agent. Far too many. And none felt right – too big, too small, too modern, too ugly, in the wrong location.

Until this one. This eighteenth-century cottage whose front door opened directly onto the pavement. This crumbling stone building, with mossy roof tiles and cracked rendering, with an archway that once would have provided access for horses and carts to the back yard, around which were a few outbuildings including a garage. This rambling ruin with its overgrown garden backing onto the marsh, its Sixties kitchen and bathroom, its peeling wallpaper and rotting carpets. The previous owner – an old man – had lived in it for many years on his own. After he died his family had just left the house empty for a couple of years before finally putting it on the market. And then no one had wanted to buy it, given its condition. Until I saw it, and somehow, it spoke to me. There was potential in that big back room, with its view across the marsh to Christchurch Harbour. There was charm in the wonky roof line and low ceilings. There was history in this house; it had a past and I wanted to give it a future.

I'd wanted a new start. I'd wanted to build myself a new life. Why not give this old cottage a new life too – we could be rebuilt together.

Nick made a few notes as we walked around the house, nodding at my ideas, suggesting a few of his own, tapping on walls to see if they were solid or just studwork, peering at the view out of the upstairs windows. 'You could knock through here, make this small room into an en-suite bathroom to that big bedroom at the back,' he said. 'And then open up this landing a little – that bit of wall isn't really doing anything. You'll get light to it from the window on the stairs, then. And what's the attic like – can I take a look?'

I hadn't been up there myself, but I had a stepladder in the garage, and Nick was able to get up using that. 'Needs insulation, and then it could be boarded as storage. You've got a few roof tiles missing. Chimney looks sound from here.'

I was warming to Nick. He seemed to know what he was talking about. But I was worried about the quote – he'd already suggested a lot more work needed to be done than Seaway had included.

'If you're worried about the cost, we can probably split the work into essentials and non-essentials,' Nick said as he climbed down from the loft, as though he'd read my mind. 'Do the essentials

– repairing the fabric of the house and giving yourself a couple of decent rooms to live in – first. Pick off the rest bit by bit. Doesn't all have to be done at once.'

'I like that idea.'

'So what I'll do, is give you an itemised quote, and mark the things you really need to get done sooner rather than later. Millie, I'll be honest, I'd absolutely love to work on this house for you. We get a lot of jobs building extensions onto 1980s houses, or converting bungalow lofts into bedrooms. I'd love to be working on an older house, especially one where the owner wants to be as sympathetic to its history as you do. That fireplace … Anyway, it'll take me a few days to get the quote sorted out. In the meantime, if you've anything more you want to discuss, here's my card. Ring me any time.' He smiled, and I noticed how one side of his mouth went up a little more than the other. A quirk that made the smile seem even warmer, more genuine, than it obviously was.

'That sounds perfect. Being honest back, I've already had one decent quote for the work but I wanted others for comparison. I'm definitely impressed by you, but you understand …'

'Of course. You're right to get a few builders in to look at it. They'll all have different thoughts as well, which might help you have more ideas. Well, I'll get the quote to you as soon as possible, and I'll look forward to hearing from you.' He paused a moment, looking thoughtful. 'Even if you don't decide to employ my firm, I'd love to know what's in that fireplace.'

I showed him out, and waved as he drove off, then wondered what on earth I was doing. You wave off old friends who've come to visit; not builders you've just met, with a strange obsession about your fireplace. Suddenly I had a horrible thought – what if Mir had taken her kittens back into the fireplace while we'd been upstairs? I rushed back in, but thankfully she and the little ones were still in the same box, which I'd tucked into a corner behind a pile of boxes where I hoped she'd feel safe. Just in case,

I found a flattened cardboard box and taped that firmly over the hole in the wall. Mir watched, a resigned look on her face. I think she'd decided it was too dirty and draughty in there for the kittens anyway.

Chapter 2 – 1783

There was to be a run tonight, landing contraband. Esther Harris felt a surge of excitement tinged with trepidation rush through her at the thought. No matter how many times she'd taken part, she always found it such a thrill to be involved, even though she was well aware of the dangers. Probably half the people in the town were involved, she realised, in one way or another. She and her family perhaps more so than many, as her father was the landlord of The Ship at Anchor pub, on Stanpit. They preferred the term 'free traders' rather than smugglers.

'What time is the run tonight, lass?' Pa asked her, as she put away a tray full of tankards on the shelves above the bar.

'Ten o'clock. There'll be a half moon. Hoping the Revenue men aren't around to see us.'

Pa was wiping tables. 'Thomas Walker was in earlier. Told me they'll keep away, as long as they get the usual.'

Esther nodded. There was a deal in place, with the Revenue men, or with most of them, at least. If they were given a portion of the haul so they could claim to have seized it and could fill in their reports accordingly, they'd turn a blind eye while the rest of it was being landed, stored and distributed. It had worked that way for as long as Esther had been involved.

'Can we trust Walker?' Esther's older brother, Matthew, asked. 'I know he gets a cut, but I don't fully trust any of them. If it paid them more to turn us in, they'd do it at the drop of a hat.'

'Walker's sound,' Pa said, with a glance at Esther. She felt herself blush. She knew Walker liked her, but she also knew he wasn't the man for her. Not while Sam Coombes lived and breathed.

Matthew shrugged. 'If you're sure. As long as there aren't Revenue men from elsewhere, we'll be safe, then.'

Pa straightened up and groaned, a hand to his back. 'I'm going to have to stay here again. Back's too painful to go down to the beach. Esther, you'll have to go in my place.'

She went over to him and put her arms around him. 'I guessed I would. It's all right, Pa. I've done it enough times. I know what to do.'

'And you'll both be careful?'

'We will, Pa,' Matthew said, with a grin at Esther. He loved the life – the night-time landing of goods, the camaraderie among the free traders, and the frisson of fear that one day they might be caught.

Pa nodded. 'Well, I'll be in the cellar and I'll be able to help at this end.'

Esther kissed his stubbly cheek. 'Thanks, Pa. I've some mutton stew for our dinner. I'll warm it up now, while we're quiet.'

Most of the men who'd normally be in the pub at this time were home, eating their own dinners or resting before the night's activities. It was like having two jobs for many of them – farming, labouring or plying a trade during the day; working with the smuggling gangs at night. Not much chance to rest, but the rewards were worth it. Without the income from helping the free traders land and distribute goods, many local families would be in deep poverty. They accepted the risks in return for a better way of life.

They closed the pub at nine that night, locking and barring the front door. If there were to be any celebrations after a successful run, they'd take place at the Haven House Inn down at Mudeford Quay, rather than at Luke Harris's hostelry on Stanpit. Esther took a rushlight through the secret entrance to the cellar – not the cellar they used for legitimately bought supplies but the other one – and Matthew followed her closely. It was always a little tricky negotiating the entrance, and she knew her Pa would struggle coming down later, with his bad back and all, but he'd manage, as he always did.

In the hidden cellar, tucked below and behind the main room of the pub, a few brandy kegs were still stacked against one wall since the last run. At this time of year contraband might be landed two or more times a week, depending on weather, tides and other factors.

Esther put the rushlight into a holder on the wall, and retrieved a bundle of clothing from a sack in the corner. This was when it got exciting – the moment she exchanged her skirts and bodice for a pair of breeches, a shirt and jacket. She twisted her hair into a bun and tucked it into a blue cap that she always wore when working with the smugglers.

'You ready, Blue?' Matthew asked, using the nickname the free traders called her when she was dressed like this.

She grinned. 'I am. Let's go.' Putting on the clothes felt like putting on a different persona, one she enjoyed being, despite the dangers that came with it.

Matthew retrieved the rushlight from its holder and pushed aside an empty beer barrel on one side of the room. Behind it was their other secret – a wooden door that led to a tunnel. They went through, down the rough steps carved into the earth, and ran along in a half-crouch. Esther was tall for a woman, and the tunnel ceiling was low. Pa was a large man – another reason he preferred not to do this part of the job anymore.

The tunnel led behind the pub, under their stables and outbuildings and common land at the back, to the edge of the marsh, where it then sloped upwards to the other entrance, hidden

13

in a dip and surrounded by reeds. The first part of the tunnel was lined with brick, but most of it had only wooden supports holding up the earth above. Pa had told Esther and Matthew how his father had built it, decades earlier. Pa had always meant to improve it, adding a brick lining throughout its length, but he never had.

'Must start work soon on strengthening this part of the tunnel,' Matthew said as they passed through it. 'Pa's not going to do it, so I will.'

Reaching the end, Esther peered through a peephole in the small wooden door to make sure all was well, and then quietly pushed it open. There'd been dry weather and no abnormally high tides lately, meaning the tunnel entrance was dry. Sometimes it partially flooded, and she'd have to wade through knee-deep water from the lowest part to the end.

A hand reached around and pulled the door wide, then caught her arm to haul her out. 'Well, Blue, here you are! I thought I'd wait for you here, and we three can go together. The coracle's awaiting us. Evening, Matthew!'

Esther grinned, and threw her arms around the man who'd waited for her. 'Sam! Thank you for waiting. We've a clear night, by the looks of things.'

'A fine night for smuggling,' Matthew said, clapping Sam on the back. 'We'll be celebrating later, eh Sam?'

'I hope so!' Sam replied.

Esther gazed at the half moon that provided enough light for them to see by, but hopefully not enough for Revenue ships to spot them. Across the marsh and the harbour, over on Warren Hill, there would be a spotter, waiting to signal to the smugglers' ships when the coast was clear. It was a clear, cold night, and she was glad of the coarse woven jacket that was part of her boy's costume. 'Come on, we should get going. Ten o'clock is the agreed time, and it's well after nine already.'

Together they moved quickly across the marsh, following a

known route that kept them for the most part hidden by tall reeds. It wasn't far to the channel where Sam had pulled his coracle up onto a bank. They jumped in, and Sam silently rowed out along the channel, into the harbour and around to a beach, where he landed it along with other coracles. Esther had kept her eye on Warren Hill throughout, and then she saw what she'd been waiting for. 'There it is, there's the flink!' She'd spotted the tiny flash of light from the spotter, which meant the ship could come in to the beach.

There was one ship tonight, a two-masted lugger. Its shallow draught together with the high tide meant it would be able to come right up onto the beach for unloading. That was always easier and quicker than if it had to anchor out from the shore and its cargo be unloaded into rowboats. They went on foot along the beach to the spot where it was due to land. There were many other men, mostly keeping out of sight in the sand dunes, also waiting for the ship to come in. Among them was John Streeter, who owned the ship, and he nodded to them as she passed. 'Well, Harris and Blue, it should be a fine haul to restock your father's cellars tonight. Tell him I'll be along to see him tomorrow.'

'Yes, sir. He'll be glad of a chat with you,' said Matthew.

'His back still crook?'

'It is, sir.'

'Ah, poor man. Not good being a publican when your back's crook. Coombes, you're working on the wagons. Harris, I want you loading the wagons before you sort your own kegs, all right?'

Matthew nodded. 'Of course, Mr Streeter. Ship's on her way, look.' He pointed out to sea. Esther could just make out the dark shape of a sail on the horizon, as the lugger tacked its way towards the shore. There was a long sandbank, a spit that led from Warren Hill and Hengistbury Head some distance across the entrance to the harbour. The ship would need to head eastwards first and then come back on the landward side of it to the beach. Streeter employed the best ship captains who knew and understood the shifting sandbanks well. Their knowledge had saved many a cargo from the clutches of the Revenue cutters, whose captains were not as experienced.

As the lugger approached, men emerged from their hiding places to await its arrival. There was an atmosphere of cautious anticipation. The men – batmen with their stout cudgels ready to defend the smugglers if necessary, wagoners and tubmen – all would be handsomely paid for their night's work. Many would earn the equivalent of a fortnight's wages tonight, just for a few hours' work landing the contraband. Esther felt her excitement bubbling up as usual, and hopped from foot to foot on the sand.

The ship – Esther could now see it was the *Phoenix* – expertly tacked into the channel between the spit and the mainland, and then the captain dropped an anchor at the same time as lowering the sails and turning the ship to beach on the sand. Once the goods were unloaded, they'd use the anchor as a pivot point to float the ship off the beach once more to make their getaway. As soon as the lugger was beached, the waiting men ran into the shallows and formed a human chain, passing kegs of brandy and packets of tobacco handed down from the ship to the shore, where they were loaded up onto wagons. Esther took her place in the chain on the beach. Matthew and Sam were loading wagons. As each one filled, it was driven away by one of the wagoners. Tubmen took two kegs, strapped one on their front and one on their back, and hurried away. Everyone worked in silence, only a few grunts indicating their efforts could be heard. John Streeter stood by the wagon chain, supervising. It was all going like clockwork.

A shout went up – 'Revenue man!' – and everyone froze. Esther scanned the beach to see who it was. If it was one of the Revenue officers who were complicit in their trade, all would be well. But not all of the riding officers based at Christchurch were sympathetic, and sometimes the smugglers were visited by new patrols from out of the area.

'It's all right. It's Walker,' said the man next to Esther in the chain. 'Come to collect his share.' It was Will Burden next to her, she noticed. He was a local fisherman, and a friend of both Matthew and Sam. She flashed him a smile.

The unloading continued; everyone relaxed now that they knew it was a friendly Revenue officer. Esther saw the man approach Streeter, dismount from his horse and say a few words. He'd leave with a couple of kegs of brandy for himself, and the knowledge of where a small stack of contraband would be left for him to 'seize' for his records, and to stop his superiors from being suspicious. Although those on the beach knew his direct superior – Joshua Jeans – was as complicit as any of them. He may be the chief Revenue officer, and one-time mayor of Christchurch, but he was as corrupt as they came.

As Esther watched, Thomas Walker turned to survey the activity on the beach. She kept her head down, turning away, and prayed he wouldn't recognise her. He knew, of course, that her father took in contraband, hid it somewhere and distributed it as well as kept some for use in the pub but he didn't know that Esther came down to the beach to actively help with the unloading. And that was the way she wanted it to stay. Walker was helpful to her father, but he could, if he wanted, make things very difficult for them. And he might decide to do just that if he spotted her dressed as a boy, blatantly helping the smugglers. It was not the way to keep him on their side.

Thankfully he didn't stay long at the beach. Of course, he wouldn't want to be seen there by other, more honest Revenue officers. That would take some explaining. When Esther risked a glance up the beach and saw Streeter standing alone once more, she breathed a sigh of relief. Walker had gone. They had almost finished the unloading. The last few kegs were passed up the chain, and then the landing party waded back up the beach and into the sand dunes. The ship's sails were quickly hoisted and a moment later the lugger turned on its anchor that was then hauled aboard, and it was afloat, sailing along the Run and into the harbour. The *Phoenix* would moor up at Christchurch Quay, and no doubt within a few days it would be off again, crossing the Channel to Cherbourg on another run.

There were hardly any men left on the beach. All had quietly melted away into the night. Streeter nodded to Esther as she looked around for her brother. 'Good job, tonight. Just your pa's load to take and you're done.' He pointed to a number of kegs stacked beside a dune, then he too disappeared.

Matthew joined her. 'Let's get the coracle loaded. Nearly finished, eh Blue?'

'She did well tonight, Matt,' said Will Burden as he too headed towards the dunes. 'As strong as any fellow, she is.'

Esther waved at Sam, who was leaving with a wagon of goods to be hidden elsewhere, then followed Matthew to load up the little boat. She was exhausted – her back and shoulder muscles screaming in pain from having hauled so many kegs of brandy that night, but they had to finish the job. It didn't take long to load the remaining contraband into Sam's coracle, and Matthew rowed it through the Run on a slack tide, across the harbour and up the little channel into the marsh. They unloaded, stacked the kegs just inside the tunnel entrance, then Esther ran back up the tunnel to check that all was well at the pub end and that her father was ready to receive the goods. She tapped on the door and Pa opened it immediately. He'd been sitting in the cellar with a rushlight and a pipe, awaiting them.

'All good, lass?'

She nodded. 'All good.' She whistled along the tunnel to Matthew, and a minute later he was there with the first two kegs. This was the part of the operation she liked least. The excitement was over, she was tired and aching, and there was still work to be done bringing kegs along the tunnel and storing them. There was minimal risk now – it was unlikely that any Revenue men would call at this hour – but even so they needed to be quiet and careful. That was the reason they brought the contraband in through the tunnel from the marsh and not by road to the front door. No one watching the pub would see or suspect any activity going on at all.

Once it was all brought up to the cellar, Pa hugged both her and Matthew, grinning at them. 'Another successful run. Well done, both of you. You'll be glad of your beds tonight, I'll warrant.'

'I certainly will,' Esther said, but Matthew put his cap back on. 'I'm off out to celebrate. There'll be drinks down at the Haven House courtesy of Streeter, I reckon. I'll be back late – don't wait up.'

'All right, lad. See you in the morning then.' Pa nodded, and Matthew let himself out of the front door of the pub while Esther made her way up to bed, where she collapsed gratefully.

Esther slept soundly and woke only when her Pa began pounding on her door. 'Lass, up you get. We need to open the bar. Your brother's not back from his celebrations yet.'

She groaned and hauled herself out of bed, washing and dressing quickly. Trust Matthew to stay out all night. He'd turn up around lunchtime, she guessed, with a sore head. Meanwhile she'd have to do all the heavy work of the pub that morning, to save Pa's back.

Later that morning, just as she was opening the pub, Will Burden came bursting in, looking dishevelled and red-faced, panting. 'Did Matthew get back here?'

'No. Not seen him yet,' she said. Her stomach turned over with fear. Something was wrong, she could see it in Will's eyes. 'What happened?'

'We were celebrating last night, in town. Got a bit rowdy in the street.' He sat down and leaned forward, elbows on his knees, and shook his head. 'Stupid, but we were so buoyed up after the run, you know? We ran into a troop of militia and they arrested us. Me, Matthew and a couple of other lads. We spent the night locked up. They had no good reason to arrest us but I think they just wanted to do something, being too late to stop the goods being landed.'

'Oh no! But you're out now?'

'I am. But …'

'What? Tell us, lad!' Pa had come out from behind the bar to hear the news.

'There was a press gang waiting as we were released. I got away – I'm a fisherman and they don't take anyone with a regular job. But Matt – they said he was unemployed, even though he said he worked here. They took him, and one of the other lads.'

'A press gang!' Esther clapped a hand over her mouth. Matthew would be away for years, forced to work on a naval ship.

Pa sat down heavily. 'Oh, Matthew. Stupid boy. And how are we going to cope without him? Just you and me, lass. And me with my back failing. But we can't afford to stop doing the runs and storing and distributing the stuff for Streeter.'

Esther put a hand on his shoulder. 'We'll cope, Pa. I can do Matthew's work. We'll be all right.' It'd be tough. But there was no choice. She thought of Sam. He would help them, she knew. He would do all he could for them, and somehow they'd manage.

They sat in silence for a while, each lost in their own thoughts as the horror of what had happened sank in. Esther noticed silent tears flowing down Pa's grizzled face but she did not allow herself to cry. One of them had to stay strong. Without Matthew the years ahead would be very difficult for them both. She realised how much she'd always relied on him being there, her big, strong, jolly brother. And now, all she could do for him was hope and pray that he survived his years in the Navy, and returned to them in time.

Chapter 3

After Nick left, I decided to walk again around the outside of my property. He'd said a few things I wanted to think about – there was evidence of a blocked-up window I could reopen, and what was I going to do with the outbuildings in the yard? On my way to the front door I pulled back the threadbare carpet in the hallway. Nick had asked about the subfloor. Underneath the carpet were large flagstones, worn smooth presumably by the passage of countless feet over the centuries. I smiled to see them. They were just the sort of original feature I'd like to bring back to life. In a sitting room they'd be too uneven, but in the hallway where I wouldn't place any furniture, they'd be perfect. I went out of the front door, which was old and in need of a coat of paint, and spent a few minutes standing on the pavement gazing at the house. Its render needed patching up, and it'd need painting. And most of the window frames, which were wood, needed repairing or replacing.

Across the street was a row of more modern bungalows and small houses, built in the last century, set back from the road. As I stood there, a woman came out of the front door of the one directly opposite mine, with several shopping bags in her hand. She looked to be about five or ten years older than me, and I knew there were a couple of school-age kids living there. Embarrassed, I realised I had not yet knocked on their door to introduce myself, though I had spoken to both my immediate neighbours on my side of the road.

Now was my chance. I jogged across the street, lifting a hand to wave at her, and went part way up her driveway. 'Hi! Been meaning to call and say hello. I'm Millie – I bought the old house opposite you.'

She smiled warmly and came forward to shake my hand. 'Hi, Millie. I'm Sharon. I live here with my husband, Brian, and you've probably heard our two kids, Jasper and Tabitha, as God knows they can be noisy enough!'

'I've seen them out playing. They were up and down your driveway on scooters yesterday evening.'

'Yes! Their current obsession. Well, they're at school right now. I was just going out shopping, but would you like to come in for a coffee? I've plenty of time. It'd be nice to get to know our new neighbour. That house has been empty far too long.'

'That would be lovely!' I followed her inside. It was a large bungalow that had had an attic conversion – a neat dormer window on each side suggested two rooms had been added up there. An open-plan kitchen and sitting room stretched across the back of the house, with patio doors leading to a tidy garden complete with trampoline and swing set. The decor was modern and bright – a good match with Sharon, I thought. I considered my own ripped jeans and shapeless T-shirt, and decided I probably also matched my house's current decor. Tatty and in need of updating.

'Coffee? Or tea? I have herbal teas if you'd prefer?' Sharon gestured to a shelf full of various types of tea in tins and boxes.

'Just regular builders' tea for me, please. Milk and no sugar.'

'Coming right up.' She filled a shiny kettle and clicked it on, took two brightly coloured mugs from a cupboard. She chose a herbal tea for herself.

We sat on a couple of armchairs that faced out into the garden to drink our tea. 'I love sitting here watching the kids play on a sunny evening, with a glass of Merlot in hand. You must come over for supper some day soon?'

'I'd like that.' It would be good to make some local friends.

She smiled. 'It's wonderful to have someone living opposite us. That house has been empty for ages. Actually I think it was empty when we moved in – the old man had already moved into a nursing home I believe. And then the family were so slow to sell it after he passed on. Do you have great plans for it? I haven't seen inside but I imagine it needs a bit of TLC?' She gave a little laugh as I nodded vigorously.

'You could say that. I don't think it's been touched for about fifty years. I want to keep as many original features as I can, while making it suitable for modern living. A tall order, but the place has such character. There are worn flagstones in the hall as though it was a really busy entrance. It makes me shiver thinking about all the people who passed that way over hundreds of years, if you know what I mean.'

She shrugged. 'Well, I can give you some recommendations of builders, if you like. We had the attic converted here, after we moved in. The kids have their rooms upstairs.'

'That would be helpful. I've had a quote already, and another chap came round this morning. But it's always worth getting a few quotes.'

'Oh, definitely. Who've you seen so far?'

'It was Marshall Construction who came round today, and I've had a quote from Seaway Renovations. They seemed very reasonable so I might well stick with them.'

'Seaway. Hmm.' She frowned.

'What is it? Have you heard of them?'

'Oh yes.' She bit her bottom lip and took a sip of tea before continuing. 'You should make sure you read their reviews on Google before deciding. A friend of mine used them, and unfortunately their workmanship was not up to scratch. They left the job half done, and she had to pay a fortune to get someone else to finish it. The fellow who runs it has been sued a few times. I'd think twice, Millie, before employing them.'

I raised my eyebrows. 'Well, thank you for the warning. I'll definitely check them out. Hopefully the other lot – Marshall – will give a good quote too. Have you heard anything about them?'

She nodded. 'Yes, the Marshall name is quite well known round here. There was a mayor named Marshall, for a couple of years. Des Marshall. Bit of a character, by all accounts. The kind who has a finger in every pie, even the less than kosher ones, if you get my drift. I think he's the father of the chap who runs the construction company. No idea if the son is like the father.'

'Do you know if they're any good? The builders, I mean?' I'd liked Nick's wonky smile and kind eyes, but of course those features didn't get houses built or renovated.

Sharon shook her head. 'I don't know. We used a company called, let me think, oh yes. Broadacre Construction. They were good. I can certainly recommend them. Do check out all the ones you're interested in. There are some dodgy dealers out there, unfortunately. And you'll want a company that specialises in older properties.'

I hadn't thought of that. 'Yes, that's a good idea.'

'Wait a minute, I think I have some details …' She got up and darted out to another room, coming back a minute later with some names and phone numbers written on a piece of paper. 'There. I knew Brian had some builders' details. He's so organised. It's why I married him, ha ha!'

'You look pretty organised yourself,' I said, with a smile. 'Not like me. I've got stuff all over the place.'

'Do you have anyone to help you unpack? I mean … or are you living alone?'

I've been reticent about telling people about my change in marital status. But Sharon was a new friend, meeting me in the post-Steve era. I could open up to her, I realised, and she wouldn't judge, not knowing Steve or anything about our background. 'I'm on my own. I was married – still am, technically, though we are in the process of getting a divorce.'

'Oh I'm sorry.' Sharon put a hand out and patted my shoulder. 'It's a difficult time.'

I smiled. 'Not really. Not for us – it's all perfectly amicable. We were together a long time. We met at school, and started going out together when we were 14. We married at 22 – mainly because everyone kept asking us when we were going to tie the knot. It was what everyone expected so we just kind of went along with it. But if I'm honest, we grew up and grew out of each other. He's still my best friend.'

'Oh, that's sad. I always think it's so romantic to marry a childhood sweetheart. Brian and I met in our mid-twenties, via mutual friends. So boring. It's nice that you and—?'

'Steve.'

'—you and Steve are still friends. Is he local?'

'Not really. But he's not far away. We lived in Southampton. I wanted a new start, somewhere different, so I chose to move here.'

'Where you can go on a date with a new man and not worry you'll bump into him, or mutual friends.'

I nodded. 'Well, yes. Though at the moment I can't imagine dating. I suppose that'll come, in time.'

Sharon tilted her head on one side. 'Well, look. I'm delighted you're here, and I think we could be great friends. I don't work, so I'm at a loose end when the kids are at school, and you're just across the road …'

'I'm starting a new job next week, though. I got a transfer from my old job – they have an office in Bournemouth so I'll be based there.'

'Lovely! What do you do?'

'Office admin. We're a small supplier of luxury food stuffs. Hampers, gift boxes, top-end chocolates and alcohol gifts – that sort of thing. We sell to boutique shops and direct to customers, via our website. I mostly handle orders and invoices.' I rolled my eyes dramatically. 'Dull, I know. But it pays the bills.'

'And buys you a characterful old house by the coast!'

'Well, it was more my inheritance from Mum that paid for the house.'

'Oh, I'm sorry to hear you lost her.'

'Thank you. Her dying was a bit of a catalyst, I suppose. Made me – and Steve – rethink what we wanted from life. We stopped needing to worry about how she'd take our splitting up. And yes, it provided the funds for me to be able to buy my own place.'

'I think it's wonderful how you're able to look at it all so positively. You're an inspiration, and I've only just met you! Well, Millie, welcome to Stanpit, welcome to Mudeford. It's a lovely area. Have you had chance to explore much yet?'

'Not a lot! I've been busy unpacking and making the house liveable and talking to builders. I walked into Christchurch town centre. That's about all.'

'Then I must show you around a bit more. How about a walk tomorrow morning? It's set to be fine, and once I've got the kids to school I'm free.'

'I'd like that.' Look at me, I silently said to all those who'd thought I'd never do it, that I never could do it: look at me. I've moved house, started the process of finding a builder to renovate it, and made a new friend. Striding out, on my own, an independent woman doing what I want, not what everyone else expects of me. For the first time in my life.

We made arrangements for the following day, and I left feeling very happy with myself. I spent the rest of the day phoning other building companies including the ones Sharon had recommended, and setting dates for them to come to look at the work needed. Mir, thankfully, was still happily settled with her kittens in the box by the sofa. Sharon's kids would probably enjoy meeting the kittens, I thought, in a couple of weeks when the kittens were bigger and more playful. Maybe Sharon would even home one of them.

I also did as Sharon had suggested and Googled Seaway Renovations. As she'd said, there were poor reviews, and worse – newspaper articles about court cases in which they'd been sued for poor and in one case dangerous workmanship. There was enough there to make me decide not to use them. I made a mental note to thank Sharon. It was good to have met a neighbour who was already looking out for me. I checked out Marshall Construction too, and found only positive reviews. Hopefully Nick's quote would be a good one.

The following day was bright and sunny though there was a chill wind. A typical April day that felt as though it could change at any moment to cloud and rain. I put on a warm coat and woolly hat, and as agreed with Sharon called on her at ten o'clock. She was wearing a smart wool jacket with matching cloche hat.

We set off to the marsh first of all. Beside my cottage was a small green on which stood a well. A sign told us it was called Tutton's Well, and it had been a source of pure water for the area for centuries, thought by some to have had medicinal properties. I had walked past it a few times since moving in but today was the first day I took a good look at it. Previous inhabitants of my house would have drawn their water from this well, though it was now capped.

'So close to the sea – it's amazing it provided fresh water,' I commented to Sharon.

She shrugged in response and began telling me about a local yoga class, held in Stanpit village hall, that I might like to join. 'It's marvellous – I feel so energised after a session! And so close to us. I go on a Friday morning but there are also some evening sessions if that would suit you better once you've started work?'

'Thanks. I might give it a try,' I said. Actually, yoga wasn't my thing. I preferred the idea of long beach walks, or cycle rides in the lanes of the New Forest, to keep me fit.

We walked on, past a scout hut, and into Stanpit Marsh – the area my garden backed onto. A walking track led around the edge of the marsh, with firm ground grazed by ponies on one side and the marsh, a designated nature reserve, on the other. There were several people with large cameras on tripods, and Sharon told me it was a popular spot with bird-watchers. I saw various birds – mostly sea birds and waders – on the tufts of grass and reeds that made up the marsh. As we walked we crossed a bridge over a channel leading across the marsh and into a reed bed. A small sign announced it was called Mother Sillar's Channel, after a local woman who ran a pub and helped smugglers hide and distribute their contraband.

'Smugglers!' I exclaimed. I'd had no idea this area had any smuggling history.

'Apparently,' Sharon said, without interest. I was getting the impression she had zero interest in local history. On the other hand, I'd always wanted to find out the history of every place I'd ever lived, and this was no exception.

Beyond the marsh was Christchurch Harbour. Looking south I could see its entrance at Mudeford Quay. 'We'll walk down there next,' Sharon said. Across the harbour was a hill on a promontory. 'That's Hengistbury Head, and the hill is called Warren Hill. A nice place to walk. There's a little ferry that runs from Mudeford Quay across to the sandbank on that side.'

We looped around by the harbour's edge, and out onto a tarmacked path I'd already walked along, that led towards Christchurch town. But we turned the other way, back towards Stanpit, and exited the marsh at the same point we'd entered it. We walked down the road past my cottage and on down to Mudeford Quay, where a group of old buildings huddled together beyond a car park. There was a pub and a café, some private cottages, and a lifeboat station. A line of sailing dinghies were pulled up onto shore, their halyards clinking against the masts in the wind. On one side, waves lapped up against the quayside, whereas on the other side were the calm waters of the harbour. A narrow channel separated the quay from a long sand-spit with a row of beach huts that stretched out from Hengistbury Head.

'Lovely area!'

'Yes. It's wonderful in the summer. You get lots of families bringing their children to catch crabs off the quayside. Jasper and Tabitha love doing that. And the fish stall there is good.' She pointed to a hut behind piles of lobster pots. But I'd spotted another information board, and wandered over to take a look.

'The Battle of Mudeford,' I read aloud, then skim-read the few paragraphs. It was something to do with a pitched battle between smugglers and Revenue officers, which had taken place in the 1780s right on that spot. I took a quick photo of the sign on my phone to read at leisure later, then followed Sharon to the café, where we bought coffee and sat inside at plastic tables, looking out over the sea.

It was a pleasant morning out, and we chatted like old friends the whole time. However, I knew I'd need to do the walks again, on my own, with time to read the information boards and really look around me, imagining what the area might have been like in the long distant past. I could feel a project researching local history coming on.

Chapter 4 – 1784

It was months since Matthew had been press-ganged. Months in which Esther had taken his place on every run, whether or not Pa's back allowed him to help out. Someone needed to row a coracle full of contraband from the beach to store at The Ship at Anchor. It was an important part of the chain, as John Streeter frequently told them. Sam, bless him, helped with the runs as much as he could. But the day-to-day running of the pub and onward distribution of the smuggled goods fell mostly to Esther.

'Lass, will you take the pony cart up to Ringwood today?' Pa asked, one rain-soaked morning in late spring. 'I'll manage the pub.' He groaned as he moved stiffly across to take a seat on a stool behind the bar, rubbing at his lower back. 'Ah, that's better.'

Esther looked at him in surprise. Usually she would run the pub while Pa took goods further up the chain, to customers across the New Forest. He'd never liked the idea of her being out on her own, with contraband hidden in the pony cart. 'Your back bad, is it, Pa?'

Pa nodded and grimaced. 'It's bad. All that jolting on the roads would make it worse. Sorry, lass.'

'No problem.' Esther looked out at the grey day where the rain was falling steadily. It wouldn't be much fun, but someone had to do it. There were Streeter's customers waiting on deliveries of rum and tobacco. At least the barrels had already been prepared – the previous day Sam had helped hide kegs of rum and packets of tobacco inside empty beer barrels. It would look as though she was returning empty barrels to the Ringwood brewery, and picking up a new consignment of ale. Indeed, she would bring back full beer barrels.

She untied her apron, pinned a shawl tightly around her shoulders and put a bonnet on her head, then went out to harness their pony, Toby, to the cart, which was already loaded with the barrels. Toby looked miserable at being made to go out in the rain, but he was a placid, obedient pony and soon she was on her way, with Toby plodding, head down, along the lanes to Ringwood. They passed by the little village of Burton and Esther found herself looking around for Sam, who lived there. But there was no sign of him today.

She pulled her shawl tighter still about her, and went on her way. By the time she was returning a couple of hours later, with the cart now loaded with full barrels of ale, she was wet through but finally the rain had stopped and the sun was beginning to glint through the clouds in the west. Even Toby was walking with his head high, sensing he was nearly home and that there'd be a manger full of sweet hay and oats waiting for him.

She was on her way through Purewell, so nearly back at the pub, when a familiar voice hailed her. She turned to see Thomas Walker on his black horse, coming along the road from Christchurch. He quickly caught up with her.

'Good day, Miss Harris. Is that ale in those barrels, or something a little stronger?' He smirked as he doffed his hat to her.

'Ale, sir. I've been to the brewery at Ringwood fetching supplies.'

'Well, I think I'll come into your pub and sample a pint of it, on condition it'll be you serving,' he said.

'Pa's behind the bar. I need to change my clothing,' she said.

'Something I'd like to see,' he muttered, so quietly that she couldn't be certain she'd heard him. Nevertheless she blushed, and turned her face away.

Thankfully he dropped behind the cart then, and she was able to drive back to the pub, unhitch the cart and stable Toby, then run upstairs to change without having to speak to him again. But when she came down to the bar, Walker was sitting at a table in a corner, chatting to Pa.

'Ah, here she is,' Pa said, with a smile. 'All well, lass?'

She nodded. 'Yes, and I'll unload the cart later when we've a quiet moment.' When Sam was next there, she thought. He'd help with the heavy lifting.

Walker smiled, then patted the bentwood chair beside him. 'Come and sit down, Esther. Your pa can spare you for a few minutes, I'm sure.'

'I can, aye,' Pa said.

Esther glanced at her father, who gave a small nod, and went over to Walker's table to sit where he'd indicated. He looked at her appraisingly, and seemed to approve of what he saw. 'You managed to change out of your wet things, then. That dress looks well on you.'

Pa brought over a tankard of ale for Walker, and stood for a moment behind Esther, leaning on the back of her chair as though his back hurt just to stand. 'You want anything, lass?' he asked, to her surprise. He'd never before served her, in their own pub!

'Ah, no, thank you, Pa. I'll only sit a minute, then I'll get on with the chores.'

'I suppose you have a lot of work to do?' Walker asked, as Pa went back to his place behind the bar.

'I have pies to make, the cart to unload, and then there'll be a rush of people in for their dinners I expect.'

'A hard life, as a publican's daughter. You deserve more.'

She shook her head. 'No, sir. It is a good life. My grandfather had this pub, then my parents, God rest Ma's soul. And I will not leave my father – he needs my help.' Pa had gone out to the yard, she noticed.

'One day you will marry and you will need to leave him,' Walker replied. There was a small smile playing at the corners of his mouth as he spoke.

'Sir, I would hope that my husband would allow me to continue to work here.' Sam would, she knew. Sam would come to live at the Ship, helping run it. Perhaps then Pa could retire, and if he didn't have to spend his days moving barrels of ale and kegs of brandy around, his back might recover.

Walker smiled indulgently at her. 'No, I suspect your future husband would not allow that. He would want you to keep house for him, and bring up his children. Where would be the time to allow you to work as a common barmaid in all that?'

'I shall not marry, then. Pa needs my help.' Esther could not help but thrust her chin forward. Who was this man, telling her what she might and might not do in the future?

He leaned forward, leering at her. 'Oh but you will marry, sweet Esther. You will marry soon, and when you do, you will obey your husband in all things.' With that he downed his ale in one swallow and stood up, knocking his chair over backwards. He did not stoop to pick it up, but doffed his tricorn hat to her and left.

'I'll do what I damned well like,' Esther muttered to herself as she picked up the chair and replaced it at the table. She grabbed a broom and angrily began sweeping the floor.

'All well, lass?' Pa had re-entered the bar room. He had an expectant smile on his face. 'Mr Walker still here?'

'No. He's left.' Esther picked up Walker's tankard and put it down heavily on the bar. 'I don't like him, Pa. I'm not sure we can trust him. There's something …'

'We can trust him. Doesn't he take his cut of the goods?'

'He does. I've seen him at the beach collecting his portion.'

Pa gasped. 'He hasn't seen you there, has he? He mightn't take too kindly to knowing you're one of the smugglers.'

33

She shook her head. 'No. I always keep my face down.'

'Good, good. We need Thomas Walker, lass. We need him to stay friendly to us. He may be on the take but he knows too much; he comes in here so often, hoping to see you. He could make things difficult for us here, if he wanted to.'

Esther sighed. 'I know he could.'

Pa limped over to her and took her hand. He was no longer smiling. 'When you say you don't like him, what do you mean?'

'I-I just find him … rude. A little frightening. Not someone I'd want to get on the wrong side of.'

'Do you not find him handsome? He is a well-built young man …'

'He's not young!'

'He is only in his thirtieth year. Not so very old. And handsome?'

Esther shrugged. Thomas Walker was still much older than she was. He had the kind of looks that most people would say were handsome. Dark hair, a strong jawline, a straight nose. Powerfully built, with broad shoulders. But she did not find him attractive. Maybe that was because whenever she was with him, she found herself comparing him to Sam Coombes. And Sam had her heart.

'I suppose,' she said, answering her father's question, 'he has tolerable looks. But that has nothing to do with his character. He's not Sam.'

Pa sighed. 'I know, pet, that your heart's always been set on marrying Sam. And I hope one day that will happen. But for now, while you're still so young and Sam hasn't yet asked for your hand … all I ask is that you keep on the right side of Walker. There are many who'd think he'd make a fine husband. As a riding officer he earns twenty pounds a year. And of course he makes more from selling any surplus of his share. He lives well. With Matthew gone, we need all the help we can get.'

Esther turned to stare at her father. 'What are you saying, Pa?'

'Just, let him think he has a chance. He'll probably tire of you and move on to someone else in time.'

'What if he doesn't? What will happen when I marry Sam? And I *will* marry Sam, Pa.'

Pa nodded slowly. 'You will, aye. We'll deal with that if and when we need to. But for now, don't rock the boat, eh, lass? Keep Sam at a bit of a distance for a while. Walker could make things h—'

He broke off as the door banged open and John Streeter strode in. He looked buoyant and elated, the way he so often did when he was planning another run. He clapped Pa on the back and chucked Esther under the chin. After checking there was no one else in the room he said, 'Haven House, tonight, to discuss the next run. I have a batch of rather nice lace and silks sitting in a warehouse in Cherbourg. And it's time I brought over some more tea – I can hardly keep up with demand. Not surprising really. With duty paid, tea is seven shillings a pound. Seven! I sell mine for two shillings and make a tidy profit. I do people a favour, really, providing them with affordable goods.'

'You do, yes,' Pa said. 'A public service. Shame not all see it that way.'

At that moment the door opened and a group of men came in for their tea-time pie and ale. Esther did not recognise them all, so it was best to stop talking about smuggling. You never knew when someone might be a spy, reporting to a Revenue officer from out of the area. While the majority of local people felt that smuggling was justified, given the extortionately high duties payable on spirits, wine, tea, fine fabrics and many other items, and the only loser was the government, there were a few who didn't think like this and who could make trouble for the smugglers if they so desired. It wasn't worth the risk of speaking freely in front of people they didn't know.

Streeter raised his hat to Pa and left. He had premises just along the lane – a snuff factory, one of his many businesses. He, of course, used smuggled tobacco in the factory. But he was careful never to hold more stock than he had paperwork for – he'd started that business with one legitimate, duty-paid batch of tobacco. When anyone in authority checked, he showed them the old invoices and demonstrated that he had no further stock. Not there, anyway. Plenty in the secret cellar of The Ship at Anchor.

A week later, another successful run had been accomplished. Esther was not involved in this one – it was the fabrics and tea that Streeter had talked about. Nothing for them at The Ship at Anchor, so she stayed working in the pub that evening, although Sam had gone to be part of the landing party. Thomas Walker was in the pub, leering at her every time she passed. Once he even tapped her on the behind. Her instinct was to smack his hand away, but Pa's eye was upon her. 'Keep Walker sweet,' he'd reminded her when the Revenue officer arrived. She'd had to smile and sidestep his groping hands, all the while thinking of what Sam would do to Walker, if he'd seen.

The following day, Esther had errands to run in Christchurch town centre. She hitched up their little pony, Toby, to the cart to drive there, skirting the northern edge of the marsh to join the road that led over a sturdily built stone bridge over the river Avon, past the ruins of the castle and on to the town centre. The castle, she knew, had been demolished after the Civil War, a hundred and fifty years earlier. That was what happened if you ended up on the losing side. Esther tied up Toby outside the George Inn. It was market day in Christchurch, and there were stalls lining the High Street. She bought the items she needed – a joint of mutton, butter, a box of tallow candles – and then walked up Church Street to the Priory where she was due to meet her friend, Lovey Warne. She was early, according to the Priory's clock, so she sat down on a low wall to wait.

When Lovey arrived, walking up the path from Christchurch Quay, Esther was surprised to see she looked somewhat stouter than usual. Could her friend be pregnant? She was unmarried, so Esther very much hoped not. Lovey's brothers, whom she lived with and kept house for, would most certainly not be happy. Lovey was a little out of breath as she sat on the wall beside Esther.

'Oof. It's warm today, isn't it, Esther? I've only got a few minutes to spare – then I must be going. Deliveries to make.' She patted her midriff.

Esther frowned. 'What do you mean? Deliveries? You're not … You can't be …' She'd last seen Lovey only a month or so earlier, and there'd been no sign of pregnancy then.

Lovey threw back her head and laughed. 'You think I'm carrying a baby under here! Oh, what a joke! Wonderful! No. Something much more precious. Valuable, at any rate. I've just come off a ship.' She looked about her, and then lifted a piece of her clothing. Under her blouse was vibrant blue silk, and suddenly Esther understood. Lovey had fine fabrics, smuggled from France, wound around her body under her clothes. It was a simple way to carry the goods off a ship. No one would think to check under a young woman's clothing.

Esther joined in the laughter. 'Oh my word, Lovey! That is so clever! But be careful, won't you?'

'I always am. And my brothers tell me the same thing, every time I come out. How are things with you? Any news of Matthew? How is your father?'

'No news of Matthew,' Esther replied sadly. They'd had just one letter, written in the West Indies, that had made its way to the Ship eventually, telling them he was well and rather enjoying life at sea. 'And Pa's improving a little, I think, but I'm wondering if he'll ever—' Esther broke off. She'd spotted two men approaching, and her heart was pounding. 'Lovey, you should go. Now.' She glanced over Lovey's shoulder giving a tiny nod, hoping her friend wouldn't turn to look but would just get up and go. But Lovey hadn't read her gesture correctly, and instinctively turned.

Two Revenue officers were approaching, in their uniforms. One was Thomas Walker, and the other was James Noyce. 'Are they with us?' Lovey asked under her breath.

'Walker is, but not Noyce,' Esther murmured in reply.

'I must be off, Esther,' Lovey said more loudly. 'I'll call and see you next week.' She began walking away, but Walker darted after her and caught her arm.

'Come and have a drink with us, ladies,' he said. 'James and I could do with some company. Esther, who's your friend?'

'L-Lovey Warne,' Esther answered, hoping her blush would be interpreted as shyness rather than guilt.

'Pleased to meet you, Miss Warne,' James Noyce said, making an elaborate bow.

Walker smirked. 'The Eight Bells does a fine glass of brandy. Join us, ladies.'

Esther glanced at Lovey, who looked pale. They had no choice. If Lovey made a fuss and insisted on leaving, the officers would be suspicious. Walker might turn a blind eye, but Noyce was not in the pay of the smugglers. Lovey would be arrested. So might Esther. 'Just the one, eh Lovey? You've time to spare?' She smiled at her friend, hoping to reassure her. A quiet drink with the men and then hopefully they'd be able to get on their way.

'Oh, I've time for a quick one,' Lovey replied, smiling brightly, although Esther could see her expression was forced and false.

Walker took Esther's arm, and Noyce took Lovey's, and the four walked the short distance across the Priory grounds, up Church Street and into the Eight Bells pub. It had a low entrance – even Esther needed to duck to enter it. She was first through the door, and as she entered she noticed a keg of smuggled brandy left in the middle of the floor. She stared at it and then at the landlady, widening her eyes. As Thomas Walker entered the pub behind her, the landlady's daughter-in-law sat quickly down on the keg, holding her baby. She spread her skirts to cover the keg, and began feeding the infant.

Esther led the others to a table at the other side of the bar, and took a seat. Hopefully the baby would feed for longer than it would take for them to have a drink and leave.

'What can I get you folks?' the landlady asked them, with a broad smile. Somehow she was managing to look relaxed, despite the fact her daughter-in-law was sitting on a keg of contraband under the noses of a couple of Revenue officers. If only she knew there was more contraband hidden under Lovey's clothes!

'A tot of your best brandy, all round,' Noyce said, and as the landlady went to fetch the drinks, he nudged Walker. 'What's the betting they haven't paid duty on that brandy, eh Tommy?'

'Ah, I'm here for pleasure, not work today,' Walker replied. 'I'm not going to ask for proof. Look, we've a couple of beautiful young ladies with us. Let's enjoy their company and not bother our heads about where the brandy came from, for once.'

'Hmm.' Noyce did not look convinced. Nevertheless, when the drinks arrived he clinked glasses with the rest of them, and knocked his back in one before calling for another. 'It is indeed a fine brandy. Suits the company we have. Esther Harris, you are from The Ship at Anchor, I believe? And Miss Warne, from where did you spring?'

'I-I live with my brothers, up at Bransgore,' Lovey replied.

Lovey's brothers were known smugglers. Esther prayed Noyce would not make the connection between her name and theirs. Maybe he didn't know them.

'What a waste, a girl like you living with her brothers,' Noyce said. 'You're a good-looking little thing. I wouldn't mind getting to know you better myself.' He leaned towards her, and for one awful moment Esther thought he was going to put his arm around Lovey's waist. He'd feel the bulkiness of the layers of silk and lace beneath her bodice.

But Lovey managed to fend him off, grabbing his arm and patting his hand, a flirtatious smile playing about her lips. 'Ah, Mr Noyce, sir. I'm beneath your notice, really. 'Tis kind of you to say such things, though.' She held on to his hand, patting it and keeping it on the table, away from her waist or leg. Esther wondered if perhaps there was more lace wound around her legs under her skirt.

Across the bar, the landlady's daughter-in-law was still feeding her child, casting anxious glances at the two Customs men. Thankfully they had not approached her too closely. Like too many men, Esther thought, they didn't want to be anywhere near a baby.

'I'm sorry, Mr Walker, I must be getting back soon,' Esther said. 'My Pa will be wondering where I've got to, and I've a leg of mutton in my basket that needs roasting. I'll have customers in the pub later, wanting their dinners.'

He leered at her, smiling to reveal a blackened front tooth. 'I shall be one of them, Esther. Roast mutton's my favourite. I'll not keep you, then.'

'Thank you, sir,' she said, getting to her feet and picking up her basket.

Lovey followed suit. 'Thank you for the drink, sirs.' She managed to bob a little curtsy, though it couldn't have been easy to do with all that fabric wrapped around her.

Esther took her hand and led her out of the pub before the Revenue officers could say or do anything to keep them there. They said not a word to each other as they hurried up Church Street, back to where Esther had tied up Toby. There they jumped up with Esther driving and Lovey sitting behind her in the cart, and headed out of town along Castle Street and over the river Avon. It was only after they'd crossed the bridge and left the bustle of town behind that they slowed their pace, looked at each other and fell about laughing.

'Ssh, they might be behind us,' Lovey said, but Esther shook her head. 'No, they left after us and turned up the High Street. And Toby's been trotting at a good pace. We're safe. Oh, if only they knew – you with the fine fabrics wound around you, and did you see that girl feeding her baby, sitting on a keg of brandy?'

'No? I was too concerned about keeping my own contraband

hidden. That was quick thinking of her, sitting down on it and feeding the baby. No one would disturb her there.'

'If they'd only known!'

'They're not paid for their powers of observation, I suppose.'

'Clearly not!' And they laughed some more, until Lovey pressed a hand to her side.

'Oh, I have such a stitch from laughing, and I'm so warm. I must go, Esther. Thanks for helping me back there.'

Esther pulled up Toby and waited while her friend climbed down. She leaned over and kissed Lovey on the cheek. 'You take care, now.'

'I will.'

It had been a bit of excitement but at the same time dangerous. Esther was all too well aware of what could happen if a Revenue officer turned against you. But keeping out of the smuggling trade wasn't an option. They needed the money, and as Streeter often reminded them, The Ship at Anchor was important to his operation.

Chapter 5

Over the next couple of days I had several more builders round to look at the work and quote for it. One was totally honest with me and said his company weren't right for the job. 'You need a bigger set-up than mine, love,' he said. 'I've only got a few lads working with me. We can build a simple extension or a garden room, but the stuff you want to do, to this old place, would be tricky for us. Building new is a lot easier than restoring old, if you get my drift. I'm not going to waste your time or mine. I'm just going to say sorry but this job's not for me.'

'Thank you anyway,' I said, showing him out. 'I appreciate your honesty.'

There was another fellow who seemed enthusiastic and nodded, saying 'no problem, we can sort that' to everything I suggested. And then when the quote came through days later it was for an extortionate amount, with absolutely no breakdown. 'This guy just thinks I'm rolling in money,' I muttered. He wasn't going to get my business.

The other two quotes were better, and as we went around the house, the builders came up with several ideas I hadn't thought of, and Nick hadn't suggested. Not all of them were what I wanted, but it was clear they were engaged and thinking about the project.

I looked forward to receiving their quotes, which would be good ones to compare with Nick's. I realised that was the only reason I wanted to see them – to compare. To make sure Nick's quote (which had arrived and was itemised as he'd promised, splitting the work into three phases of 'essentials', 'desirables' and 'icing on the cake') was competitive. I really hoped it would be, especially now I'd ruled out using Seaway Renovations.

As it turned out, Nick's quote was right in the middle. One of the others came out more, and the other one less, but that company wouldn't be able to start work on my house for at least six months. And I was impatient to get going. Nick Marshall's company could start within a couple of weeks. And so it was a no-brainer for me. I phoned Nick to tell him, feeling strangely nervous.

'Millie, that's great news. May I come round on Saturday to take some measurements, so I can order supplies for the first phase? I'm really pleased we'll be working with you on this project.' He genuinely sounded delighted, and by the time I hung up, having arranged a time for him to call, I was feeling very excited to be getting going with the project. I spent the rest of that day listing everything I really wanted done in that first phase – all of Nick's 'essentials' and a few of his 'desirables' that I could afford now, while still keeping some savings for contingency.

That evening, I had a phone call from Steve. That wasn't unusual – we were still friends, and had agreed to call each other every fortnight or so for a catch-up.

'Hey, Millie. How's it going? Settled into the new house?'

'Yes, I love it here,' I answered. 'I'm about to get some work done on it. I told you, I think, that it needs complete renovation?'

He laughed good-naturedly. 'Yes and I think you're mad taking it on. What's wrong with a nice, neat new-build? You saw the details of the one I've bought? It's immaculate. All I've had to do is arrange some furniture in it. And I'll have to mow the lawn soon. No maintenance means more time to enjoy myself.'

'I think I'm going to enjoy the renovation project.' Why an image of Nick floated through my mind as I said that I wasn't sure.

'I hope you do, Millie, but I reckon you might find it quite stressful at times. Bloke I work with is in the middle of a major project – he took the back off his house and rebuilt, extending outwards and making it all open plan. His builders discovered a water main underneath where the new foundations were going, and it wasn't deep enough, and he's had all sorts of hassle getting that sorted. And then a neighbour complained about something or other, and work had to stop while that was looked into. Back on track now, but I swear he's got more grey hairs than he had before.'

I'd only half listened to Steve. I didn't want to hear second-hand tales of woe about building projects. I was well aware it could be stressful, but the end result would be worth it, and every step along the way, every little bit that was completed, would bring excitement and a glow of satisfaction, I was sure of it. 'I'll be all right, Steve. I'm actually looking forward to getting started. This house desperately needs some TLC to give it a new lease of life.'

'I still don't understand why you bought it. I wouldn't have touched it with a bargepole.'

'Well, we realised we like different things, didn't we? I can't say exactly why, but it spoke to me. This house feels as though it's got history oozing out of it, and I just fell in love with it at first sight.'

'Do you know much about its history?'

'No. But I'm going to research it. It'd be lovely to know when it was built and who lived here. And Nick – that's the builder I'm employing – and I are going to ensure that all alterations are as sympathetic as possible to its age and character. I don't want it to be a shrine to its past though – it's got to be a home fit for the modern day.'

'Sounds good.' But he sounded bored, I thought. It had been Steve who'd chosen our marital home. Looking back I think I'd have picked something with more character, something more individual with a bit of history. It's funny how you can get to the age of 29 before discovering what your tastes really are.

'Oh, did I tell you Mir had kittens?' I said, to lead us onto a different topic.

'Wow, did she?'

'Yes. I hadn't even realised she was pregnant until moving here. She had three, born just a couple of weeks after I moved in. They're so cute.' As I spoke I was watching two of them making their wobbly way across the sitting-room floor. The third was more timid, still sitting in the box where they slept. Mir was in the kitchen having some food. As the kittens grew, she was becoming more prepared to let them out of her sight for short periods.

'Aw. Are you going to keep them all?'

'I'll probably keep one. Not sure yet.' Steve had never wanted pets. Another way in which we were different. Growing up I'd had a cat, and some rabbits and hamsters at different times. Steve's brother had kept gerbils and goldfish but Steve had always said pets were too much bother, too restrictive.

'Well, I'll let you go. Keep in touch, hey? And I'd like to come and see the house, if I may. Perhaps when the building work's done.'

'Sure. I'll have a barbeque or something.' I tried to imagine introducing him to Sharon or Nick at a party in my back garden. Nick? Why would Nick be at this future party?

'Great! Well, best wishes and all that. See you, Mils.'

'Bye then.'

We would always be friends, but I had a feeling it might dwindle to only a superficial friendship as time went on. We'd drifted too far apart. And if either of us found new partners, it'd be awkward meeting up. I felt a momentary pang of loss. Not for Steve himself, but for the kids we'd been, the teenagers who'd got together at the school disco and discovered our first love. For our youth, which was now in the past.

'It's called growing up,' I told myself, sternly. 'And you're far from old yet, Millie.'

The kittens were fast becoming bigger. By the time Nick's company arrived to start work on the house, they were at the stage when they were into everything. I left a sewing basket out, and returned to find they had pulled out all the reels of thread and offcuts of lace and cord, and got them all into a huge tangle. I left a newspaper on the floor and hours later there were shreds of paper like confetti all over the house. A USB cable was chewed and a sock was attacked and killed by all three of them working as a team. I mean, it was cute to watch them but I had to be so careful to keep anything important out of their reach.

'You need to discipline your children!' I told Mir, as I disentangled two of the kittens from a curtain they had climbed halfway up. Good job they were old curtains, inherited with the house, that I would soon be throwing out. Mir just sat in the middle of the floor, regarding their antics with an expression of maternal pride. It was going to be fun keeping the cats and builders apart, I thought. I had a plan to shut them all in a bedroom with litter tray, food and a bed whenever the builders were in. The kittens were too little to be allowed outside yet.

I'd just moved the kittens and their things into a bedroom and was searching for Mir, when the doorbell rang. I closed the bedroom door and hurried down to answer it. It was Nick, with some fellows in tow. They'd parked a van outside the house. 'Hi, Millie. These two are Keith and Aaron. They're my best lads, and they'll be here most days along with me.'

'Hi, guys. Come on in!' I led the way through to the sitting room. 'So, shall I get you some tea before you get going?' The way to a builder's heart and best work is via cups of tea, as my mum had always said.

Nick laughed. 'Let us get started. Tea would be great in about an hour or so, though.'

The two lads (well, they were in their thirties and older than me – I should call them men, I suppose) looked disappointed but laughed good-naturedly. Nick talked them through what was to be done and a few minutes later they were bringing in armfuls of tools and supplies. The plan was to start on some remodelling downstairs first – a dividing wall to come out, a patio door to put in, the fireplace to be opened up. It was going to be messy and disruptive, but I'd end up with a beautiful big sitting room stretching across the back of the house. After that the kitchen would be ripped out and replaced, and then we'd get started upstairs.

They shifted my furniture out of the way. I'd already moved the smaller items to bedrooms but the lads and Nick moved my table and chairs and bookcases into one of the outbuildings. A skip was delivered while they worked, and manoeuvred into position on the pavement in front of my house. I'd parked my car in the yard around the back of the house. Soon the skip was half full with the old carpet and plasterboard from a stud wall that had divided the living area into two. It was amazing to see the space change. As they worked, Nick kept glancing over towards the blocked-up fireplace. 'Looking forward to opening that up,' he said to me, as I handed him the second of the cups of tea I'd made. 'All right if we do that next? Too late today to cut the patio door opening.'

'Whatever you think best.' I was already trusting Nick implicitly.

The younger builder – Keith – armed himself with a sledge-hammer and approached the old fireplace. I stood to watch, but at that moment the doorbell rang so I had to leave them to it, closing the sitting-room door behind me in a futile attempt to keep building dust out of the rest of the house.

Sharon was at the door. She glanced behind me as I answered it, as though checking whether there was anyone else around. 'Do you have a moment? Can I speak to you in private?'

'Of course.' She gestured to me to come outside, so I did,

pulling the front door over. It was on the latch already as Nick, Keith and Aaron had been in and out all morning.

She led me a few steps away from the house, and stood by the skip, nodding towards Nick's van. 'You went with Marshall, then? Were the other companies I recommended to you no good?'

'They were fine. But one of them couldn't do the work for months, another's quote was really high. Marshall's seemed the best of the lot.' I sounded defensive, even to myself.

'Hmm. I'm sorry if you think I'm interfering, but I thought I'd warned you about the Marshall family. Millie, I'd hate for you to have trouble – I know how much this building work means to you. And, well, I just don't think any Marshalls can be trusted.'

'Why? What have you heard?' I must admit, I was worried by this. I'd read reviews on Nick's website and on Google of course, and they'd all been good, but mostly I'd picked him because I liked him and felt he had the same vision as I did for the house. I'd had a gut feeling that he was the right builder for the job.

'His father is Des Marshall. He used to be the local mayor.'

'Yes, I think you told me that before. Well, that's good, isn't it?'

'He was – oh, how shall I put it? – known for dodgy dealing, I think is the phrase. You know the sort of thing – if you wanted something done, a little bit of a backhander to Dodgy Des and it'd smooth things over. There were a number of developments in the town where the tenders went to Des Marshall's cronies. And building projects that shouldn't have got planning permission, but managed to despite objections. Money changed hands, if you know what I mean.'

'But that's Des Marshall. It's his son, Nick Marshall, that runs this business.'

'Ah, but an acorn doesn't fall far from the tree, does it? You're not local, of course, so you weren't to know. But all the Marshalls are … well … not really to be trusted.' She leaned in conspiratorially. 'A Marshall was mixed up with drugs in the past. Not just taking them – dealing, or bringing them into the country or something. I don't know all the details, but it was definitely one of the family, and to my mind it's worrying. I mean, maybe this fellow will do a good job and prove me wrong, but I'd watch him carefully if I were you.'

'Well … all right. Thank you for the warning. His company had some great reviews online so I thought …'

'But those could all be fake, couldn't they?'

'And I looked at one project, from the outside, that he'd done …'

'But you can't really tell the quality from the outside.' Sharon's tone was verging on triumphant. I was not enjoying this conversation. I was about to say something more when the front door opened, and Nick stuck his head out.

'Millie? Sorry to interrupt, but we've uncovered something … I think you're going to want to see this.'

'All right, on my way.' To tell the truth I was very glad to have an excuse to end the conversation with Sharon. I hoped she would not want to see what Nick had found too.

'Well, think on what I said, and take care. I'll let you go.' Sharon waved a goodbye and set off back across the road.

I took a deep breath. She'd worried me a little. I did trust Nick – my instincts told me to – but was there anything in what she'd said? After all, she'd been right about Seaway. Maybe I should do some digging online, ask around a bit more, get some other opinions. But whatever I found out, Marshall Construction had started on my house and I couldn't drop them now in favour of anyone else, could I?

I went back inside, and through to the sitting room where the guys had removed the breeze blocks that had closed off the old fireplace. I could see Nick had been right – it was the size of an inglenook fireplace, far too large for the room especially after it had been divided. No doubt that was why it had been closed off. But it wasn't the size that had made Nick come to fetch me.

'Look at that.' He pointed to the back of the fireplace. There

49

was a low door, made of some sort of blackened metal, set into the brickwork.

'What's that for? Ventilation?' I moved closer, and saw that it was about a metre high – at a crouch an adult would be able to squeeze through.

'No, I think it leads somewhere.' Nick stooped and shuffled forward into the fireplace. He pushed on the door but nothing moved, and then he tugged on its handle. It began to open, the bottom edge scraping over the base of the fireplace. Nick had to push rubble out of the way, until the door was far enough open to peer around. 'Do you have a torch?'

'Only my phone.' I switched on the torch function and passed it to him.

He angled the phone to light up the space revealed behind the door. 'Oh my word! This is amazing!'

I couldn't see. 'What? Come on, tell us!'

'Steps down. Looks like a cellar.'

'Accessed from inside a fireplace? There's no cellar I know of in this house.'

'We've got to get this fully open and have a proper look. Aaron, Keith, let's clear out this rubble.' Nick backed out of the fireplace and the two lads moved in to remove the debris. They made short work of it, and with the addition of a squirt of oil on the hinges of the metal door they soon had it open. Keith had also fetched an inspection light and an extension lead from the van, as well as some safety helmets.

'Let me go first,' Nick said, donning a helmet. He entered the fireplace once more, opened the door fully and held the light ahead of him. I could see a set of rough stone steps leading downwards, into a gloomy space. Nick set off down them, his tall frame bent double. As he progressed, more and more of the space was lit up. 'Bloody hell. It's huge!'

'Can I come down? Is it safe?' I couldn't wait to see.

'Put a hard hat on. But yes, looks sound from what I can see.

50

I'm under your outbuilding, I think. The one where we stored your furniture.'

I strapped on a helmet and ducked into the fireplace, following Nick down the steps. The space at the bottom was low-ceilinged. I could stand upright but Nick had to bend his head a little. There was a bit of debris in there – some packing crates, a pile of bricks, a couple of small barrels stacked against one wall. 'What was this place? And why on earth is the access to it from a fireplace? That's just crazy!' The barrels had put me in mind of a pub storeroom. Was that what this was?

'Not if you wanted to keep it hidden,' Nick said. He'd hung the inspection lamp from a nail in one wall, and was looking around the edges of the cellar. 'I wonder if there's another entrance. I bet there is.' He began shifting a stack of broken packing crates that were on the opposite wall to the steps. 'These are empty. Wonder what they're hiding.'

He was right. Behind them was another door, this one wooden and partly rotted at the bottom. Nick tried to open it but the handle came away in his hand. 'Keith? Pass down a crowbar, would you?'

Keith brought one down, and Nick used it to lever half-rotten strips of wood from the door. Eventually it gave way. I unhooked the inspection lamp from the wall and brought it nearer, shining the light through the doorway he'd revealed. Beyond was a tunnel, sloping gently downwards. It was lined with bricks and the floor was packed soil. 'What on earth …?' I said, feeling lost for words. A hidden cellar, a tunnel – what was all this for?

'Shall we see where it leads? This brickwork looks sound …' Nick tapped the top of the tunnel. 'Actually, let me go first.'

'But you need the light,' I said, and he nodded. Cautiously we both made our way slowly into the tunnel.

'Hey, you're leaving me in the dark!' Keith said, and faintly I heard Aaron, still up the steps in my living room, laugh.

'Use your phone, mate,' Nick called back to him.

We crept along, Nick checking the ceiling and walls of the tunnel as we progressed. The idea of it collapsing on us was not a thought I wanted to dwell on. The extension lead was a long one, and every now and again Nick tugged more of it into the tunnel behind him. After a while the brickwork stopped, and from there on the tunnel was lined only in rotting wood. Just beyond that point it was clear we could go no further. 'It's collapsed just up here,' Nick said. 'Completely blocked. And I'm not confident this section is safe, either. Go back into the part that's lined with bricks.'

I turned around and did as he said, and he followed. 'Actually, Nick, let's get out of here,' I said. 'It's beginning to give me the creeps.' I gave a nervous laugh.

'Of course. You go ahead with the lamp and I'll be right behind you.' He put a gentle hand on my shoulder as we made our way back. It felt warm and reassuring – he was there, I'd be safe, we'd soon be out.

We emerged into the cellar where Keith was waiting. 'Where did it lead? What did you find?'

'It goes about twenty metres or so, round a bit of a bend, and then it's collapsed. Only the first section is lined in brick. Millie, are you OK? Do you want to get back up into the house?'

I think I must have been looking a bit scared still. I nodded, and went back up the steps and out through the fireplace entrance. Aaron gave me a hand getting out, and I straightened up grate-fully and grinned at him. 'Well, that was all a bit unexpected!'

He grinned back and nodded, as Keith and Nick also came back up.

Nick switched off the inspection lamp. 'You know what I think you've got there?'

'No idea,' I replied.

'A smugglers' tunnel and storeroom. Can't imagine what else it would have been built for.' His eyes were bright with excitement.

I gasped, and let my mind run riot, imagining gangs of men

carrying kegs of rum through the tunnel and into the cellar, while oblivious Customs men rode horses up and down the street outside. Now I knew I needed to know more about the history of my house. Why store contraband here? Where had the tunnel led to?

Chapter 6

Life went on for Esther, over the next few weeks, as spring gave way to summer in much the same way as always. At least once a week she was involved in a night-time smuggling run, unloading the goods on the beach, transferring them to a rowboat and bringing them up the channel through the marsh, to The Ship at Anchor to be stored in the hidden cellar. Most of these runs were small and went smoothly, though Streeter liked to vary the pattern. Some goods were rowed up the Stour and distributed in various villages further up. Some would be taken to Place Mill in Christchurch, and hidden inside sacks of flour. If Revenue men were spotted approaching the town while goods were being distributed in Christchurch, it was common for a farmer at Purewell to 'accidentally' allow his sheep onto the bridge to block it, thus keeping the authorities away from the town centre and giving the smugglers more time to distribute and hide the goods.

At the pub, once the goods were safely stored Esther and her father would lay a fire in the fireplace, complete with kindling and animal fat smeared on the logs. It was ready to light at a moment's notice and would flare quickly, hiding the cellar entrance and making it impossible for anyone to access it from the pub. Anyone coming in would see a roaring fire and wouldn't for a moment suspect there was a secret cellar accessed from the back of the fireplace. It had saved them on more than one occasion, when Revenue men had entered the pub and demanded to inspect the contents of the cellars.

Each week Esther would set off in the little pony cart to the brewery up at Ringwood, and come back with barrels of ale. Pa used to make this trip, but he found it too uncomfortable now that his back problem had worsened. Inside some of the empty barrels she was returning would be hidden kegs of brandy and packets of tea and tobacco for onward distribution by the brewery. And now and again Streeter's customers would come directly to the pub, where after giving Esther or her Pa the correct code word, they'd be taken round to the yard and a packet of tobacco would change hands.

Back when Ma had been alive and Matthew had still been with them, it had been Esther's job, as a young girl, to keep a lookout for Revenue men. She'd play out on the street and if she spotted anyone coming near, she was to run in, shouting that the puppy had run off. That was the signal to light the fire. Matthew would do this, while Ma and Pa checked there was no contraband on show and that all their customers, for they were not always sure which of them they could trust, were not suspecting anything.

Ma had done her share of helping land and store the goods too. It was she who'd first dressed in men's clothes to go down to the beach. The blue cap that Esther always wore had been Ma's, though the nickname of Blue had only ever been Esther's.

Ma had died suddenly and unexpectedly, one summer when Esther was about 12 years old. One day she'd been fit and strong, working in the pub all day, teaching Esther how to make the mutton pies the pub was famous for. She'd helped land a run of contraband that night, and had returned to the pub late and exhausted, along with Pa and Matthew, who at 15 was already helping the smugglers.

And then the next morning Ma had complained of chest

pains, struggling to keep going. Pa had sent her to rest after the lunchtime rush, and when Esther went upstairs to check on her later she'd found her lying cold, still and grey, tucked under the counterpane. Esther had closed Ma's eyes and kissed her cheek, lying on the bed beside her for a moment before going downstairs to tell Pa and Matthew the terrible news.

They'd buried her in the Priory churchyard, with all the towns-people in attendance to pay their respects.

Losing her mother at such a young age had been hard for Esther, who'd had to grow up very quickly, taking over her mother's responsibilities in the pub, baking pies, pouring pints of ale and cleaning up. A year later she helped land her first haul of contraband, using her mother's set of clothes.

Throughout all this, Sam had been part of her life. Pa and Sam's father had been close friends, and old Dick Coombes was a regular in the pub. When he was there, Luke Harris would take off his apron and sit for a while, chatting with his old friend and leaving Esther to run the pub. Sam would often accompany his father on these visits, and would end up sitting near the bar, where he and Esther could talk, and flirt, between customers.

Dick Coombes died a few years later, leaving his house in Burton to his sons, Sam and George. They both worked as farm labourers, supplementing their income by helping on smuggling runs, just as their father had before them.

This was how it was, Esther thought. How it had always been, and always would be. The only thing that would change was that in time, she and Sam would wed, and take over the pub when Pa was too old or frail to run it. They'd been waiting only until Esther was of age. Pa knew and Sam had his blessing. At least … he'd had it up until Thomas Walker started showing an interest in her. Meanwhile, life went on with a run taking place every week or so, and goods ebbed and flowed through the tunnel and cellar just as the tide rolled in and out of the harbour.

* * *

One memorable cargo was unloaded in broad daylight, with the lugger at anchor in the harbour. Revenue men from Lymington, not the friendly Christchurch men, had rowed alongside, asking what the ship was carrying, and the ship's captain had invited them on board. They'd been wined and dined by the ship's officers with the best the ship had to offer, while the rest of the crew quietly unloaded the contraband and rowed it to shore. Sam Coombes had been involved in this one, and Esther had enjoyed hearing him tell the tale, entertaining him in return with the story of Lovey Warne taking a drink with James Noyce, while actually wearing contraband under her clothes.

'They have no idea, do they?' Sam said, laughing.

'Those who know are on the take. Those who don't know must be blind and deaf, as well as stupid,' Esther replied. She regarded Sam thoughtfully. 'Do you ever feel guilty? I mean, what we are doing is against the law, isn't it? My own brother had to pay the price when he was caught.'

Sam shook his head. 'No, I don't feel guilty. The only ones losing from what we do is the government, and it's their fault we need to do it anyway. If the duties on these goods weren't so stupidly high, there'd be no profit in it, or at least not enough to warrant the risk. Look, the duty on some of the things we bring in can be six or seven times the value of the goods! The government are squeezing people dry. Everyone benefits from the free traders – the men involved in bringing it in and distributing it are paid more than their weekly wages, the rich get to enjoy their drinks and smokes and silks, the trades depending on those goods make more profit. Streeter sources and pays for the goods honestly, and transports them at his own expense. The goods are in demand, by people who could not otherwise afford those things. This is how he puts it, and I have to agree. It might be illegal, but it's all good.'

Esther nodded. She'd heard all this before, she believed it herself. It was how things were, in communities all along the south coast. Just occasionally, she would wonder if there was a better way – if duties weren't so high; if the government could raise their finances by some other means, perhaps by taxing the rich; if wages for common working people could be higher so they didn't need to take risks to supplement their income … But all that would need change to come about, and that didn't look likely to happen any time soon. 'As long as no one gets hurt, I can handle it.'

'No one gets hurt,' Sam confirmed. 'Worst that ever happens is we tie up a Revenue officer while we unload the goods, then we leave him someplace where he'll be found and set free in the morning. He gets an uncomfortable night, that's all.'

Esther smiled. She'd heard before of such things happening. It all seemed a bit of a joke at times. So many of the Revenue officers were in the pay of the smugglers anyway. There weren't many who were a problem. Of the Christchurch officers, only Noyce was not on the take. The rest were born and bred locally and many had family members taking part in the trade, or had even been directly involved themselves before becoming Revenue officers. The free traders needed to be careful not to be too blatant about their activities, but on the whole they were safe. It had been going on for decades, centuries, even, and seemed unlikely to change any time soon.

But that night things did change. Sam did not come to the pub, although he'd said he would after taking part in landing some goods. Esther had not been involved this time. The following day Sam called at The Ship at Anchor in the late afternoon, looking tired and drained.

'Blue, I'm in need of a strong tot of brandy,' he said, and she fetched the drink for him. He sat near the fireplace, head in hands.

'What's happened?' She spoke quietly, for there were a few people in the bar whom she didn't recognise.

'The run last night. We'd unloaded and were just getting going with the carts when Noyce and a couple of officers from

Lymington arrived on horseback. They gave chase. We lost a cartload of goods – it overturned and we had no choice but to abandon it. One of the batmen decided to put up a fight, and he laid into a Lymington officer with his cudgel. Noyce wasn't standing for that, and he fired his musket. Our man – a fellow called Ramsden – was shot in the shoulder.'

Esther gasped and clapped a hand to her mouth. 'Was he … Did he …'

'We let the Revenue men take the goods, and lifted Ramsden onto the cart. He lives in Bransgore so we drove the cart there, to his home, and laid him on the kitchen table. His wife looked at the wound and saw the musket ball was still in there. We knew he'd have no chance unless we could get that out, but no one was willing to try.'

'He needed a doctor.'

Sam nodded. 'George and I saddled up a couple of horses and rode back to Christchurch. We knocked on Dr Quartley's door.'

'Quartley's no friend to the free traders!'

'We had no choice. George and I, shall we say, *persuaded* him to come with us, back up to Bransgore. We gave him no choice but to come with us, on the back of my horse. It was about three o'clock in the morning. We took Quartley in to see Ramsden, and he operated on him – he managed to get the musket ball out, stitched him up, dressed the wound. Then we took the doctor back home. We didn't hurt him at all, though he was complaining loudly.'

'Did he recognise you?' Esther was worried the doctor might report Sam to Noyce or other authorities.

'We had masks over our faces. We barely spoke to him. He won't know who fetched him and took him back.'

'Will Ramsden be saved?'

Sam shrugged. 'He has a good chance, now. He'd have died for certain without the doctor's ministrations. Now, as long as the wound doesn't become infected, he should probably live.'

Esther was relieved to hear this. Shooting of muskets felt as though it went against an unwritten code between the Revenue men and the free traders. 'Why did Noyce fire his musket?'

'Ramsden had lashed out with his cudgel, hitting one of the other officers. Noyce was defending them. From his point of view, I suppose he felt he had to fire.'

'It's awful. I wish there was never any need for violence.'

Sam shrugged. 'The Revenue officers are always going to carry firearms to defend themselves. They're usually outnumbered by us. And we have to be able to defend our goods.' He softened his voice and put a hand on her arm. 'Don't worry, Blue. It's not often something like this happens. Neither side wants bloodshed. We have to watch out for Noyce, we know that.'

'What if it had been you who was shot?'

'That wouldn't happen. I'm not a batman. Any violence involves them only, and as I said, Ramsden provoked it, the silly bugger. We could have abandoned that cartload and got away safely. Streeter always says he can afford to lose one complete cargo out of every three, and still make a profit overall. And last night, it'd have only been one cartload lost, which wouldn't have bothered him a bit. The others – another six full wagons – had already got away. Ramsden's a fool to have lashed out.'

'I'm glad the doctor was able to help him.'

'So were we. And tonight we will pay him – George is leaving a keg of brandy on his doorstep in lieu of payment.'

Esther had to admit that seemed fair. And after all, people got hurt in any job, didn't they? Even in the pub, fights could break out, people got injured, accidents happened. Maybe she just needed to toughen up a little. After all, no one had died. Ramsden would hopefully survive his injury thanks to the doctor's work. Even so, it made her blood run cold to think that one of the free traders could be killed on a run. She shivered. Imagine if it was Sam?

'Any chance of service around here?' The shout made her jump.

She'd been talking to Sam for far too long. Thomas Walker had entered the pub and was banging on the bar. She looked around for Pa but he must have gone through to the yard for something.

'Of course, sir,' she said, hurrying behind the bar to get him whatever he wanted. Sam, she noticed, downed his brandy in one and got up to leave. He didn't like staying in the pub when any Revenue men were there, even if they were friendly ones like Walker.

She served Walker the brandy he asked for. 'And how goes it with my little Esther Harris?' he asked. His tone was a little overfamiliar for her taste, but Pa had returned to the bar and she dared not be at all rude to Walker.

'All well, thank you, sir,' she replied. She headed across the floor to collect some empty glasses and tankards but Walker put up a hand to stop her.

'Wait. You were talking to Coombes, I think, when I walked in?'

'Yes, sir.'

Walker nodded. 'Keep away from him. He and his brother are trouble. The Revenue service has its eye on them. I don't want you caught up in it, if they get arrested.'

'What could they be arrested for?'

'Trouble last night, so I was told by Noyce. He's after them. He'll find a reason to arrest them sooner or later, and I won't be able to stop him.'

'Thank you for the warning,' she replied. She in turn would pass on the warning to Sam. Perhaps there were some uses to keeping Walker close, as Pa had always said.

'My pleasure. And for my further pleasure, sit a while with me. I've brought something for you.'

She was surprised but took a seat. Walker reached into his jacket pocket and pulled out a small packet. He opened it, to reveal a length of fine lace. 'I thought it'd look well around the neckline of your gown. The blue one that suits you so.' He smiled, and for once looked kind rather than wolfish. 'It's the best, Flanders

61

lace, of course. I've no idea whether any duty was paid on it or not, of course.' He winked at her.

No one had given her such a gift before. Not even Sam. Her instinct was to refuse the gift, but she dared not, in case she offended him. 'Thank you, sir. It's beautiful.'

Across the bar Esther caught Pa's eye, and he nodded. A moment later he passed by, a clutch of empty tankards in hand. 'You sit there and rest, lass. I'll serve the customers. You keep Mr Walker company as long as he wants, eh?'

She would rather have gone back to serving, but Walker had given a useful warning to pass on. If payment for that warning was for her to allow him her company for half an hour or so, then so be it. Apart from the occasional pat on her behind, Walker didn't attempt to touch her in any way. He was harmless enough, and Pa treated him as a friend, so Esther supposed she must, too. Walker had never attempted to get close to her, and she hoped that would remain the case.

Chapter 7

I made Nick and the lads another cup of tea after we emerged from the cellar. I realised I'd brushed against the tunnel wall and my T-shirt was filthy, as were my jeans, from crawling through the fireplace. Good job Sharon hadn't come to the door at this moment, I thought, as I handed out the cups of tea. She'd have been horrified at the state of me. We sat on stools in the sitting room to drink the tea.

'I guess we need to discuss what you want to do with that cellar and the fireplace,' Nick said. 'There's lots of options. We could put a new set of stairs down from inside the outbuilding so it's accessible from there, and close off the fireplace entrance. Or just block the whole thing off if you don't want to use it for anything.'

'I don't know. I'll have a think,' I replied. 'But first I want to try to find out something about the history of this place. I mean, if it was really used for storing smuggled goods …'

'There's a local history society, isn't there?' Aaron put in. 'I saw a display about them at the library.'

'Or you could ask at the Red House Museum,' Keith added. 'They've got a bit in there about smuggling, if I remember correctly.' He sniggered. 'Mind you, last time I went there was when I was in Year Six. Miss Royston's class, it was. I was only interested in dinosaur bones in museums back then.'

Nick looked thoughtful. 'There's a bloke I did some work for, once. He was in the history society, I think. Had a stack of books about local history. Old fellow. We were putting in a patio door and building some decking. Aaron, you were on that job I think?'

Aaron nodded but looked as though he didn't remember it.

Nick turned to me. 'I'll find the name of that fellow. I'll give him a call if you like. I reckon he'd be interested in taking a look, and would probably be able to tell you more about the smuggling trade back in those days.'

I smiled. 'That would be awesome, thank you.'

Nick and the lads got on with other work over the next few days, leaving the fireplace tidy but unchanged. There was so much to do in every part of the house they were always able to progress one part or another. It was the messy phase – the phase that Nick had warned me was the hardest, when everything looked worse than it had before, and it was hard to see what the end result would be. But when walls came down and spaces were opened up, when a patio door was put in and the sitting room was flooded with light, when ugly ceiling tiles were removed and original beams exposed, I found I could visualise the end result, and see how the house would look when it was done.

They'd also put a scaffolding tower up and repaired the roof, replacing missing roof tiles and repointing the chimney brick-work. The roof was done, and soon they'd repair cracks in the rendering and repaint the outside. The window frames were to be replaced room by room as the work progressed.

And Nick gave me the name and phone number of that histo-rian he'd mentioned. His name was Arthur Watts, and I phoned him on Saturday afternoon when there was no work going on in the house. He sounded excited at what I told him, and asked if he could come round to see the cellar right away.

'I don't see why not!' I said, and gave him the address. It was only fifteen minutes before a small car pulled up outside. I went out to greet him. He looked to be in his late seventies, tall and thin with wispy grey hair. He was wearing a pair of thick-framed glasses, a checked shirt and a pair of jeans.

'Millie? I'm Arthur. Pleased to meet you.' He smiled and put out a hand for me to shake. I warmed to him instantly.

'Lovely to meet you too. Come on in. I have some coffee on, or I can make tea if you prefer?'

'Would you mind if we just get straight to it? I'm longing to see what you've discovered.'

I ushered him inside, and through to the sitting room. He went over to the fireplace and bent to look inside.

'It's really dirty, and the steps are a little steep …' I said, unsure if he'd be able to manage them.

He grinned at me. 'I'm in my oldest shirt and I'm steady enough on the old pins. Is there any light?'

Nick had left his inspection lamp and extension lead with me, so I plugged that in, passed Arthur a hard hat and went ahead of him, into the fireplace and down the steps, holding the light so he could see. He grunted a bit but managed it, and once he was in the cellar I hung the lamp on the nail we'd used before.

'This is incredible. What a find!'

'There's a tunnel as well, but it's partially collapsed so you can't go far.' I hoped he wouldn't want to go down it and thankfully he seemed happy to just peer in.

'This is undoubtedly the work of smugglers,' Arthur said, and I nodded.

'That's what we thought. But why here? Why this building?'

Arthur looked at me over the top of his glasses. 'Well, I think we should go back up, sit somewhere comfortable perhaps with that cup of coffee you offered, and I'll tell you. I know a little bit about this building's past life.'

'Sounds like a plan.'

65

Shortly afterwards we were sitting outside on deckchairs in the scruffy back garden with coffee and biscuits. As I had no sofa (Steve had kept ours) and all my other furniture was stored away in an outbuilding it was the most comfortable place to sit. And not at all unpleasant, even though the garden was a terribly overgrown mess. If you stood up, you could see over the reeds across the marsh and harbour, to Hengistbury Head. Sitting down it felt completely private. Mir came out to join us – with the kittens a little bigger she was now comfortable with leaving them for short periods. Arthur leaned over and stroked her, in a way that suggested he was as much a cat lover as I was.

'So, Millie, what I can tell you is that your house used to be a pub. Until the late 1800s, it was known as The Ship at Anchor – kind of a sister pub to The Ship in Distress just up the road.'

I nodded. I'd passed The Ship in Distress a few times but as yet had not gone in. 'The Ship at Anchor sounds a bit more welcoming than The Ship in Distress!'

He chuckled. 'Many of the pubs around here were connected with the smuggling trade. It made sense – they helped store the contraband, they'd keep some of it and then they'd sell the spirits and wines in the bar for far less than the duty-paid prices. There are rumours of tunnels under several other pubs in town. The area was rife with smuggling back in the eighteenth century, when customs duties on many items were sky high. It was thought of as a victimless crime. Many people couldn't afford to buy duty-paid goods. Tea, for instance, could cost seven times as much if the duty was paid. Also, helping the smugglers brought in extra income for ordinary people who were involved in landing and distributing the goods.'

'I've heard a bit about it. I saw the sign down at Mudeford Quay about a battle.'

Arthur nodded. 'Yes, that happened at the height of the smuggling trade in 1784. Quite a dramatic event, by all accounts! I've got a little book on it, which I can lend to you. A Revenue officer was shot dead in the scuffle. It had a huge impact locally – the smugglers lost a lot of support from local people who felt things had gone too far. Before then, over half of the adult population of Christchurch was involved in helping the smugglers unload, store or distribute goods. By the size of your hidden cellar I'd say quite a lot was stored here. And no doubt the contraband was brought in via that tunnel. I expect the other end of it is somewhere hidden on the edge of the marsh.'

'Why is the entrance in the fireplace?' I'd been wondering this. So inconvenient!

'I suppose so that if Revenue men were in the area the publican could quickly light a fire to hide that entrance. I know of another house in Bournemouth, built by a notorious smuggler, that had a secret room accessed by a door six feet up inside a chimney. It was only discovered when the house was demolished in the 1950s. They had all sorts of tricks. Although many Revenue men here in Christchurch were corrupt, and in the pay of the smugglers.'

'No need to go to such lengths to hide the goods then,' I said.

'They couldn't be sure of all of them, and they couldn't be sure that one they thought was a friend mightn't turn on them.' Arthur took a sip of his coffee. 'And there's rumours a Revenue officer was done away with by the free traders, after the battle. You really didn't want to get on the wrong side of the smuggling gangs.'

We chatted for a while longer. Arthur told me all sorts of little anecdotes about smuggling in the area. A doctor who'd been abducted by the smugglers to help tend to one of their own who'd been injured; then years later, that smuggler came across the doctor in a pub and bought him a drink, thanking him for saving his life. Smugglers carrying goods in broad daylight through Christchurch Priory courtyard, just as a congregation were leaving. A tombstone for a fictitious person that could be pushed aside revealing a hiding place for smuggled goods; small orders of contraband would be left there to be collected by the customer. A convoy of smugglers meeting Revenue officers on horseback, exchanging a bit of banter and passing over some of their haul voluntarily. It all sounded rather good-natured, apart from one story about a young lad who was sold into slavery by the smugglers, to force his family into compliance. I was pleased to hear that hadn't happened in the Christchurch area.

'Is there some way I can find out who lived in this house, or rather this pub, back in the eighteenth century?' I asked. 'I'd love to have some names of who might have built and used the tunnel.'

'There are business directories of the town from that era. I'm sure the pub would be listed,' Arthur replied. 'I have access to the ones held by the historical society. So I shall look it up for you. If you have an email address, I could send you all the details I find.'

'Oh, don't put yourself to any bother for me!' I said, but Arthur waved my protests aside.

'No bother at all. It's nice to have a little project to do. Retirement can be a bit tedious at times.' Arthur stood up and stretched. 'Well, I must leave you for now. I will find out what I can and hope to email you some news within a week.'

I got up to write down my email address for him and to see him out. 'Thanks so much. It's been so interesting, and I am intrigued by all the smuggling stories.'

'I shall lend you some books on the subject. Lovely to meet a young person who's interested in local history.' He nodded and left. Across the road I noticed Sharon at a window in her bungalow. I waved to show I'd noticed her. She did seem to be the kind of person who kept an eye out on comings and goings of her neighbours, and I wasn't sure how much I liked that. Maybe she was just taking an interest. Maybe it was coincidental she'd been at that window as Arthur left. We were due another coffee and a chat. I decided to send her a text and invite her out for coffee. No point bringing her to my house while it was in such a mess. I couldn't imagine her coming round in her white jeans and heels while the builders were in.

* * *

Arthur had recommended the Red House Museum for me to visit. I looked it up online that evening, and discovered it was in the centre of Christchurch, near the Priory, and housed in what had once been a workhouse for the poor. It was open on Sundays. 'That's my outing sorted for tomorrow then,' I told myself. I was starting my new job the next week so I'd have to visit at the weekend or not at all. I wondered about asking Sharon if she'd like to go, thinking perhaps we could take her children, but I remembered how bored she'd seemed by the local history boards I'd stopped to read on our walk. No, it wasn't her thing. I'd be better off going by myself.

So the following morning I set off after breakfast to walk into town and go to the museum. I'd done this route before, skirting around the edge of Stanpit Marsh and then crossing the river Avon. This time I kept an eye out for Dr Quartley's old house – Arthur had told me the doctor's house was still marked by a brass plaque bearing his name. I spotted it – right by the river. There was the step where I guessed the smugglers had left a keg of brandy as thanks. Local history came alive when you were in the actual locations where things had happened.

I passed Ye Olde George Inn and turned left, down the High Street towards the Eight Bells gift shop. Arthur had told me that it used to be a pub and that along with Ye Olde George Inn, it was rumoured to have smugglers' tunnels beneath. 'But no one's ever found any evidence,' he'd said. 'You're the first to actually find a tunnel.'

Ahead was the Priory Church but the way to the museum took me up a small one-way street to the right. It was housed in the old workhouse, an impressive red-brick building opening directly onto a narrow street. To one side were well-maintained walled gardens.

Inside I found a typical small-town museum, with a jumble of old items donated by various people and businesses in the area. Everything from wallpaper printing templates from a long-gone local factory to an impressively large wooden mangle. Part of the museum told the building's history as a workhouse. One room was styled as a 1930s sitting room and reminded me of my grandparents' old house. The upstairs rooms were dedicated to the archaeology of the area – Christchurch had a long history going back to Saxon times.

In a corner downstairs I found a small display dedicated to smuggling, and I spent an absorbing half-hour or so browsing it. I'd heard some of the stories already from Arthur but it was good to read more about it and to see pictures depicting smugglers and a few items of smuggling memorabilia. There were kegs that had once contained brandy, very like the ones still in my hidden cellar, I thought. There were clay pipes and a skeleton of a dog that had been found in another hidden cellar under a now-demolished pub at Iford. There was a cudgel of the type used by smugglers for defence, and a drawing of a typical 'lugger' – the type of shallow-keeled boat that could be run up onto a beach for unloading, favoured by a notorious local smuggler named John Streeter. Who was he? I wondered. I made a note of his name. Perhaps I'd be able to find out more about him.

And tucked into a corner of a display case containing a rather random assortment of old costumes was a faded blue woollen cap, with a caption that said it was thought to have been worn by a woman named Esther Harris, who worked with the smuggling gangs unloading contraband from the ships. My imagination ran riot at the idea of a woman smuggler – I'd always assumed it would have been only men involved. I made a note of her name too.

All in all it was a pleasant and informative visit. I bought a book on local history, one with plenty of photos of Christchurch in the nineteenth century, and left the museum to walk home. I'd only just reached the corner beside Ye Olde George Inn when I heard my name being called. 'Millie! Wait up!'

I turned to see Nick waiting for a gap in the traffic to cross the road to me. He was grinning broadly. 'I thought it was you!

Just legged it down the High Street to catch up. Phew. Fancy a coffee? They do them in here.' He indicated the pub and I nodded.

'Yes, why not? I've just been in the Red House Museum and was heading home, but I've plenty of time.'

We went into the little covered courtyard of the pub and ordered coffees, which were brought out quickly. I told Nick about Arthur's visit – after all it was Nick who'd put us in touch. He seemed genuinely interested in all that I'd learned, and I enjoyed having someone to talk to about it all. 'Arthur's going to look through old town directories, to see if he can find out who owned my house back when it was a pub.'

'It used to be a pub? Right, well I know where I'll come for a drink next time then!' Nick said. I laughed, a little embarrassed and unsure how to take Nick's joke. Was he saying he'd like to come round for a drink? Or was it intended only as a joke?

'Well you'd better build me a bar!' I retorted, and he laughed.

'Just tell me what you want and where you want it, and I'll do it,' he replied, raising his eyebrows in what could be interpreted as a suggestive way. Was he flirting with me? I'd been with Steve so long – since school days – I had no idea how to tell when someone was interested in me.

I decided he couldn't possibly be. He was my builder. He was interested only in the house, and he was a pleasant bloke enjoying a coffee out with a client. That was all.

I laughed, and told him a little about what I'd seen in the museum, to change the subject.

'Sounds fascinating,' he said. 'I haven't been there since I was a kid. Must go again. My dad's always on at me to check it out. He donates quite a bit of money to it.'

'That's lovely of him,' I replied, remembering how Sharon had referred to Des Marshall as Dodgy Des who was not averse to taking a backhander.

'Yes. He tries to do his bit for the community. To give something back, as he puts it. Well, shall we make a move? I'm actually

71

parked over at Stanpit – I was in that area and decided to leave my car there and walk into town. So I'm going back your way, if you're ready and would like company?'

I smiled. 'That would be lovely.'

We paid the bill – Nick insisted on paying – and set off, walking back the way I'd come. At Stanpit Marsh, Nick suggested we take the longer way round, with its views of the harbour. It was the route I'd done before with Sharon, in the opposite direction, but I was happy to walk it again. A few ponies grazed alongside the path, moving lazily away as we passed. We walked along the harbour beach, over Mother Sillar's Channel, and back past the little visitors' centre, following the track at the edge of the marsh. But then, near the end, I spotted a turn off the path I hadn't seen before. 'What's down this way?'

'Don't know,' Nick said. 'Never been down that path. Isn't that the back of your house?' He was pointing across the reed beds.

'Yes, think so. That's my bedroom window on the left and the bathroom to the right. And you can see the chimney.'

The little track led through the reeds almost in the direction of my house. We followed it as it twisted and turned. It was clear not many came this way. I wondered if perhaps only the ponies used the path to graze. There was certainly some evidence they'd been that way – hoof prints and manure.

The path ended beside a small, rather muddy pool. We were closer still to the back of my house, which was now only about fifty metres away – just thirty metres to the end of my garden.

Nick bent and swirled the water of the pool with his fingers, then cautiously sniffed them. 'Brackish water. I wondered if the ponies come to drink here, if it was fresh, but I guess not.'

'Peaceful spot,' I said. 'Very secluded and hidden. If there was a little bench just there it'd be quite nice to hide away here with a book.'

Nick laughed. 'You'll be able to do that in your own back garden, with much the same view, once you've got everything organised.'

'I can't wait. I'm thinking I might do some work in the garden sooner rather than later. I was going to leave it till next year but it'd be so nice to be able to sit out there this summer.'

'I agree. Now's the time to do it.' Nick led the way back to the main path. I wondered whether to invite him back for coffee, but we'd just had one, and actually it was lunchtime and I had no food to offer. We parted at the little Stanpit car park, where he'd left his car. I'd be seeing him again the next day anyway.

Later that day I sat down to browse through the local history book I'd bought. It contained plenty of nineteenth-century photographs of Christchurch and environs, and a few earlier drawings including one of a smuggling ship being unloaded at Mudeford Quay. On another page was an old photo of The Ship in Distress and beside it, a line drawing of its sister pub, The Ship at Anchor. I gasped as I recognised the shape of my house, the window beside the front door that was now my kitchen window, the upstairs gables, the archway that led to the back yard and my parking spot. Not much had changed on the front of the building for over two hundred years. And not much had changed underneath in the cellar and tunnel, either, I thought.

Chapter 8

The pub was quiet. Just a couple of men from a nearby farm, and the wife of one of them, sitting in a corner, drinking steadily but not talking much.

Pa turned to Esther and spoke quietly. 'Go on down to the Haven House. Find out Streeter's plans, eh lass? I hear rumours he's planning another big run.'

'You sure?' Esther wanted to go – Sam would very likely be there.

'Quiet enough here. Off you go.'

She nodded, removed her apron and wrapped a shawl around her shoulders. It was not quite dark yet – the last of the sunset lit up the western sky. Hengistbury Head and the lookout spot on Warren Hill were silhouetted against it, and the pink and red light reflected off the water in the harbour. It was a beautiful place to live, she thought as she walked down the lane leading to Mudeford. Not that she'd ever lived anywhere else to compare it with. She'd been born in the pub, and her plan was to die in it too, whatever the likes of Thomas Walker said about any future husband not allowing her to work there. If she had any say in it, her future husband would be Sam, who would gladly run the pub with her. Not Walker. She shuddered at the very idea of being married to the Revenue man.

She reached the point where the road crossed the little river Mude. There was a bridge there now, it was no longer only a ford. Just after the bridge was a turn that led to the beach and to the Haven House Inn, perched at the end of a promontory between the open sea and the harbour.

The Haven House Inn stood alone, with only a couple of cottages beside it. Its isolation was the main reason John Streeter chose it as a meeting place to discuss his business. It was easy for someone to stand at an upstairs window and keep an eye on the road from Stanpit, warning the free traders if any Revenue officers turned towards the beach or pub.

Tonight, Streeter was sitting with two men in the furthest corner of the inn. One, Esther recognised, was William Parrott, the captain of the *Phoenix*. The other man she didn't know. Also in the bar was the landlady, Hannah Sellars, whom Esther knew well, and a few other men, mostly sailors from the *Phoenix* who were making a good start on drinking away their earnings from the last run.

'Esther!' Sam appeared from a dark corner, and kissed her cheek. He was there with his brother, George, who was a few years his senior, and their friend Will Burden. Esther greeted them all, delighted that she'd have company.

'Pa sent me to find out Mr Streeter's plans,' she said. 'And I need to warn you. The Revenue officer Noyce is after the two of you. You'd better keep out of his way. Thomas Walker told me he was looking for you.'

'Good of him to pass the warning on,' George said, but Sam was frowning. Esther knew Sam suspected Walker of having more than a passing interest in her, and he was no doubt jealous.

Hannah Sellars walked by their table after delivering a round of drinks to Streeter and his companions. 'Hello, Esther, love. John's just coming to a decision, I think. Sure he'll let us all know soon. Meanwhile, you'll have a glass of ale, the three of you?'

Esther nodded. 'Thank you, I will.'

Hannah went to fetch the drinks. George, Esther noticed, watched Hannah's every move. She caught Sam's eye, and he raised his eyebrows at her. Clearly he'd noticed the same thing she had. Even Will Burden smirked at the sight. Hannah was a widow who'd inherited the pub from her husband, but she was still quite young and certainly a fine-looking woman.

'Here you are, my chicks,' Hannah said, putting four mugs of ale down on the table. 'Get those down your neck. I think we'll be cracking out a brandy keg shortly. Got to celebrate our recent successes, haven't we?'

'We have indeed,' Esther said with a smile.

'Cheers then,' Will and Sam joined in.

'Aye, Mrs Sellars,' said George.

'Oh call me Hannah. Everyone calls me Hannah.' She gave George a playful smack on the upper arm, and he grinned, looking delighted with the interaction. 'I've more people to serve. You behave now, George Coombes.'

'Difficult to, with you around,' he said with a wink.

'Ah, be gone!' She bustled across the bar to serve some rowdy newcomers, men whom Esther recognised from previous smuggling runs.

'What's Streeter planning next?' Sam asked George, whose eyes were still on Hannah.

'I don't know. Think we'll find out soon though.'

Esther glanced across at Streeter, who was still deep in conversation with the two men. It certainly looked as though decisions were being made. As she watched, Streeter slapped his hands onto the table and leaned back in his chair, looking pleased with himself. He stood up and made his way over to the middle of the bar. The customers gathered around him – they were mostly sailors who worked on his ships and locals who helped land the goods – waiting to hear what he had to say. Streeter scanned the pub making sure there was no one there who posed a risk, and then spoke.

'Some of you know, I have a new ship, named the *Civil Usage*. I want to send her over to the Channel Islands on a run. *Phoenix* needs a few repairs so she will stay in the harbour. *Civil Usage* will sail tomorrow. I know this is short notice after the last run, so I understand if some of you wish to stay onshore and see your families – perhaps you can go on *Phoenix* in another week or so. But do I have a crew for my new ship?'

'Aye!' Several heads nodded and hands went up.

'Over there, then. Meet Captain William May, who will be the skipper of the *Civil Usage*. A fine man, who I trust absolutely and who will stand for no nonsense from his crew.' One of Streeter's companions stood up and nodded to the assembled men.

Captain May counted the men. 'We need more. Any more sailors among you? Or anyone want to learn the ropes?'

'I'm going to volunteer,' George Coombes said to Sam, as he raised his hand and then followed the group of men gathering around Captain May at the back of the bar.

'I'll go,' Will Burden said. 'Might as well fish for brandy. More lucrative.'

Sam glanced at Esther, questioningly. He wanted to go, along with George and Will, she realised. Sailing on a smuggling ship could be dangerous – anything could happen out at sea. But she would not stop him, if he wanted to go. She gave a small nod, which he took as assent, for he raised his hand too, grinning, and went after the others. Esther bit her lip. She'd miss him while he was away. There was no question of her going too – while she might dress as a boy to help land the goods, she couldn't do that on a voyage that might last a week or more. She couldn't leave her father that long.

'We have a crew,' Captain May said to Streeter, who nodded, looking satisfied.

'Thank you, men.' He raised his glass. 'To the *Civil Usage*, and all who sail in her. May she bring us all prosperity!'

'The *Civil Usage*!' Everyone drank to the new lugger.

Arrangements were made for the crew to meet up the following morning, to make the ship ready to sail from Christchurch on the outgoing tide late that night. Sam came back to Esther's side and put an arm around her.

'I'll only be away a few days. I've always wanted to learn to sail. This is the perfect opportunity.'

She smiled up at him. 'As long as you don't decide to join the Navy or go on merchantmen to the Far East!' She thought of Matthew, in the Navy against his will, sailing who knew where.

He shook his head. 'Not likely. I'll stick with Mr Streeter's ships, just back and forth across the Channel. That'll be enough for me. Just think, next time you're on the beach unloading, I'll be on the ship passing the goods down to you!'

She gave him a squeeze. 'You'll be careful, won't you?'

'Of course. And George will be with me. He'll look after his little brother, and bring me home safe and sound to you.' Sam leaned in close and whispered, 'As well as bringing himself home safe and sound to Hannah, I'm thinking!'

She giggled. 'I do think he has designs on her. She must be quite a bit older than him.'

'Ah, but she's a fine woman. Don't worry, though, Esther, I only have eyes for you.'

The evening passed all too quickly. Esther enjoyed the banter and camaraderie of the Haven House Inn. She was of course very used to the environment of a pub but it was different when it was your father's pub that you worked in. Being here was much more fun. The Revenue officers never came to the Haven House for a drink, so everyone was able to relax and enjoy the evening. The news of Mr Streeter's second ship and promises of riches to come when its first cargo landed had put everyone in high spirits. Literally, Esther thought, as she watched Hannah Sellars distribute another round of brandies among Streeter and the two ships' captains drinking with him.

At last Esther and Sam left, though George had decided to stay for a final drink. 'He'll stay until Hannah kicks him out,' Sam said, and Esther laughed. She took Sam's hand and the two of them went back up the road to The Ship at Anchor. Sam's lodgings were in the little village of Burton just outside Christchurch so he had further to go. It was a beautiful night, with a full moon in a cloudless sky, and Esther wanted the walk to go on forever. She thought she had never enjoyed an evening so much. And with Sam leaving on the ship the following day, who knew when they would get a chance like this again – just the two of them, alone, under the stars.

As though he was thinking the same thing, Sam did not let go of her hand as they approached the door of the pub. 'It's been fun tonight, hasn't it?'

'Yes,' she replied, and leaned against him a little. His arms snaked around her, and she rested her head on his shoulder. The Ship at Anchor was closed for the night – she could see no lights in any window. And hopefully Pa was not looking out of an upstairs window. She was supposed to be keeping Sam at a distance, to keep Walker sweet. 'You're leaving tomorrow. In the morning.'

'I am. But it will only be for a week or so, and then I'll be back, and there'll be more money for us. One day soon, Esther my love, you and I will wed and set up a home together. We'll be glad then of the income from free trading.'

She smiled. 'Yes, we will. But what about Pa?'

'He will come to live with us. Or we will run this pub for him. Whichever you prefer.'

It was her dream to run The Ship at Anchor with Sam by her side. But she could not imagine Pa giving it up just yet. And there was still the situation with Thomas Walker to resolve.

'I'd like that, so much,' she whispered, and Sam dipped his head to kiss her.

'Then we will make it happen. You're my port in every storm, Blue, you know that. After this run, I shall speak to your father.'

'Wait a while. I need to prepare the ground. I will tell you when it's a good time.'

'Of course. Let's make it soon, though.' He kissed her again, and she felt herself melting into him. If only this moment could last forever! She held him tight, wishing he was not going on the ship, praying her father would accept him as a son-in-law and Thomas Walker would simply disappear somehow, both fearful and hopeful for the future.

At last he broke away. 'I must go, and so must you. Will you be part of the landing party when *Civil Usage* returns, Blue?'

She smiled at the use of her nickname. 'I suspect that's very likely. Take care, dearest Sam. Take no risks.'

'And the same to you.' He squeezed her to his chest one last time and then let go, waving back at her as he turned to walk up the road that led towards Christchurch and on to Burton.

She watched him go, and only when he was out of sight did she go through the archway to the pub's yard, and in through the back door.

'Out with Sam again?' Pa's voice startled her – she'd assumed he was upstairs in bed and even asleep.

'He and George were at the Haven House. I sat with them. I have news, Pa, of Mr Streeter's plans …'

'I'll hear them in a minute. First though, come and sit in the bar.' Pa picked up a candlestick and led the way through, walking stiffly, a hand pressed against his lower back. His tone was stern. Esther guessed he'd seen her outside with Sam, seen the kisses they'd shared. He'd tell her to keep her distance from him, no doubt. He'd remind her she needed to keep Walker on their side for a while longer. But for how much longer? Sooner or later she needed to put Walker off for good, and marry Sam. Sooner, not later.

Pa put the candle on a small table and sat down with a groan. His back must be paining him again, Esther thought. She sat opposite, her hands in her lap, and what she hoped was a meek, obedient expression on her face.

Pa was silent for a moment, regarding her, as though he was trying to find the right words. He looked disappointed rather than cross, she thought, and she felt a pang of guilt. She wanted her father to be proud of her, not disappointed. Finally, with a huge sigh, he spoke. 'My pet, I know how much you love Sam Coombes. He's a good lad. In any other situation I would want the two of you married as soon as possible. But …'

Esther held her breath waiting for him to continue. This was not what she'd expected to hear from him tonight.

Pa sighed again. 'Thomas Walker was in here this evening. He asked where you were. I told him I thought you were up at the Eight Bells with Lovey, as I didn't want to send a Revenue man down to the Haven, knowing Streeter was there making his plans. And then he asked me for my approval.'

'Approval?'

'Pet, he wants to marry you. He wants to do it right, with my blessing.'

Esther raised her eyes to his, and spoke in a small voice. 'And does he have your blessing?'

Pa nodded, slowly. 'He does, for if I said no, he hinted that he would make trouble for me. He would tell Noyce and Jeans, and he'd organise a raid by the militia.'

'They'd find nothing.'

Pa gazed at her sadly. 'Walker knows about the tunnel.'

Esther's blood ran cold. Walker might be one of the Revenue officers who accepted kegs of brandy in return for their complicity, but there was a limit. It was not good for him to know all their secrets. As far as she'd been aware, to date Walker had thought their pub was only a customer of the free traders, buying the contraband to sell on, not actively trading and storing goods themselves. She'd always been careful not to let him see her when she was helping land the goods. 'How, Pa? How does he know?'

'He came in early, round the back, before I'd opened. A couple of days ago. You were out running errands. He caught me just coming out of the fireplace, bringing up a keg of brandy. He said nothing, but he'd seen, and he had a cunning look in his eye, like he knew he'd be able to use that knowledge for his own ends.' Pa shook his head sadly. 'I'm sorry, lass. I wouldn't ever have forced you to marry him, you know that. I'd thought you liked him. He's always been charming enough when he's in here. He says he needs a wife. The Revenue service like to have married men in charge of Customs houses, and Walker has his eye on Joshua Jeans's job, when Jeans retires in a few years.' He sighed. 'I know your heart is set on Sam. Mine too, if I'm honest. But if – or when – Walker asks you … you know what you need to do. For our safety, lass. I wouldn't ask it, otherwise.'

Esther stared at him. He was asking her to accept Walker's proposal, when it came. He was asking her to marry a man who made her skin crawl. Walker wasn't a bad man, but he was not Sam, and she felt absolutely no attraction towards him. How could she marry him, and give up the chance of a future with Sam whom she loved? She could not trust herself to say anything more about it to Pa, now. She stood up slowly and brushed down her skirts. 'I'm away to my bed now, Pa. We'll talk about this tomorrow.'

She patted his shoulder as she passed him. It wasn't his fault, and he looked aghast at the situation. It was his fault Walker had found out about the tunnel, and gained a hold over them. But it wasn't Pa's fault that Walker wanted to use that hold to gain her hand in marriage. If only she were a year or two older and already married to Sam; that rosy future she'd dreamed of could have been their reality.

The following morning, the first of July, Esther told Pa she had errands to run in Christchurch and walked up there hoping to be able to see Sam before the *Civil Usage* set sail on the high tide from Christchurch Quay. She watched from the quayside for a while but sadly she did not spot Sam on board, and did not dare interrupt the sailors who were all busy making the new ship ready for her maiden run. *Civil Usage* was a fine-looking ship, with two masts and lug sails. John Streeter was there too, checking all was well, and he gave her a wink as he walked by her. 'They'll be all right, Blue. They'll be back safe and sound, your Sam included, in no time at all.'

She felt more reassured by Streeter saying this, and had a sudden urge to confide in him about Walker's interest in her. But no. If she said anything, she'd end up blurting out about Walker knowing about their tunnel. Streeter would be angry, and The Ship at Anchor would no longer be used as storage for the contraband. That would mean less income for her and Pa. Maybe it would be a way out for her – if they stopped using the tunnel and cellar, it wouldn't matter if the pub was searched for there would be nothing to find. Walker's hold over them would come to nothing.

But the free traders did not take kindly to anyone who betrayed them. A year before, a farm labourer had got drunk in the Eight Bells and had talked loudly about the cache of brandy kegs he'd hidden in a hayrick. James Noyce had been in the pub and heard him, and the brandy was lost. Streeter had sent a couple of batmen who'd given the labourer a thorough beating. He'd left the area, as soon as he'd recovered enough. Streeter was liked and respected, as long as you kept on the right side of him. Get on the wrong side and he was a man to be feared.

'They won't be sailing until late tonight,' Streeter told Esther. 'Don't be hanging around hoping to see them off.'

'No, sir. I need to get back before the lunchtime trade anyway.' As Esther walked back home, she forced herself to stop thinking about it too deeply. Sam would be safe, as Mr Streeter had said, and she'd find a way to put Thomas Walker off without antagonising him. Everything would continue as it always had.

Chapter 9

The building work progressed well over the following week. I'd started my new job, so I was out most of the day and returned home in the evening to check on the work. So far Nick and his lads had repaired the roof, opened up the sitting room, added the patio door, removed the old boiler and begun to install a new one and new heating system. Nick had phoned me at work a couple of times to check exact requirements, and each time we'd then ended up chatting for twenty minutes or so. He was beginning to feel like an old friend.

When I arrived home from work on Friday evening he was still there, covered in building dust. He removed a pair of safety goggles, revealing pink skin around his eyes that contrasted with the grey and white of the dust. 'Sorry, Millie, I must look a state. Been drilling through the wall to put some pipework in. I wouldn't go in your sitting room until you've changed – there's a lot of dust in the air.'

'You're here late! Thought you'd have gone by now.'

'Ah, I let the lads go, but I wanted to get this bit done. It's the messy stage. We'll be able to start making it look better from Monday, at last – get some plastering done. Plasterer's booked for Monday so I wanted to finish this today and then there's the whole weekend for the dust to settle.'

I smiled. 'OK, well I'd better make you a cup of tea then.'

But he shook his head. 'No, I'm all right, thanks. I'll get this cleared up then I'll be off.'

I felt a pang of disappointment. I'd begun to think he liked me – all those phone chats in the week had seemed so friendly. And here was a chance to spend a bit of time together. Ah well. Maybe I'd misread the signals. Anyway, what was I thinking? I'd only just moved out of the house I'd shared with my ex-husband. It was a little soon to be thinking of a new relationship, wasn't it?

I went upstairs to change, and to check on Mir and the kittens, whom I was having to shut in a bedroom all day while the work was going on. The kittens were growing fast, and I'd soon need to find homes for the two I wasn't keeping. They were fine, though a fluffy pom-pom I'd given them to play with had not survived the day and there were pieces of wool strewn all around the room.

By the time I came back down, Nick had cleared his tools, vacuumed up the worst of the building dust and ensured the house was in a usable state. I was grateful for this – I had to live here over the next two days before any more work was done, and I wanted to let the cats come downstairs. He took the last of his tools out to his van, then came back inside to the kitchen where I was beginning to investigate options for my dinner. 'We'll be back by eight on Monday, then.'

'Sure. Have a great weekend.'

I expected him to nod, say goodbye and go, but he hesitated a moment, staring at the floor as though trying to work out the right words. I busied myself taking a quiche out of my freezer, and gathering a few salad ingredients for my dinner. At last he spoke. 'Millie, if you are free tomorrow … I wondered … the weather's due to be good. Would you like to have a bit of a picnic, perhaps? Down at Mudeford Quay. We could take a basket, a bottle of bubbly or a couple of beers … if you're not doing anything …'

It sounded awfully like a date. Wonderfully like a date. I smiled broadly. 'I can't think of anything nicer! Yes please. I can prepare a bit of food here …' I glanced around at my kitchen – so far it had been untouched by the building work but it wasn't the most inviting place to work.

He shook his head. 'I'll sort the food, and the drink, don't worry. Any particular likes or dislikes?'

'I'll eat or drink anything.'

'Great! Then I'll call for you around midday? We could walk down, take a rug to sit on or nab one of the benches …' He looked delighted that I'd agreed, and I wondered if my own expression was as excited as his. What was happening here? A date, or simply the start of a friendship? I didn't have much to compare it with. Steve and I got together at school, when we were 14. Neither of us had ever had any other romantic relationship.

'Perfect.'

He nodded, blushing a little – at least I thought he might be, it was hard to tell under the grime – and then he left. I continued preparing my meal while deciding what to wear for the picnic, wondering what we'd talk about for the day, wondering what would happen. *Was* it a date? Did I want it to be a date?

I'd just about finished eating and had let Mir and the kittens come downstairs, when there was a tap at the door. I'd come to recognise the way Sharon knocked – a sharp double rap that somehow always made me want to scurry to the door and open it quickly as though I'd be in trouble if I didn't. Sharon was standing on my doorstep with her children, holding a foil-wrapped cake of some sort.

'Millie! The kids and I were baking this afternoon and thought you might like this.' She held it out. 'It's banana cake. I hope you like it.'

'It's the one I made,' the little girl – Tabitha – said.

'I absolutely love banana cake. That's so kind, but are you sure you don't want to eat it yourself?'

'We're going to eat mine,' Jasper announced. 'Tabs's cake

cracked on the top but mine didn't, so Mum said we should give hers to you.'

'Jasper! Both cakes are equally good,' Sharon said, sounding a little embarrassed that her son was hinting the reject cake was the one being given to me.

'Well, thank you so much!' I could take that to eat at our picnic tomorrow, I thought. 'Would you like to come in and see my kittens? They're big enough now for you to pick up and play with.'

Both kids gasped with delight and nodded enthusiastically, so I stood back and let them past. 'Go through there. It's a bit of a mess because of the building work but it's safe.'

'How's it coming along?' Sharon asked, looking around as she followed the children through to what would become my sitting room, when I had some furniture.

'All going well so far. They've made great progress.' I pointed to the corner of the room where the kittens were terrorising a dust sheet Nick had left neatly folded. 'Look, the kittens are over there, kids. It's OK to pick them up if you want.'

'They're so cuuuute!' Tabitha squealed, diving down onto her knees beside them.

I gave Sharon a tour of the changes made so far. 'This patio door's new. I'm going to have some decking built out there soon. And I thought I'd put a sofa here, to make the most of the view out towards the marsh.'

'Yes, that's lovely, and you'll get the evening sun all year round.' Sharon nodded with approval. I was glad she was not repeating what she'd said about the Marshall family. Not today, the day before what might be a date with Nick – I didn't want to hear it. 'How much longer will they take, do you think?'

I shrugged. 'To be honest I don't know. I think they're making good progress but we never really agreed on a schedule. There's all this to finish, and the kitchen to do, for this phase. Then there might be a bit of a gap for the sake of my sanity, before they tackle the rooms upstairs and the bathroom. And I'm thinking of doing some work in the yard with those outbuildings. Did you know we found a hidden smugglers' cellar and tunnel?' I was pretty sure I'd told her but as always with anything related to local history, she hadn't seemed interested.

'Oh yes. Well you'll be bricking that up, I imagine. That huge fireplace – I'd put a big TV there I think, with some seating around here to watch it.'

'Hmm. Perhaps.' I had different ideas.

'Mu-um?' Tabitha and Jasper had both approached, holding a kitten each. 'When the kittens are ready to go to their new homes, can we have one?'

'Or two?' Tabitha said, hopefully.

'One at the most, but of course Millie might already have found homes for them,' Sharon said, with a glance at me.

I tried to read whether she was hoping I'd say the kittens were already spoken for thus letting her off the hook, or whether she was genuinely happy to take one. She'd never struck me as the sort of person who'd have pets. 'To be honest I haven't thought as far as who they'll go to. I want to keep one myself – that one,' I said, pointing at the one in Jasper's hands. 'That's a female, and the other two are males.'

'Can we have this one, then?' Tabitha asked, holding up her kitten – the gingery one.

'If your mum and dad are happy to take on a cat, yes, you can.'

'Mum? Can we? Pleeeease?' they chorused.

'Well, yes, I suppose so. They're short-haired, so there shouldn't be too much shedding of fur, right?'

'Mir doesn't moult much,' I confirmed. I'd expected Sharon to be most concerned about her immaculate house than about the well-being of a pet.

'Yes!' Jasper punched the air, put down the kitten he was holding and went to stroke the other one. 'We can call him Tigger.'

'No, he's Crookshanks,' Tabitha said. 'Like the ginger cat in Harry Potter.'

'Hmph. He looks nothing like Crookshanks,' Jasper complained.

I'd have called a ginger cat Jasper, only they'd already used that name for their son. I thought it best not to say this. Sharon and I left the two to argue it out while I showed her around upstairs and talked her through my plans for it. 'Well, the building work is certainly coming on nicely' was Sharon's verdict, as she shepherded the children out twenty minutes or so later. 'So far so good, with Marshall, then. I'm glad it's working out. I was worried for you.'

'No need to be. I'm delighted with them.' I wanted to shut her down before she got going again with her remarks about Nick's dad. 'Well, bye then. Another couple of weeks and you can take the kitten. Meanwhile, kids, any time you want to come and see him just knock on my door, all right?'

On Saturday morning after much soul-searching I decided to wear a pair of loose cotton trousers and a lace-trimmed top. Much more 'girlie' than anything Nick had seen me in so far. I added a pair of chunky walking sandals so he wouldn't think I was too high maintenance. Not that it mattered – I was dressing to please myself, not him. Nick called for me on the dot of midday. He was carrying a rucksack that I guessed contained the food. I had a shoulder bag ready, with a bottle of chilled wine in a cooler jacket and some plastic glasses, a pot of olives, the banana cake and a picnic rug. My paltry contribution.

'Ready?' he asked, as I picked up my sunglasses and threw a cardigan into my bag as an afterthought. The day was sunny but there was a bit of a breeze. We walked down Stanpit and around to the grassy area on the harbour side of Mudeford Quay, where we put our two rugs down on the ground and sat near the water's edge. It was a perfect early summer's day – the sky was bright blue with seagulls wheeling and soaring above us, white against the azure. Paddle-boarders were making their way slowly around towards the Haven House. A bright yellow sailboat moored in the harbour looked so photogenic I had to take a number of pictures on my phone.

I lay back on the rug, taking it all in. 'When I die, I want to be reincarnated as a seagull,' I mused.

He laughed. 'What brought that on?'

'Look at them.' I waved a hand above my head. 'Not a care in the world. Swooping and gliding with zero effort. Not like, say, pigeons, that have to flap manically with their stubby wings to get airborne. That looks too much like hard work.'

'OK then. Be a seagull. Nice on a day like this, but on a stormy winter day when you've got to dive into the freezing cold sea to hunt fish, probably not so good. Me, I'd rather come back as a cat.' Nick stretched his back then lay down beside me to watch the seagulls.

'Yes,' I agreed, thinking of my pampered Mir, 'cats have a good life.'

'But we humans have the best life of all. I brought a bottle of bubbly. Fancy a glass?'

'Mmm, yes please.' I propped myself up on my elbow to take the glass he'd poured me. Drinking in the daytime always seemed so decadent, but today, with this glorious weather, it was the perfect thing to do. We opened my pack of olives, and Nick pulled out a platter of cheeses, cold meats and crackers, sticks of cucumber and celery, and a selection of dips. The kind of summer food I love. And we finished with the banana cake and huge juicy strawberries. As we ate we chatted about our lives, our backgrounds and my plans for the house, as well as touching on local history.

'This was where it happened, of course,' Nick said. 'The Battle of Mudeford. I always felt that was such a dramatic name for what was not really much more than a skirmish.'

'Someone died, though,' I added.

'Yes, and a smuggler was executed afterwards. So yes, I suppose it was more than a skirmish, at least for the people at the time. It happened after a record-breaking run, when double the usual amount of contraband had been brought back all in one go. You know, there was a re-enactment of the battle staged here a few years back. I came down to watch some of it. Dad was mayor at the time, and made a little speech.'

'Wow. That must have been interesting to see. What was it like having your dad as the mayor?'

Nick laughed. 'Made no difference to my life. He's always been on the council, chair of governors at my school, best friends with the police commissioner. He's that type, you know? Got to have a finger in every pie, likes to mingle with all the local bigwigs, wants to be involved in every decision made in the town. Drives me mad sometimes, but on the whole he does a good job.'

'Sounds like a pillar of the community.' What Nick was saying was entirely at odds with what Sharon had told me.

Nick nodded, slowly. 'That's the image he's always wanted to put across. He's not perfect though, by any means. He has his faults.'

'Don't we all?' I gave a little chuckle.

'He got in trouble once,' Nick said, quietly. 'I was a very young kid at the time. But he'd done some sort of shady deal. Greased a few palms to help a mate, something like that. I never knew all the details. He was up in court, found guilty and did a couple of months in prison.'

'Oh!' I wondered if this was what Sharon had been referring to.

Nick smiled at my reaction. 'Sooner or later people always hear about it, so I thought it better you hear it direct from me first. That my dad was once a bad boy.'

'But also a good man? Mayor and everything?'

'Yes. How he got himself elected back onto the council after that, I don't know. But he did, and he said he'd learned his lesson, and that I should always remember things aren't always black and white. There are countless shades of grey.' He took a sip of his drink. 'Anyway. Enough about him.'

His phone chirped at that moment, alerting him to an incoming text. He glanced at it and frowned, then quickly thumbed a response, angling his phone away from me. 'Sorry about that. Work,' he said, slipping it back into his pocket.

'No problem. Any other family?' I asked.

Nick shrugged. 'I don't see much of Mum. Once a year or so. She lives in Cornwall. They divorced when I was about twelve. Mum moved to Cornwall with her new man and I moved in with Dad. My older half-sister – Dad's daughter from his first marriage – died a year or two before, and Dad never really got over it. I think it helped that I chose to stay here with him rather than go with Mum. Although actually I was more concerned with staying near my friends.'

'Sorry to hear about your sister.' I couldn't imagine what it felt like to lose a sibling. I wasn't hugely close to my own brother, but we'd grown up together and we kept in touch by both visiting our parents at the same time.

'Mmm. What about you? Your parents? Do you have any brothers and sisters?' It was as though he wanted to change the subject, and not talk any more about his family, particularly the loss of his sister. Fair enough, I thought. She must have died fifteen years or more ago, but even so, I could understand him not wanting to dwell on the subject. And now it was my turn to tell him about the loss of my mum, which I still felt all too keenly.

'That's hard, losing a mum like that,' he said, when I'd finished. I had managed to talk about Mum without crying, which might have been a first. She'd been gone over a year, and it was her dying that had changed my life – shaken me out of the rut I'd been in with Steve, brought me to Mudeford and, I found myself thinking, allowed me to meet Nick. I missed Mum immensely, I always would, but some good had come from her passing. Things that might not have happened otherwise.

'Yes, it is.' I smiled brightly at him, to indicate it was time to talk of happier things. He took the hint, and steered the conversation onto amusing anecdotes from previous building jobs, and soon I was laughing loudly at some of his stories.

We stayed there for hours. When we felt stiff from sitting on the ground we packed up the rucksack and moved to a nearby bench, where we sat drinking the wine I'd brought. Later we bought takeaway coffees from the Haven House café, and sat on a different bench overlooking the entrance to the harbour, which Nick informed me was known as the Run. 'See the sandbank?' he said, pointing it out. 'It's constantly shifting. Every spring a new safe channel through it is marked out for pleasure craft to use. I think that had something to do with why smugglers liked Christchurch as a base – they knew the way through the sand-banks but the Revenue ships didn't, and couldn't follow them.'

I nodded. Arthur had said something about this too. I loved the way history was all around us here, as though it was a living, breathing thing.

It wasn't just history around us. As we sat there gazing out to sea, Nick suddenly pointed again. 'There. See it?'

I followed his finger and yes! I saw it! A dolphin, no, a couple of dolphins, lazily swimming just beyond the sandbanks, occasionally breaching the water. 'Wow! Magical. I had no idea there'd be dolphins here.'

'It's rare,' Nick said, 'but I've seen them on occasion before. What a perfect way to end a perfect day.'

As he said that, I realised I didn't want this perfect day to end. Not yet. The sun was still up, but it was time for another meal. 'Would you like to have dinner? Maybe over there in the Haven House Inn?'

To my delight he agreed, and we headed over to the pub. It was only basic pub food but was well prepared and we were both hungry. Afterwards, as darkness fell, we walked slowly back up the road towards my house. Should I invite him in? We both fell silent as we approached, and I had the impression he was

93

thinking the same as me – what would happen now, what did we want to happen? As we reached the house, he stopped and turned to face me. 'What a wonderful day we've had. I've really enjoyed being with you, Millie. I hope we can do it again, soon. Or at least have an evening out, maybe next week.'

I smiled. 'Yes, I'd like that.'

And then he held me by the shoulders, dipped his head to mine and kissed me. I snaked my hands up around his neck but the rucksack was in the way, and I couldn't find a way to hold him. Arms around the rucksack, or hands squeezed between it and his shoulders? I tried both, and we ended up both giggling uncontrollably.

'Ah, well, on that note, I think it's time to say goodnight.' Nick released me gently. 'I'll see you Monday. Maybe we could go out for a drink some night midweek? The Ship in Distress, perhaps?'

'Perfect,' I replied, and we kissed once more, just briefly, and then he left.

I stood for a moment watching him walk the short distance up the road to the Stanpit car park where he'd left his car. I touched my lips. Apart from a boyfriend I'd had before Steve, who had lasted about three weeks, that was the first time I'd kissed anyone other than Steve. And yet it had felt so natural, so right. I was only sorry it hadn't gone on a bit longer, and maybe even led to something more … But perhaps it was better to take things slowly.

I needed advice, I realised. My old schoolfriend Arwen. Maybe she'd be free to visit soon and I could talk to her about Nick.

Chapter 10

The *Civil Usage* had set sail on the first of July, but it was almost a fortnight before she was seen again. On the morning of the twelfth of July she made her way through the sandbars and into Christchurch Harbour. Esther spotted her from the upstairs windows of The Ship at Anchor, as she rounded Hengistbury Head. She'd been looking out many times every day ever since the ship had left.

She ran downstairs and into the bar, where Pa was getting ready for the lunchtime trade. 'Pa! It's Mr Streeter's ship! May I go and meet Sam? Can you spare me?'

'What? Lass, it can't be. We'd have heard if there was cargo to be landed, and it wouldn't be coming in at this hour. And it wouldn't be coming to Christchurch Quay neither.'

'It is, though. I recognise it. Please, Pa?'

'Something must be wrong for it to be coming up to the town.' Pa spoke almost to himself, looking worried.

Esther felt a surge of dread run through her. She had been so excited to see the ship she had not for a moment considered the possibility that things had not gone to plan. But Pa was right. There had been no calls to put together a landing party. The ship had been away far longer than expected. She'd thought she'd see

Sam and the *Civil Usage* next on the beach some time during the hours of darkness, dressed in her boy's clothes while they unloaded quickly. She knew the spotters had been stationed on Warren Hill day and night for the last week but they must have received no signal, otherwise John Streeter would have mustered a landing party.

'If something's wrong, I must go, Pa. I must find out if Sam is safe. Pa, I can't bear not knowing!' She was twisting her apron in her hands. Pa regarded her solemnly and at last nodded.

'Go, lass. I hope all is well.'

'Thank you, Pa.' She kissed his grizzled cheek, pulled off her apron and ran out of the pub before he could change his mind.

She walked as fast as she could around the marsh, over the bridges and into the town centre, past the colonnaded Town Hall, the Priory and down to the quay. She arrived just as the ship was tying up. Sailors were disembarking – they looked tired but also jubilant, laughing and joshing with each other. Some headed off home almost immediately, others went into the nearest pubs – the Eight Bells or the George Inn. Esther stood on the quayside scanning the ship and the disembarking sailors for a sight of Sam … and then, at last, there he was.

'Sam! Oh, Sam!' She ran headlong towards him. He noticed her at the last moment, so she almost bowled him over.

'Esther!' He opened his arms and she fell into them, showering him with kisses. 'Esther, steady on! I've so much to tell you. But not here, not now. Let's go somewhere quiet.' He nodded at a group of figures across the quay: two men on horseback. Revenue officers. From that distance she couldn't tell who they were, but one of them might have been Thomas Walker. Sam, of course, didn't know about Walker's conversation with her father, and it wouldn't do for Walker to see her in Sam's arms. He'd make trouble for them both. But she couldn't tell Sam about Walker. Not yet, not when he'd only just come back to her.

'All right, let's head back towards Stanpit,' she said, and they walked back through the town, over the bridges and onto the path that skirted the marsh. Part way along was a little piece of woodland, and in it there was a fallen tree. Esther led him to it, and they sat on the trunk, hidden from the main path. 'What happened? Is Streeter paying duties on this cargo?'

He laughed. 'Not at all. And actually, no duties are due. Do you know what's in the hold of the *Civil Usage*?'

She'd assumed wine, spirits, tea and other luxury goods – the usual. But he had a mischievous glint in his eye, so she shook her head.

'Ballast. That's all! Let me tell you the full story.'

Esther settled herself leaning against him while he spoke.

'We sailed on the first of July. We spent a night anchored off Hurst Spit, and then sailed over the Channel to Guernsey the following day, where we loaded the ship with wine, spirits and tea. But she wasn't full, so we then went to Alderney to pick up some more, before heading northward again. It was all going so well. I thought we'd be back home by the sixth.'

'Under a week!'

'Yes. The more experienced lads said that's quite usual. With the right winds, a decent ship can cross the Channel in just eight hours. Anyway, we were struggling a little with the winds being wrong when we spotted a Revenue cutter – the *Rose*. She'd seen us, and was gaining on us.'

'Oh no!'

Sam grinned. 'There's more to the story, just wait. The Revenue service can't do anything while we're at sea, because at that point, there's been no crime, of course. For all they know, the captain's intending on paying duties on all his cargo. All they can do is follow us and watch, and take action if we start unloading without having paid any duties.'

Esther nodded. She already knew this was how it worked. For legitimate cargoes, a tidesman would board the ship before unloading began, checking the goods and listing everything. Once duties were paid at the town's Customs house, permission would be granted for the ship to be unloaded.

'But of course we didn't want the cutter following us. So Captain May ordered us to suddenly go about and head south, back towards Alderney, where we hid.'

'How on earth can you hide a ship?'

'We tucked in behind the island, out of sight of the *Rose*, and then it grew dark. Then we sailed during the night to Cherbourg, and went into the port. The Revenue ships can't touch us there, in a French port. The *Rose* was patrolling back and forth, outside of French territorial waters, but could come no closer. Finally a couple of days later we set sail again, but soon saw the cutter, and turned tail once more, back to Cherbourg. I'll admit, it was all a bit frustrating at this point and I wondered how on earth we'd get the cargo back. The *Rose* obviously knew we were up to something, and was refusing to leave the area.'

'What a situation!' Esther's eyes were wide as she listened to the story.

'Then Captain May went onshore to speak to some contacts he has, and when he came back he ordered us to unload the cargo, and store it in a warehouse in Cherbourg. Streeter's got other goods there too, waiting to be brought across. A real treasure trove it is – you should see it!'

'You left the goods over there?'

Sam grinned again. 'Yes. And loaded up the *Civil Usage* with ballast. We sailed again yesterday, and as expected soon saw the *Rose*, who followed us all the way back across the Channel. The cutter's captain must have assumed we were simply going to try to outrun him. Oh, Esther, you can imagine how we laughed on board, especially when we got close to Christchurch in the early hours of this morning. They hailed us then, and sent a boarding party.'

Esther chuckled. 'And their faces when they found there was nothing on board!'

'We were all laughing and taunting them, but there was absolutely nothing they could do. We'd broken no laws! They left, we sailed into the harbour and docked. We've all been paid for the voyage. Captain May's meeting John Streeter at lunchtime in the Haven House Inn, to see what's to be done next.'

'Meanwhile, you're back. You must be tired. Maybe go home and sleep, and I'll see you tomorrow.'

But Sam shook his head. 'No, I'll go down to the Haven. I'm thinking Streeter will want to sail again to collect the cargo, sooner rather than later as there's so much of it. The *Rose* has gone – last seen heading westward with her tail between her legs.'

'You won't sail again immediately?'

'If Streeter wants to send his ships – and I noticed the *Phoenix* was in port too and ready to sail – then I'll go. It was funny, but it was also frustrating coming back with nothing. I want to see this through. We picked up a huge cargo, and Captain May said there was the same amount already in storage in Cherbourg. Imagine, Esther – about three times the biggest haul I've ever helped land!'

Esther felt a pang of annoyance that he might be leaving again so soon. She realised she may have to get used to this life – of worrying whenever Sam was away on a run, longing for him to come back. She decided not to tell him about Thomas Walker today. Not if he was about to go to sea again – it could wait. She was still hoping that somehow Walker would tire of her, or find someone else he wanted to marry. She forced herself to smile at Sam. 'Yes, of course you must go, and finish the job, if Streeter is really going to send the ship again soon. I will try to come down to the Haven too, this afternoon. Right now I had better go back and tell Pa that you are safe. He will want to know.'

She gazed at him, then leaned in and kissed him. It felt so good, and so right. And yet, if she did end up having to wed Thomas Walker, she could never again kiss Sam or even hold him in her arms. Maybe she should stop now. It wasn't fair on Sam to let him go on thinking there was a chance for them.

When he came back from this run, she promised herself. As soon as he came back, she'd find a way to tell him about Thomas Walker, and gently begin the process of pushing Sam away. He'd find someone else. He was handsome and kind and would make someone a wonderful husband. But he couldn't be hers. It broke her heart to think of it, but unless by some miracle Walker changed his mind about her, then she and Sam could never be together.

They walked the short remaining distance to The Ship at Anchor, where Sam left her. He went straight down to the Haven House Inn. 'I'll get myself something to eat there,' he said. 'Hannah's pies aren't a patch on yours but I want to be in place when Streeter decides his next plan. Hope to see you later.'

She kissed him briefly once more, and went into the pub. Pa was busy in the bar, where a couple of early customers were already nursing tankards of ale. 'Sam's all right,' she told him quickly. She went through to the kitchen, out of earshot of the customers, and Pa followed her through, stretching his back as he entered.

'Oof. My back. I'm glad you're back. I could do with sitting down. So, what news?'

'The *Civil Usage* was chased by a Revenue cutter, and ended up leaving the cargo in Cherbourg. She returned with just ballast in the hold. Mr Streeter's going down to the Haven House to meet with his captains and decide what next.' She half-wished Streeter would hold his planning sessions in their pub. But the Haven House was more isolated and not frequented by any Revenue men, so it made sense for him to meet them there.

'They brought back nothing but ballast?' Pa was incredulous.

'The Revenue cutter tailed them all the way back, and a boarding party checked the *Civil Usage*'s hold as soon as they were in coastal waters.'

'And found nothing.' Pa grinned, a toothless lopsided smile that Esther had always loved.

'Exactly. But now Streeter's got a warehouse full of goods in

100

Cherbourg. Sam thinks he'll want to do another run to collect it soon.'

'You go on, lass. Go down to the Haven House and find out what's afoot. I'll manage here. It's going to be a quiet one, I think. Send my regards to Mrs Sellars.'

'Let me just get some pies made ready for the lunchtime trade,' she said, already donning her apron. It took just minutes to make some pastry, fill dishes with a mutton stew left from the day before and add pastry tops. She left them ready to go in the range oven and gave Pa some instructions. 'I'll be back as soon as there's news,' she said, and headed off down the road to Mudeford Quay once more.

Chapter 11

I phoned Arwen on Sunday, after my day out with Nick. She was free to come for a visit the following Sunday. She'd offered to come on Saturday, but I'd dithered, wondering whether Nick would invite me out again, and she'd picked up on my hesitation.

'I get it, Millie.' She laughed. 'I'm second best! No problem. I am free either day, because Colm's away in Ireland with his mates. Going to a Munster rugby match. I'm a rugby widow, remember? So let's book it for Sunday, and if perchance this new fellow of yours wants to see you Sunday rather than Saturday, just say the word and I'll come over on Saturday instead.'

'Thanks, you are such a good mate.'

'I know, and I can't wait to see the house, hear all about this Nick bloke, and just generally catch up!'

I couldn't wait either. Arwen lived in Southampton, not too far from where we both grew up and went to school together. It would take her about forty-five minutes to drive over, and I was hoping she and Colm would be regular overnight visitors once I had the house in order and a guest room made up. Next weekend would be just a lunchtime visit, but it'd be so good to catch up and get her advice on how to handle a new romance, if that's what Nick was.

We'd met on our first day in secondary school, being assigned adjoining desks in our tutor group. We'd come from different primary schools, and I remember feeling initially a little daunted by the idea of making new friends, but Arwen had been open and friendly right from the start and we'd quickly become the best of friends. She was the one who'd told me Steve Galton from our French class fancied me, and it was Arwen who'd nudged me at a school disco until I plucked up the courage to approach him and ask if he wanted to dance. He'd turned bright red, said yes, and that was it. We became an item and stayed together for the next fifteen years.

Arwen had been the person I confided in when I finally admitted to myself that our marriage was over, too. She'd listened for hours, on several occasions, as I worked myself into a lather trying to decide what to do, and she'd gently but insistently told me to speak to Steve. 'You have to tell him. You have to discuss this with him – there is no other way forward, Millie. No other way.'

But then Mum got sick, and dealing with that took all my emotional energy. Steve had helped me so much through that time, being a solid, dependable rock I could lean on. After the funeral I'd finally taken Arwen's advice and broached the subject of the future of our marriage. As we talked I watched Steve's face fill with what could only be described as relief. Sadness, yes, but predominantly relief. He'd been feeling the same way, for years. After Mum's death he'd been waiting, it transpired, until a decent interval had passed. 'A year or two, I suppose. Until you seemed as though you were coping with losing her,' he'd said with a shrug, when I asked him how long he'd have waited to tell me he wanted to split up. I'd loved him for that. For being so sensitive. But we both knew it was over; the relationship that began at that school disco had run its course and now it was time to move on.

Arwen had been there for me with Prosecco and hugs and practical advice when I told her we'd finally made the decision. She was on her second marriage, and knew how to go about getting a divorce. It took us a while, and even now we hadn't yet finalised it, but Arwen had been there every step of the way. Of course she was the right person to advise me now, about this fledgling new relationship.

Work went well on the house during the week. I barely saw Nick, as I had to leave for work within minutes of his arrival each morning. We didn't mention Saturday, or our kiss at all. Most days Keith and Aaron were there by the time Nick arrived and it would hardly have been appropriate in front of them. But we did manage to set a date to go to The Ship in Distress for a drink, on Thursday night.

I arrived home on Thursday to discover fabulous progress in the house – the living room had now been plastered. It looked amazing – I could really begin to see what it would be like when finished. Soon I'd need to choose paint colours and floor coverings. As I looked around, I noticed a little note tucked under a tub of sealant that had been left in the fireplace. It was from Nick, just confirming that he'd call for me at 8 p.m. to go to the pub. It was signed off with a couple of kisses. There was something about getting a handwritten note rather than a text that I loved – so old-fashioned, such fun to find it! And he'd known I would spot it there. I spent a lot of time gazing at that fireplace, imagining smugglers lugging kegs of brandy up and down the steps to the secret cellar, squeezing themselves through that narrow entrance.

I made myself a light dinner, showered, and then faffed for ages deciding what to wear. I'd never had this problem when going for a night out with Steve, I realised. And this was only a drink in my local pub. God help me if we ever went out for a really special occasion. In the end I picked a pair of black jeans and a pale pink T-shirt, with my trusty leather jacket over the top. And on a weird impulse that rarely struck me, I added a pair of black heels. The Ship in Distress was only a short distance up the road. It had been there even when my own home was a pub. Odd to have two so close together, and not in a town centre. But Stanpit had been lined with fishermen's cottages two hundred years ago, some of which were still standing, and I supposed there were enough of them and enough farm labourers living or working nearby to provide enough trade. Especially since both pubs had links with the smugglers.

Nick was punctual, as always. That was something I liked about him – he'd never kept me waiting either when working or on a date. He gave me a brief kiss in greeting that made my stomach flip over, and then we went straight out. I'd been keen to try The Ship in Distress, to see if I could imagine what my own house would have looked like when it was a pub. But I had the impression it had been altered so much over the years that now there was little left of how it would have been in smuggling times.

We chose a table tucked into a corner, and Nick ordered a pint of Guinness while I had a rosé wine. As we chatted, it felt as though I'd known him for years. I couldn't help but compare the evening with the last few times I'd gone out with Steve, a couple of years ago now. We'd sat almost in silence, and every attempt at conversation had faltered. We'd grown too far apart and had found we actually had very little in common despite all our years together. It was the opposite with Nick – we found we liked the same films and books, we both enjoyed walking up mountains and adored the Lake District, we both had an interest in local history. Despite all our time together on Saturday, we still found there were endless topics to discuss, jokes to share and little secrets to find out about each other.

Nick talked about his past – the long-term girlfriend he'd had, who'd eventually dumped him for someone she worked with. 'We'd grown apart anyway,' he told me. 'Like you and Steve, only I'd never found the courage to suggest we should end it.' He smiled. 'It was a relief when she told me about her new man. We sold the house we'd been living in.'

'Where do you live now?' I only had a business address for him – he rented a small unit on a nearby trading estate.

He laughed. 'With my dad, believe it or not! After Susie and I split up, I bought, renovated and sold a couple of properties. In between each I moved in with Dad. I'm there now, but hunting for another place in need of a facelift.'

'Good to have somewhere you can use. But don't you miss having your own place?'

He shrugged. 'I've been on my own a few years now. I suppose if I had someone special in my life, I'd want to build a home with them, but for now, this suits me. And Dad admitted he rather likes my company. He's got a huge house – I don't just have a teenage bedroom I've outgrown when I'm there. I have an en-suite bedroom and another room I use as a sitting room and study. I do share the kitchen with him though.' He smiled. 'Fabulous kitchen, Dad has. Even though I say so myself.'

'Did you install it?' Of course he did – I knew the answer as I asked the question.

He nodded. 'Talking of kitchens, do you know what you want yet?'

I shook my head. 'I'm struggling for ideas. I want something that isn't jarring with the age of the house. And yet it needs to be modern and practical. I don't want country stripped pine, nor do I want glossy white and chrome.'

'Hmm. You should see Dad's kitchen. It might inspire you. In fact, we could pop round there and look at it now, if you like? When we've finished our drinks?'

'Yes please. If he won't mind.' I must admit, I was curious to see where Nick lived, and it was a good idea to get some kitchen ideas.

Soon after, Nick, who'd only had one pint, was driving us to his dad's house, which was on the edge of the New Forest, along a private road in the countryside. The midsummer evening was still light as we drove there, and the last part of the road was up a gentle hill past some woodland, eventually arriving at a large house that I guessed to be a couple of hundred years old, set on the top of the rise, with magnificent views across the Avon valley.

'What a wonderful place to live!' I said, as I got out of the car.

'Nice house, bit isolated for my liking,' Nick replied. We went in through the front door into a spacious hallway. 'Kitchen's to your left. I'll make us a coffee, or would you prefer a glass of wine? There's some Sauvignon in the fridge.'

'Wine would be lovely. Thank you.' I followed him to the kitchen and immediately fell in love. The cupboards were a pale grey-green, with small cream rectangular tiles in a brickwork pattern. The floor was warm terracotta quarry tiles, and the work surface was a similar coloured granite. The whole effect was one of classic, timeless warmth and elegance. 'Wow. I see what you mean. This style of kitchen would be perfect for my house.' Even though my kitchen was far smaller than this one, I could see it would work.

'I thought you'd like it. Here.' He handed me a glass of wine and began talking me through some of the design decisions he and his father had made.

Part way through, the door opened and a middle-aged man with a shock of grey hair came in. 'Nick, thought I heard you in here! I came back early. Clive wasn't able to stay out to play. His better half wanted him home as soon as we'd finished golfing. Ah, hello!'

I guessed this was Des. He'd taken a moment to notice me but when he had, he stepped forward, hand outstretched. I shook it, smiling.

'Dad, this is Millie Galton, from the house I'm working on over at Mudeford. I brought her back to have a look at your kitchen, to get some ideas. Millie, this is my dad, Des Marshall.'

'Pleased to meet you,' I said. Des smiled, and I noticed his eyes crinkled in the same way as Nick's.

'I've heard a bit about you. Your house was once a pub, with a smugglers' tunnel beneath, is that right?'

'Yes, that's the one.'

'Fascinating! Always love hearing a bit of local history. I've got some books on the smugglers of Christchurch, if you're interested?'

'Ooh yes. I'd love to borrow them if I may?' Arthur had said the library was well stocked with local history books but I hadn't as yet had a chance to check it out.

'I'll dig them out, give them to Nick to pass to you. Sauvignon, is that? I'll have a glass myself, I think.'

Nick poured it for him and we went through to the enormous sitting room that had a massive window overlooking the valley. Nick's phone rang then, and with an apologetic glance at me he went to the kitchen to take the call. I sat on a huge soft sofa while Des took an armchair. 'The smugglers would have brought their goods up through here – up the valley, hiding out in the woodland. For all I know, some of the contraband could have been hidden here. Not that I've any secret cellars.'

'That you know of,' I said, and he laughed.

'True! But I think it's unlikely.'

Nick returned from his call and a look passed between him and his father that I couldn't read. He sat beside me on the sofa. The three of us chatted for half an hour or so, watching the last of the sunset. I found myself liking Des immensely. He was charming and knowledgeable but didn't try to hog the conversation. He seemed genuinely interested in me, my job, my house, and told me a little about his latest business ventures. Nick sat there grinning, as though delighted that we were getting on so well.

'Of course, smuggling in those days was simply part of the local economy,' Des said. Our conversation had turned back to my tunnel and hidden cellar. 'Everyone who lived within five miles of the coast was involved, according to one of the books I read. And you can't blame them. The duty on so many goods was extortionate.' Des chuckled. 'If I'd been around back then I'd have been involved in that game, I reckon. I'd have bought a ship or two and brought back wine and brandy. There was a good living to be made from it!'

'There probably still is,' I said, without really thinking what I meant by that. Nick shot me a warning look.

'Hmm,' Des said, stroking his chin. 'These days drugs are about the only commodity that gets smuggled.' He looked thoughtful, and I frowned, unsure what to say to that. Once more Nick glanced at his father and gave a small shake of his head. I was reminded of Sharon's warning about the Marshall family and her mention that they'd been involved in the drugs trade in the past. Were they still? Was that why Nick kept getting mysterious calls and texts that he kept hidden? Or was I simply suffering from too active an imagination?

'Well, more wine, Millie? Dad?' Nick had leaped to his feet, filling the awkward silence.

Des shook his head sharply, as though both declining the wine and dislodging an unhappy thought. He then smiled broadly, though there was a falseness to it that hadn't been there before. 'Not for me, lad. I'll be taking myself off to my bed now, I think.' He stood up. 'Lovely to meet you, Millie. I hope the house renovations continue smoothly. I'm sure they will – Nick's the best there is, and no, I'm not in the slightest bit biased.' We all laughed, and he said goodnight.

'Another glass for you, Millie?'

I shook my head, not wanting to drink too much when Nick wasn't drinking at all. 'I should probably be getting back. Work tomorrow.'

'Ah yes. I'll be busy tomorrow picking up kitchen design catalogues for a certain client, now she knows what she wants!'

He drove me home, parking just up the road and walking me back to my front door. 'I'd love to come in, but I fear I'd never leave,' he said quietly, as he held me close. I could only make a little squeak in reply, which made him laugh, and then we kissed, a proper kiss this time – long and deep, and I was able to pull him close, my hand running over his muscular shoulders with no rucksack getting in the way. I felt as though I could stay like that for ever, in his arms, kissing him, the cool night air making us squeeze yet closer for warmth.

But at last he pulled away with a sigh. 'I really must go, Millie, or it'll only become more difficult.'

'If you really must,' I said, smiling.

'I must. I don't make a habit of this, you know. Dating clients, I mean.'

'I met one of your previous clients. Arthur Watts. Lovely man but I'm not too surprised you didn't date him.' Nick laughed, enjoying my teasing.

'Maybe I should have. Maybe he's lonely.' Nick's tone was only half in jest.

'I'll invite him round again,' I said. 'I want to try to work out the route of the tunnel. You could help.'

'That's a good idea.' Nick kissed me once more and then he left.

The following day, Friday, Nick and the lads had left before I got home. I was just opening my front door, wondering what progress had been made, when I heard Sharon calling me from across the road. 'Millie! Oh, I'm glad I caught you. Can you spare a few minutes?'

'Er, yeah. Sure,' I said, though actually I'd rather have had a chance to change out of my work things and grab a cup of tea first. But maybe it was a minor emergency. It did seem like she'd been watching out for my return. I hadn't seen her since she'd brought the children round, although Jasper and Tabitha had been over to see their kitten-to-be a couple of times during the week.

'Oh, good. Can we go inside?' She didn't wait for my reply but went ahead of me into the house. She wrinkled her nose at the smell of drying plaster and looked around for somewhere to sit. Downstairs, there wasn't anywhere, other than my garden furniture. I didn't want to take her upstairs, which was a mess, so I led her out through the new patio doors.

'This is the only place we can sit, sorry,' I said.

'It's all right.' She smiled tightly but did not sit down. Not in those white linen trousers, on my rather tatty deckchairs. 'I just wanted to ask, how is the work coming on? Looks like some things have changed.'

'Yes, it's all moving on nicely,' I replied. 'Good progress since you were last here with the kids. I'm nearly at the stage of needing to pick paint colours. I was thinking of having …'

She flapped a hand impatiently. 'Well that's good. You're still using Marshall. And I see you've been seeing him socially as well, like last night. You'll say it's none of my business, but I really feel it's my neighbourly duty to warn you …'

'It's none of your business, Sharon,' I said, quietly but firmly.

'I knew you'd say that. I said to Brian that you'd say it, but even so. You'll hear me out.' It was a statement, not a question. I folded my arms and waited. I already knew she didn't think much of Nick Marshall, or at least of his father, but for her to feel the need to come over and accost me like this seemed serious. And short of throwing her out, I didn't have much choice other than to listen to what she had to say.

'I'm worried for you,' she continued. Her voice was soft and sounded kind. Whatever she wanted to say to me, it was clear she meant well. 'You're not from here, you don't know the background. That family are … toxic. Crooked. Desmond Marshall – that's the father of your builder – he's been caught up in so many dodgy deals. He's acquired property by underhand ways and circumvented planning laws by paying off councillors. That new housing development, up beside the bypass – he's got a stake in that. And the piece of land nearer town – where the old Chinese restaurant was – rumour has it he's bought that too. Lord knows what he'll build there.'

'So he's a developer? Wasn't he also the mayor once?' I decided not to tell her I'd met Des and liked him.

She nodded, pursing her lips together. 'Yes, he's been mayor a couple of times. Though goodness knows how, given his background. He was arrested once, charged with corruption and found guilty. I believe he was in prison for a while. He likes the pomp and circumstance, I think, and all the dressing up in robes and chains. And of course it's a way to get to know all the other local dubious businessmen.'

'They can't all be dubious. I heard he'd been in prison. Nick told me.' I was glad he had, so I hadn't given Sharon the satisfaction of hearing me gasp at this news. 'But Nick also said his dad had learned his lesson. What makes you think he's still doing dodgy deals?'

'That's what I hear, from friends who'd know,' she said.

'And what does it have to do with Nick anyway?'

'There's more. Drugs. It's not just the old man. Whole family is involved, so I've heard.'

'What?'

'Des Marshall's daughter was involved with drug smuggling. Probably for her father. I'd guess he pushed her to do it.'

'His daughter? The one who died young?'

'That's her. And the son – the fellow you've been seeing – he's no doubt all mixed up in it too. If I were you, I'd back off. Plenty of better men out there if you're looking for one. My friend used a dating app – she was in touch with loads of suitable fellows in no time. They match you up according to your likes and dislikes and background, you know. All very clever. I can send you the link, if you like?'

'Er, no. Thank you.'

'Well, I've said my piece. I'll go. Oh, I wondered if you'd like to go out for coffee one day soon? I know you're working now, but maybe on Sunday? Brian takes the kids out to swimming lessons so I have a free couple of hours.'

Thank goodness Arwen was booked in for Sunday. 'Sorry, I have a friend coming to visit then.'

Her face clouded. 'Nick Marshall?'

'No, Sharon. An old school friend.' I'd had enough now. I wanted to think about what she'd told me, and digest it on my own. I went back in through the patio doors and thankfully she followed me, as I led her to the front door.

'Well, think on what I've said. As I said, I'm sorry if you feel it wasn't my place to say anything, but I hope you think of me as a friend and realise I am only telling you all this in friendship, as a warning. To avoid you making a mistake you might regret.'

'Thanks. I do understand.' I didn't want to say anything more.

She put out a hand and patted my shoulder. 'Well, I'll be off. I'm only over the road, if you want anything, or to talk ...' The look in her eye showed me she might be regretting poking her nose in. She looked as though she was wondering if she'd spoiled any chance of us being close friends. I was wondering that too. I needed to think about it. But she'd been right before, about Seaway Renovations, and her warning then had possibly saved me from making a costly mistake. What if she was right now, as well?

'OK. Well, er, thanks, Sharon. See you ...' I held the door open for her, and with a sigh she went through, and I immediately closed it after her and leaned back against it.

Drugs. I had no real reason – beyond worrying about the calls and texts he received and was so secretive about – to suspect Nick was in any way associated with any drug crime, but ... was his father? And was it true about Nick's sister being involved in smuggling drugs for her father? I'd have assumed it was simply Sharon causing trouble, but the way she'd seemed so regretful that she might have spoiled our friendship as she left made me think that she was genuinely worried for me.

Nick had said his father had learned his lesson after his short spell in prison. He'd stopped doing his underhand deals and all his business activities were now above board. At least, that's what

Nick had implied. I couldn't help but remember Des's thoughtful expression when he mentioned modern-day smuggling and the look that passed between him and Nick. Could there be something in what Sharon had said?

I went into the kitchen to make myself a drink. On the work surface was a little pile of books. All local history, with a couple about smuggling in Hampshire and Dorset. A Post-it note stuck to the top one read: *Books from Dad. Enjoy! Nick xx*

Chapter 12

At the Haven House, John Streeter and his two ships' captains, May and Parrott, were sitting at their usual table near the back. The inn was busy, with several crewmen milling around, drinking ale, waiting to find out what was happening next. Esther went to join Sam, who was there with George again. The two men were chatting about their experiences on the run, laughing once more at the trick played on the Revenue service.

'Here she is,' Sam said, pulling Esther into an embrace while George watched, smiling.

'You going to make an honest woman of her, little brother?' George asked, and Esther blushed. How she would like that! But it was impossible.

Sam was looking at her with affection. 'One day, I hope, if she'll have me. What about you and Hannah, eh?' He nodded over to where the landlady was bustling around the bar, taking a tray of drinks to Streeter and the captains.

George adopted a wistful expression. 'I can but dream, brother, I can only dream.'

Hannah looked over at that moment, as though she'd heard him, and winked at George. A moment later she joined them. 'Well, lads, another drink? And hello Esther, love. How's business up at Stanpit?'

'Good, thanks Hannah. Pa sends his regards. I'm here to find out—' She broke off as John Streeter stood and cleared his throat, ready to make an announcement to all who were present. As last time, he first glanced around the pub to make sure there was no one present he didn't recognise.

'Well, lads, I need two crews. One for the *Civil Usage*, and one for *Phoenix*. A number of *Civil Usage*'s sailors went home this morning, when the ship came into port, but I want her crewed and ready to sail this afternoon, on the next tide.'

'That's short notice, sir!' a man standing beside the bar called out. 'We've no time to see our families.'

'I've two full shiploads of goods waiting to be picked up. The Revenue cutter that caused us problems on the last run is now well out of the way. The tides are right and the wind is perfect. It'll be a quick trip, there and back, just a day or two if we're lucky, and it'll be the biggest cargo we've ever landed. Who's in?'

Shouts and cheers went up from the men, including Sam and George. Esther had known Sam would go again, but even so, she found herself wishing he wouldn't. She'd miss him, and he'd be in danger again. But she smiled and joined in with the cheers.

Before long the two captains were organising the men into crews, and telling them to be on their ships by two o'clock on the Priory's clock.

Streeter needed to arrange the landing party. As he passed by Esther, he caught her by the arm. 'Blue, this is going to be the biggest haul ever. Can you ask your regulars, the men we can trust, if any can help with wagons and horses? It'll only be a couple of days before the ships are back and we're going to need to have a proper army of a landing party if we want to pull this off.'

'I'll do what I can, sir. I'll put the word out.'

'Good. And you'll be there?'

'Of course.'

Streeter nodded in approval, and left the inn. Sam and George were assigned to Captain May, to sail on the *Civil Usage* once more. Esther managed a quick hug and kiss with Sam, accompanied by jeers and laughter from the other men. Over his shoulder she noticed George giving Hannah a squeeze, but the landlady shrugged him off.

She hurried back to The Ship at Anchor to report the news to Pa. Thomas Walker was in the pub, sitting at his favourite table by a window, from where he could watch all the comings and goings along Stanpit. All the other customers were positioned well away from him. She bobbed a little curtsy to him as she passed, but didn't stop. She went straight through to the kitchen, hoping Pa would follow.

He took the hint and made his way to the kitchen. 'What news, lass?' He kept his voice low, even though he'd pushed shut the door that led back through to the bar.

'They sail this afternoon. Sam's going again. Both ships – *Phoenix* and the new one. Streeter reckons it'll be a quick crossing – the wind's good. We've to help muster the landing party – get the word out among our regulars who can be trusted.'

Pa nodded. 'I thought as much. Right, we'll get onto that. You'll have seen Walker's in the bar?'

'Walker's in the kitchen now.'

Esther turned with a gasp. She hadn't heard the Revenue officer come in. Neither had Pa, who turned puce, and hurried past Walker back to the bar, muttering about customers to serve.

'Oh, Mr Walker, is there anything I can get you?' Esther smiled at him, and indicated the unsold pies that were lined up along the kitchen table.

Walker regarded her silently for what seemed like minutes but was probably only a few seconds. 'Not at present. I will let you know what I want, when I am ready.' He gave her a twisted smile, and his gaze travelled slowly down her body and back up again, as though he was undressing her with his eyes. She suppressed a shudder. 'So Streeter's sending his ships back to France, is he?'

'I … I don't know for sure,' Esther stuttered, wondering how much Walker had heard, and whether it mattered, given he was in the pay of the smugglers.

'I'll make sure Joshua Jeans knows, and he'll make sure Noyce or anyone else we can't trust is not working when the goods are being landed. You see, you need me, Esther, whether you want me or not.' He nodded to her, and went back to the bar.

Esther let out a huge breath. She couldn't make out Thomas Walker. One minute he was lecherous and leering at her, using what he knew about their business as a hold over her and Pa, and the next he was helping them out, being a friend to the free traders. Could she trust him? He was a Revenue officer, but a corrupt one. By definition he was untrustworthy – his own employers were wrong to trust him!

Over the next couple of days Esther was kept busy both in the pub and helping Mr Streeter find enough men and women for his landing party. She spoke to everyone she knew who came into the pub, and also called on many friends and neighbours, especially those who had carts and horses. She called on Lovey Warne, but Lovey said her brothers were no longer allowing her to be involved in the movement of contraband, since the near miss when she'd had to fend off Noyce before he noticed the smuggled fabrics around her waist. Her brothers were still involved though and would form part of the landing party.

'I still help in one way,' Lovey said. 'I put on my red cloak, and walk about on the high ground outside town if there are Revenue men in the area. It tells the free traders to take another route when distributing the goods.' She smiled at Esther, and caught her hand. 'Listen, Esther, tell me you'll keep yourself safe – don't take any risks. If that Revenue man who's sweet on you knew what you do when a run is landed, you'd be in a lot of trouble.'

'He takes his share,' Esther told her. 'He knows quite a lot.'

'But not that you actually help unload?'

'Not that. I stay hidden. Don't you worry, Lovey. I'll be all right. It's going to be a busy night. Two ships to unload, and Streeter wants it all done and the goods away in under an hour.'

'That'll take some doing. Well, good luck, Esther. Keep safe.'

'I will.'

And then at last one morning the news came that the ships would land their cargo on Avon Beach that afternoon. 'Going for a daylight landing,' Streeter said, as he rushed in with the news for Esther and Luke to pass on. 'Sooner the better. Got no choice. There's a Revenue ship in the area. It's gone for the moment so if we're quick, we can pull this off. We've about 300 men lined up, plus you of course,' he said, nodding at Esther, 'though you won't be the only lass on this run. Pass on the word.' He left and a moment later they heard his horse galloping up the road, spreading the news.

It was a hectic few hours, as Esther ran around to tell the local people who'd agreed to help. Pa stayed in the pub to serve customers and spread the word there. Many men coming from villages such as Burton and Bransgore were stopping at The Ship at Anchor anyway, for a bite to eat before the hard work of unloading cargo began. One of their neighbours arrived to borrow Toby and their cart, to help out with the distribution. At two o'clock Esther went down to the hidden cellar and changed into her boy's clothes, then exited the pub via the tunnel. There was, of course, no Sam to meet her this time. Sam's coracle was still pulled up in its usual place, and she struggled a little to push it out into the channel and row it round to Mudeford Quay on her own. She tied it up behind the Haven House Inn, then ran along to Avon Beach. There were dozens of men, and a few women – some dressed in breeches like her but most in their skirts – all gathering near the beach, hiding in the sand dunes or behind the few buildings nearby. There were many more in the Haven House Inn and its outbuildings, and all roads leading to the beach were clogged with horses and wagons. Esther had never seen so many turn out to help.

She watched as the two luggers – *Civil Usage* and *Phoenix* – rounded the end of the sand-spit and beached. Men immediately ran into the water and began unloading, and some horses and wagons were even driven down across the sand and into the water, to help. Esther took her place in a gang loading up wagons. The unloading seemed more frantic than ever, and not just because it was daylight. The men kept glancing out to sea, and following their gaze Esther saw a Revenue cutter standing a little way off. Its captain had clearly seen them and was watching proceedings. It must be the one Streeter had mentioned, she thought.

'Will they come closer?' she asked the man beside her.

'No, Streeter's ships have more gunpower, and manpower. The cutter won't dare come closer. But they've seen us, so we need to get this all away before they can do anything.'

Esther knew that although landing a haul was dangerous, so was distributing it. Convoys of wagons could be intercepted and seized inland. The goods needed to be spirited away, hidden in cellars and outbuildings, as fast as possible. Especially a haul as large as this one, and particularly when a Revenue ship was watching and would no doubt report everything it had seen.

She worked her hardest, hauling tubs of spirits up the beach and onto the carts. Part way through the afternoon, she spotted one of the Revenue officers talking to Streeter, come for his share. Streeter organised a team of men to load a few wagons with a hundred tubs that had already been put aside. That was the 'seizure' the officer could write up in his report. It wasn't Walker who'd come, and for that Esther was grateful. No need for her to hide her face.

She spotted Sam on board the *Civil Usage*. He'd waved to her but not yet set foot on land. It was enough to know he was safe. She carried on working quickly, focusing only on the tubs she was hauling and loading, ignoring her screaming muscles, thinking only of the job at hand.

And so she didn't notice a second Revenue man approach Streeter and then walk onto the beach, towards the area she was working.

'Those kegs there – they're to be put aside, Streeter says.'

Esther spun around at the familiar voice, and too late realised she should have done the opposite. Walker's eyes widened as he recognised her under the cap. 'What the hell are you doing here?' he hissed.

'H-helping out. It's a big haul – Mr Streeter needed as many hands as possible …'

'You're a girl!'

She tilted her chin upwards, defiantly. 'There are other women helping too. I'm strong, from working in the pub. I'm perfectly capable, Mr Walker.'

'Dressed like that – you disgust me! You won't help on the beach or wear clothes like that when you're married to me, that's for certain.'

'Sir, you haven't asked me to marry you, and I have no intention of marrying anyone.' The words were out before she could stop herself, but then she realised she didn't care. If she disgusted him, then she wouldn't marry him, no matter what.

He stared at her, opened his mouth as though to say something more, but then turned and walked away. By the tension in his shoulders Esther could see he was seething with rage. Well, so was she.

She resumed her work, throwing the tubs onto wagons with such force one of the men working with her admonished her to be more gentle. 'Streeter won't be happy if you split them kegs,' he said, and she took the advice and was more careful how she handled them. Whatever the consequences of upsetting Walker, annoying Mr Streeter wouldn't be a good idea either.

A few minutes later she stopped working to stretch her aching back muscles. She gazed around at the men working on the beach – fewer now that many of the wagons and tubmen had left with their loads, each wagon guarded by a batman or two. Some of the haul was to be stacked at the Haven House Inn and moved on over the next few days. Streeter, standing nearby to direct activities, looked agitated.

'That Revenue cutter's seen everything we've done. I was hoping she'd have sailed further east but she turned back. I'm going to have to get my ships away sharpish, or I'll lose them. And *Civil Usage* is so new! Come on, men. Get the cargo unloaded quickly. I need more time before that cutter can do anything.'

'Yes, sir,' Esther said, and got back to work.

'And that doesn't help.' Streeter nodded to where a man sat on horseback, a little way off. Esther recognised the uniform of the riding officers, but it wasn't Walker, or Bursey who'd been there earlier.

'Is that Mr Noyce?' she asked, and Streeter nodded. 'What's he doing here?'

'Nothing good,' Streeter replied. Noyce was the only one of the Christchurch Revenue officers who couldn't be bribed to turn a blind eye. As Esther watched, he turned his horse and galloped off in the direction of Lymington. Streeter swore. 'He's gone to raise the militia at Lymington, I bet. They'll try to intercept some of our goods as they're taken inland. Dammit. This is too big a cargo to lose.'

'Sir, it won't all be lost. Much of it has already been taken away.'

'You're right, Blue. All we can do is keep on moving. Hurry up there, lads! Need to get the ships away and ballasted, so they can sail again pronto!'

At his shout, everyone worked harder and faster than ever, and it wasn't long before the last of the goods were off the ships, and the ships were brought round into the harbour, behind the Haven House Inn, so they could be filled with ballast and made ready to sail the next day. Esther realised that meant she probably wouldn't have a chance to see Sam. And she so wanted to see him.

Soon they were finished. A pile of contraband was stacked by the Haven House – some of this was to be taken to The Ship at Anchor. Esther looked about for someone to help her load her coracle but most of the men had left with the carts, and the luggers' crews had largely dispersed; only a few were left who'd decided to stay overnight at the Haven House. The Revenue cutter had sailed away – to fetch help, Esther guessed. This was far from over yet.

Esther went into the Haven House Inn, where the atmosphere was very different to the usual. Despite it being the largest haul ever landed, Streeter was concerned and the men were subdued. Sam, thankfully, was in there, quickly eating a bowl of stew and drinking some ale.

'Esther!' He rose and embraced her. He too looked drawn and worried. 'I'm to help ballast the ship. Streeter wants them gone from here as soon as possible.' He leaned in close to whisper to her. 'He's really worried he'll lose his ships. That Revenue cutter – the *Resolution* – will be back with reinforcements. I know Streeter's forfeited a ship before, but not two at once. He's furious. We have to be away on the morning tide.'

'What can I do?'

'Get your share of the goods back to The Ship at Anchor. Get some sleep.'

'What are you doing?'

'I'll stay – help with the ballasting and anything else needed. If they're short of crew, I'll sail again. George is doing the same.' He indicated his brother, who was eating a meal while sitting at the bar, near Hannah Sellars. 'If there's enough sailors, I won't go, Blue. I'll come and see you then. But so many of them have gone to their homes for a bite to eat and a rest. Streeter's scared there aren't enough of us to get the ships ballasted. And there's all that contraband still to be distributed.'

123

'There are men coming back for that,' Esther said, and indicated through the window. Men with carts and horses were arriving – they'd presumably delivered one load and were now coming back for more.

'Good.' Sam ate the last mouthful of stew. 'Let's get your coracle loaded and you away. Your pa will help you unload?'

'I can get it into the tunnel myself. It might have to stay there overnight. Pa can't do much with the way his back is.'

Sam nodded, and went outside with her to load the little boat. 'You sure you're all right rowing it? Only I'm needed here …' Ballasting work was already underway, overseen by Streeter and the two captains of the luggers. It was back-breaking work – shifting baskets of gravel into the hold. Each ship would need around fifty tons for stability before it could sail.

Esther nodded. 'I'll be fine.' She kissed him and left, wondering when she'd see him again and what she would do about Walker. Chances were, he'd be in their pub that evening.

Chapter 13

I had the house looking as good as possible for Arwen's visit. Tricky to do, as there was still no furniture in the sitting room, bare plaster on the wall (still not dry enough to paint) and only rough, broken floorboards to walk on. But I cleaned the kitchen and tidied the bedrooms, put cushions on the deckchairs and swept the hallway flagstones thoroughly. Thankfully the forecast was for sunshine. The previous day, Saturday, it had rained all day – Nick had called to cancel a walk we'd planned to Highcliffe. No point doing it in the pouring rain. I'd felt a mixture of relief and disappointment at the cancellation. On the one hand I'd looked forward to another day out with him, but on the other hand I wanted to talk to Arwen first, get some advice, and decide how or if to ask Nick whether there was any truth in what Sharon had told me about his family.

I'd spent the day instead reading through the books Nick had left, lent by Des. In one of them, there was a detailed account of the Battle of Mudeford, which read like a thriller. At the time of the battle the chief Revenue officer in Christchurch had been a man named Joshua Jeans. He'd also been the mayor of Christchurch on a couple of occasions prior to that, yet he was corrupt, taking a portion of each smuggling run for himself in return for turning a blind eye, and making sure his men did the same.

He sounded a bit like Des Marshall, I thought, if Sharon was right about him. On the surface an upstanding member of the community, but beneath it all involved in the shadier sides of local business. But surely Des was not involved in drugs at all? It was one thing to take a bribe to allow a development to progress smoothly through the planning stages – that felt like a victimless crime, like the smuggling of old. But anything related to dealing or smuggling drugs was a different matter.

I had a salad made, a quiche ready to go in the oven and a bottle of something bubbly but low alcohol chilling ready for Arwen's arrival. I'd not seen her since moving house.

She arrived promptly, bearing a huge potted fern that would look amazing by my patio doors when the sitting room was finished, and a box of chocolates. 'Millie!' she squealed, as she dumped the plant in the hallway and gave me an enormous hug. 'So good to see you! And this place! Wow. I want a tour right away! And I want to meet your kittens!'

I laughed, and showed her around, talking her through the work that had been done already and the plans ahead. The kittens and Mir were in the sitting room, for once all asleep but they woke as soon as we went in. Arwen fussed over Mir more than the kittens. 'I bet everyone ignores you now that there are kittens to play with,' she crooned, and Mir nuzzled against her hand appreciating the attention.

'It's awesome!' was Arwen's considered opinion of the house. 'And it'll be even more awesome when everything's done. I cannot believe you've got a secret tunnel under your house. A secret tunnel used by smugglers! You've found a good builder in that Nick of yours. So come on, tell me how the new romance is going.'

'Yep. Well, I need to talk to you about that anyway. Shall we go for a walk and I'll tell you as we go?'

'Sure! I brought my trainers.'

I led her on a loop that took us down to Mudeford Quay, along to Avon Beach, then crossed through a housing estate to the little river Mude. We walked downstream along that for a bit and then across to Stanpit. A long walk but a good way of showing her all the local points of interest. We had a lot to talk about.

She listened carefully as I told her what Sharon had said regarding Des Marshall and his possible links to drug smuggling and distribution, and that strange expression of his when he'd mentioned drugs. 'So I'm worried Nick's involved in some way. Or if not directly involved, he must know what his dad does, and must turn a blind eye. I don't care if Des is on the fiddle in the council or takes bribes or whatever, but drug smuggling … that's a different matter. Arwen, it makes me really uncomfortable.'

Arwen nodded. 'I know. Remember Josie?'

'Exactly.'

Josie was a girl we'd been at school with. Same school year as us, but not someone we mixed with very much. She'd always been the first to do everything – smoke, drink, sleep with a boy – and it seemed inevitable that she'd be the first to experiment with drugs. But she didn't just smoke a joint or try a tab of acid. She was on heroin by 16 and was thrown out of school. She was arrested and convicted of drug dealing at 17, when she was caught trying to sell Ecstasy to kids at the school gates. She was imprisoned for four years, and I hadn't seen her since, but word on the grapevine was that she'd gone back on drugs and was now living in a squat in London, working as a prostitute or shoplifting to finance her next fix. I had no idea whether any of this was true but I could believe it of her. She'd had a rubbish home life and little support from school or elsewhere. And she'd always been easily led astray.

The only good thing Josie had done was open the eyes of the rest of us in school to what drugs could do to a person. I'd always felt sorry for her. I'm pretty sure she was the only one of our year group who'd got caught up in that shady world.

'If your fella's dad is in any way part of the chain that puts drugs into the hands of kids like Josie … well, if I were you, I'd want to know. I'd want to know exactly how much your Nick is involved or how much he knows about it all. If he lives with his dad, he must know what he's up to, at the very least. And then, if it was me and it turned out Nick's involved, I'd have a real problem with that …'

I nodded. 'Yes. I would too. And yet …'

'Nick sounds so nice. I'm sure he has no idea. We don't know if what your neighbour says is even true. Might she simply be stirring?'

'I wondered that, but she didn't come across in that way. She sounded like she was genuinely trying to look out for me, to be a good friend. Also, she'd warned me earlier about another builder I was about to employ, and when I followed it up she was right. She saved me from making a bad mistake there.'

'Mmm. Well, I think you're going to have to talk to Nick. Find out the truth directly from him. Either that or run a mile, if you think for a moment there could be any truth in what your neighbour says.'

She was right, but I didn't much like the sound of either option. A difficult conversation that might ruin everything, or zero chance of a relationship with Nick. Neither appealed.

We turned the conversation onto local history then. Arwen wanted to know all that I had learned from Arthur and my reading about smuggling in the area. 'It's odd,' she said, 'how we're totally happy with the idea of those eighteenth-century smugglers bringing in brandy and tea, but aghast at the thought of the Marshall fellow bringing in drugs.'

'Bit different,' I said. 'Avoiding duty on legal goods is a victim-less crime. At least, only the government lost out by not getting the revenue on those goods. Everyone else gained. Whereas drugs smuggling hurts so many people – those at the bottom of the heap who are users. And their families.'

'Yes, you're right. Good way to see it.'

At last our route brought us around to Stanpit. 'We'll just do a quick loop here, and I'll show you the marsh land at the back of my house, then I think it's time for our lunch,' I told her, and she nodded.

'Yep, I am starving!'

We did the loop around the marsh, on paths that were muddy after the previous day's rain. I pointed out Hengistbury Head on the other side: 'from where the smugglers signalled to the ships when it was safe for them to land', and Mother Sillar's Channel: 'she ended up running The Ship in Distress pub, just up the road from me'. And then we headed back along the path towards the Stanpit car park. I'd intended showing Arwen the little path leading to a pool not far from my back garden that I'd discovered with Nick.

As we approached the car park I noticed a commotion – vehicles were on the track that led along the edge of the marsh. Not just any vehicles – they were the type with blue flashing lights on top.

'What's going on?' Arwen said.

'No idea. Look, that's the back of my house, right there. Whatever the police are doing here, it's a little bit too close for comfort.'

'We could ask, when we get nearer.'

'Yes. I will.'

As we walked I realised the police were congregating right by the turn off the main path that led to that hidden pool. They'd hammered in stakes and put some tape across that read, 'Police line, do not cross'. A couple of police cars had driven up the main track a little way and were parked beside that turn. A uniformed officer was standing guard.

'Excuse me, can you tell us what's going on?' I asked.

He was a young man, and must have been at least six and a half feet tall. 'A body's been found. Just down there. You can't go any closer, miss.'

'A body! Oh! My garden backs onto this marsh. Where was the body found?'

'In a pool. Dog walker reported it. Where exactly is your house, miss?'

I pointed it out, and he made a note. 'There'll be door-to-door enquiries ordered, I expect, miss.'

'OK. I don't think we'll be able to help. We've been out on a long walk this morning.'

'Body may have been there since last night. Anyway, expect a call from one of my colleagues, miss. For now, it's best you move along.'

'Will do.'

Arwen and I squeezed past the police cars that almost blocked the track, and returned to the little car park. That was clogged with more emergency vehicles and as we approached, a fire engine arrived.

'What do they want that for?' Arwen wondered.

'Maybe they'll be pumping water away or something. Though how that can get near the pool I have no idea. Come on. Lunch is beckoning.'

We went back to my house, and I put the quiche in the oven to heat up while Arwen took some cutlery and condiments out to the garden table. 'The police are really quite close to your back garden,' she reported when she came back inside. 'From out there I can hear them, indistinctly. Can't see them because of those tall reeds.'

I followed her outside and stood on my garden table to see if we could get any kind of view. 'Be better from upstairs,' I said, feeling very nosey but given what had happened I felt it was understandable.

We both went upstairs, and into my bedroom, which was at

the back of the house and had a view across the marsh from the window. Sure enough, from there we could see the heads of the police officers gathered about twenty or thirty metres away from the fence at the end of my garden. 'Good God, that's closer than I realised!' I said. When I'd visited the pool with Nick it was hard to tell how near it was to my garden, due to the height of the reeds. From the window it was not possible to see the pool itself, only the heads and shoulders of the police milling about near it.

We stood and watched for a while, as both uniformed and plainclothes officers came and went, and a couple of people in white forensics suits arrived. Eventually a stretcher was carried out. 'There they go, the poor soul, whoever it was. Wonder what happened?' Arwen said. 'Accident, or not?'

'I don't know.' But I had a bad feeling about it. I supposed it was possible someone walking out there might have slipped, knocked themselves out and drowned in the pool. Or had a heart attack. But it seemed more likely they'd gone there to die – found that peaceful, unfrequented spot and quietly killed themselves. Twenty metres from my garden.

I heard the oven beeping downstairs and turned away from the window. 'Sounds like the quiche is done. Come on, let's go and eat and try to forget about all this.'

'Lead on,' Arwen said, and we went down for lunch and to try to salvage the good mood of earlier, but somehow that poor person's death so close to my home seemed to be hanging over us, dampening our spirits.

We'd finished eating and were beginning to wash up when there was a knock at the door. I had a strong feeling it'd be the police on their door-to-door enquiries, and I was right. Two non-uniformed detectives introduced themselves and asked if they could come in and ask us a few questions about an 'incident'.

'Certainly. But I am in the process of renovating the house so there is nowhere to sit downstairs, other than the garden,' I warned them.

'The garden will be fine,' said the older one, a man I guessed to be in his forties with a sprinkling of grey hair. I took them through and introduced Arwen. We told them about our walk and coming across the police presence on the path at the end.

'Do you know the area well?' the older detective, who'd introduced himself as DS Michaels, asked.

'Not really. I moved in only a few weeks ago. But I have seen the pool – was that where the body was found?'

'How did you know there was a body?'

'Ah, we asked a policeman who was stopping people from walking that way. He told us a body had been found at the pool.'

DS Michaels nodded, and I wondered if I'd got that policeman into trouble. Perhaps he wasn't supposed to have said why they were there.

'Did you hear anything odd, maybe late last night or early this morning? Or see anything? Perhaps from upstairs? In fact, can we take a look at the view from your upstairs windows?'

'Of course. And no, I heard or saw nothing. First I knew about it was when we walked around that way. Can I ask, what or who have you found?'

'A body, as you know. A young woman. And that's all I can say, for the moment.'

I led the two detectives upstairs and they looked out of the windows with interest. 'I need to ask, where were you last night?'

'I was here. Arrived home from work about six-fifteen, and the builders left shortly after.'

'Anyone with you in the evening or night?'

'No.'

'And do you sleep in this room? What time did you go to bed?'

I must have raised my eyebrows at the questions, because DS Michaels smiled reassuringly. 'I'm just trying to establish whether you would have heard, if there'd been any noise from that part of the marsh last night. It might help establish a timeline.'

'It's all right. Yes, I sleep here, and I went to bed around eleven. The windows were closed because it was raining. Rained quite heavily for a while. That might have drowned out any sounds I'd otherwise have heard.'

'That's a good point, boss,' the younger detective said, as he made a note.

'Well, I think that's all for now. I'll take your name and contact details, please. We may need to come back and check a few more details. You've been very helpful, Miss …'

'Mrs Galton. Millie Galton.'

'And was Mr Galton not here last night?'

'No. We're divorcing, it's only me living here.'

'All right. Thank you, Mrs Galton. We can see ourselves out.'

I came down after them anyway, and went back to the garden where Arwen had waited for me. I sat down heavily and blew out noisily. 'Phew. Glad they're gone. What a horrible thing to happen. It's a young woman, apparently.'

'Suicide?'

'They didn't say. Maybe they don't know cause of death yet. I imagine it'll be on the local news. That poor young woman, whatever happened. Doesn't bear thinking about.'

'No. It doesn't.' Arwen shook her head sadly. 'And somehow not knowing what happened makes you feel so helpless, doesn't it?'

'Yes. I can't help thinking, if I'd heard anything, might I have been able to do something, to save her somehow?'

'Don't think like that. If it was suicide it could all have happened very quietly. Like, if she walked there, sat down and took an overdose, you wouldn't have seen anything suspicious or heard anything.' Arwen came over to me and wrapped her arms around me. 'Don't be thinking you could have done anything, whatever happens next. You heard and saw nothing, and had no reason to think there was anything out of the ordinary.'

She was right, I knew she was. But I also knew I'd worry about this until I heard the truth of what had happened to that poor young woman. I had an overwhelming urge to talk to Nick about it. For some reason I felt I needed his reassurance too, despite my niggling doubts about him.

Chapter 14

It was tough, rowing around the harbour to the marsh and up the channel by herself, against an outgoing tide, and in a coracle full of kegs of spirits and packets of tobacco. This wasn't all they were due to store at The Ship at Anchor either – Esther would need to return at some point for more. But she was strong and eventually, in the early evening, she made it. She tied up the coracle and unloaded, stacking goods just inside the tunnel entrance. There they would need to stay until the following day. Esther needed to rest, but there was no chance of that yet. She ran up the tunnel to the secret cellar and quickly changed into her women's clothing.

In the pub, Pa was busy serving dozens of sailors from the two luggers. As in the Haven House, the mood was more subdued than usual. That Revenue cutter sitting in the bay, watching their every move had spooked the men. Esther took Pa into the kitchen and gave him a brief update.

'Thomas Walker saw me, on the beach,' she said. 'It's fair to say he was not happy.'

'Dressed in your men's clothes?' Pa looked at her with horror.

She nodded. 'It was daylight. I couldn't help it. But Pa, he said

I disgusted him, dressed like that. Maybe he'll no longer want to marry me now.'

'Did he say that?'

She thought back to what Walker had said on the beach that afternoon. 'No.' Her shoulders slumped.

'Well, we'll see. Try not to do anything more that annoys him, eh lass?'

She bit her lip. All she could do was to hope that Walker had been put off marrying her, but wouldn't cause them any trouble. If only he could just disappear so she never saw him again. She didn't wish him any harm, but if he was out of the way, however it happened, then she'd be free to marry Sam.

'Well, lass, there's customers in the bar, and from what you say, a lot of men with more work to do tonight or early tomorrow. Let's get them fed and watered, eh?'

She smiled. 'Yes, Pa.' The sooner the bar emptied out, the sooner she'd be able to rest. There was plenty more heavy work ahead of her the next day. She went through to the bar and made herself busy serving the thirsty sailors. The time passed quickly as the bar was busy, and she had no chance to rest or think about the events of the day. It was late evening, and most of the free traders had left, when Thomas Walker arrived. He strode in, barely glancing at Esther, and ordered ale from Luke Harris. Pa looked over at Esther to serve the Revenue officer, but she gave a tiny shake of her head. Until she knew Walker's mood she didn't want to go anywhere near him.

Walker drank his ale quickly, looking around as if to see who was in the bar, but seemed to be purposely avoiding catching Esther's eye. He spoke to Pa only to order his drink and then as he left, to bid him goodnight, in what seemed to be a friendly enough manner.

'Well, lass, I don't know what to make of that,' Pa said to Esther as they cleared away the last used tankards and plates. 'But you get off to bed now. I know you're tired.'

'Yes, and I'll be up early to go down to the Haven House and see what's what,' she replied, kissing him on the cheek and heading up the stairs.

Esther rose early, soon after dawn, dressed and breakfasted quickly and set off down the road to Mudeford Quay. It was a bright morning with occasional gusts of a gentle breeze. Hopefully the two luggers would be fully ballasted and ready to sail on the outgoing tide later in the day.

As she approached the Haven House she looked out to sea. There in the bay was not only the Revenue cutter they'd seen yesterday, but also two other ships. Another cutter, and farther off a larger ship. Esther couldn't tell from that distance, but if the larger one was also a Revenue ship then Streeter was in trouble. She hurried to the inn to see if he was there. He wasn't. All was quiet in the Haven House. The men had probably worked half the night on the ballasting, and Hannah Sellars would have stayed up to provide refreshments for them. Esther called out and knocked loudly on the door leading to the upper floor. Some of the sailors would have stayed there for the night, she was sure.

At last a bleary-eyed Hannah came downstairs, in her night-gown with a shawl wrapped around her shoulders. 'What is it, Esther?'

'Is Mr Streeter here? Or the two captains? Only I think there are three Revenue ships out in the bay now …'

'Streeter left a few hours ago. The captains are upstairs.'

'And Sam?'

'He and George bedded down on the *Civil Usage* a few hours ago. Ballasting isn't quite finished yet but they were exhausted, poor lambs. I'll wake the captains now.' Hannah turned and went back upstairs.

A few minutes later both Captain May and Captain Parrott clattered down the stairs, still tugging on jackets as they came.

They went outside and peered at the ships in the bay. Captain May had an eyeglass. 'It's the *Orestes*,' he said, pointing to the larger ship. 'Naval ship. If that comes closer, we're outgunned.'

'With three of 'em they could block the harbour entrance,' Captain Parrott said. 'Best finish that ballasting and get the luggers out of here before they do. Someone needs to tell Streeter.'

'We need more hands,' Captain May said. 'Some of the lads were off to sleep at Will Burden's house in Christchurch. I'll fetch them.' He took a horse from the inn's stables and was soon riding off up the road.

'If Mr Streeter's at his Stanpit address I can run up and find him,' Esther offered. Streeter's tobacco factory was very near The Ship at Anchor.

Captain Parrott nodded. 'Look for him there.' He strode over to the two luggers to resume the task of ballasting. Esther followed him over, hoping to be able to spend a few minutes with Sam, but Parrott waved her away. 'Go on, lass. Find Mr Streeter. And hurry.' He was looking out to sea where one of the Revenue cutters looked to be making its way closer to the harbour entrance. Esther suddenly understood the worry. If the Revenue ships blockaded the entrance to the harbour and trapped Mr Streeter's ships, the Revenue crews would then be able to lower their rowboats, come round to where the luggers were tied up and seize them. As one of them had witnessed the unloading the day before, they had all the evidence they needed. Even though the contraband had almost all been distributed, Streeter would not want to lose his ships. Esther knew that once before, the *Phoenix* had been seized and Streeter had had to buy it back. He would not want to do that again, especially as this time there were two ships involved.

She turned to head back up to Stanpit, but as she set off there was a shout. 'Blue! Come down here before we sail on the high tide and I'll have a few minutes to spare then!' It was Sam, waving at her from the gunwales of the *Civil Usage*. She waved back and shouted her agreement, then hurried up the road to look for Streeter.

He wasn't at the tobacco factory or the lodgings attached to it. He owned other properties in the town, so she sent a man from the factory away on a horse to search him out. A man on horseback would be quicker. Besides she had work to do at the pub – all that contraband was still just inside the tunnel. If there was a very high tide, the tunnel sometimes flooded. She needed to move the goods along to the cellar where it would be safe.

Later that morning, Esther spotted the fisherman Will Burden and a number of others walking down the road towards Mudeford. Captain May must have tracked them down to help with the ballasting. Shortly after, Streeter went galloping past. Esther was relieved he'd been found and could make decisions.

Pa watched him go by from the window of The Ship at Anchor. 'Go to the Haven House, lass,' he said. 'You've moved enough of the goods to the cellar. Mr Streeter might be needing you there – as a messenger if nothing else. We've no customers here.' He kissed her head. 'But keep out of the way of Thomas Walker, if he happens to be around.'

'Thanks, Pa. Walker won't go near the Haven House.' Esther was pleased to be allowed to get away. She hoped that if Burden had brought enough of his friends then perhaps Sam wouldn't be needed sailing out of the harbour. In which case, she could bring him home with her.

For what seemed like the hundredth time over the last couple of days, Esther hurried down Stanpit to Mudeford Quay once more. As she neared the beach she could see the Revenue ships were closer. The third one was not a cutter – it was a sloop, a man o' war, heavily armed. And it had rounded Hengistbury Head. What the captains had feared had happened – Streeter's boats were trapped.

* * *

Esther ran into the Haven House. Streeter was there, with his two captains. He was furious. 'If I lose both those ships it'll wipe out most of my profit from this run. The biggest haul ever, the most risk, and it'll be all for nothing.' He slammed his fist down onto a table. 'I'll not give them up without a fight, you hear me? *Civil Usage* is brand new, dammit! I want those luggers saved.'

'We're blocked in,' Captain May replied. 'We've no chance of getting them out. The *Orestes* is anchored out there, and her guns have a range of half a mile. Her captain's experienced, too. If we tried to sail or tow the luggers out and *Orestes* opened fire, we'd be sitting ducks.'

'Bloody hell. What can be done?' Streeter was pacing up and down. All Esther could think about was Sam – whatever happened she didn't want Sam on board if the naval ship opened fire. He'd be in real danger for his life.

Captain Parrott tried to stop Streeter pacing. 'All we can do is save what we can from the luggers. Take their sails off, store them here somewhere. Remove their masts, spars, guns – anything that can be moved we should take off. Then if we do have to relinquish them, the Revenue men get just a keel filled with ballast. Nothing of any real value. You've the men here, who've been ballasting the ships. We've missed our chance to sail out, but we've the men here to work on stripping them. Say the word, get them onto it. It's all that can be done.'

'Not quite all,' Captain May interjected. Streeter turned to stare at him questioningly. 'We have enough muskets to give out to the sailors. If the Revenue cutters launch their rowboats and come to try to board our ships, we can defend ourselves. Defend your property.'

'Fire on them, you mean?'

May nodded grimly. 'Only if they fire first. In self-defence.'

Parrott agreed. 'It's all we can do.'

Esther watched open-mouthed as Streeter looked from one to

the other of his captains, and then made a decision. 'Very well. We'll strip the ships. And arm the men.'

She gasped, and looked around for Sam. Where was he? Surely he would not need to be involved in this. As she turned, Sam entered the inn, looking filthy from the ballasting work, and exhausted. George was with him. She ran over to them and told them what she'd just heard.

George nodded. 'I'll do my part. Mr Streeter's been good to me, and I'll help him defend his ships.' He went over to the captains to volunteer his services.

Sam took Esther in his arms. 'I'll help strip the ships but I'll not take a musket. That's a step too far. Let me go and help with this first stage. That I must do, but I'm not getting caught up in any fighting.' He spoke quietly, so only she could hear. 'I'll talk George out of it, too. He's only wanting to look the big brave hero in front of Hannah.'

She smiled. 'Yes, stop him getting involved in any of that. But it won't come to it, will it? I mean, there won't be any actual firing of muskets?' She imagined there'd be posturing, the free traders waving weapons at Revenue men to try to stop them boarding, but surely nothing more.

'I expect shots will be fired over heads, to try to frighten off the other side. Streeter's going to have to accept he's lost his ships though.'

As Sam said that, the two ships' captains began rounding up any men in the pub who could help with the work stripping assets from the luggers. 'You too, Blue,' Streeter said, as he passed. 'We'll store everything in Hannah's outbuildings. You can help organise it.'

'Yes, sir.' She followed the men outside and Hannah showed her an empty stable where the ships' gear could be stored.

'I don't like this, Esther,' Hannah said, once the men had returned to start work on the ships. 'I don't like this idea of handing out guns. If things go wrong, if shots are fired, it's not going to go well for us. If our men shoot them, they'll be arrested and hanged. If their men shoot ours …' She shook her head sadly. 'Either way we lose. Why can't Streeter just take the loss this time? There'll be other runs, other chances to make a profit. Even if he loses the ships.'

Esther stared with mounting horror at the older woman. She didn't like what was happening either, and had a bad feeling about what might happen in the hours ahead.

Chapter 15

Arwen left in the late afternoon, promising to visit again soon. 'Hopefully next time will be a little less dramatic,' she said, as we kissed goodbye. 'Thanks, and I hope you'll sleep all right. Don't be worrying – there was nothing you could have done. And best wishes with Nick.'

'Thanks. For all of it.'

As I shut the door behind her I leaned back against it. I would not sleep that night, I knew it. I'd be thinking of that poor girl and wondering what happened to her. I went upstairs to look through the bedroom window once more, to see what was going on in the marsh. There was still a lot of activity there, and an incident tent had been erected, presumably over the exact spot where the body had been found.

I was still standing there, staring out of the window when the doorbell rang, and I hurried down to answer it. I was sort of hoping it might be Nick, but expecting it was more likely to be Sharon.

It was neither. A journalist was on the doorstep, with a camera crew hovering behind. 'Hello, I'm Fay Morton from South Coast News. Am I right in thinking your property backs onto the marsh? I was wondering whether you knew anything about the body found there, and whether you saw or heard anything?' She thrust a microphone under my nose. Behind her, the crew had a camera pointed right at me.

'No, I'm sorry, I don't know anything—' I began, but Fay interrupted.

'Can we come through, and look at the scene from your side? We can't get anywhere near with the police cordons ...'

There was something about this woman I didn't like. I knew she was only doing her job, but to have her and the cameraman in the house would feel like an invasion. 'No. Sorry. I've had a long day ...'

'We'd only be a minute and wouldn't disturb you at all.' She actually took a step forward as though I'd agreed.

'No, really. I've spoken to the police and ...'

'What did you tell them, may I know?'

'I had nothing to tell them. Now, please, I need you to leave.'

She shrugged and scowled, but got the hint and turned away. Across the road I could see Sharon peeking out through a front window. I so nearly lifted a hand to wave at her but stopped myself in time. I was not ready to discuss it with her just yet. It was time for a glass of wine, a snack, and a bit of me-time. As I closed the door I noticed the journalist heading over the road to have a word with Sharon. She'd have more luck there, I suspected.

A little later that evening I opened up my laptop to search for any further news about the grisly discovery. It didn't take long to find the headlines: *Body of woman found in beauty spot, police suspect murder.*

Murder! I shivered. The thought that she might have been killed there, within earshot of my bedroom where I'd been sleeping, was too horrible to contemplate. I read on. *Investigations continue to determine the identity of the woman, and whether she was killed at the spot or elsewhere and her body dumped. Pumps are being brought in to drain the pool in the hope that further clues will be found.*

There was a generic picture of Stanpit Marsh, and a short video clip of a police officer, not one who'd come to my house, appealing to anyone local who might have seen or heard anything unusual in the last twenty-four hours. I racked my brain. Was there anything I'd heard? I felt as though I wanted to help, somehow.

There were brief interviews with a couple of local people. The TV journalist who'd called at my house had clearly had better luck with others, including a young man who regularly walked his dog near where the body had been found. 'Can't believe it, like. Could have been me who found her.' He shook his head. 'Glad it wasn't, but horrible thing to happen. Normally so quiet round here.'

The next interview was with Sharon, filmed on her doorstep. 'Of course, living so close to where it happened, it's all been a terrible shock. I hate to think of murder happening so close to home. I imagine she'd been out late with the wrong sort of people. Not saying it's her fault, but you do wonder, don't you? This sort of thing shouldn't happen here, it really shouldn't.'

Typical of Sharon, I thought, listening to her. She had a slightly gleeful look about her, as though she was lapping up the attention. I didn't like the way she'd suggested it might be partly the woman's own fault. Murder was *never* the fault of the victim!

Nick phoned, and when I answered he sighed with relief. 'I know it sounds mad, but when I heard the news that a woman's body was found in Stanpit Marsh, for a moment I was scared it was you. But you're all right?'

'Of course I'm all right. That poor woman. They're saying she was probably murdered, and her body was found so close to my house. It's awful.'

'Where was she found?'

'That little pool, just off the main track. It's only about twenty metres from my garden.'

'I remember the place. Millie, do you want me to come over? Are you sure you're all right?'

'I'm fine, and no, don't come. I'm still clearing up after Arwen's visit and I think I just need some time to chill on my own. And there's work tomorrow.' Truth was, I was still processing what Sharon had told me and couldn't face Nick yet. Not until I'd worked out how to ask him if he knew anything about his father's involvement with the drugs trade.

'Oh. OK. If you change your mind, and feel you don't want to be alone, you know where I am. I'll be round tomorrow anyway. I'll get there early, before you leave …'

'Honestly, Nick, I'm fine.' Even to myself I sounded a bit short with him.

'Right, OK. See you tomorrow then.'

'Yes. Bye.'

I hung up, perhaps a little swiftly.

Not much more news came out that night, though there was a short piece on the national news about it on TV, with Fay Morton presenting it. She'd managed to find some other local person to interview, but they had nothing new to say.

Sharon, predictably, knocked on my door later on, after the TV news bulletin. 'Have you heard? A murder! Right on our doorstep, too. Brian was wondering, can you even see the site of it from your upstairs? Did you see anything last night? It's all rather exciting, isn't it, although perhaps a little close to home. They interviewed me about it. Did you see me on TV? Very nice reporter, she was.'

'I saw you on TV. But I saw and heard nothing last night, as I told the police. Not sure I'd call it exciting, either.' Sharon's glee-fulness was a bit distasteful. A woman had been killed, after all.

'Oh, I'm sorry. I don't mean exciting as such. Interesting, maybe. I mean, you see all those real-life crime programmes on TV and it's so fascinating following how they investigate and then solve the case, and here we are right in the middle of one, and being interviewed for TV too.'

I gave her a tight smile. 'Yes, I guess it'll be interesting seeing what happens. But that poor woman …'

'Of course. The poor woman. Well, I must report back to Brian that you don't know any more than we do. You'll come and tell us, of course, if you hear anything more? Like who she was, how she was killed …'

I nodded, and she left. How did she think I'd hear anything before her? Just because my garden backed onto the marsh it didn't mean I had a direct line to the police investigation.

Twice now, Sharon had come over to say something that I hadn't liked to hear. It was a shame. I'd thought initially that we would end up being great friends, but it wasn't looking that way now. Well, I told myself, other neighbours and friends were available. I'd keep Sharon at a distance, a superficial friendship.

I left for work early the next day, texting Nick with some excuse saying I'd been called in a bit early but as he and the lads knew what they were getting on with I hoped it was not a problem. I got a simple thumbs-up in response.

I spent half the day at work fending off enquiries from colleagues who knew I lived in the area where the body had been found. They didn't know quite how close though, and that helped. I could detach myself from it a little and concentrate on work.

I heard it first on the radio on my drive home. *Police have drained a pool where a young woman's body was found yesterday. There appears to be an entrance to a tunnel in the hollow revealed beneath the pool. Local historian Arthur Watts has suggested it may have been a smugglers' tunnel, connected to a local house that was once a pub …*

I had to switch off the radio, for fear that I'd crash my car, concentrating too much on the idea that my house, my tunnel might have linked up with the place where that poor woman's body was found. There was only one thing I could do and that was get home and phone Arthur, find out exactly what it was

147

he suspected. I realised I'd given no thought regarding the other end of my tunnel. It seemed it had led to the edge of the marsh.

As soon as I was home I called Arthur.

'Ah, I thought I might hear from you! So now we know where your tunnel led.' He sounded almost gleeful. I supposed that from a local history point of view, it was quite a discovery.

'You're sure that's the other end of my tunnel?' I asked.

'What else could it possibly be? It's so close, and the marsh end of the tunnel is very near the water's edge. The free traders, as they liked to call themselves, could have rowed contraband to a point near the tunnel entrance, carried the goods through the reed beds, which would have been perfect for staying hidden, and then through the tunnel for the last part to the pub. Without that tunnel they might have been seen from the road bringing goods in via the front of the pub. And of course, coming up into that hidden cellar was perfect.'

'What I don't understand is how there could have been a tunnel entrance under a pool of water. Not very convenient!'

Arthur laughed. 'We have to suppose that it was dry in those days, and the pool has formed more recently. I would expect they might have had trouble with the entrance flooding on occasion though, and perhaps had to dig drainage channels.'

'Maybe the water getting in is what has caused the tunnel to collapse.'

'Perhaps you are right. I wonder, if there's some breed of surveyor who'd be able to map out the entire route of the tunnel? It would be fascinating to walk above it from your house to the pool, even though we can't walk through it.'

'I'll look into it. My garden is horribly overgrown at the moment – only the patio is usable. I need to get the house into some sort of liveable condition first and then tackle the garden. Maybe once the overgrown shrubs are cut back or ripped out it'll become clearer. I'd need to do that before any surveyor could work out the route of the tunnel, I think.'

'Of course. But if or when you do, keep me informed, eh?'

'I certainly will. Have a good evening, Arthur.'

'I shall. I've begun researching the various families who lived in your house over the years. I'll let you know what I find out. It feels even more important to get on with this research now that a current-day mystery is connected to the past.'

'Thank you.'

I made myself some dinner and afterwards, sat upstairs in my bedroom where I'd set up a TV temporarily. I managed to catch a news programme later on that covered the discovery of the tunnel. It also mentioned a new snippet of information – that the police were now definitely treating the case as a murder inquiry.

Murder, quite possibly carried out more or less on my doorstep, and I had heard nothing.

Chapter 16

They worked hard and fast – the men on board the luggers –
removing sails, spars, masts, ropes, guns, gear. Anything movable
was taken off the ships and stored in Hannah's outbuildings.
Esther made sure it was all tidily stowed away. At some point it
would go back on the ships, or maybe would be used on new
ships if these were seized. Now and again she went out and
stood on the quayside, checking on the position of the Revenue
cutters and the Navy sloop *Orestes*. They weren't moving – they'd
anchored just off the mouth of the harbour. There was no way
out. Streeter had made the right decision – about stripping the
ships, at least. She was still uneasy at the prospect of issuing guns
to the free traders.

Captain May and Captain Parrott had gone back and forth
between the inn and the ships, and Esther had seen them distributing muskets and ammunition. So it was really happening. As
far as she was aware, Sam had not taken a gun but George had.

And then in the afternoon something changed. The stripping
of the luggers was almost complete, and Esther was hoping to find
Sam and go back with him to The Ship at Anchor. She left the
stable to look for him, and noticed there were several rowboats
and a pinnace in the water, launched from the three Customs

150

ships. All were making their way slowly, against the outgoing tide, through the Run and into the harbour. There were marines on board the boats, also armed with muskets.

Captain May came to stand alongside her. He was looking through his spyglass at the pinnace. 'That's William Allen in charge there. Dammit.'

'Who's William Allen?'

'Sailing master from *Orestes*. He has a commission from the Board of Customs too. Young but very able. He looks to be leading this expedition. They'll try to board the luggers and seize them. He's good. Damn.' Captain May turned and hurried off – Esther guessed to confer with Parrott and Streeter. A moment later she spotted men taking positions on the luggers, behind their gunwales. And another couple of men with muskets, including George Coombes, running across the yard and into the Haven House. Upstairs, several windows were opened and Esther could see musket barrels pointing out.

'Oh God. Where is Sam?' she muttered to herself. It was time to get away from there. If there was to be a battle, and she really couldn't believe it but that's what it looked like, she wanted Sam and herself to be as far away as possible, safe and sound in her father's pub. She ran towards the *Civil Usage* where she'd last seen Sam. It was a sorry-looking hulk of a ship now, stripped of its masts and sails. It had made two voyages only, and that seemed as though it might be all it would ever make.

Sam was climbing down a rope ladder over the side of the ship. He spotted Esther and ran towards her. 'We should go. But I don't know where George is.'

'He's inside the inn. He has a musket, but if he's in there he'll be safe.' To Esther's mind, joining the battle from an upstairs window of the inn would be safer than staying on one of the ships, given that the aim of the marines was surely to seize the ships, refloat them and take them away.

'I wish he would not take part in this,' Sam said.

'He must make his own decision.' Esther took hold of Sam's arm. 'Shall we go?'

But Sam was watching events in the harbour, where the rowboats and marines had now made their way around the headland and weren't far from the luggers. The pinnace – the largest of the rowboats and which carried William Allen – had become stuck on a sandbank. 'They don't know what they're doing, those marines. It's only us who know these waters well enough to get through,' Sam said.

As they watched, William Allen, resplendent in his naval uniform of blue jacket and white breeches, jumped out of the pinnace to try to refloat it off the sandbank. As he heaved against it, they heard the sound of a musket shot. Whether it had come from one of the luggers or from the Haven House Esther could not tell. But Allen gave a shout and fell back in the water, obviously hit.

'He's been wounded!'

'But not badly, look,' Sam replied, and Esther saw that Allen was pulling himself back to his feet, and over the side of the pinnace.

There was another shot and this time they saw that Allen had been hit in the chest. The marines still in the pinnace hauled him over the side and into the bottom of the boat. And then they opened fire with their muskets on the men on the luggers.

'Run!' Sam grabbed her arm and pulled her away from the firing, around to the far side of the Haven House. There was a huge explosion and shards of masonry fell about them. 'The sloop's firing its guns on us now. We have to hide!' He pushed her ahead of him into the inn.

Hannah was pacing up and down, twisting her apron in her hands. Streeter was there too, sitting at a table looking worried. Hannah went over to him. 'This was not what I agreed to, Mr Streeter. I was always happy for you and your men to use this place to make your plans and store your goods. Not to have a pitched battle!'

'They're just firing to frighten us. No one will get hurt.'

'Mr Streeter – we saw a man from one of the rowboats get hit,' Sam told Streeter.

'It was William Allen, the sailing master,' Esther said. 'Captain May recognised him.'

'The sailing master?' Streeter went white. 'Pray to God he survives, or we'll all be done for.'

'And what of our own men?' Hannah said, her hands on her hips. 'With all this firing—' She broke off as there was another loud crash and the walls of the inn seemed to shake around them. 'I'm not going to have a pub left at this rate. And who's to say our men aren't taking casualties too? If we've hurt one of theirs, they'll aim for ours. They'll not be shooting over heads like you told me they would. They'll be aiming to kill.'

'George!' Sam ran to the stairs. Esther followed him, terrified they might find George shot, bleeding out on a bedroom floor up there. But he wasn't. He was at a window, firing his musket at the marines who were trying to climb on board the *Phoenix*. 'George, leave them! If you're caught, having fired weapons on the marines, it'll not go well for you.'

'Ah, who's going to catch me? No one will say I was here. We'll all keep quiet, won't we, all we free traders, and no one will know who did what. Got to protect our livelihood and Mr Streeter's boats. It's our way of life, Sam!'

Esther could see there was nothing Sam nor she could say that would change anything. George was caught up in the heat of the moment. Perhaps Hannah Sellars could talk some sense into him. She ran back down the stairs.

'Mrs Sellars, stop George! He's shooting at the marines. He'll end up killing someone!' She caught the older woman's arm.

But Hannah shook her off. 'What makes you think he'll listen to me? He's made his own decision. I'm not happy about it, about any of this. But it's not anything I can stop right now, is it? These men, thinking it can all be resolved by fighting. I've had enough,

153

but all I can do now is wait for it to be over and hope my pub's still standing at the end.' Her voice was filled with suppressed anger. She leaned in towards Esther. 'Get yourself away. You and Sam. You want nothing to do with this, believe me.'

'But what about George?'

Hannah flapped her hands at Esther. 'Never mind him. Just go, girl, if you know what's good for you.'

It was enough for Esther. She turned and shouted for Sam. He came clattering down the stairs, but was stopped by Mr Streeter. 'Coombes, you're needed. Come with me.'

'Sir, I'll not use a gun,' Sam said, but Streeter shook his head. 'I'm not asking you to. There's other work needed.'

Sam turned to Esther. 'Go back to your pa. I'll be all right here. Don't worry.'

'Yes, Blue, go to your father. Tell him to try to keep any riding officers away from here. We don't want anyone who can recognise and name us witnessing this battle.'

'Yes, sir. I will.' Esther was glad to have a job to do, a reason to go, although it broke her heart leaving Sam. She kissed him quickly and left the inn. The gunfire was sporadic, but taking place on the other side of the building, so she did not feel in danger of being hit. More worrying was the ordnance being fired from the Revenue ships. Most were hitting the waters of the harbour or the sand-spits, sending plumes of water, sand or gravel flying high into the air. A few shots were hitting the buildings, taking chunks out of corners, smashing roof tiles or breaking windows. So far it looked like the Haven House was holding up. It was solidly built.

She ran to the road, then walked fast up to Stanpit and back to The Ship at Anchor. She was almost there when she spotted Thomas Walker coming down the road the other way on his black horse. Her instinct was to pretend she hadn't seen him and duck inside the pub. After the previous day's events he surely didn't want to speak to her. But Streeter had said to try to keep

Revenue officials away. She had to do what she could. She raised her head and kept walking.

'Esther Harris. Good afternoon.' He raised his tricorn hat to her. Esther was surprised at his politeness. Perhaps he'd forgotten his fury at her yesterday. Perhaps it meant he still expected her to marry him.

'Good afternoon, sir,' she replied, dipping her knees in a small curtsy.

'I heard reports of gunfire. Down at the Haven. Is that true, do you know? You've come from that direction?'

She couldn't deny it. Even from this distance the shots fired from the ships could be heard. 'Yes. Mr Streeter's ships are trapped in the harbour by two Revenue cutters and a man o' war. There are marines trying to board the ships and … they are firing on the free traders.' She'd stopped herself before saying that the smugglers had opened fire first.

'That sounds serious.' Walker rubbed his chin as if deciding what his course of action should be.

She nodded. ''Tis like nothing I've seen before.' If he went down there, she suddenly realised, he'd be in danger. He'd get caught in the crossfire, or worse – the hot-blooded free traders might turn on him as the enemy. She reached up and caught hold of his sleeve. 'Sir, stay away. It's not safe.'

He looked down at her, seeming startled by the contact. For a moment she thought he was going to just brush her off and carry on riding down towards the quay. But instead he covered her hand with his own. 'Thank you, Esther, for the warning. I think you are right. This is for my superiors to decide how to act. I can't ignore it, you understand. I will report to Mr Jeans.'

He gave her hand a squeeze, then turned his horse and rode back up the road towards Christchurch at a canter. Esther breathed out heavily. She'd done her best. She'd turned him away, so that he wouldn't be able to identify any of the smugglers with guns. And so that he'd be safe. Whatever happened, however much she might not like the man and wanted him gone from her life, she didn't want him hurt. She went into the pub and found Pa upstairs, standing by a window that faced towards the harbour. 'Lass, what's happening? Gunfire? Sounded like cannon. I've heard the shots, and there's been puffs of smoke …'

She told him the events of the day. 'I couldn't get back, till now. And Sam's still there. Pa, I'm so worried for him.'

Pa took her into his arms. 'He'll be all right, you'll see. It's all just for show, is it? No one's been hurt?'

'A sailing master from the marines' ship was hit. Looked bad. I don't know about our men. There's that much musket fire, it could be bad for the men on Streeter's ships.'

Pa visibly slumped hearing this. 'I'm glad you're back, lass. We must just keep our heads down and keep out of the way. I hope Mr Walker and the other riding officers aren't anywhere near.'

She told him then about her encounter with Walker. 'He was off to talk to Joshua Jeans. It'll be up to him to decide what to do.'

Pa gave a hollow laugh. 'Jeans won't want anything to do with it. He'll keep his head down even more than us.'

'Any chance of service here? There's thirsty men waiting!' A yell came from downstairs.

'Coming,' Esther called back, as she hurried down. The pub had been quiet, Pa had said, as people rested after their hard work landing the cargo the day before. But now that the working day was over and evening was here, men were coming to the pub for a pint or two of ale before returning to their homes. And, she suspected, to find out what was going on down at Mudeford Quay.

They were kept busy for a little while, serving a steady stream of customers, all of whom were desperate to hear about what was happening. Among them was Will Burden, who looked white and frightened. He arrived an hour or so after Esther, and she was pretty sure he'd come from the quay. The gunfire could still be heard, though more sporadic now.

Later, in the early evening, there was the sound of a horse

galloping up the road towards the pub. Esther looked out, and saw Captain May. He dismounted and barged in through the pub door. 'You men! Get down to the Haven House now! You're needed there to fight, not sit in here slurping ale. You're the ones who benefit from our trade. Get down there and defend it!' He grabbed at Burden, pulling him to his feet.

Burden yanked himself free. 'I'm not shooting at people who're only doing their job. Get off me, man.'

May moved on to another couple of men who'd been drinking with Burden. 'You? What about you? Come on, we need all the help we can get!' He looked crazed, specks of spittle flew from his mouth as he shouted at them. But all the men shook their heads and turned away.

At last Captain May gave up, and left the pub, muttering something about needing more ammunition for the brave souls who were fighting. Shortly after, Esther saw him galloping back the other way, to the quay, with a cask of ammunition on his back. They then heard the gunfire pick up again.

'What of Sam?' she said to Pa. 'I'd hoped he could get away.'

'You saw what that captain did here to Burden and the others. I reckon they're hanging on to the men they've got. Just hope no one's hurt.'

'Should I go down there? I could … help tend to any injuries?'

'You're not going anywhere until the gunfire ceases completely,' Pa growled at her. 'You're staying right here, where it's safe. You've done enough.'

She nodded, and to take her mind off worrying about Sam, got to work cleaning pots and plates, washing tankards and setting the kitchen to rights.

As evening wore on and darkness fell, at last the gunfire became more sporadic and eventually stopped. 'They can't see what they're doing now,' Pa said. 'Let's just hope it doesn't start up again at first light.'

Esther nodded. The idea of another day of fighting was too

much to bear. All she could do now was pray that Sam was all right and would be back with her soon. And that none of the free traders had been injured.

An image of the sailing master William Allen falling into the water after being hit by musket fire flitted across her mind. She prayed, too, that he survived his injuries. Free trading was supposed to be about bettering the lives of local people. It shouldn't ever be the cause of any loss of life. And yet … things had escalated today, so horribly. The way Allen had been hauled into the pinnace by his men … It didn't look good for him.

Chapter 17

Sharon called round again one evening that week, shortly after I'd got home from work. Nick had once again left before I arrived home. I wondered if he was keeping his distance. Perhaps he'd picked up on my hesitancy when he last called me on Sunday evening.

I wasn't entirely sure I wanted to see Sharon, but she was a neighbour, and I wanted to stay on friendly terms with her.

'Millie, how are you? I wanted to check that this business with the murder on our doorstep hasn't upset you too much – I know you felt awful when her body was originally found.' Her tone was much more sympathetic than the last time I'd seen her.

'I'm all right. It is horrible, though. Knowing she was killed there and yet I didn't hear a thing.'

'Brian says that maybe she was killed elsewhere and her body dumped. We don't know, do we? The police aren't giving much away yet – I suppose before they've identified her they can't, really. They won't have been able to even notify her next of kin. But someone must be missing her, somewhere.' Sharon shook her head. 'The poor thing. I feel bad that I saw it as just a piece of excitement when it first happened. You told me off about that.' She gave a little rueful smile. 'You were right. I'm sorry. Friends?' She held out her hand to me to shake.

I took it and smiled. 'Of course we are friends. Don't worry.' I wanted to say, as long as you don't lecture me about who I go out with, but refrained.

But I didn't need to say it. With impeccably awful timing, Nick's car pulled up on the road outside, at that exact moment. Sharon and I were still on my doorstep, and she watched, thin-lipped, as he walked over to us.

'Millie? I wanted to come and see you, check you were all right. Just, with the latest news ... and I haven't seen you for a bit ...' He glanced at Sharon, as though wondering who she was and waiting for me to introduce them.

'I'm fine, Nick, honest. This is Sharon – she's my neighbour from across the street. Sharon, Nick Marshall. My builder.'

Nick threw me a confused look as I put a slight emphasis on the word 'builder'. But it seemed the right way to introduce him. Especially to Sharon. I still wasn't sure whether Nick and I would ever have a closer relationship, after what Sharon had told me about the family.

'Hello,' Sharon said, with a slight nod at him. She didn't offer him a hand to shake. He must have picked up on her reserve as he didn't offer a handshake either, just nodded back at her.

'Millie, can I come in? Couple of things to discuss ... about the house, I mean.' His look was pointed, as though telling me to get rid of Sharon.

'Sure. Go on through. I'll be just a moment.'

He pushed past me into the house. Sharon pulled me away from the door and hissed in my ear. 'Keep your distance, Millie. Honestly. I don't want you to get hurt, and I ... don't trust them. His family, I mean.'

'I'll be all right,' I said, and stepped away from her, back to my doorstep. She took the hint. Just as well, as Nick was still very near and I wondered if he'd heard what she'd said about his family.

'Well, I'll be off ... you know where I am if ... you need anything.'

160

'Yeah, thanks. Bye then.' I closed the door and went inside.

Nick was standing, hands in pockets, in the middle of the sitting room, gazing at the fireplace.

'She was murdered at the other end of your tunnel, then,' he said, as I walked in. 'At least we now know where the tunnel led to.'

'Yes.' I didn't trust myself to say anything more.

'Murdered. But you heard nothing.'

'No.' I bit my lip. To my horror tears were pricking at the backs of my eyes. I hadn't cried when Arwen, who was my oldest friend, was here. Nor when talking to the police, the reporter, my work colleagues, Arthur or Sharon. But something about Nick's presence made the tears want to flow.

'Ah, Millie. Even though you're not involved, it's so close. No wonder you're stressed and upset. Come here.' He stepped forward and wrapped his arms around me. It would be the most natural thing in the world to rest my head against his chest, let the tears flow for a bit, put my arms around his waist. I almost gave in to the urge to let him comfort me. But if I did that, I'd be admitting he was important to me, treating him as a boyfriend, a partner, and accepting that we were at the start of a romantic relationship.

And none of those things were true, were they?

I gently backed away, and lifted a hand to tell him no, stop, don't hug me.

His brow was furrowed. 'What's wrong, Millie?'

I shook my head. What could I tell him? He needed, and probably deserved, some sort of explanation. We'd had a wonderful couple of dates and it had seemed as though our relationship was going somewhere. Yet now I was pushing him away. My mind frantically scrabbled around for something I could tell him, that wasn't along the lines of *my neighbour Sharon whom you just met has warned me off you, telling me your family are a bad lot and that your dad whom I found so charming is a drug baron.* 'It's just … It's all a bit sudden. A bit soon.'

'You mean, after your divorce?'

I nodded. 'That's not even finalised yet. And I've only just moved here, I've started a new job ... and living in a building site is stressful, and then the tunnel, and the murder ... It's all a bit much, I suppose.' I gave a crooked smile that I hoped looked apologetic. 'I'm sorry. I'm just not ... I can't ...'

'All right. I'll back off, for a bit, then. But Millie ... I think we could have something special here, when you're ready. I hope you'll give me another go, later on? When the work's done, and your divorce comes through, and all the fuss dies down?'

'I guess ... we'll see.' It was all I could say. There were too many unknowns. Too much for me to think about and work through, before I could give him any definite answer.

He looked hurt and confused, and my heart broke for him, but I knew I couldn't say anything else if I didn't honestly feel it. 'I'll be off, then. Oh, tomorrow I won't be here. Just the lads – they know what they need to get on with. See you later in the week. Phase one of your work should be more or less finished by then – all bar the decorating. You can decide if you want to continue with the next phase ... or wait a bit. Whatever you want.'

'Thanks.' I was going to say I'd see him out, but he was already heading down the hallway to let himself out.

When I heard the door close I went upstairs and threw myself down on my bed, like a teenager who'd been grounded. Why was that man affecting me so much? I'd only had two dates with him. Why did I care that he seemed hurt by me?

I spent the following day trying not to think about Nick. When I arrived home that evening Aaron and Keith were still working, and the house was looking amazing. They'd got so much done. They'd replaced the floorboards in the sitting room and had repointed and cleaned up the stonework on a wall we were leaving unplastered as a feature. The old flagstones in the hallway had been cleaned and polished too. They were gloriously uneven but beautiful, and once again I wondered about all the feet, all those pub customers – some of whom would have been free traders – who'd walked over them in years gone by.

'Painter's coming tomorrow, then it'll really look good,' Keith said. He looked proud of their progress. 'And Nick said to tell you he won't be back here until next week. Oh, and have you seen the new entrance to the cellar? We got that started today.'

'Oh! No, haven't seen it.'

'Shall I show you now?' Keith looked like an excited puppy so I let him lead the way, out to my garden and into one of the outhouses that was above the hidden cellar. They'd cut through the wooden floor and added a set of wooden steps. 'Still need to add a handrail but you can see the potential of this space now. It could be a games room, or home cinema,' Keith said proudly as he made his way down the steps and flicked on a newly installed light. I knew he was imagining a pool table, a little bar in the corner and a huge screen showing back-to-back football matches. A boy den.

'It could, or it might just be somewhere I store Christmas decorations,' I said, realising I sounded old and boring. 'Steps are lovely. I'm really happy with this.'

'We moved those old barrels over to that corner. Few bits of rubbish there too – old stuff. Didn't know if you wanted to keep it all or not. If you don't want it, Aaron and I can help shift it tomorrow. It'll be much easier to clear it out now.'

I looked where he pointed. I'd forgotten about the barrels, what with the excitement of finding the tunnel. The door to the tunnel was still in place. I hadn't decided what to do about it yet – perhaps leave a little piece of tunnel intact but made safe, just for posterity. But now, knowing a woman had been murdered at the other end of it, I didn't feel quite the same. I walked over to the small stack of barrels. 'I should check if there's anything in these, I think.'

'Some feel light – as though they're empty. But those two' – Keith indicated two barrels stacked to the left of the tunnel door – 'might have something in them. And then there's these bits. Really old. I reckon no one can have come down here for a couple of hundred years.'

'It's quite possible, that after the tunnel collapsed no one used this cellar anymore,' I said.

Keith nodded. 'Well, I'll be off now. Anything you want doing, leave a note for us. Otherwise we'll get on with the scheduled work.'

'Thanks, Keith.'

He left, and I stayed in the cellar for a little longer, trying to envisage how I might use it. It didn't feel like anywhere I'd want to use as a living space, so it would almost certainly end up being just for storage. I'd probably leave a couple of empty barrels here … just to help tell the story of the room's origins. I went over to the other items Keith had uncovered. There was an ancient lantern, with a stub of candle still inside. A mouldy pile of fabric. I picked up one item and held it out. A jacket, made of some sort of brown cloth. It was very fragile, more or less disintegrating in my hands. Beneath it was a pair of trousers of some sort, and a rough tin plate and mug. Had someone lived down here for a while? I'd almost certainly never be able to know. But Arthur had promised to find out who'd lived in the house. I couldn't wait to hear from him again.

I gave one of the barrels by the tunnel entrance a little push. It certainly felt as though it contained something. There was some worn writing on the side but nothing I could make out. Whatever was inside, even if it was alcohol, was surely unusable after all these years.

I went back upstairs, flicking off the light. It was a beautiful evening so I decided to have my dinner in the garden. It was only pasta and a ready-made sauce so took me minutes to prepare and carry outside to my tatty garden table and chairs, along with a bottle of beer and my phone, in case of any calls.

My garden faced west, so the evening sun lit up the terrace. It felt private and peaceful. What was once a lawn was now thigh high, flanked by overgrown bushes. I'd need to tackle this at some stage, and the sooner the better as it was only going to keep growing. I made a mental note to check my finances and see if I could afford to bring in a gardener. It definitely felt beyond my capabilities. The end of the garden gave way to the reeds of the marsh. A little further on was the pool. I shuddered, and wondered if I'd ever be able to forget about the murder.

Probably not. I wished I knew a bit more – who was she, how was she killed? Who had killed her and why? I hoped so much that her killer would be found and brought to justice, but as yet, there was no more news.

I'd just about finished eating when my phone rang. It was Arthur. 'I have news about the various people who lived in your house, when it was a pub,' he said. He sounded exhilarated. I imagined he got a thrill from tracking down snippets of local history.

'Go on, then. Do tell. Or come round – I can make tea or there's a couple of beers in the fridge if you prefer.'

'Oh my dear, a glass of beer and a chat about your house's history would make for a perfect evening for me. I shall be there shortly.'

I just had time to wash up my dishes and find two suitable glasses for the beers when he arrived, brandishing a folder of papers. Some were handwritten and some printed from websites. He greeted me and the cats before we sat down. 'Hello, little ones. I didn't know your cat had kittens!'

I explained how while the building work was going on I'd had to shut them in a room upstairs. The kittens were on good form – wide awake and excited to meet a new person. 'So it's only recently that I've been allowing them downstairs in the evenings,' I said, watching as he picked up one and held it close to his face, apparently enjoying the feel of its warm little body against his cheek. I smiled, wondering if possibly he'd give a home to the remaining kitten. I poured his beer and we went through to the garden. I loved these midsummer evenings when it stayed light until nearly ten o'clock.

'Let's start at the beginning,' Arthur said, after he'd settled himself into a garden chair and had a good long sip of his beer. I'd shut the patio door so that the kittens stayed inside. 'I've gone back through all the business registries I have access to. Your house was built in 1734 and was a pub right from the start. It was called The Ship at Anchor, and up the road was its sister pub The Ship in Distress, which of course still exists. The pub's first landlord was a fellow called Masters, and then the Harris family ran the pub for a couple of generations. At the time of the Battle of Mudeford in 1784 it was a Luke Harris who was landlord here. Later on in the nineteenth century it was owned by a fellow called Coombes. It stopped being a pub in 1865, which is around the time that the smuggling trade in this area finally died out. A man called Matthew Coombes was the last landlord of it, and it looks as though he sold it when he retired, and from then on it was a private house.' Arthur nodded towards my sitting-room patio door. 'I would bet good money that your cellar was boarded up then and no one ever used it again, given it wasn't very convenient to access it.'

'Yes, and the fireplace was too large to be practical.'

'You found some items down in that cellar, didn't you?'

'Yes. Want to see? I've some nice new steps going down there now – no need to crawl through the fireplace.'

Arthur grinned his acceptance and I took him down the new steps, flicking on the light as I entered the cellar. I showed him the pile of rotting clothing.

'Hmm, I wonder …' he said, as he picked up what remained of the jacket.

'You wonder?'

'There's a local legend of a young woman who would dress in boy's clothing and help the free traders landing the goods.'

'Oh! I went to the museum and saw a blue cap that belonged to a girl like that.'

Arthur nodded. 'Yes, and her name was Esther Harris. I wonder if she was related to the Luke Harris who ran this pub at that time. Perhaps she was his daughter, and perhaps these were her clothes.'

I gasped. 'And maybe she would change into her boy's clothes in here and go out through the tunnel to join the smugglers!'

'That's very possible, if the tunnel was still in use at that time. We don't know when it collapsed, of course.'

I regarded the dirty brown jacket he was still holding. The thought that it could have belonged to a smuggler girl was intriguing. And the idea that Esther Harris, she of the blue cap and legendary status among the smugglers of old, might have lived in this house and worn these clothes was so exciting.

Arthur must have recognised the expression on my face. He grinned. 'I love feeling as though I am almost physically in touch with real history and real people who lived long ago, don't you?'

I nodded. 'Yes. This is so much more fascinating than dry facts in dusty textbooks. People who stood right here, wore these clothes, and in their own way had an impact on the local area.'

'You're catching the local history bug.' Arthur looked pleased with himself.

I had to laugh. He was absolutely right.

Chapter 18

By the time it was fully dark it seemed that the battle was completely over. From the front windows of The Ship at Anchor Esther saw smugglers walking back up the road towards Christchurch in ones and twos. A few called in to the pub for late refreshment. Will Burden stayed in the pub, also staring out of the window, watching who was going past.

At last Sam and George arrived, and Esther brought them into a back room to hear their stories of the end of the battle.

'We've lost the ships,' Sam said. 'We defended them as long as we could, but in the end they had more firepower, and we had to pull back to the Haven House. Marines are on board them now. Once we'd lost the ships and darkness had fallen, there was no point carrying on.'

'We've seen the men coming back up towards Christchurch,' Esther said. 'What of Mr Streeter and the two captains?'

'The captains were just behind us,' George said. 'And Mr Streeter left a while ago. He's going into hiding.'

'Was anyone hurt? I mean, I saw that sailing master in the pinnace was hit. I hope he was not too badly injured. But were there any more?'

'Think I hit a marine in the shoulder,' George said, with a hint of pride that turned Esther's stomach. 'He fell back into the same pinnace the other fellow was in. And I'm sure a few others said they hit marines.'

'What about the free traders?'

George shrugged. 'Couple of minor injuries. Nothing too bad. Hannah was seeing to them, patching them up.' He sighed and rolled his eyes. 'She didn't want me to stay down there. Think she's cross with me. Don't know why.'

'I don't think she approved of the fighting,' Esther said quietly. 'Sam, what were you doing all this time?'

'Running around handing out ammunition and passing on messages,' he replied. Esther was pleased he hadn't been persuaded to pick up a gun.

'We didn't lose any of the haul,' George said, with a grin. 'That's the main thing, isn't it? We'd got it away before all this started. You've some here, haven't you?'

Esther nodded. 'Some of it's still in the tunnel though. Not had a chance to move it up.'

'Tomorrow, I'll help you,' Sam said. 'I'll stay here tonight. I'm too exhausted to get home.'

'George, you can stay too,' Esther said. 'No need to go back to Burton. We can make up beds down here for you both.'

'Thanks. Been an exhausting couple of days.'

'Esther? Come out to the bar, pet.' Her father's voice called through from the bar.

She went to see what he wanted, and gasped to see Thomas Walker in the bar. She prayed he had not heard any of their conversation from the back room. It wouldn't do for him to know for certain that George and Sam had been involved in the battle. 'Good evening, sir. Is there anything I can do for you?'

Walker shook his head. 'I just called in to check you were safe, Esther. I care about you, you know. Despite what I said the other day … and I'm sorry for that. It was in the heat of the moment. The shock of seeing you on the beach. I hope you will forgive me.'

169

'Sir, yes. I did not take it to heart. You don't need to apologise.' Keep him sweet, Pa had said. He knew too much.

'Good, that is good.' He leaned in close to whisper to her. 'You recall I was going to speak to Mr Jeans when I last saw you, to enquire what should be done about the kerfuffle down at Mudeford?'

She nodded.

'Well, Officer Bursey was there as well. And Mr Jeans just told us to ignore it and go to bed. There was nothing we could do. In any case, it seems to be over now?' He phrased the last part as a question.

'Yes, sir. I have heard no more gunshots since darkness fell.'

'And have you heard anything else? Do you know what occurred? Who was involved, whether anyone was hurt, whether Streeter's ships were seized?'

'Sir, no, I don't know. I have been here since you met me in the street.'

'But men have been in and out. Will Burden was just leaving as I walked in. And he's a face I know from the beach. They must have said something.'

Esther did not know how to answer him. He was still speaking softly, as though trying to get her to take him into her confidence. But however friendly he was, he was still a Revenue officer, and she and Sam and her friends were free traders. They were on opposite sides. She could not betray her friends. Her mouth opened and closed a couple of times as she tried to formulate a reply. In the end, to her surprise, Walker chuckled, and patted her cheek as though she was a child. 'All right, young Esther. I won't push you to say anything against your friends. Not now. One day, soon I hope, your loyalties will be to me rather than them, but until that day, I'll let you be.'

'Th-thank you, sir.' She dipped in a little curtsy. 'Now, may I get you a drink? Or something to eat?' Please say no, she thought. She wanted him gone, so that Sam and George could come out safely.

'No, I'll be getting on home now.' He paused, then took her hand and lifted it to his lips and kissed it gently. 'I want the best for you, Esther Harris. I know you don't believe me, but I do. And I'll prove it to you, somehow.'

With that he dropped her hand and pushed his hat back on his head. There was a movement at the back of the pub, and Walker must have spotted it, for instead of leaving as he'd been about to, he frowned at Esther and strode over to the door to the back room. He flung it open. Inside, Sam and George stood, with expressions like boys caught stealing from an orchard.

'The Coombes brothers. Good to see you, gentlemen. As all other free traders seem to have dispersed, perhaps you two can inform me of the evening's events?'

'Sorry, Mr Walker, sir. We know nothing. Been here helping Esther and Harris in the pub all day, haven't we, Sam? Shifting stock around, chopping wood and such. You know how Harris's back is too crook to do it himself.' George spoke defiantly, as though goading Walker to question him further. Sam simply kept quiet, but cast a worried glance at Esther.

'Hmm. Well, I'll not say a word.' Walker tapped the side of his nose. Then he looked at Esther and smiled. 'Soon, I'll have married into the free traders, won't I, Esther my sweet?'

'What?' Sam's expression was one of shock and disbelief, as he looked from Esther to Walker and back. 'What do you mean?'

'I mean, Samuel Coombes, that Esther will soon be my wife. She'll not consort with smugglers after that, not directly. She won't be working here.'

'Esther, is this true?' Sam stared at Esther, horror and hurt in equal measure in his eyes.

'I'll leave you to it, I think,' said George with a wry smirk, and he sidled out of the room into the bar. At the doorway, Pa stood, having clearly caught the gist of what was going on. He shook his head sadly and followed George back to the bar. It'd soon be closing time, Esther thought, wondering if they could use that as an excuse to get rid of Walker.

'Is it true?' Sam said again.

'Mr Walker hasn't ever actually asked me to be his wife, and I have never actually agreed to it,' she said, holding her head high and proud. Walker had only ever hinted that she would marry him, and had made an assumption that she would after his discussion with Pa.

'But I will, and you will.' Walker gave her a wolfish grin.

Sam looked to be only just keeping himself under control. 'You'll only wed her if that's what she wants, Thomas Walker. And I wouldn't be too sure of that.'

'She'll marry me if she knows what's good for her. And what's it to you, anyway, Coombes?' Walker's eyes widened as the likely answer to his own question dawned on him. 'Ah, you wanted her for yourself, did you? Well, bad luck, son. She's had a better offer, and she'd be a fool to turn it down.'

Esther was trying to formulate a response – she hated the way Walker was talking about her as though she wasn't even present. Did she not have a say in all this? She was about to make a retort when Walker turned to walk out. It was clear he thought he'd won. He didn't know, Esther realised, how close she and Sam had been, or he wouldn't have turned his back like that. Sam was bigger and stronger than the Revenue officer. Too late she realised what Sam was going to do, as he let out a roar and launched himself through the door at Walker's back. The two men fell to the floor, with Sam on top of Walker punching any part of him he could reach. Esther was reminded of small boys scrapping, but they were grown men and they might hurt each other badly. She screamed at them to stop, and her screams brought Pa and George running.

George pulled his brother off the Customs man, while Pa helped Walker to his feet and made an attempt to brush him down. 'Get off me, man,' Walker said impatiently. The only injury

172

was to his pride, Esther thought, but the way he glared at Sam as he straightened his clothing was ominous. 'You. I will remember you, and you will regret this moment.'

Sam stepped forward, fists raised once more. 'You'll regret it too, Walker, if I pass it on to your superiors just how many times you've been paid off by Streeter.'

'You do that and you'll be the one who lands in gaol.' Walker's tone was tough but he looked rattled, Esther thought.

'He meant nothing, he's sorry,' she said. 'Please, sir, he wouldn't have hurt you.'

'I'd kill him if he hurt you in any way.' Sam was red in the face, but submitted to George tugging him away to sit down at the back of the bar.

'We'll talk about this again another day,' Walker said to Esther. 'When we're *alone*.' He raised his eyebrows in a suggestive manner.

Sam swore and made to attack him again but George managed to hold him back for long enough that Walker was able to leave the pub. He was the last customer so Esther bolted the door behind him. She was going to have to explain things to Sam, but she'd prefer to wait until Pa had gone up to bed. Right now he was in the kitchen, keeping out of the way. It was all his doing, promising her to Walker as though she were some sort of tradeable commodity, as though she were a keg of brandy to be bought and sold. If she thought about it for very long in those terms, she became furious with him. But then she remembered he'd had no choice. Walker could make things very difficult for them if he wanted. He knew too much. He knew about the hidden cellar and the tunnel. He'd seen her on the beach unloading contraband. They'd already lost Matthew to the press gang as a result of his smuggling activities. Pa was too old to be press-ganged into the Navy but not too old to serve a prison sentence, and the same fate could await her, if Walker became vindictive. No, Pa had done what was best for them both. She could not blame him.

Even so, it was tough to think that she might have to give

up Sam and marry Walker, to keep herself and Pa safe. She still hoped there'd be some other way out – that Walker would tire of her or find someone else he preferred.

'Has he gone?' Pa had emerged from the kitchen, where he'd been hiding.

'Yes, Pa. You get on off to bed now. I'll clear up down here.'

But Pa hobbled over to her and put his arms around her. 'I brought this on you. I'm so sorry, pet. And I'm sorry for you too, Sam. You're a good man.' He nodded sadly at Sam then let go of Esther and made his way upstairs to bed. George went out to the privy in the yard, leaving Esther and Sam alone.

'Blue, what's going on?' Sam gazed at her looking sad and confused.

She sat down beside him but did not touch him, although she longed to put her arms around him and kiss him. She explained as best she could the dilemma they were in. 'Walker knows of the tunnel. And he saw me on the beach yesterday. So he has a hold over us. He's asked my father's permission to marry me. And Pa had no choice but to say yes.'

Sam nodded slowly. 'I understand. But if you don't want to wed him, you don't have to, Blue. We could go away, where he can't reach us. We could start somewhere new …'

'But my father …'

'He would come with us. We'll take care of him.'

'He'll never leave this pub. He was born here.'

'Then we stop our work with the free traders. We'll have enough to live on. If there's no contraband stored in the cellar then it doesn't matter who knows of its existence, does it? Walker can tell whoever he likes, and when they check there'll be nothing there.'

Esther shook her head. 'But if we do that, we'll fall foul of the smugglers. They don't take kindly to people who turn against them.'

'Mr Streeter wouldn't hurt you or your father. He thinks too much of your family.'

'Probably not, but what about those two ships' captains? Captain May – there's something about him I don't like. He was the one calling for guns to be used yesterday.'

'Yes, and I think he was the one who fired the first shots, and hit that sailing master. I don't know for certain, but I think it was him.'

'I don't like him. He's changed things. He's influencing Mr Streeter. And if word got out we weren't helping the free traders, who knows what he might do in retaliation. This pub's too important a link in the chain. We store a lot in that cellar, and deal with a lot of Streeter's customers.'

Sam put his head in his hands. 'What are we to do? I won't see you wed Walker if you don't want to. I can't, Blue. Even if you won't be mine, I can't bear you to be forced into something you don't want.'

She put a hand tentatively on his shoulder, and he caught hold of it and nuzzled his face against it. 'Sam, don't despair. Something, anything might happen, to change things. I'm not married to him yet, or even engaged. You need to get to bed now. It's been a long, hard couple of days.'

'That it has. And you're right – everything's changing. Maybe there'll be some other way to get Walker off your back. But if not … who knows.' He kissed the back of her hand and went to set up beds for himself and George, leaving her with a few chores to do to tidy the bar ready for the next day, before she too could collapse in her bed. Though not to sleep – her head was buzzing with so many questions and worries, and the events of the day to relive over and over.

Chapter 19

It was another couple of days before the police made a breakthrough in their investigation into the murder of the young woman, who had still not been named. I heard the latest on the local radio station that I listened to in the kitchen while cooking and washing up.

The police had found a car abandoned some miles away, partially burned out. They'd discovered evidence that the woman whose body had been found yards from my back garden had been in that car. It was still not clear from the report whether she'd been killed elsewhere and her body brought in that car to Stanpit, or whether she'd been in it when still alive. The police also believed that items retrieved from the burned-out car might provide some clues as to the woman's identity.

I hated the thought that they still did not know who she was. That there could be a family out there, not knowing their daughter or sister was dead. Maybe not even aware she was missing. Whatever had happened to her, my heart broke for her and her loved ones.

Did she have any loved ones? Someone somewhere must be missing her.

I said this to Sharon, whom I bumped into as I went for a

walk down to Mudeford Quay, making the most of a warm, light evening.

'Pfft. She was probably a drug addict. I heard rumours that she was, and they're saying there was something in the burned-out car to do with drugs. She could have been living in a squat somewhere, stealing or prostituting herself to get money for her next fix. Bound to be. No real loss to society.'

I hadn't heard about the possible link to drugs. It made me shiver, and I was reminded of Josie, the girl Arwen and I had been at school with, who for all we knew was living just like that these days. 'But even if that's the case, she was still a human being, still someone's daughter, and she almost certainly had friends somewhere who'll miss her. Honestly, Sharon, I don't care who she was, I still feel for her and her loved ones when they find out who she was. And I think it's so sad to think of her body lying in a morgue somewhere with not so much as a name tag.'

Sharon smiled at me – a smile that I expected to be indulging or condescending but that actually came across as warm and admiring. 'You're too nice a person, Millie. You're always looking for the best in people, aren't you? Whereas I …' She shook her head. 'I can't help assuming the worst. I should learn from you.'

'Well, while we don't know the whole story, I just think we should keep an open mind and try not to judge her.'

'You're right, as always. Well, I must get back. I only popped out to pick up a loaf of bread for the kids' sandwiches tomorrow. Jasper came home from school and ate about six slices, straight off. Honestly I swear that boy has hollow legs. Well, enjoy your walk.' She waved a loaf of sliced white at me and went on her way. I walked on down to the quay, and on a whim went to the Haven House Inn and ordered myself a pint of lager. The sun would soon set over the harbour and it was such a nice evening I wanted to make the most of it.

As I sipped my beer and watched the sun sinking across the water, a couple came to sit at the table next to mine. They barely looked at the sunset – they were too wrapped up in each other. Hands held, heads leaning so close they were almost touching, occasional little kisses and plenty of laughter. Clearly in love.

I couldn't help but think about the dates I'd had with Nick. They seemed so long ago now, but it had only been two weeks. We could have been like that pair. He might have been here with me now.

But not if he and his family were involved in drug smuggling. Involved in the very thing that might have played a part in the death of that young woman. My young woman, as I had begun thinking of her. I hoped the police would hurry up and identify her. Tell her story, and allow her a decent burial.

Arwen visited again the next weekend. She found me in a despondent mood.

'What's wrong, Millie? You don't look yourself.' She said this before she'd even sat down, so I knew I must look really bad.

'I'm sorry, Arwen. I don't know what's wrong with me. Can't sleep for thinking about the murder inquiry.'

'Have you spoken to that bloke? Nick, wasn't it?'

I shrugged. 'Not really. Not about the drugs thing. I kind of told him there was too much going on in my life and I wasn't ready yet for a relationship. I haven't seen him since. So it's all kind of on hold at the moment.'

Arwen pulled a sympathetic face. 'Could be for the best. I mean, if your neighbour's right about him and his family …'

I sniffed back a tear. It was hard to explain how much I didn't want Sharon to be right, but at the same time had a horrible feeling that she was. And Arwen, who knew me so well, was right to suggest that if Nick was caught up in the drugs trade, I'd want nothing to do with him.

'Ah, babe.' Arwen crossed the kitchen and put her arms around me, twisting me so I could lean on her shoulder. 'I know, it's so hard to know what's best to do. Maybe just let it lie, at least until you know for sure one way or the other? Kettle's boiled, anyway.'

I gave her a weak smile and made the tea. We took the cups through to the garden. Yes, let it lie, keep my distance until I knew for sure. But how would I find out the truth?

Arwen was suitably impressed with the wooden flooring and new plasterwork that had been done in the sitting room since she last visited. 'What's next in there?'

'Second-fix electrics and finish off the decorating,' I replied. 'And then I had better buy a few sticks of furniture.' I hadn't kept much from the marital home. I hadn't wanted it. It was all stuff Steve and I had chosen together, suitable for a character-less suburban semi. Mostly from Ikea. There is nothing at all wrong with Ikea furniture but I didn't think it would work in an eighteenth-century ex–public house. I wanted old, dark oak, or stripped pine, mismatched chairs, battered leather sofas. Not white laminate and smoked glass.

'Ooh, can I come furniture shopping with you?' Arwen practically clapped her hands in glee at the idea.

'Sure, if you'll traipse around endless second-hand shops with me. It's going to take time to find the right pieces.'

'You're in no hurry though, are you? This is a long-term project.'

'It is, indeed.' I looked around at the back of the house that already I had grown to love. 'I can't imagine ever wanting to move again. This place is home.'

A couple of days later a text arrived from Nick. My stomach lurched as I opened it. *Millie, I don't know what I've done wrong, but whatever it is I'd like a chance to make it right again. I'll come round Thursday evening*, it read.

I replied with a thumbs-up. After our dates, our kisses, this was what we were reduced to now. But perhaps we should have a frank talk, however hard it would be, and get everything out in the open no matter where it led us.

When I arrived home from work on Thursday, Keith and

Aaron were finishing a bit of work upstairs. A plumber had been there earlier in the day and had put in my new bathroom suite. Aaron, who seemed to be multitalented, had started work on the tiling. It was going to look amazing. Keith was sweeping the floor, making the room usable for me overnight. It was one thing I loved about these workmen – every day they left the house tidy and all rooms usable.

The lads finished up and left, and I changed quickly out of my work things, wondering what time Nick would come round and how long he'd stay. A quick chat on the doorstep, or a long sit-down heart-to-heart with tea and biscuits?

The doorbell rang and with a rush of nerves I went to answer it, wiping my sweaty palms on the back of my jeans as I did so.

To my surprise it was not Nick standing on the doorstep, but Steve. He was holding an enormous bouquet of flowers and smiling broadly. 'Hi, Millie. I hope this isn't a bad time – I was passing and thought I'd call and have a look at your new place.'

'Passing?'

He laughed. 'I know, but honestly I was! Had to attend a conference that was held just down the road, in the Harbour Hotel. So, literally, I was driving up this road on my way home. Can I come in?'

'Sorry, yes, sure.' I stood back and let him pass, taking the flowers off him. I had a large vase somewhere in the kitchen so I went in there to sort them out. Steve followed me in.

'This is quite a place. You're still having work done?'

'Yes, it'll take a while. Pretty much everything needed doing and I want it … the way I want it.'

He nodded. 'Quite right too.'

I made him tea and showed him around the house, telling him what work had been done and what I was planning. He seemed genuinely interested, and pleased for me. 'You know, this place suits you, Millie. You always liked history and old places. I couldn't have lived here. My new-build is much more suited to me. Couldn't be more different to this house.' He shrugged and gave a little smile. 'Kind of proves we weren't compatible, doesn't it? We should have called it a day years ago.'

'Maybe. But we had some good times together anyway.'

'Ah, Millie. I miss you.' We were in the kitchen, by the window, and Steve stepped forward and wrapped his arms around me. I leaned into him, the way I always used to, his scent so familiar, his embrace feeling like returning to a much-loved childhood home. Nothing romantic about it, but there was comfort in his embrace.

He held me for a minute, before letting me go with a sad little smile. We went through to the sitting room to chat. Steve was on good form, telling me the latest gossip from his group of friends. In the end he stayed for dinner – I rustled up a quick pasta with tomatoes – and a beer. We had a good evening, lots of chat and laughter. There was no question of a reunion with Steve but it was somehow comforting to know that we could get on so well, even now after having lived apart for a few months. This was how divorce should be. No regrets, just a friendly parting of the ways.

Steve told me, shyly, towards the end of the evening, that he had begun dating a woman who'd joined his company. She was also divorced and had a small child. 'She's fun,' Steve said, 'and kind. The type who always finds little ways to make things special. I like her. A lot.'

I smiled. 'I am genuinely pleased for you, Steve. You deserve someone lovely in your life.'

'So do you, Millie. I hope you find someone soon.' He hugged me again then and kissed my cheek. 'I should go. I've taken up enough of your evening. Thanks so much for dinner, and remember, any time you need a friend or a shoulder to cry on, or anything, I'm here for you.' He gave me a squeeze and then he was gone.

I checked my phone and saw another text from Nick. *Tonight not convenient. Will catch up with you re work in a day or two.* I'd forgotten he was supposed to be coming round, what with

Steve turning up out of the blue like that. Ah well, as he said, we'd catch up in a day or two.

After Steve had left I felt just a little bit lonely. He would see his new girlfriend at work the next day. Maybe they'd go out on a date on Saturday night. Maybe they'd progress their relationship a step further in some way. Whereas my love life, if you could call it that, had gone from vaguely promising to non-existent again.

Chapter 20

The day after the battle, Sam and Esther walked down to the Haven House Inn, to see if there was any news. The two luggers were gone, and a bleary-eyed Hannah Sellars told them the Revenue cutters had entered the harbour in the early hours on an incoming tide, pulled the carcasses of the luggers off the beach and towed them away.

'There were no free traders left defending our ships by then,' she said with a shrug. 'Some were sleeping in my bar, the rest had gone to their homes. No one saw *Orestes* or the cutters sailing out. Mr Streeter's not going to be happy when he finds out.'

'Where is he?' Sam asked.

Again, Mrs Sellars shrugged. 'Not at his place on Stanpit, so I hear. Probably at one of his other properties, hiding, but I expect he'll be down here later on today.'

They left her trying to clear some of the mess around her property. The inn had taken a few hits from the ships' artillery, and there was loose masonry all over the yard. Some windows were broken. The outbuildings where Esther had supervised storage of gear from the luggers were in disarray. 'Looks like the marines searched in here in the early hours for contraband,' Sam said, and Esther nodded.

'What a state.' She started trying to move some items but Sam pulled her away.

'Not our job, Blue. Let Hannah get any men left in the Haven House to sort it, or else Streeter can. We've done enough. Maybe George will come down here later and help her.'

They walked slowly around the end of the spit. In the harbour there was little evidence of the previous day's battle. Out to sea there was no sign of the *Orestes* or of the cutters or luggers. Only the damage to Hannah's buildings was left to show for it all. And the contraband that was safely distributed throughout the countryside. That reminded Esther – they still needed to move the rest of the kegs up to the cellar from the tunnel, back home. They walked back up the road, into the pub where Pa was beginning to prepare for the day's trade, and entered the cellar via the hidden entrance in the fireplace.

Once inside, out of sight of anyone, Sam turned to Esther. 'I barely slept. You, and Walker … I can't believe it. I can't understand it. I wish … I wish things could be as they used to be.'

'Sam, I'm sorry. I was going to talk to you about it earlier. It all happened when you were away on the *Civil Usage*, and there's not been a chance since to tell you.' She sighed. 'And I was hoping it'd all just blow over and Walker would set his sights on someone else. He just wants a wife. It doesn't have to be me.' She stood before him, hoping he would open his arms to her and let her sink into them, the way she always used to. She needed the feel of his strong arms around her, comforting her, promising her he could make it right. But he stepped aside, as though to say she was someone else's now, and not for him.

'Let's get this work done. Then I need to get back home.' He pushed aside the cask that hid the entrance to the tunnel, and opened the little door behind.

She had no choice but to follow him, and the next half-hour was spent bringing the goods up to the cellar and stacking them. On one of the many trips back and forth, about halfway along the tunnel,

Esther noticed that a part of the wooden planking lining the walls was bowed and cracked. 'Better get that repaired,' she muttered to herself, making a mental note to tell Pa about it. It wouldn't do for the tunnel to collapse and become unusable. Bringing contraband into the pub via the front entrance was too risky.

Once the goods had been moved, Sam bade a cold farewell to Esther and her father, and left to return to his own home in Burton. He had not been back there for a couple of weeks, since he'd first sailed on the *Civil Usage*. George had left a while earlier, intending to head down to the Haven House Inn to see Hannah Sellars, before going back home.

The following day brought some unwelcome news. It was Will Burden who carried the news to The Ship at Anchor – he'd heard it from someone else in Christchurch town centre.

'He died, you know,' he said conspiratorially to Esther as she poured him his ale. 'That sailing master who was commanding the marines. The one who was shot at the very beginning of the battle.'

'Died?' Esther's hand flew to her mouth.

Burden nodded. 'Yes. He was hit twice. They pulled him into the bottom of his pinnace, and later took him back onto the *Orestes*, but he died early yesterday morning. They're holding an inquest today, over at Cowes on the Isle of Wight.'

'Who was he?' Esther asked. She thought one of the captains had told her but couldn't remember the name. She handed a tankard of ale to Burden.

'Young chap, name of William Allen,' Burden replied. 'Well thought of, apparently, and considered to have a great career ahead of him.' He snorted. 'Not now, he hasn't. If you ask me, this all got out of hand. Streeter and those two captains of his have a lot to answer for.'

Esther could only agree. 'Yes, I think you are right. That poor young man, and his family.'

'This is going to turn people against the free traders, I reckon.' Burden took a long pull of his ale. 'They're happy enough buying the cheap goods Streeter brings in, but they won't be happy about killing a man. There won't be so many willing to help. I for one am not going to have anything more to do with it.'

Esther pressed her lips together to stop herself saying anything – she was sure Burden would continue to buy smuggled brandy and tobacco and tea. Everyone did. Otherwise they had to pay three or four or up to seven times as much. Duty-paid goods were priced beyond the reach of most ordinary people. 'Has anyone seen or heard from Streeter?'

'No. He's lying low.'

Another fisherman, named Carter, heard this last exchange. 'Ale and a mutton pie, Esther, when you're ready. People are talking, Will, about the battle. Asking who fired first, and why, for goodness' sake? None of this had to happen. Streeter had the contraband away by the time the shooting started, didn't he?'

Will Burden nodded slowly as Esther poured Carter's pint. 'He did, aye. All I know is, it was Streeter's men who fired first, not the marines.'

Esther noticed he had not said '*we* who fired first'. He seemed to be trying to distance himself from the whole affair. He'd been involved with the free traders for years though; he'd sailed on runs to France and the Channel Islands; he'd helped unload contraband; he'd roped in other fishermen friends. And he'd definitely been at the Haven House for the first part of the battle. She'd seen him there. She passed Carter his ale and went to fetch him a pie from the oven. When she returned, the men were still discussing it, and a couple more had joined in. All were men she'd seen on the beach unloading contraband.

'What did they think they'd achieve, by starting the battle?' Carter said. 'They knew *Orestes* was there, as well as the two cutters. They knew there was no hope Streeter could save his

186

ships. They had the goods – and they were worth a damn sight more than the luggers. What was the point?'

'Once that first shot was fired, there was only ever one way this would turn out,' another man said, 'and that was always going to be bad for the free traders.'

'It was that Captain May,' someone answered. 'I saw him.'

'No, you never did,' Carter told him. 'You was upstairs in the Haven House with me, and the first shots were fired from the *Phoenix*.'

'I thought the first shots came from the windows of the inn. Anyway, it was May who gave out the guns. So it was him who started the fight,' the man said, defensively.

Carter nodded. 'I won't argue with that. Poor decision. Why did Streeter go along with it?'

'That's the big question,' Will Burden said. 'Futile attempt to save his ships I suppose. Madness, because he was always going to end up losing them, from the moment *Orestes* arrived. He had no chance. He was well outgunned and outnumbered.'

'Yes, and he's lost *Phoenix* before and bought her back. He could have done the same this time.'

'He'll have made a huge profit anyway, from the amount of goods in this haul. Didn't he always say he only needed two runs out of three to be successful to make a profit? And this was a much bigger run than the usual.'

'He did, aye. I suppose it must be greed that made him agree to shoot a man dead rather than lose his ship.'

'Poor bugger William Allen was only doing his job.'

'Aye, he was.'

Esther listened as the men discussed the events. It was clear that despite knowing and working with Streeter, they were sympathetic to the poor sailing master, who they all agreed had not deserved to die. Who had fired the fatal shot was a key question. No one seemed to know, although there were some who wanted to point the finger at Captain May. 'Coombes would probably know best,'

Carter said. 'Wasn't he – George I mean – alongside May the whole time? He'll know who fired the shot.'

'Maybe it was Coombes himself? He'd do well to keep quiet if it was.'

'No, gentlemen, I'm sure it wasn't George,' Esther put in. 'He was back here afterwards, along with Sam, and it can't have been him.'

'Well, it weren't Sam Coombes. He never picked up a musket once, even though Captain May gave him a direct order to join in,' one man said. 'Do you think we'll all be questioned?'

'Why would we be? Who's going to tell the authorities who was there? It's only us that know who was there and who did what, and we'll not tell, will we? None of us would say a word. Neither will Streeter nor the captains. We'll all be safe. Joshua Jeans isn't going to tell on us either, is he? Not after all the contraband he and his men have had off us.' Carter sat back in his chair looking satisfied with himself as he ate his pie.

'What about Noyce? Didn't he see the stuff being unloaded on the beach?' Burden asked.

'Aye, he did, but so what? He went to raise the militia. He didn't see any part of the battle. They've been searching for the goods since then, but they've found nothing. It was all magicked away as it always is.' Carter winked at Esther. 'Probably some beneath my feet right now, eh, Esther?'

She smiled and shrugged. No one other than the Coombes brothers, John Streeter, herself, Pa and Matthew, and now Thomas Walker, knew about the hidden cellar and tunnel. But of course all suspected there was more to the pub than met the eye. The same was true of all other pubs in the town. The Eight Bells was rumoured to have a secret cellar. The George Inn supposedly had a tunnel running all the way down to the Priory Church, where contraband was sometimes hidden in the vestry. Esther had never seen them, and the landlords of those establishments would never admit to their existence, but everyone local was pretty certain they were there. It was the entrances to secret places that had to be kept well hidden, not the cellars and tunnels themselves. She risked a glance towards the fireplace. No fire was lit, but it was, as always, set ready to light at a moment's notice.

John Streeter came into the pub a couple of days later. He looked drawn, Esther thought, as though he had not slept for days. But even so, he seemed upbeat, despite recent events.

'Well, Blue, we pulled it off, eh?' he said, as he slammed his hat down onto a table with a flourish. 'Biggest ever haul anywhere, I'll wager. Shame I had to lose the luggers but it can't be helped.'

'Shame a man lost his life too, sir. What can I get you?' Esther had not been able to stop thinking about William Allen. So young, and only doing his job, and he'd been shot, almost certainly by someone she knew.

'A finger of your best brandy, if you would. And yes, it's a shame about that poor fellow. He was just in the wrong place at the wrong time.'

She poured the brandy, from one of the bottles brought over in a previous run, and handed it to him. 'I'm glad no more were badly hurt.' If only all the firing had been overhead, not aiming at bodies.

'Couple of marines took shots in the arm and shoulder I heard,' Streeter said with a shrug. 'And one or two of ours were hit. But nothing too serious. It was Allen's funeral yesterday, so I heard. Over in Cowes. Weather was appalling, as you know, but they say the whole town turned out to pay their respects.' He scoffed. 'And yet they all partake of smuggled goods over there on the island as much as we do here in Christchurch.' He downed his brandy in one, and held out his glass for Esther to refill. 'It's the duplicity of it that angers me, you know, Blue? The way they're happy for me and my men to take all the risks, doing the runs, unloading and storing the goods and defending ourselves, but soon as something like this happens they're all pretending they

189

never approved, that they'd like the trade to stop, that we shouldn't be dodging customs duties. Yet they wouldn't want to pay five times as much for their brandy and tobacco, and even more for their tea now, would they? Two faced, the lot of them.'

Esther nodded. She'd heard many such conversations lately, from people who'd played a part in smuggling runs but were now turning their backs on the trade while still drinking the smuggled spirits on offer in the pub.

Pa approached and shook Streeter's hand. 'Good to see you, John. We thought you'd disappeared off the face of the earth.'

'No, I was just having a quiet few days while I waited for things to blow over. Good to see you, Luke.'

'And has it? Blown over, I mean?'

'There's an inquiry starting. Fellow called Arnold leading it, over in Cowes.'

'Who's that then, anyone you've heard of?'

'Chief Revenue Officer, based in Cowes.'

'Ah, like our Joshua Jeans, then?'

Streeter grimaced. 'No, because I hear he's completely incorruptible. He's written to Jeans, to say he wants to use this case as an example and stamp down hard on all those involved. He was asking Jeans for information to try to bring what he called the "murderers" to justice.'

Esther gasped, but Streeter just laughed. 'Don't you worry, Blue. Jeans came straight to see me when he got that letter, to warn me. He won't tell on any of us, you can be sure of that. Our secrets are safe with him and his men. They'll never catch any of us. Another brandy, my dear, and perhaps your pa will join me?'

Chapter 21

The day after Steve's visit, I saw on the TV news that the police had made another breakthrough in the murder inquiry. Two breakthroughs, in fact.

Firstly, at last they had discovered who the young woman was, and had released her name. She was called Tiffany Coles, and she had been 22. She was from the Southampton area.

As Sharon had suspected, drugs had played a large part in her life. Tiffany Coles had been a heroin user, who'd been arrested a few times for stealing to fund her habit. But it wasn't her drug use that had killed her – not directly anyway. She'd been raped and strangled. There was still no news as to who the murderer might have been.

But it was the second breakthrough that had me gasping, clapping my hand over my mouth as I watched TV. Over footage showing the burned-out car in which Tiffany Coles had been taken to the place where her body was found, a reporter announced with poorly disguised excitement that the car had been registered to one Desmond Marshall, a well-known businessman and former mayor in the town where Tiffany's body had been found.

Nick's father.

Nick's dad owned the car.

I knew the doorbell was going to ring a split second before it happened. It was Sharon, of course, who'd seen the news and had immediately run across the road to discuss it with me.

'So this proves it! I had my suspicions, as I told you, and then I wasn't sure of myself as you were telling me not to judge before we knew the facts. But here we are – the girl was a drug addict who'd been in trouble with the police, and the car she was most likely killed in belonged to Des Marshall. You need to keep well clear of that family, I'm telling you. And this time I won't have you say anything in their defence. It's awkward I know as you've employed Marshall's building company and the work's not complete but honestly, if you could tell them to stop and find someone else to finish the job, I would do that if I were you. I warned you not to use them. I hate to say I told you so, but …'

'Then don't, Sharon.' I raked my fingers through my hair. 'Honestly, I don't know what to think. There might be perfectly innocent explanations. Maybe the car was stolen … I don't want to jump to conclusions!'

'Here you go again!' Sharon said, triumphantly. 'I knew you would. Making excuses, explaining it away. But sometimes, Millie darling, the obvious explanation is the right one. That car was Des Marshall's. So very likely he's the killer. Or someone else who had access to the car …'

She was implying it could have been Nick. He lived with his father. It was certainly possible that he might use the car.

'I'm sure the police will be questioning Mr Marshall,' I said tightly. Her attitude once more was winding me up. I hated her excitement, the way she seemed to get a thrill out of it all. And I needed to process the news myself, first.

'Of course. But what are you going to do? Sack Marshall? I suppose you'll have to pay them for work done so far. I'll ask Brian for recommendations for someone to finish your project instead of them. And of course you won't even consider that fellow as a

192

boyfriend now. In a way it's helped you out – it will have made the decision to drop him so much easier …'

That was enough. I could not listen to any more of it. 'Sharon, I have no intention of finding a different builder. Even if Des Marshall does turn out to be involved, that does not mean Nick has anything to do with it. They are an excellent building company and the two fellows who've done most of the work here can't be faulted. Also, whether or not I go out with Nick is absolutely none of your business. Go away, Sharon. I can't listen to any more of what you have to say about this. Not today. Not ever.'

'Well, really. I only have your best interests at heart, Millie. Since you moved in all I've done is try to help and advise you. But if you won't listen then on your head be it. I've done my best, done my neighbourly duty. I listened to you when you told me I was jumping to conclusions, but you won't do me the courtesy of hearing me out. I just hope you don't regret carrying on your association with that family. They're dangerous, as I've told you before.'

With that she turned on her heel and walked out. I was left standing by the front door, staring after her as she crossed the road back to her own house. With a sigh I closed the door and went to the sitting room where I flopped down onto a chair. I'd lost her for good, probably. But was it any loss? I'd thought we might be friends, but I couldn't take any more of her prejudices and sniping. I felt like telling her she couldn't have a kitten after all, but that would be petty and unfair on the children. Maybe I could be friendly to them while keeping Sharon at arm's length.

'Ah, who cares about Sharon anyway?' I said to myself. My worries were about Nick. I had to know the truth, one way or another. Before I had a chance to think about it too much, I picked up my phone and brought up Nick's number. I'd call him. Right now.

My finger hovered over the call button. A hundred 'what ifs' went through my head. I needed to know the truth, but what if I didn't like the truth? Maybe not knowing was better.

No. It wasn't. Not knowing was agony. And anyway, I found myself worrying about how Nick was taking all this. If his father was being questioned, that must be a stressful situation to be in, whatever the outcome. Maybe Nick himself would be called in for questioning, if he too had access to the car. I was his friend, wasn't I? At least I had been for a while. Not just a client.

I pressed the call button.

But there was no answer. I left a message – my voice sounding shaky even to myself. 'Nick, I heard the news, about your dad's car … I just wondered … how are you? Is everything OK? Is there anything … I can do, maybe if you want to talk about it … or whatever? Anyway, call me back … if you want to. Thanks, bye.'

What a rubbish message. Why had I signed off with 'thanks'? I tutted at myself but hey, it was done now. Time for a fortifying glass of wine and a surf of the internet to see if there was any more information on the investigation. Whether or not Nick called me back, I wanted to know all the facts that were out there.

I emailed my boss and asked for a couple of hours off the next morning. I wanted to wait at home until the lads arrived to work. There were a few good reasons, only one of which I put in the email. Firstly, Keith and Aaron were due to start work on the kitchen. I had boxed up most of my crockery and pans and food, ready for them to begin taking out the old units that must have been installed in the 1970s. I needed to finish that job and also wanted to talk to them about the new kitchen layout. And secondly, privately, I was hoping that Nick would come round to supervise the start of this new phase of work. I knew he'd ordered all the units – a similar style to his dad's kitchen.

When I got up the following morning there was a reply to my email, saying yes, sure I could take a couple of hours, assuming I'd make them up the following week. I emailed back a thank you and promised to be there by midday. And then I spent another hour making sure the kitchen was ready for dismantling. Nick had told me this phase might feel one of the most disruptive, and to be prepared to eat a lot of takeaways.

Keith and Aaron arrived at eight-thirty – their usual start time.

'Kitchen today, Millie?' Aaron said, and I nodded.

'Yes. Will you move the fridge into the sitting room for me? I need to keep using that old one until the new one is delivered next week.'

'Sure. In the corner by the fireplace?'

'Perfect.' I waited while they did that. Still no sign of Nick. 'Aaron, are you expecting Nick here this morning? There's a couple of things I wanted to discuss …'

There was a glance between Aaron and Keith – an uncomfortable look that seemed to say *will you tell her or shall I?*

'What is it?' I asked.

'Um, we don't think he'll be here this morning, no,' Keith said at last. 'Something's come up that he has to deal with …'

'I saw the news last night,' I told them.

'Yeah. His dad's car. It was nicked, then used in that murder and burned out. Police are talking to Des today.'

'It was stolen?'

Keith nodded. 'From outside Des's house. He only reported it a week later, Nick says, as he'd been away and didn't realise it was gone.'

'Nick's got to make a statement too,' Aaron added. 'As he is living at his dad's house. They'll want to know when he noticed the car was missing and all that.'

I nodded. It made sense. I wanted to tell Sharon the car had been stolen. Though she'd no doubt say Des had only reported it stolen to deflect suspicion from himself. 'So is that where Nick is, this morning?'

'Um, yeah, think so,' Aaron replied. I had the feeling there was more to it – perhaps Nick had said something to them about not wanting to see me.

'OK. Thanks, lads. I'll let you get on, now. I'll be off to work in a bit.'

But not before I'd had another go at contacting Nick. I went upstairs along with the cats for some quiet and privacy while the lads started the noisy work of demolishing the old kitchen, and tried calling Nick once more.

It went to voicemail again. I sighed. 'Nick, it's me, Millie. Just checking everything's OK with you. Hope—' I broke off. What did I hope? 'Um … I mean, hope to hear from you soon.' There. Not much better than the last message but it would have to do.

Over to Nick to call me back, or come round. He knew where to find me.

Chapter 22

As the summer wore on, the battle and its aftermath began to gradually fade from the forefront of Esther's mind. She had too much else to think about. Thomas Walker was in the pub almost every day, watching her every move, persuading her to sit with him and have a drink now and again. He had changed his tactics, it seemed, and rather than talking as though her marrying him was a done deal, these days he was more pleasant, chatting in a friendly way to her, asking after her health, and generally trying to woo her. He was proving, or trying to, that he was a decent man and would make her a good husband. If he'd always been like this, and if Sam hadn't been around, then maybe she would have liked him enough to agree to marry him. She could not imagine ever loving him the way she loved Sam, though she might have liked and respected him.

But from time to time, Walker would speak harshly to another customer, perhaps even threaten them, and she would be reminded of the other side of his personality and the fact that he could not be trusted.

Sam had not been near. George had called in a few times, but would not be drawn on his brother's state of mind. 'Leave him be, Blue,' was all George would say on the matter.

One day a week or two after the battle, Esther woke to the sound of Pa crying out and groaning. She hurried in to see what had happened, and found him sitting stiffly on the side of his bed, a hand pressed against his lower back, his face distorted in agony.

'Pa, what is it?' She rushed over to him.

'Tried to get out of bed, and something's … just gone, popped like, in my back.'

'Here, let me help you,' she said, catching his hand to help pull him up. But he pushed her away.

'No, lass. I can't move. Arggh!' He tried to shuffle forward but it was clearly too painful.

'What can I do?'

He looked at her and shook his head. 'You'll have to run things. I can't get up at all.' He eased himself back onto the bed amid much groaning, and lay down. 'Maybe it'll ease up later on.'

'I'll bring you something to eat,' she said, tucking a blanket over him. Should she fetch a doctor? Dr Quartley might come out to them. But she'd known other people with bad backs, and all a doctor ever prescribed for them was rest. Rest for Pa, and hard work for her.

Later that day Walker came to the pub, and asked after Pa. She told him he was resting, not wanting to let on that he was bedridden.

'If you agree to marry me,' Walker said, 'you will not have to work like this. And we will give your father a home with us. Not here. I'll build us a large property on the edge of town where there'll be space for all of us, and for all the children I'm sure we'll have in time.'

Despite herself, Esther felt grateful to him for that offer, and began to consider if it might be best all round for her to marry him. It would provide both her and Pa with security for their future. She made herself a lace collar with the piece Walker had given her, and began wearing it whenever she was serving in the bar. Walker noticed, and nodded approvingly. It felt a little like a betrayal of Sam and an acceptance of Walker, but what choice did she really have, if Sam was dropping her? In the long term, running the pub and nursing Pa would be too much for her to take on by herself, and she couldn't afford to pay anyone else to work for her. Perhaps after nearly fifty years it was finally the end of the Harris family at The Ship at Anchor.

Late in July, word came that the Revenue service was offering a reward for information about the smuggling run and the battle. A large amount of money was to be paid to anyone who could identify men who'd been involved in the shooting. Streeter was still convinced he was invincible, and that no one would breathe a word. For the smugglers, the reward was not as much as they might earn over a year helping out on runs. 'I have it on Joshua Jeans's authority,' he said proudly. 'He's not said a word to Arnold, and he won't. Mark my words, Blue, this will all have blown over by the end of the summer.'

She couldn't help but think, while it might all blow over for them, things would never be the same for William Allen's family and friends.

And then one blustery night in August, George Coombes came barrelling into the pub, just before Esther closed for the night. There were only a couple of men left, finishing their pints. George cast a worried glance in their direction, then gestured to the kitchen. Esther nodded, and followed him through.

'What's the matter? Is it Sam? Oh, please tell me it's not Sam …'

George shook his head. 'Sam's all right. He's at home. But I … I'm in trouble. Sam says you might be able to help, for old times' sake. Oh God, save me, Esther. I need your help!'

'I'll do anything I can,' she said. 'Sit down, gather yourself. I'll just close up.' She went back through to the bar and bustled about, making it clear to the remaining drinkers that she wanted to shut up shop.

'Aw, Esther, you turning us out on a night like this?' one of them said.

'She's got her fancy man – he just came in. Coombes, isn't it?' said the other.

'He's not my fancy man. He's a friend. Now, come on, lads. It's not raining at the minute – you'll make it to your homes still dry if you go now.' She picked up a broom to sweep the floor around them. They took the hint, and left, while still grumbling good-naturedly.

She went back through to the kitchen, with a tot of brandy in a glass for George. He'd looked like he needed it, and indeed he took it gratefully. 'Do you want anything to eat, George?'

'No, not hungry. Where's your pa?'

'Upstairs, in bed. He'll not come down. Now then, what's happened?' She pulled over a chair and sat opposite him, waiting patiently for him to open up.

'Will Burden. I thought he was a friend. God's sake, he *was* a friend. I've known him all my life.' George shook his head in sad disbelief.

'What has he done?'

'That reward. The one the Revenue service offered for information. Seems it was too tempting for Burden. Carter told me that Burden went to the Customs office in Lymington. He's told them everything he knows. Everything that happened on that run, and that night.'

'But he was on the crew of the *Civil Usage*! And he was involved in the battle – didn't he have a musket, and fire it too?' She remembered that Burden had left the site of the battle early however, and had come up to The Ship at Anchor.

'Yes, but he told them he fired overhead and left as soon as he could, and they've agreed to give him immunity in return for his information. He's taken the reward, Carter said.'

'If Streeter finds out …'

'Streeter knows, and has sent men to look for him. But Burden's disappeared. He's told them Streeter organises everything as well.' George finished his drink and got up, pacing the room. 'Will Burden knows he'd be in danger of his life if Streeter got hold of him. I imagine he's taken the money and gone to settle far away from here, far from anyone who'd recognise him. Inland. He had no family here, nothing to keep him.'

'A traitor.' Whatever she might have felt about the shooting of William Allen, Esther's loyalties remained with the free traders. The one thing they'd all been certain of is that no one would inform on them. Their only danger, they'd felt, was from people like James Noyce, and he'd known very little of what went on, thanks to Joshua Jeans assigning him to patrol any part of the coast where no goods were due to be landed. But Will Burden knew it all. 'So what does this mean, for us? For all of us?'

George stopped pacing and stood before her. 'It means trouble. There's arrest warrants out, for several of us. Streeter. The two captains, May and Parrott. A couple of lads we were sailing with, on *Civil Usage* – Henry Voss and Jonathan Edwards.' He took a deep breath. 'And me. Not Sam, but me. Will Burden, may he rot in hell, has told the authorities it may have been *me* who fired the fatal shot at William Allen. It wasn't, Esther. You believe me, right?'

She stared at him for a moment. There was anguish and remorse in his gaze, but not guilt. 'I believe you.'

He caught hold of her hands. 'Sam believes me too. That's enough for me.'

'And Hannah Sellars?'

He shook his head, his mouth twisted. 'No. She says it might well have been me, for all she knows. Truth is, Esther, she's had nothing to do with me since that day. Won't even look at me if I go in the Haven House. She hates the fact that the deadly shot was likely fired from her premises. Carter says she's been considering claiming the reward herself.'

'Not Hannah!' Esther couldn't believe that. Of all the people locally, Hannah Sellars had always been known as a true friend to the smugglers.

'No. I don't think she would. Just Carter making mischief. But with the information from Will Burden, if they catch any of us, they're bound to want her to give evidence. And she's said she'll not lie before the court. That's perjury, and she'll not do it.'

'What are you going to do? I mean, if there's a warrant out for your arrest …' Esther was horrified at the implications of what he was telling her.

George looked up at her. 'Same as John Streeter and the captains, I suppose. Same as all of us who've been named. Lie low. Hide. Streeter's gone to Guernsey, I believe.'

'Hide, hide where?' As she said the words, she suddenly realised why George had come here, today, and what his real purpose in talking to her was. 'You want to hide here? In the secret cellar?'

'Esther, please. You're my only hope. I have nowhere else. Streeter and the captains have already sailed or I'd have gone with them. It'll blow over soon enough, I'm sure. But for now …'

She stared at him, imagining him tucked away in that windowless cellar, her taking food to him. 'But you can't *live* down there!' It was good for storage, but not to live in.

'I thought … perhaps I can live here, sleep on a truckle bed in the bar like Sam used to. In the daytime I'll stay hidden away upstairs. And if word comes that the authorities are searching in this area, I'll go to the cellar then. I could run through the reeds and come in via the tunnel, if there was anyone in the bar. Esther, please, will you do this for me? I will pay you for food of course, and I will do any heavy work for you, but it'd have to be overnight. No one can know I am here.' He looked at her with desperation in his eyes.

'Is there really nowhere else? I mean, the authorities are bound to search here. This is a pub, near the site of the battle – of course they're going to suspect us. Wouldn't you be better off going inland somewhere?'

'But where? I have nowhere. Everyone I know is a free trader and just as likely to be questioned as you are. But no one else has anywhere that I could hide without risk of being discovered. Esther, Sam said you would help. He *promised* me you would.'

It was not Sam's place to make promises on her behalf, Esther wanted to say, but she bit her tongue. She would hide George, of course she would. He was one of them, and he was Sam's brother, and even though Sam had distanced himself from her, she knew she'd do anything for him, now and always. 'If you've nowhere else, then yes, you must stay here. I am worried, though, about how we'll manage it. Pa of course will need to know you are here.'

'But he won't tell.' George framed his words as a statement rather than a question. Esther nodded in agreement, even though she couldn't help but remember that Pa had let on to Thomas Walker about the existence of the cellar and tunnel. That was a danger, and one George should know about, before committing himself.

'George, you should know that one of the Christchurch riding officers knows about the cellar. Thomas Walker. He's in Streeter's pay as you know, but that doesn't mean that we can trust him.'

'The one who's got his eye on you.' George nodded. 'He's the reason Sam's keeping away, isn't he?'

She sighed heavily. 'Yes. Mr Walker thinks I'll marry him. But …'

He nodded. 'But there's Sam.' He caught her hand. 'I do understand. So I'll need to keep out of sight, and we will need to hope that Walker keeps quiet about the cellar if there's any danger of the militia coming here to search.'

There was nothing more to say. Esther pulled her hand back, and went to find bedding for him. Sometimes she wished she and her family had never had anything to do with the free traders. Life would have been a lot simpler, and a lot less dangerous.

The days grew hotter and work harder as August progressed, and

Esther was busier than ever. With Pa bedridden – it was as much as he could manage to get up to use the chamber pot – and George to take care of, there was more to do than ever before. George did what he could to help at night, when the pub closed. He'd carry kegs of ale up from the cellars to the bar, sweep the floor, mend broken chairs or tables. He didn't set foot outside at all, other than to use the privy. He kept the hidden cellar equipped with food, water and bedding, in case he needed to hide in there for an extended period, but so far he'd been able to sleep in the bar downstairs and hide in Esther's bedroom upstairs during opening hours. The system was working, and only Esther, her Pa, and Sam Coombes knew where George was.

At least Esther assumed Sam knew, but as he never came to the pub anymore she couldn't be certain.

Walker, however, came at least twice a week, sometimes daily, for a drink and a pie in the early evening. 'You're a fine cook, Esther,' he would say, appreciatively, as he tucked into the pies. Mutton was his favourite, and she found herself feeling pleased that he enjoyed them and putting more effort into decorating the tops of them with little diamond pastry shapes. She spent a few minutes with him each time he came in, sitting and talking at his table. She told herself it was to see if she could find out any information about the arrest warrants, but she was beginning to enjoy these moments. Walker made an effort to entertain her with little stories about his day, and frequently made her laugh.

But sometimes he had a snippet of more serious news. 'Noyce has given evidence about the run and the battle,' Walker told her one day. 'At Lymington. No one is giving evidence here at Christchurch.'

And another day, he told her that the warrant for Streeter's arrest was only for evasion of duty, not for murder. 'He'll be back, soon as he hears this, won't he?' Walker said with a chuckle. 'He'll pay his fines and be back in business. Which is good for us, eh, lass? I miss my little share of the goods.'

Esther smiled and nodded vaguely.

But the arrest warrants for the two captains, George Coombes, Henry Voss and Jonathan Edwards were still in force, and they were all wanted for murder or aiding and abetting a murderer. George still had to lie low.

One evening Walker arrived late at the pub, looking dishevelled. 'I've ridden from Poole. Why the Revenue service there can't manage their own affairs I'll never know. Been there all day, and not a drop to drink nor a bite to eat. What've you got on the menu today, Esther?'

She poured him a brandy, and went to check on the food. There was only one pie left, which she'd put aside for George to eat when the pub closed and he could come downstairs. She'd have to rustle him up something else instead. She plated it, and brought it through to a grateful Walker, who tucked into it with relish.

'Thank you. I knew I could rely on you. You're a good woman, Esther. Sit a while and talk with me.'

She did so, and heard the full story of his day's activities as he ate. The pub emptied out, until there was only Walker left. 'I must start the clearing up, Mr Walker,' she said, picking up his empty plate and cutlery.

'Call me Thomas, Esther. Please.'

She smiled. 'Very well, Thomas. Do you mind if I start the chores? It's all right for you to stay sitting there and rest a while.'

He leaned back in his chair, a refilled brandy glass in his hand. 'Thank you. I do need to take a few more minutes before I get back on my horse. This is a hard job. We're not paid enough for what we do.'

She nodded but said nothing. The low pay of Revenue officials was the reason so many of them were willing to take a cut from the free traders, in return for turning a blind eye. She began to gather up empty tankards and glasses, taking them through to the kitchen. She'd wash them in the morning, in daylight. Or if she was lucky, George might wash them before she was up, as he often did. Walker watched her work in silence, a half-smile on his face, as though he was imagining her clearing up around him in their own home, in some possible future. She wondered if she was in danger, being here in the bar alone with him. He knew Pa was bedridden these days, and unable to come to her rescue if she cried out, and of course Walker did not know George was in the building. But no, Walker had recently proved himself an honourable man, and she was no longer frightened of him.

And then the door to the stairs opened, and George came through. He'd obviously heard the sounds of her cleaning up and thought the bar was empty and the coast was clear.

'Esther, I'm famished! If you'll tell me what I can have, I'll sort myself out … oh!' He'd spotted Walker sitting at a corner table. Walker was staring at him, his mouth slightly open. George stood still, as though frozen, not knowing what to do or say.

'George … go back upstairs …' Esther began.

'There's no need. I've seen him now,' Walker said. 'Tell me, is he here as your guest, your lover perhaps? I thought it was the other Coombes brother who'd been sweet on you.' There was a cold menace in his tone.

'Sir, he's most certainly not my lover,' Esther protested.

'I told you to call me Thomas. You're hiding him them. He's one of the group the Revenue service have an arrest warrant for, isn't he?'

Esther nodded without thinking. George was still standing silent, watching and waiting to see what Walker would do.

'So what's the plan? He hides here while the pub's open, sleeps somewhere, and disappears into the secret cellar if there's news of a raid? Oh, I know all about the cellar and tunnel, Coombes. Harris told me.' He fell silent, thinking, calculating. 'I'm guessing you don't want anyone to know you're here, Coombes?'

'That's right, sir, if that's possible—'

Walker put up a hand to stop him talking. 'It's possible. So, we will make a deal. The three of us. I will hear if there are to be any searches locally. All communications come to Joshua Jeans, and he passes the information on, so I will be informed in advance. If I hear, I will come directly here to warn you.'

'Thank you,' Esther began, but again Walker raised his hand.

'And in return, for there *has* to be something in it for me, in return you agree to marry me, Esther. Willingly, and before the year is out.'

She stared at him, and was aware of George staring at her. His safety depended on her saying yes to Walker.

'I should add that if you don't agree, I might well decide to use my knowledge of Coombes's whereabouts for my own advantage in other ways. It would mean certain promotion for me, I think, if I were to bring him in. And a reward.' Walker rocked back on his chair, his hands clasped across his stomach. 'But I will forgo those rewards in return for your promise.' At this he reached for her hand.

She flinched instinctively, and his face hardened. 'Esther, I have been good to you and your father, for more years than you realise. And lately, have I not been attentive and kind to you too? You're wearing the lace I bought for you. I realise you may not love me, but that might come in time. Meanwhile I am offering you comfort and an easier life than you have here, as well as security for your invalid father and safety for your friend.' He nodded at George, who seemed to be holding his breath.

What could she do? If only Sam was there to advise her ... but as soon as she'd had this thought she realised that Sam couldn't help her here. He'd kept away, he'd freed her to make her choice. There was no longer any real choice. She could not do anything that might harm George, and possibly Sam and Pa too.

Slowly, cautiously, she nodded. 'Yes, sir. Thomas, I will marry you, if you promise to do all you can to keep George, Pa, me and also Sam Coombes safe.' She took a small step towards him.

Walker stood and took both her hands in his. This time she

did not allow herself to pull away. He kissed her forehead, and it was all she could do to smile at him and not rub the kiss off.

'Thank you, Esther. You have made me very happy. You won't regret this, I promise.' He nodded at George. 'Good luck, Coombes. I will warn you if you are in any danger.' And with that, he left the pub.

'Esther, thank you,' George whispered. 'What a great thing you have done …'

She could not answer him. She picked up her broom and put it away. The rest of the clearing up could wait until the morning, for she was in no mood to do it now.

Chapter 23

Nick finally called me back on Friday afternoon. I was still in the office at work. 'Sorry, Millie, for not getting back to you sooner. I've been snowed under this week. I hope you're happy with the progress Aaron and Keith are making?'

'Oh, yes, they're great. I wasn't calling about the work.' I felt ridiculously flustered and knew I was blushing profusely. I swivelled my chair so I was facing away from work colleagues who were looking at me questioningly. 'I just wanted to catch up … you know, about the police investigation and all that … wanted to check you were all right and it's not been too stressful …'

There was a long silence, as though Nick was weighing up how to answer me. I felt my palms sweating. Had I done the wrong thing in calling? Had I upset him so much when I told him I wasn't ready that he never wanted to speak to me again?

'Nick? Are you still there?' I was wondering if we'd been cut off somehow.

I heard a huge sigh. 'Yes, Millie. Still here. You're right, we should probably talk, about the investigation and other things. I expect your neighbour's been gossiping again. You need to hear the truth, and from me. If you are free this evening, I could meet you down at the Haven House for a drink and a chat. About seven-thirty? What do you think?'

'That sounds … good.' Weird, to be revisiting the spot where we'd had our date, which seemed so long ago but had been only a few weeks; but I thought it best to simply agree with his suggestion rather than come up with anywhere different.

'Right then, I'll see you then.'

He hung up without waiting for me to say goodbye.

'You all right, Millie?' my colleague Louise asked. 'You look a bit shaky.'

'I'm fine. Just …' I waved a hand vaguely at the phone.

'Men troubles?' She tilted her head on one side and gave me a sympathetic look.

'Well, kind of. Complicated. Anyway, with luck we'll sort it out tonight.' I didn't want to even begin going into Nick and my history, or what it was that we needed to discuss tonight. I liked my colleagues but as yet none of them counted as close friends. With the work going on in my house I had not gone along on any post-work drinks or the like – I'd been clocking off and rushing straight home each day. That would need to change soon. It would be good to have friends at work, now that things hadn't worked out with Nick or Sharon.

'OK. Good luck.' She smiled at me. 'If you need to talk it through any time, we could have lunch together, or a drink after work?'

'Thanks. Let's do lunch one day next week?'

'Sure.'

I'm not sure how much work I did for the rest of the afternoon. I could not drag my thoughts away from what would happen that evening. How would we get on, what would he tell me about his dad, the car, drugs, the police investigation? What should I wear, how should I greet him (friendly, reserved, warmly?) and how would he greet me? It was ridiculous. I was a grown woman who'd been married for eight years and I ought to know how to handle this sort of situation. 'Pull yourself together, Millie,' I muttered to myself, earning a wry smile from Louise who'd clearly overheard.

I left on time, as usual, and went back to find Aaron and Keith had begun fitting the new kitchen. The floor had been tiled and the carcasses of the new units were in place – no doors or worktops yet. But it was taking shape nicely. I spent a little time walking around it, imagining cooking, washing up, storing groceries away. In which cupboards would I keep the plates, the cutlery, the mugs and glasses? I'd spent ages planning it on paper and on a kitchen-planning app, but it's always different when you see it for real.

Who would I cook for, in this new kitchen? Myself, of course. Arwen, now and again. Sharon and family, if we ever managed to make friends again.

Nick?

Would we, could we, ever get back to that kind of relationship, where I'd invite him round for dinner? The kitchen design had been inspired by his father's kitchen, so whatever happened, every time I walked in here I was going to think of Nick and what might have been. I just hoped I wouldn't also be reminded that I'd nearly got myself involved with a drug baron.

Talking of dinner, it was time I ate something, before getting ready to go out. I had a ready meal in the fridge that I could microwave. It wasn't great – just fodder, really – but would soak up any alcohol I ended up drinking. Such as the glass of Chardonnay I poured to fortify myself.

I had the usual clothes crisis, and ended up in a pair of loose cotton trousers and a floaty T-shirt, with a pink fleece to cover up if it got chilly later in the evening. I left the house in good time to walk down to the pub. Nick was always on time and I didn't want to keep him waiting.

When I reached the pub he was standing outside, waiting for

me, his hands thrust deep into his pockets. He wasn't smiling. 'Hello, Millie. Shall we get a table on the terrace at the back?'

'Hi, Nick. Yes, sounds perfect.'

'Happy with progress on the kitchen?' he said, as we walked around to the back.

'Yes, it's looking good.'

'It'll be done by end of next week. Then there's only a few more bits to do on the list, and we'll be out of your hair. You'll enjoy having the house back to yourself, no doubt.'

'It's been fine. They're good workers and I'm out at work most of the day anyway.' Our conversation felt stilted. So different to the last time we'd been out together socially. Nick went in to order the drinks while I saved our table.

He came out with the drinks, sat down diagonally opposite me and took a long pull of his pint. He stared down at it for a minute, while I wondered how to start the several conversations I knew we needed to have.

'Nick, I—' I began, but at the same time he started talking.

'Millie, I'm going to tell you some things I don't usually talk about. It's because I know something has changed your opinion of me, and I am guessing you have listened to gossip. I overheard something your neighbour said to you. I need to set the record straight. And yes, this is all linked to the murder of that poor girl, Tiffany Coles.'

My stomach lurched when he confirmed there was a link. Although, maybe he was referring only to the fact his father's car had been stolen and used to transport the body. I really hoped so.

'All right. I'm listening.'

He gave a small nod and took another sip of his beer. 'Right then. I told you about my sister. Half-sister.'

I nodded. 'The one who died young.'

'Yes. What I didn't tell you is that she died of a drug overdose. It's not something we have ever wanted to talk about much, Dad and I. It was a tough time. She'd rebelled as a teenager, against my dad and all he stood for. He was the mayor at the time. Her mum had died young, Dad had remarried – my mum – and I was born, and I think she felt sidelined by his new family. As a teenager she had several body piercings and tattoos done and dyed her hair various startling shades, which her school couldn't cope with so she was excluded. She'd been caught shoplifting as well. She'd try anything to shock Dad, to make herself central in his world even if it was for the wrong reasons. She and Dad had an enormous row and then she left home. Ran away to London and lived on the streets for a week. Dad found her and brought her home, but she kept leaving and then when she was 16 there was nothing more he could do about it. She lived in a squat for the next few years, and became involved with drugs.'

Nick stopped speaking for a moment, and drank more of his pint. He looked sad as he told the story. I kept quiet, waiting for him to resume, and wondering what all this had to do with Tiffany Coles's murder.

'Dad visited her every month. He was torn between wanting to give her money to live on, yet knowing that money would only get used to buy drugs. I was only 10 but I remember so clearly how he'd come back from London after seeing her, and he'd be sitting with his head in his hands, his face looking drawn and tired as though he was twenty years older. People – my mum, for example – told him to forget about her. Mum used to tell him my sister had made her choices and needed to deal with the consequences by herself, and that until she was clean and off drugs, he should keep his distance. I was kind of proud of the fact that he wouldn't give up on her. "She's still my daughter, even if she's a drug user," he'd say. "I do what I can for her. Whatever she'll allow me to do. I still love her and I will be here for her, whatever happens."'

Nick sniffed, took out a tissue and blew his nose. This was hard for him to talk about, I could see.

'Dad saw her as a person still, whereas so many saw her only as a drug addict.'

I nodded. Sharon saw Tiffany Coles only as an addict, as though she was less than human due to her life choices, and so less deserving of our pity.

'And then my sister got involved in drug smuggling,' Nick went on. He lowered his head and shook it, sadly. 'She would go abroad and bring stashes of heroin back, hidden in her luggage and on her person. Taking enormous risks. I only knew about this much later, but I remember Dad calling her on the phone and saying to her that she was mad, that she'd be locked away for life if she was caught, that she should stop, come home, get clean … How he found out about it I don't know.'

'Perhaps she told him, because he was so supportive. Perhaps she wanted to hear what he thought of it.'

'Mmm. Or perhaps she told him as a way of rebelling still further. She knew he'd try to talk her out of it. Anyway, Dad thinks she did about two or three runs successfully. And then on another run, something went wrong. One of the condoms filled with heroin she'd swallowed burst open inside her, and she absorbed so much of the drug it killed her.'

His voice was matter of fact as he said this, but he kept his gaze fixed on the pint glass in front of him. I wanted to reach out and take his hand, express my sympathy in that way, but I didn't dare. I didn't want him to break down, not here in such a public place. 'Nick, I'm so sorry.'

'Why do people say sorry when they hear about a death? It's not like it was your fault in any way.'

'I mean, I feel for you, and your dad. Having to deal with that. Losing her in that way. It's an expression of sympathy. There are no words that really work in this context, are there?'

'Of course. Sorry for snapping.'

'And I'm sorry if I sounded trite.' I was sorry too, that I'd listened to Sharon's gossip and even for one moment thought that Des might have been the one who got his daughter involved in drugs smuggling.

He smiled a little then. 'You'll be wondering why I'm telling you all this. But I felt I needed to. Anyway, it's been a tough thing for Dad especially to come to terms with. She was 22 and he'd really loved her, despite everything. He'd never stopped believing that one day she'd get herself off the drugs. He'd never stopped trying to help her however he could, in whatever ways she'd allow. But suddenly she was gone. And he felt he could have, perhaps should have, done more. He threw himself even more into his public works after that, as though if he kept busy, he'd be able to forget. Mum couldn't cope with him working every hour there was, so she ended up leaving him for someone who'd pay her more attention. So then it was just the two of us. Dad and me. And, Millie,' – he looked up at me then, his eyes sparkling with unshed tears – 'he's a good man. The best. I'm still proud of him, for all he does.'

There was silence for a while, and we both sipped our drinks. Finally, I broke it. 'Nick, your dad's car ...'

'It was stolen. Dad hadn't reported it immediately as he'd been away, then he thought I had borrowed it. I sometimes did, if I needed a bigger, smarter car rather than turning up in my builder's van or my little Renault. Dad was questioned, of course, but he had an alibi for the time Tiffany Coles was murdered.'

'Were you also questioned?' As I said the words I grimaced, knowing it sounded as though I was suspicious of him.

He nodded. 'Yes, as I had a key to Dad's car. But I also had an alibi, thank goodness. And you may not know this – I don't think it's been reported in the press yet – but the detective in charge of the case, whom Dad knows pretty well, told us that clues from the car have pointed towards someone known to the police. Someone on their database, who's previously been in prison for various offences. They are tracking him down, and they told me it'll only be a matter of time.'

'That's good.'

'Yes. So she wasn't murdered by Dad, or by me, in case you were wondering. And Dad was never involved in the drugs trade in any way. Despite all the other sometimes dodgy deals he'd been involved in, he always said, "Not drugs, never drugs", since my sister's death. He'd done all he could for Tiffany, and would never …'

'Tiffany?' I frowned.

'Yes. My sister's name was also Tiffany. The fact the murdered girl had the same name, and also turned out to be a drug user, has hit Dad hard. It's like he's reliving those awful events from twenty years ago.'

'OK. Has he, I mean, is he getting help? Counselling, or anything?'

Nick snorted. 'Dad never looks for help from outside. His way of coping is to be busy. To find some way to make something good out of a bad situation.' He smiled. 'And he's decided to do something tangible to try to help other people in Tiffany's situation.'

'Which Tiffany?'

'Either. Both.' Nick smiled. 'Plans are a bit vague at present and I'm not supposed to say anything, but believe me, he'll do it.'

'That's wonderful. I only met him that one time but I liked what I saw of him then. He's a good man.'

'He is. So now, you'll believe me and not some gossipy neighbour spreading malicious rumours and turning you against anyone with the surname Marshall, eh?' There was a little twinkle in Nick's eye as he said this.

I smiled. 'Absolutely. God, I've been mad. I'm so sorry. Can you forgive me?'

'I hope so. In time.' He downed the last of his pint.

'Shall I get you the same again?' I asked, as I stood up ready to go to the bar.

'No, it's all right. I can't stay for another. I'll be off, unless you want me to walk you home?'

'No, no. I know the way.' I smiled weakly at my feeble joke. Why did he want to rush off like that? I'd thought, having told me the whole story and cleared the air between us, that he'd at least have another drink with me, a chance to make friends again, to chat and hopefully enjoy each other's company.

'All right then. I'll be round next week to check on progress. About six o'clock on Wednesday – if you're there we can go through outstanding work and any snags.'

'Yes, I can be home by then.'

He stood up, lifted a hand in a half-wave, and left.

So that was that. I now knew the truth, and it was what I'd fervently hoped – that Nick and his father had absolutely no links to the drugs trade. And yet, despite this, we had not reconnected. What had started out as a promising potential romance had petered out into nothing. I felt tears pricking at the back of my eyes. Leaving what was left of my wine I got up and walked home as the sun set, alone.

Chapter 24

Over the next few weeks, Esther gradually became resigned to the idea that her future must lie with Thomas Walker, whether she liked it or not. It was the only way to ensure George's safety. She told Pa about the engagement. His reaction was a mixture of relief that Walker had promised not to inform on them, sadness that it wasn't the marriage she'd hoped to have, and like her, accepting that although it wasn't what she'd dreamed of, it would probably turn out all right in the end.

As far as she knew, word of her betrothal had not reached Sam. As yet, beyond Pa and George, who both never left the pub, no one knew.

Walker proved true to his word one day in late August. There'd been a few days of heavy rain and Esther had barely left The Ship at Anchor. Walker entered the pub in a hurry, rain dripping from his hat, and went through to the kitchen, gesturing to Esther to follow him. 'Militia in the area,' he said, breathlessly. 'They're heading across from Lymington. I don't know if they'll come here – they're following a tip-off about Captain May but just in case …'

She nodded and ran upstairs to alert George. Esther promised to tell him as soon as it was safe to come out. 'Might not be until after closing time,' she warned him.

George nodded. 'It's all right. I have everything I need in the cellar.' They'd kept it stocked with food, water and a candle lantern as well as rushlights, and the fireplace was set ready with logs and kindling, hiding the entrance. 'Please thank Walker for me.'

There were a number of customers in the bar so he could not access the cellar via the fireplace entrance. Instead he climbed out through a window at the back of the pub, letting himself drop from the windowsill. From there he crossed through the reeds to the tunnel entrance at the edge of the marsh, and into the cellar from that end.

She thanked Walker as he'd asked. And it turned out the warning was justified, for within half an hour a Lymington Revenue man with four soldiers accompanying him entered the pub. Walker had left by then. The drinkers – men who'd helped unload hauls of contraband in the past – all stood to leave but one of the soldiers blocked the door.

'Just a few questions, gentlemen, please,' said the Revenue officer, and he proceeded to question everyone. Walker was right – they were looking for May. They all shook their heads – in all probability truthfully, Esther thought. No one local had seen Captain May since the battle in July. It was thought he was hiding out in Guernsey, where Streeter had gone, but no one knew for sure, or would tell if they did.

'Miss, we need to check upstairs and in your outbuildings,' the Revenue officer said after all customers had been questioned. Most left as soon as they could, and Esther didn't blame them. She led the way upstairs, where they spoke to Pa and Esther silently prayed that he wouldn't say anything about George. Thankfully he didn't. Next she took them outside, into her stable and legitimate storerooms. There was no access from there to the hidden cellar, and of course no contraband was stored in any of those outbuildings.

'Nice lawful business you have here, miss,' the Revenue officer concluded, as he doffed his hat to her and left the pub.

Esther breathed a sigh of relief, and after thirty or so minutes had passed when she was certain they wouldn't return, she pushed aside the logs and tapped on the doorway at the back of the fireplace to let George know it was safe to come out. With no customers in, he could emerge via that entrance rather than use the tunnel. He had a broad grin on his face.

'It's working. Good old Walker. He's come through for us. We can trust him. Though I'm going to need to repair that tunnel lining soon. A bit fell away as I ran through, and I thought I heard more fall a few minutes ago. This rain's not helped it any.'

'Walker warned us this time. We don't know if—' She broke off, as there was a huge crash at the door. She'd bolted it before George emerged from the cellar, but whoever was out there was ramming it. There was a splintering of wood and the door gave way. George was halfway back to the fireplace but it was too late – the militia and Revenue man who'd been in earlier were back.

'Stop! What do you think you're doing? You've damaged my door! You'll pay to repair that!' Esther waved her arms around as she shouted at them, hoping she could provide enough distraction to allow George to hide. Hoping that they perhaps wouldn't recognise him. But it was all for nothing.

The Revenue officer pointed at George. 'You. George Coombes, unless I'm very much mistaken. We were told you were likely to be here. Don't know where you were hiding earlier but no matter, we have you now. Restrain that fellow.' Two of the militia men stepped forward and grabbed his arms. George struggled, but there was no chance of escape, as one of the other men drew a pistol and pointed it at him.

'Let him go! He's done nothing!' Esther screamed and dashed forward to try to help him, but the Revenue officer caught hold of her. He was a burly man, and despite her strength he held her back easily.

'Oh, but he has. He's wanted on suspicion of the murder of William Allen, late sailing master of the *Orestes*. At the very least aiding and abetting the murderer. We have him now. Take him outside, bind his hands and tie him to my horse. I'll have him transferred tomorrow to the prison in Winchester to await his trial.'

'He didn't murder anyone! It wasn't him who fired the shot that hit Mr Allen! Everyone knows that!'

The Revenue officer kept a hold of her. 'And do you know who *did* fire that shot, eh, miss? Did you witness it at all? Because if you did, you will be required to give evidence. We have witnesses that say Coombes here was definitely firing a musket in the direction of the pinnace when Allen was shot.' He gave her a shake. 'So tell me, were you a witness?'

'N-no, sir. I came back here. I didn't see …' She needed to defend herself, but on the other hand she needed to defend George.

'Came *back*? So you were there at the start, were you? It was early on in the fracas that Allen was hit.'

She shook her head. 'I saw nothing. But I know it wasn't George.'

While he'd been holding her, the militia men had dragged George from the pub. Only now did the Revenue officer let go of her. She ran outside, where the rain was still falling. George was tied by the wrists on the end of a rope secured to one of the horses. 'Esther, keep away. It's all right. They've no evidence. This will all blow over,' he called to her. 'But tell Sam, will you? Let him know …'

The Revenue man had come out after Esther and now mounted his horse. 'If you're hiding anyone else – Voss, May, or even John Streeter himself – we'll find out and we'll be back. It'll go badly for you, miss, if that happens.' He kicked his horse and set off at a trot, George stumbling along behind him and the militia men following on.

Esther watched after them. Never had she felt so helpless in her life. That could have been Sam being dragged away, she realised.

Thank goodness he'd refused to take a musket and so no one could give evidence against him. Tell Sam, George had said. Yes, she needed to do just that, and as soon as possible.

She hurried inside and secured the door as best she could, although the militia had broken its bolt. She ran upstairs to her father's room and burst in. He was asleep despite all the commotion, but woke as soon as she entered. She quickly told him what had happened.

'Pa, I'm going to go now to Burton and find Sam. There's no one in the bar. I can leave it closed unless you're able to come down?'

'What time is it, lass?'

'About three o'clock.'

'There'll be a rush in a couple of hours, when the men come home wanting their ale and pies. We can't afford to lose that custom. Will you be back by then?'

'Ah, Pa, I don't know. I'll take the pony. I don't know how long it'll take to find him.'

'I'll come down, lass. I can do it if you help me.' Pa grimaced with pain as he heaved himself upright and swung his legs out of bed.

'Pa ... well, if you're sure ...' Esther helped steady him as he got to his feet. There was a determination in his eyes. She helped him dress and let him lean on her as he staggered down the stairs and took a seat on a stool behind the bar.

'Go, lass. Find Sam. I'll manage here.'

She kissed him, grabbed a shawl and went out to the yard, where she saddled up their little pony, Toby, and rode straight to the farm where Sam worked. Thankfully the rain was easing off now. She found the farmer's wife, who confirmed which field he was working in, repairing a fence. Esther followed the directions she'd been given along a lane, over a stream and into a field, and spotted Sam at a distance, his shirt off, vigorously digging holes for fence posts. Despite the circumstances she couldn't help but stop and admire his rippling back muscles for a moment. This was what she was giving up by promising to marry Walker. Though now, with George arrested, was that agreement now broken?

'Sam! It's me, Esther!' She shouted to him and waved, and began picking her way around the edge of the muddy field towards him.

He turned, laid down his spade and mopped his brow. 'Esther. How are you?'

She pulled on the reins to bring Toby to a halt and for a moment stood still, a couple of yards away from him, and just gazed at him. It seemed so long since she'd seen him, and oh, how she'd missed him! But where to start, telling him all that had happened?

'Sam. It's George. You know, I think, that he was hiding in The Ship at Anchor? Using the cellar if there was any danger, or upstairs during the day?'

'I sent him to you. I thought you might help.' He gave a small nod of thanks.

'Thomas Walker saw him one day. And promised he'd warn us if there was to be a raid by unfriendly Revenue men or militia, so George would be able to get to the cellar. But in return ...' She stopped herself. Did she need to tell him what she'd agreed to in return? She decided that yes, she did. If now that the agreement with Walker was meaningless, she wanted there to be no secrets, nothing hidden between them. Delaying telling him of Walker's interest in her before had only led to problems.

'In return?' he prompted.

She dismounted and took a deep breath. 'In return he made me promise to marry him.'

'I see. Well, I thank you for doing what you are doing for my brother, and I wish you well.' He picked up his spade and began to turn away from her.

She took a couple of steps forward and caught his arm, the muscle firm under her touch. 'That's not the end. Walker came by earlier today and warned George of an imminent raid. George went to the cellar. It seemed to work, the militia searched everywhere and then left. Half an hour later George came out, but soon afterwards the Revenue man and militia came back and …'

'And?'

'Oh, Sam. I couldn't stop them. They've arrested him, and they're taking him to the prison in Winchester awaiting trial.'

'Arrested! Oh God! Why didn't Walker warn you they were coming back?'

'I don't know …' As she said it, the likely truth dawned on her, and looking at Sam's face it appeared he'd come to the same conclusion.

'He told them, didn't he? He must have seen them leave, and suggested they go back after a short while, when you'd have dropped your guard and George would have come out. He betrayed you. The two-faced bastard! If I ever see him, I'll …' Sam shook his fist.

'I don't know … that might be what happened. I'm sorry, Sam. I believed him when he promised to warn us. And I thought it had paid off when he came to say they were on their way. But now … you might be right, he could have crossed us.'

'Have you seen him since?'

'No. I came straight here. Pa's manning the bar.'

'It's that damned Will Burden. He's the one who gave information against George. And he was our friend, or so we thought.' Sam spat to one side. 'Have you seen Will? I haven't. I went to his house to ask him why he did this, but he's gone. Cleared out.'

'He did it for the reward,' Esther said.

'Aye, I know, but why pick on George? They were friends since childhood. I used to tag along behind them, as the annoying little brother. I don't understand. And now … George in prison! It *wasn't* him, was it? It was Captain May, or so I heard, that fired the fatal shot.'

Esther caught his arm again. 'Sam, if you know for sure it was Captain May, the only way to help George is to become a

224

witness. Tell them what you know, and they'll then look for May and release George.'

But Sam shook his head. 'They're looking for May anyway. They wanted George on a charge of aiding and abetting a murderer.' He looked down at his feet. 'That's still a hanging offence, Esther. And now that they've caught him …'

'No one will give evidence against him.' Esther made her voice as firm as she could, in an attempt to reassure Sam.

'Someone already has. Will Burden. And for all we know, there could be more who are tempted by that reward.'

Chapter 25

It was reported the next day that the police had arrested and charged someone for the murder of Tiffany Coles. I assumed this was the person Nick had mentioned that they'd been tracking down. There was a shot of a man being escorted into a police station, handcuffed and head bowed. He looked like someone you might pass in the street without a second glance. I realised I'd been expecting some kind of monster and yet he looked perfectly normal. His name was given as Simon Johnson – pretty much the most mundane, everyday sort of name you could possibly imagine.

Details were also reported of how Tiffany had died. She'd been raped and strangled, not at Stanpit Marsh but at some other location. Then her body had been put in the boot of Des's stolen car and brought to the marsh, driven up the track and dumped in the pool. Johnson had links to the local area and knew exactly where he could leave her without being spotted. I still felt pangs of guilt that I had not heard or seen anything at the time. But she was already dead by the time she was brought to Stanpit so I couldn't have saved her. At best if I'd seen or heard something I could have helped the police find her killer sooner.

Simon Johnson was middle-aged, and part of a gang of drug

traffickers. More details emerged over the weekend and on Sunday there was a long write-up of the case in a Sunday paper that I read online. He'd been trying to force Tiffany Coles to work as a mule. Just like Nick's sister Tiffany. He'd been in prison a couple of times for drug-related offences but clearly had never changed his ways.

On Wednesday I made sure I was home before six, ready for Nick's visit. I felt nervous once again. He'd made it clear he wasn't interested in me, so I should have been able to simply switch off and treat him the way I treated Keith and Aaron – friendly but as purely business acquaintances. But it didn't matter what I told myself. I still found my palms sweating and my stomach churning at the thought of seeing him.

He arrived at ten past six, just as Keith and Aaron were leaving. My nerves did not improve having him in the house. We ran through a few things on the snagging list and compiled a list of outstanding work for this phase. We also discussed when his team would come back for phase two – replacing the bathroom, knocking through to create a larger landing, updating the wiring, plumbing and heating upstairs. I'd been scared Nick might say he didn't want to do the later phases of work. I'd thought perhaps he'd want to end our business relationship as well as the embryonic personal one, but he was as professional as ever and seemed genuinely keen to complete the project. For that I was grateful.

'I see they've arrested a chap for the murder,' I said, when we'd finished the business talk and were making our way back downstairs.

'Yes. And it's a name my dad recognised.' He sighed. 'Simon Johnson lived in the same squat as my sister back in the early 2000s. Dad met him a few times when he went to see Tiff. Maybe he had something to do with my sister getting involved in drug smuggling too.'

'Oh my God! That must make it even harder for you and your father.'

He nodded. 'It's certainly made Dad even more resolved than he already was to do something to help. He's started having talks with relevant people about his plans.'

'Can you tell me them yet?'

'Not yet. I will when things are more settled.'

We were back downstairs. I found I didn't want him to leave just yet. But if I offered him a drink, or a cup of tea, I was pretty certain he'd turn it down. 'Nick, before you go, could you take a look at the garden? I'd welcome your thoughts on some ideas I've had …' It was a bit desperate, I know, but there, the words were out.

'Millie, we're not a landscaping company,' he protested.

'I know, but I … value your judgement. And maybe you'll be able to recommend someone to take this on.'

He nodded. 'All right, I'll take a look. I do know a decent landscaper whose details I can pass on to you. It's a chap who's worked on gardens after we've built garden rooms. He's sound.'

'Thanks. Well, let's go out through the patio doors and I'll show you what I'm thinking of.'

He gave a small smile and followed me out. We crossed to the edge of the patio – the only piece of garden I'd used so far – and gazed across the overgrown lawn and tangled bushes that lay between the house and the edge of the reed beds in the marsh.

'So you see along there' – I pointed – 'there's a kind of dip. I'm thinking of having that area dug out to make a pond. I'd love to encourage wildlife into my garden. And then a path from here over to it and along one side. Over there' – I gestured to the right – 'a row of hedging plants to screen my garden from people wandering around Tutton's Well. And some flowerbeds on the left of the patio, with the rest laid to lawn.'

Nick nodded at everything. He turned to me and smiled. 'All

sounds good – I can picture it. I will give Dan a ring and pass on your number, if that's OK. He'll call you if he can fit you in.'

'Thank you.'

Nick was looking around the garden as though picturing what it might look like. I found myself doing the same, only in my mind he was there with me, sitting beside me on the patio sipping an early evening drink, walking hand in hand around it discussing the planting scheme, pointing out dragonflies and tadpoles in my pond. Enjoying the garden alongside me. But it could never happen.

'Right then, I'll be off. Expect to hear from Dan Bradshaw soon. He's a good lad.' And Nick went back inside, carefully wiping his feet on the mat before stepping on my new wooden floor. He picked up his folder of notes, nodded to me and left.

'Damn Sharon and her stupid accusations!' I said aloud, thumping the back of a chair. If only I hadn't listened to her, or at least hadn't said anything about it to Nick. If only I'd trusted him, and my gut instinct about him, right from the start. I'd been so, so stupid, and the result was I'd ruined all chances of a relationship with the one man I'd met with whom I thought I'd shared a spark.

I poured myself a glass of wine to drown my sorrows and sat down in the sitting room, which was still furnished only with garden furniture. I had a sofa on order but still needed to buy a dining table and chairs, a couple of bookcases, a TV cabinet and something to go on the walls.

I needed to talk to someone. But who? Arwen was the first to come to mind – she's the one I usually spoke to for advice. But hold on – it was Arwen who'd advised me to drop Nick if I had any suspicions about him being involved with drugs. Maybe Arwen didn't always get things right. What would she tell me this time? I sat back and considered, picturing her here beside me discussing the problem. She'd tell me to move on, I concluded. She'd point out there were plenty more fish in the sea, and I should get out and be sociable and find someone new. She'd sign me up for online dating and have me out several nights a week meeting new men until I found one I gelled with.

And would I take that advice? No. I might have, if I hadn't met Nick. But now I couldn't imagine dating anyone else, anyone new. I wanted him.

An image of Steve flitted into my mind. And suddenly I wanted more than anything to talk to him. To get his advice. My ex-husband, but also the person I'd been closest friends with for so many years. And we were still friends – he'd said he would always be there for me if I needed a friend, hadn't he?

I picked up my phone and called him, willing him to be in and able to talk to me. Too late I wondered what if he was out on a date? Well if he was, I'd make a quick excuse and hang up, then apologise by text. I didn't want to get in the way.

He answered quickly.

'Millie! Good to hear from you. Hold on two ticks – I was just pouring myself a beer.'

'You're at home then?'

'Yes, home alone.'

'I wanted a chat … actually I wanted your advice about something …' I sounded hesitant even to myself. Was this a stupid idea? Steve hadn't met Nick. How on earth could he advise? But perhaps it was worth a go.

'Of course …' There was the sound of beer glugging into a glass, and a little grunt and sigh as he sat down. I pictured him relaxing in the old sofa we'd bought when we were first married. It needed replacing, but he'd always liked it, so I'd been happy to let him keep it when we split our belongings. We'd had many an evening snuggled together on it, watching TV or, in the early days, just chatting and laughing together.

'All right, Millie. Go ahead. How can I help?'

I loved that. The assumption that whatever it was, he would be able to help. 'It's kind of delicate. But we're friends, and we said—'

'We'd always be there for each other,' he interrupted. 'And that's absolutely true. We always will be.' He fell silent, waiting for me to continue.

'So … it's about a chap. My builder … but we went on a couple of dates.' It was odd – asking your ex-husband for advice about a new relationship, but here we were, and as I spoke, I knew that Steve would do all he could to help and advise me. We had so much history together, we knew each other so well and wanted only the best for each other. I took a deep breath and continued. 'I liked him. A lot, if I'm honest. But now, I've … fucked up, I think is the best way of describing it.' I went on to outline all that had happened. Steve made all the right noises to show he was listening, he was sympathetic, he was considering the best way to resolve the problem. It was only as I was telling him everything that I remembered Nick was supposed to be coming round that evening when Steve had called unexpectedly. 'Also, he'd said he was coming round that day you turned up here. What if he did, and he saw you hugging me in the kitchen?'

'Ah ha!' If I'd been with Steve I think I'd have seen him punch the air.

'What?'

'You muppet.' It was said with fondness. 'I bet that's what happened. He saw you and me cuddling through the window and probably assumed we were getting back together. That's if he even realised I was your ex. If he thought I was anyone else, he'd have assumed you were dating someone else as well as him and therefore not taking him seriously. Either way, backing off is what any decent man would have done. I don't blame him.'

'Oh. God, yeah.' I thumped my forehead. Stupid woman. Of course Nick would have jumped to conclusions. Why had I needed Steve to point it out? If Nick had seen us, he'd have no way of recognising Steve, and even if he had, how would he know we were only good friends? Besides, for all he knew, I was dating other men as well as him.

'So what you need to do,' Steve continued, trying his hardest to suppress a giggle, 'is phone this Nick, who sounds like a decent kind of bloke, tell him it was me you were hugging that day but that of course we are not getting back together. We are simply good friends, as we have been since we were 10.'

'Eleven.'

'What?'

'We met aged 11 when we started at Woodfield School.'

'Ah, OK. Tell him also, if it helps, that I've met someone new – Amanda, her name is, and she's fabulous and I'm very happy. And I'd love for you to feel the same.'

'Amanda?' He'd mentioned he was dating someone from work when he'd come round. I was delighted he sounded so happy with her. 'Is it serious?'

'Ha, it's only been two months, but yes, it might become serious. I really do like her a lot.' His tone changed as he continued, becoming serious but warm and loving. 'Talk to him, Millie. Sort it out. Tell him how you feel and what you want from him, and if he feels the same you'll be back on track in no time. And if he doesn't – well, it's better to find out sooner rather than later, isn't it?'

'I guess so. Thanks, Steve. I feel better now. There's a way forward.'

'Yes, and a very simple one. Good luck, Millie. Let me know how things pan out, eh?'

'Will do.'

I ended the call with a grin on my face. If Nick had seen me with Steve then of course that would be part of the reason he'd been so cool with me. And I realised now, that when we'd gone out for that drink and he'd told me all the history of his sister, he'd been expecting me to also come clean and tell him who he'd seen me with in my kitchen. But I'd said nothing. No wonder he'd decided to leave me after one drink and go home alone. Steve was right. I really was a muppet.

Chapter 26

Nothing would ever be the same, Esther felt, as summer ended and autumn began. With George Coombes imprisoned in Winchester gaol, and John Streeter still a wanted man and keeping a low profile, the mood among the free traders was muted. There'd been no smuggling runs of any size – certainly none that Esther had been involved in. Jonathan Edwards and Henry Voss had also been arrested. Pa was still largely bed-bound, though each day with Esther's help he'd get up, walk around and exercise a little. It was beginning to work, Esther thought. Pa missed the life of the bar, and was keen to get back to it full time, as soon as he was able.

One thing, however, had changed, and for the better. Thomas Walker had not been seen since the day of George's arrest. Esther had assumed he was keeping out of her sight, owing to his guilt at causing George's arrest, but Carter told her one day that no, Walker had not been seen anywhere. ''Tis like he's simply disappeared,' he said. 'He's not showed up for his work, which makes Joshua Jeans very unhappy, so I heard. His house looks abandoned. He's run away, I reckon.' Carter snorted. 'Perhaps there's a warrant out for his arrest too, that we don't know of. Perhaps they've discovered how corrupt the man is.'

'If that's so,' another man sitting with Carter said, 'why haven't they arrested Bursey and the others, and for goodness' sake, Jeans himself? They're all as corrupt as each other.'

It was a mystery, that was certain.

And the other change in Esther's life was that Sam was gradually beginning to return to her. He began calling in at the pub now and again. Not every day, as before, but weekly, then twice weekly. They were becoming friends again. Whether they could ever be more to each other, only time would tell. But Esther was happy to see him, even though Sam's mood tended to veer between depressed and angry about what had happened to his brother.

'Do you think Walker will ever come back?' Esther tentatively asked Sam one day.

He shrugged. 'I don't know. If he does, it'll be at the worst possible moment, that's for sure. He's done us a lot of damage, but he could do more, and I bet if there was a chance to, he would.'

'He'd warned us the militia were coming. I don't understand why he didn't come back and warn us again. I thought …'

'You thought you could trust him. That's where you went wrong – the man's corrupt and can't be trusted with anything. I hate him, Esther. I'd kill him if I saw him again.' Sam's eyes flashed with anger.

There was no point continuing the conversation. Sam blamed Walker for what had happened to his brother, Esther knew.

A rumour reached them one day that Walker had been seen far away in Poole. 'Maybe he's moved to a different Customs house,' Sam said.

And on another day while driving the cart pulled by Toby to Ringwood, Esther thought she'd seen a man on a black horse further up the road. When she reached that spot however, there was no one to be seen. 'Do you think it was him?' Sam asked her, when she told him what she'd seen.

Esther shook her head. 'I don't know,' she replied. 'I think I'm so scared of seeing him, it's like I spot him when he's not there. I really don't want to see him so my imagination conjures him up.'

It was Carter who brought the news, in October, that Streeter had arranged another run. Using intermediaries, he'd purchased another ship and was due to bring back a cargo of tobacco and brandy. 'He's asking will you store the goods, like before?' Carter muttered to her as he sat at the bar sipping a glass of the previous haul of smuggled brandy.

It would be the first run since the big one in July. A part of Esther wanted to say no, to have nothing more to do with the free traders. But on the other hand, it had been their way of life as long as she could remember. It was a large portion of their income. It was what the community did. And despite Streeter's lower profile, she still feared what he might do if she didn't agree to help. She conferred with Sam when he was next in, and to her surprise, he grinned.

'It'll be like old times, Blue. There'll be no trouble, as it's a small run. We'll just be part of the landing party, like we used to. You and me, working together again.' That, more than anything else, clinched it for her. Working side by side with Sam once more, landing and storing the goods. She sent word back to Streeter to say yes, she would help.

Her only worry was that resumption of the runs might bring Walker out into the open once more. While part of her wanted to know what had happened to him, and wanted to hear if there was any explanation for why he hadn't returned to warn them, the larger part of her hoped he'd stay out of their lives for ever.

On the night in question, a blustery autumn one where heavy showers constantly threatened, Sam arrived at the pub before closing time and hung around in the kitchen while she cleared up. The beaching time was due in the early hours. They had time to sit and have a brandy together, alone, while Pa slept upstairs. In the old days they'd have laughed and joked and kissed and held each other given this sort of opportunity. But now she found their conversation stilted, with an awkwardness to everything they said to each other. As though there were words unsaid, a subject too big to tackle, sitting between them. It was different when he visited the pub during opening hours. Then, there was noise and chatter all around, and she was kept too busy to do much more than exchange a few pleasantries with him. Tonight the hours passed slowly, until at last the chiming of her pendulum clock told her it was time to get ready and make their way to the beach. She went down to the hidden cellar first to get changed into her boy's clothes. They'd not been used for months but she'd left them down there. Then Sam came down, and helped her move the beer barrel that covered the tunnel entrance. Using a rushlight, they set off down the tunnel.

Part way along something felt wrong. There was loose earth underfoot, not the usual well-trampled ground. The tunnel smelt of wet soil. A little further, around the bend, Esther realised why.

'Sam, stop. Look.' She held the rushlight in front of her. Ahead, the tunnel was completely blocked with earth and rubble.

'What the …' Sam reached out and touched the blockage, and as he did so, more earth fell from the tunnel ceiling. 'It's collapsed. Turn back, Blue! Hurry!'

She needed no second telling, but turned and hurried back to the cellar, with Sam on her heels and the sound of more falling earth and rock behind them. It was those rotten planks that had lined the tunnel, she realised. The ones she'd meant to talk to Pa about, to get them replaced. They must have given way. The tunnel hadn't been used for months, not since Sam and George had helped bring up that massive load in July. Who knew when it had collapsed – it could have happened at any time since then. Suddenly she remembered that George had used the tunnel once since then – on the day he'd been arrested, when he'd first hidden from the militia. He'd said something about part of the tunnel lining falling, then.

Back in the cellar Sam grabbed her and pulled her to him in a tight embrace. 'Oh my God, Blue. That could have happened when you were in there. That could have killed you.' He nuzzled into her neck, and she realised he was stifling sobs.

'It's all right, Sam. We're safe. Thank God it didn't happen when you and George were moving the stock in July, or when George used it to hide. We're safe. But the tunnel's unusable.'

'We'll have to bring the goods by road. Or walk them from the edge of the marsh.' He'd pulled himself together and let go of her, blushing a little.

'It's dangerous by road. So many Revenue officers ride up and down Stanpit. But there's no way to carry goods by land over the marsh. The reeds are too thick.'

'It'll have to be by road, then. With some batmen for protection.'

She nodded. This was not the way she liked it, taking the risk of bringing smuggled goods by cart. She'd always enjoyed the night-time rowing through the harbour and up the channel under the stars, when all was peaceful and still. But like so much else, it seemed that too had changed for good.

Thankfully the run went smoothly. John Streeter was there at the beach, dressed in a crude disguise as a farm labourer. Esther told him about the tunnel collapse, and he groaned. 'Get that tunnel rebuilt, Blue. Your cellar's too good a storage area to lose, and as you say, taking the goods by road is risky.'

The unloading on the beach was accomplished quickly, and they loaded goods for the pub onto the cart pulled by Toby. Five batmen walked alongside, just in case they met with any trouble, but there was none. Esther kept a careful lookout at the beach to see which of the local Revenue officers would turn up to take their cut, in case it was Thomas Walker. But it was Bursey who arrived. She wanted to ask him if he knew what had become of Walker but she didn't dare. As before, it was best to keep her head down, her face averted from the Revenue men.

Sam stayed to help unload at the pub and move the goods into the hidden cellar via the fireplace entrance. When the work was done, she considered asking if he wanted to stay, sleep on the truckle bed in the bar as he used to, but she feared he'd be embarrassed by the suggestion. Despite their embrace earlier after the fright with the tunnel, they weren't as close as they used to be.

But it was he who suggested it, shyly. 'That old truckle bed, is it still … available?' He looked at her sideways.

'It is, yes. George used it, before … I can make it up for you.' She turned and ran upstairs to fetch bedding before he noticed the flush that she knew was creeping up her face. Was it possible that they might be able to rebuild what they had? Become close again? And if after some time there was still no sign of Thomas Walker, perhaps she could dare to consider herself released from her promise and free to be with Sam, if he'd have her? If he still wanted her?

Sam had been a regular at the pub since the discovery of the tunnel collapse. After the harvest season ended there was no need for him to be in Burton, and he gradually began spending more and more nights at the pub. Esther was grateful for his presence, his company, his help with the heavy work of the pub, and his friendship.

At last, in November, George's case was brought before the Winchester Assize. But, there was a technical issue, reported in the local papers. It seemed that because William Allen had been shot at while below the high tide line, and then died in his ship, the Winchester Assize was not the right place for the trial. It was a case for the Admiralty, as effectively the victim had died at sea. Coombes, Voss and Edwards were transferred to Newgate Prison in London, awaiting their case to be brought at the Old Bailey, under the High Court of the Admiralty.

'If ever I find Thomas Walker,' Sam said, for the hundredth time, 'I won't be responsible for my actions. I'll kill him. For if my brother is found guilty, that's what will happen to him.'

'He won't be,' Esther soothed. 'There won't be enough evidence, against any of them. It's Captain May they need to find.' May had not been seen in Christchurch since the arrest warrants were issued. He was probably still in Guernsey, but no one could or would confirm that. 'And besides, we don't know that it was Walker who betrayed George.' She wasn't sure why she was sticking up for Walker, but it felt right to do so. In those last weeks he'd proved he could be a decent man.

Sam shook his head. 'Who else could it have been? Why else would he have disappeared as soon as George was arrested?'

'I don't know. I really don't. If he's gone for ever then that's good ... for us ... but he might return at any time.' A thought occurred to her. 'You don't think Streeter, or one of the captains, might have ... had something to do with his disappearance?'

'Finished him off, you mean?' Sam shrugged. 'It's possible, I suppose. I wouldn't put it past May, especially. But he's been in hiding since the battle. And why would he do anything to Walker and not any other officer?'

Esther had no answer to that. Walker's fate remained a mystery, one she spent many sleepless nights thinking about.

At last George's trial came up. 'I want to be there,' Sam said to Esther. 'I want to be in the courtroom to support him through this.'

'I want to be with you,' she said, and he stepped forward and took her in his arms, resting his chin on the top of her head.

'Thank you, Blue. But the trial may take days, or weeks. You are needed here, with your father.'

She nodded, trying not to let the tears come. He was right. But the thought both of him being away for an unspecified length of time and of what he would be going through was hard to bear.

Sam left her the next day, travelling first to Winchester by way of a local carter he knew, and then by stagecoach to London. He was not the only local person to go – Hannah Sellars was called upon to give evidence. She too travelled to London, but was back within a couple of days after giving her evidence.

Esther went immediately down to the Haven House Inn to see her, on learning she was back. What evidence had Hannah given? Was it possible she'd said something that would cause harm to George? She couldn't believe Hannah would, but … these were strange times.

Hannah was busy in her bar, bustling around with an apron tied around her middle, looking a little more flustered than usual. 'Esther. Oh, yes. Just a moment. I suppose you want to …' She hurried off, served another couple of fellows, and then untied her apron and began to take it off before apparently changing her mind and retying it. She gestured to a corner table away from her other customers, and Esther followed her over.

'How goes the trial?' Esther asked. 'How is George?'

Hannah bit her lip and shook her head. 'I fear … I don't know what will happen. Esther, I told them as little as I possibly could. They said I had to give evidence otherwise I'd be arrested. They know Streeter made his plans here, and the shots were fired from here and I'd allowed them access, so they're saying I could be charged as an accessory to murder. And I had to swear on the Bible to tell the truth. It was horrible, Esther. George is a good man. I had thought maybe we'd …' She trailed off and once more shook her head.

Esther knew what she'd been about to say. There'd been a chance, once, that George might marry the widow. There was an age gap between them, but George had always been smitten with Hannah. 'What did you tell them, Mrs Sellars?'

'Just that they had muskets, that they fired from both the luggers and from upstairs, here. All that they already knew, from the testimonies of the marines. But they wanted names – who had I seen with a musket, who was firing them, where were they firing from? I told them George … was holding a musket but I hadn't seen him fire it. Which is the truth. And I told them

240

Captain May had handed out the muskets. I wanted to say it was he who shot the sailing master but I didn't know for sure. I never witnessed it.'

'Better that you didn't say. But everyone says it was May. Why they're after George and the other two, I don't understand.'

'They're trying Jon Edwards for murder, and George and Henry Voss for aiding and abetting. There's some who say they've not enough evidence for any of it to stick.'

'Let's hope that's so.'

Sam returned to Mudeford a few days after Hannah. He came straight to The Ship at Anchor, and Esther waved him through to the kitchen where they could talk in private. His face was as drawn and haggard as Hannah's had been, and Esther was sure that was not just the result of a long and uncomfortable journey.

'What news?' she asked, as she made him sit down with a glass of fortifying brandy.

He knocked the drink back in one go. 'There wasn't enough evidence—'

'That's wonderful news!' she interrupted, but he waved a hand to silence her.

'Not enough evidence to convict Edwards or Voss. Both were acquitted. But they found George guilty of the murder of William Allen. Even though they know he did not fire the fatal shot. They just want to make an example of someone.'

'Guilty!' She clapped a hand to her mouth. 'What will become of him?'

'It's not over yet … There's still a chance …' Sam poured himself another brandy from the bottle she'd left out and took a swallow of it. 'His counsel, Fielding, had a trick up his sleeve. He said that the trial was invalid. He said because the shot was fired from land the trial should have been held at the Winchester Assize after all, and not at the Admiralty Court.'

'So the trial would have to be held again?'

241

Sam shook his head. 'A man cannot be tried for the same crime twice. If the court wasn't the right one for the trial, then the trial is void and George should be released. That's what Fielding is arguing.'

'You said they found him guilty …'

'They did, and it was after the verdict that Fielding stood up and said his piece. But the counsel for the prosecution said that as Allen died at sea it was right for the trial to be held at the Admiralty Court. It's kind of between the two – the shot fired from land but the death occurring at sea. In the end the judge said he would defer sentencing until he'd consulted with other judges. At least he's taking it seriously. George was taken back to Newgate. All we can do now is wait, and hope that Fielding's right and that the trial is invalid. Blue, I'm so worried. I have a bad feeling about this.'

'Oh, Sam.' Esther slid off her chair and knelt at his feet, wrapping her arms around him. She knew what he meant. His bad feeling was that if the guilty verdict was upheld, George would be hanged.

Chapter 27

I left it a couple of days before sending Nick a text. By then I'd had a call from his friend Dan Bradshaw, who'd agreed to come and look at the garden work on Wednesday afternoon. I decided to work a half-day so I could be there and take as much time as we needed to talk things through. Maybe it'd be helpful to have Nick there too – Keith and Aaron were due to have completed their work by that day so it was a chance to check it all with Nick.

And hopefully there'd be an opportunity to talk to him once more.

I was home by lunchtime, ate a quickly made sandwich and then wandered around the house checking all the work had been done before the time Dan and Nick were supposed to be here.

They arrived together, and I had the impression they'd probably been at a pub for a catch-up before coming to me. Dan was a brawny chap with a deep suntan as could be expected on someone who worked outside all day in all weathers. He had a pleasant, open-looking face and was clearly passionate about his work.

I made them tea and we went to the garden to talk through the plans. Dan made notes as I pointed out where I'd like a hedge, lawn, a path, flowerbeds. He paced out the size of the garden and checked the health of a few trees and shrubs I'd thought could be kept.

'Here, where there's a natural dip, I thought it'd be good to dig a pond,' I said, indicating the area.

Dan nodded, and then hunkered down, patting the ground in that area. 'It's odd, this dip. It's as though something's collapsed underneath. Do any drains run under here? If so, we couldn't dig a pond right here.'

'No, mate.' Nick answered him. 'The drains all run out to the front of the property. We've done some work on them.'

I was looking from the house to the marsh and back again. 'Could be the tunnel, I guess.'

'Tunnel?' Dan looked intrigued.

Nick nodded. 'I think you're right, Millie. Let's show Dan the start and see if we can work out its route.'

Dan followed us into the outbuilding and down the new steps to the hidden cellar. I opened the door to the tunnel and shone a torch in. 'This place used to be a pub, and this cellar was used to store contraband. The tunnel led from here to the edge of the marsh. That pool—'

'The one where that girl's body was found?' Dan interrupted, his eyes wide.

'Yes. That was the other end of the tunnel. It's collapsed, just a little way in.'

Dan rubbed his chin and nodded. 'I bet that dip is over the collapsed section. Let me take some measurements and we can try to work it out, to trace the route of the tunnel across the garden.' He pulled a large tape measure out of his pocket, and passed one end to Nick. 'Is it safe to go in, a little way?'

'Should be. First section is brick-lined. The collapse is after that – looks like the next section was only ever lined with timber that's rotted.'

'OK, I'll just go to the end of the brick section.' Dan took the torch from me and went into the tunnel, unspooling the tape measure as he went.

A moment later he returned. 'About eleven metres to the end of the bricks and I'd estimate another three to the collapse. A slight curve to the right.'

We left the cellar and went back up, and he went through to the garden and stood by the wall, right over where the tunnel entrance was. 'So, fourteen metres from here, in a gentle curve. No need to use the tape measure. I'll pace it out.' He did so, taking large metre-long strides. It brought him exactly to the beginning of the dip. 'We were right, then. It is the tunnel collapse beneath here.'

'What does that mean for my ideas, then?'

'I'd suggest you get Nick here to brick up the end of the tunnel inside, so you can't go past the safe section. Then we can dig for your pond, but bear in mind we will soon hit the tunnel cavity and in places we'll need to fill in rather than dig out, to get the right shape pond. That might work in our favour – there probably won't be any need to take spoil away, we'll just reuse it. It'll be good to work out the rest of its route from the other side of the collapse to the edge of your garden and fill that in as well, so there's no chance of further collapse and a new dip forming.'

'We could take a walk around to the other end of the tunnel, and take a bearing from there to this point. If we assume the tunnel was more or less straight, that'll give us a clue as to its route,' Nick said.

'Good plan. Now let's put a marker here that hopefully we'll be able to see above the reeds.' Dan looked around the garden, and finding nothing suitable went out to his van. He brought out a length of timber, left over from some project, and pushed that into the soil, upright, at the marsh end of the dip. 'Right then, lead the way. This is far more exciting than most quotes I'm asked to do!'

I grinned, and the three of us trooped back through the house, up the road, through the little car park and along the path leading to the pool. The police had long since packed up, having finished their investigation, and the path was once more open to the public.

The pool had not refilled. We'd had barely any rain since Tiffany Coles's body was discovered so that wasn't surprising. The path to it was much more well-trodden than when Nick and I had first walked it. Obviously a lot of police and curious locals had walked it since. Where the water had been was now a muddy hole, and at the back of it there was a low, waterlogged wooden door set at an angle into the ground. It had police tape across it, and a sign on a board hammered into the ground warned people not to approach or enter the tunnel, due to extreme danger of collapse.

'I heard the council will soon come and make this end safe,' Nick said. 'Dad's been pushing for it to be done quickly, anyway.' He turned to me and gave a half-smile as he said this, as though to highlight that once again his father was acting in the community's best interests.

'I can just see the top of our stick,' Dan was saying, as he stood on tiptoes and craned his neck.

Nick was taller. He elbowed his friend. 'Short-arse. I can see it easily.' Dan rolled his eyes and pulled out a compass – he seemed to have everything in his pockets – to take a bearing.

'East-north-east. Which means from the pole in the garden we need to go west-south-west to head in this direction. Millie, if you employ me for this job, I'd want to dig out the whole tunnel under your garden and fill it in, to be safe. I wouldn't feel happy leaving it.'

'That's fine,' I said. 'I'd want it done anyway, and yes, assuming your quote doesn't end up being way beyond my means I'd like you to do the work.'

'I'll do the tunnel for nothing, and quote you for the rest,' he said, as we walked back round to my house.

He marked the line of the tunnel with a few short stakes in the ground. 'It'll be clearer when we start digging. So, I think I have everything I need in order to prepare a quote. It will be a lovely garden, this, when it's done. Being surrounded by reeds rather than a boring old fence makes for a lovely boundary. And you're right to want a pond there. You'll get all sorts of wildlife and bird visitors to it, being so near the Stanpit nature reserve.'

'She'll get bird-spotters wanting to camp out in her garden,' Nick said with a laugh.

He and I had been getting on well, I thought. With luck he'd stay and we could chat when Dan had gone. But it seemed he'd had a lift here with Dan, his own car being at the garage for servicing. 'You OK to drop me off at Dad's, mate?' he said as Dan was packing up his things and getting ready to leave.

'Oh, I was hoping we could have a quick chat …' I said.

'What about? The work's all done, Aaron told me. Are there any problems with it?'

'Not at all, it's just …' I glanced at Dan, and he seemed to grasp that a private chat was what I wanted.

'Listen, mate, you stay here. I'm off to do another quote over in Highcliffe. I could pick you up on the way back, if you want.' He glanced at me and then gave Nick a meaningful look.

Nick appeared supremely uncomfortable. I turned away and went to the kitchen. 'Right then, I'll make us another cup of tea, Nick,' I called over my shoulder. 'You make yourself comfortable in the sitting room.'

'I'll get that quote to you tomorrow,' Dan said as he headed towards the door. He stuck his head into the kitchen and spoke to me quietly. 'Good luck. He likes you. I heard the whole story.' He nodded and winked, and I blushed horribly. And with that he left.

'Here. Milk, one sugar, not too strong. Just as you like it,' I said, handing the tea to Nick, who was perched on a garden chair. One of the kittens was nosing around him, begging to be played with. He stroked it absent-mindedly. 'My new sofa's coming next week, thank goodness. About time I had some proper furniture in here, don't you think? And I'm going to buy a rug to go in front of the fireplace and a bookcase against that wall.'

'Sounds good. Millie, what is it? I thought we'd said everything that needs to be said, between us.'

'Not everything.' Best to come straight to the point, I thought. 'Look, I think when you were going to come round a couple of weeks ago you might have seen me in the kitchen … with my arms around someone.'

He shook his head. 'It's none of my business, Millie. You and I had a date or two, very pleasant, but we're free to see whoever—'

I put my hand up to silence him. 'You don't understand. That was Steve, my ex-husband.'

He stared at me. 'Ah. I see. Well, the same applies, and I wish you all the best if you're trying to make it work …'

I smiled. 'He said you'd assume we were trying to get back together. Oh, Nick, we are really not. Steve and I are simply good friends now. We have known each other since we were 11, and I love him to bits, but only as a friend, now. To tell the truth, we should never have married. We'd just been going out for so long, since we were 14, and neither of us had ever had any other relationship. And everyone just expected we'd stay together for ever, and started asking us when we'd get married. Eventually we just kind of succumbed to the pressure and married when we were 22, right around the time we ought to have been calling it a day and finding ourselves new partners. We stuck it out for eight years, knowing it was wrong, that the spark had long gone and we'd grown up and grown apart, although we were still good friends.'

He listened in silence, his head hanging, not meeting my eyes.

'I told you before it was an amicable split, I think? It really was. I phoned him for advice the other day. Advice for what to do … about you, actually. As I was talking to him I realised you might have seen him here and jumped to conclusions. All the wrong conclusions.' I smiled, as he looked up at me, with what I thought was a glimmer of hope in his eyes. 'He told me to come straight out with it. To tell you there's no chance, of course there isn't, of he and I getting back together. Besides, he has someone new and I wish him all the best with her, and I …'

'You …?'

'I'd like to think you and I could start over again. I … I really like you, Nick. I loved being with you on our dates. I'd dearly like more days like those. And now we understand each other better, and know each other's backgrounds … is there any chance?'

There. I'd opened my heart to him. It was all up to him now. He could pick it up, or trample all over it. His choice.

He sat in silence for a minute longer, his head bowed, a little muscle at the side of his jaw working away. He was thinking, considering, deciding how to answer me. Deciding how best to gently turn me down, I thought. Well if so, at least I'd given it a shot. There was nothing more I could do or say. I took a sip of my tea while I waited.

At last he lifted his head, looked at me and smiled. 'We've both been a bit daft, haven't we, Millie? You believed all that crap your neighbour said about me and Dad, and I believed you were just messing around with me, not looking for anything serious. And all we needed to do was talk openly to each other.' He reached out a hand to me, and I reached back. Our hands joined, midway between our chairs. 'Yes. Let's give it another go. I'd like that very much. And this time, if anything's bothering us, we just talk about it, right?'

I grinned back at him. 'Right.'

And then he put his cup of tea on the floor by his chair, slid off onto his knees in front of me and wrapped his arms around me. I just had time to put my own cup down before it was spilt, and then his lips were on mine, I was kissing him back, and all was well with the world once more.

Chapter 28

The winter wore on, with George languishing in Newgate Prison and Sam taking up permanent residence in The Ship at Anchor. Esther had cleared out a small room upstairs for him, with Pa's blessing. It was more comfortable for him than sleeping in the bar on a truckle bed. She needed his help with the running of the pub, and he needed her emotional support to cope with what was happening to his brother. With still no hint of what might have become of Thomas Walker Esther had begun to think that it was only a matter of time before she and Sam could wed, even though sometimes during sleepless nights she still pictured Walker striding back into the pub to claim her.

There were smuggling runs, and Streeter was still the venturer behind them, but he was largely in hiding and kept off the beach when the goods were landed. Instead he managed things from a distance. No one knew quite where he was staying, but there were no more meetings in the Haven House Inn, and no visits from him to Pa.

It was a cold wet day in January when George returned to court. Once more Sam travelled to London to witness the proceedings – a long and difficult journey in appalling weather, with the roads in a treacherous state. 'I have to go,' he'd said to Esther, and she'd nodded. Of course he did. Maybe his presence in the court would lend George some comfort, whatever happened. And if by some miracle Fielding's defence was upheld and the trial was ruled unlawful, George would return to Mudeford with Sam, as a free man.

While Sam was away Esther wanted to prepare bedding for George, in case he was coming home. She bought a rib of beef ready to roast, in case there was to be a celebration. But she dared not do too much, for fear of tempting fate.

'Will he come back?' Pa said to Esther, as he lay on his bed the day after Sam had left.

'Who, Pa? Sam, or George?'

'Either, pet. I'm wondering if you've lost both.'

Esther sighed. 'Sam will come back. George will if his trial is ruled invalid. We can but hope.'

Pa nodded slowly and tried to sit up, his face contorted in agony. 'Aye. Fetch me a brandy, pet? For the pain.'

She did so, knowing that it would send him to sleep. Maybe sleep was the best thing for him. Maybe he would get better if he just rested.

Sam arrived back at the pub within a week, in the middle of the night. Esther was woken to the sound of him hammering on the door, and calling up to her window. She hurriedly got out of bed, wrapped a shawl around herself and went downstairs to let him in. He fell in through the door, and collapsed wet and shivering on the floor of the pub.

'Sam! Oh, Sam, let me help you up. I'll fetch you a brandy. And a blanket.' He allowed himself to be hauled upright and sat in a chair by the fire, which still contained glowing embers from the evening's trade. She wrapped a blanket around him, put wood on the fire to get it going again and poured him a generous glass of brandy. 'Drink this. It'll warm you up.'

His eyes were wide and staring, his skin cold and clammy. He tried to say something but his lips were cracked and his jaw seized up with the cold.

'Ssh,' Esther said, although she longed to hear the news. 'Don't try to talk. Let's get you warm and dry first.' She gently began removing his sodden boots and jacket, and he submitted to her ministrations like a sleepy child. The fact he'd come home alone, and in this state, told her what she needed to know. There was no hope for George.

Gradually as the fire began to blaze and the room warmed up, Sam stopped shivering. Esther had brought him a set of dry clothes down from his bedroom, and he changed into them while she stayed in the kitchen to give him some privacy. While there she found some bread and cold ham, and a piece of apple pie that she added cream to and brought through to him. She had no idea when he'd last eaten, but thought that it might warm him up. He wolfed the food down.

At last he leaned back in his chair, looking tired and defeated.

'Can you talk about it now? Or would you rather go to bed and sleep?' she asked.

In answer, he pulled a chair to the side of his own and patted it. 'If you can bear it, Esther, I-I'd like to talk now, about all that has happened. I can't deal with it all myself, alone.' His voice dropped to a whisper, as though forcing the words out was almost too much effort.

She sat down by him and took his hand. 'Talk, then. Tell me. Share it with me, and let me take some of the burden.'

He took a deep breath. 'George appeared pale and wasted when he returned to court. The months in Newgate had not done him any good. His counsel, Fielding, looked subdued as he entered the court, and I feared the worst from that moment. The judge read out a long explanation of the decision reached, which was that because William Allen had died at sea on board a naval ship, the High Court of the Admiralty was the proper place for the trial. All other judges he'd consulted were of the same opinion. And therefore ...' Sam let out a shuddering sigh. 'Therefore the judge ordered that George should be returned to Newgate awaiting hanging.'

Esther had guessed this would most likely be the verdict, but even so the stark words hit hard and she let out a little gasp. She held his hand still tighter. 'When?'

Sam turned his face to hers, and she saw the truth there. 'It ... it has already happened. George was back in Newgate only for the weekend. He was taken at midday on Monday to Wapping and there he was hanged. I was there, Esther. I saw him brought out of Newgate in a cart, his hands bound behind him. He was escorted by officers of the court, and a silver oar mace was carried before the cart, as a symbol of the court's authority. There were people out in the street, watching silently as he passed.'

'Did ... did he see you? Did he gain strength from your presence?'

Sam nodded. 'Yes, he saw me, and I think ... I hope it helped. He was calm and dignified, Esther. He went to his fate quietly. There were those in the crowd who'd come to jeer but were won over by his behaviour and, by the time the procession reached the gallows at Wapping, were sobbing openly. I followed the cart, trying to keep eye contact with my brother, trying to take some of the pain for him.' He sobbed and ducked his face into his hands. 'And then they hanged him. I looked away then, Esther. I couldn't help it. In his final moments I-I could not watch.'

'He would not expect you to.' Tears were streaming down Esther's face as she listened to Sam's account, wishing she could have been there to lend Sam some support but at the same time, thankful that she had not had to witness this terrible event.

'I let him down there, at the end. I turned away once the noose was around his neck. I heard him fall, I heard the gasp of the crowd, and I heard a woman near me quietly praying for his soul. I could not pray.' Sam raised his head again and gazed at

Esther. 'My only brother, hanged, for a crime he didn't commit, by a court that knew he did not commit it. They just wanted to hang someone, *anyone*, to set an example. And because they couldn't catch Captain May, they picked on George, just because it was known that he was there at the Haven House, with a musket in hand.' He shook his head sadly. 'That's all they had on him. A witness, I suppose it was Will Burden, telling them that.' Sam spat into the fireplace as he said Burden's name.

All Esther could do was hold him. She slid off her chair to her knees in front of him, and wrapped her arms about him, pulling his head onto her shoulder. If he could cry, she thought, truly cry the way small children did, would it help? Get the feelings out of him rather than bottled up inside like a keg of explosives?

And cry he did. Huge, shuddering sobs, his tears soaking through her shawl and nightgown. He clutched at her as though he was a drowning man and she his rescuer. His body rocked with the effort and she held him tighter still, squeezing him, patting him, stroking his back – anything to take away some of the pain.

At last his sobs subsided and he gently pushed her away. 'We should get some sleep, Blue. The morning will soon be here, and there'll be customers wanting their ale and pies. There's wood to chop and brandy kegs to be brought from the cellar. Work to be done.' He breathed deeply. 'Life to live – for George now, too. I will need to go and tell Hannah Sellars.'

Esther nodded, and with a poker spread the remains of the fire around in the grate. She put the plate and glass he'd used in the kitchen to wash, spread his wet clothes on a chair to finish drying, and folded the blanket she'd wrapped around him. And then she took him by the hand and led him upstairs, to her room with its larger bed. 'Sleep here tonight,' she whispered, 'so I can continue to offer you comfort.'

He stared at her, his mouth a little open, and then nodded. Carefully, silently they made themselves ready for bed and slipped between the sheets. Esther pressed herself against his back, wrapping her arms tightly around him once more. He was not on his own, through this. She was there with him, and she'd stay with him, doing what she could for him.

It wasn't long before his breathing became even and quiet, and she realised he was asleep. She stayed in the same position, not daring to move for fear of waking him. And although she could not sleep herself, knowing she was doing her best for him helped rest her mind, and his presence beside her, where he belonged, soothed her soul.

In the long, dark hours of the night, she made herself a promise. Even if Walker did come back, she would not forsake Sam. Not now, not ever, whatever the cost.

Despite only having a couple of hours' sleep, Sam was up early the next day. 'I have to go to see Hannah. It's only fair. You know he loved her, and she, I believe, was fond of him. In time, who knows, they might have …'

Esther nodded. 'Yes, go. But be back soon. You need more rest.'

She busied herself making a batch of pies and getting the bar ready for the day's trade. The more she did the less she brooded on what had happened to George. She hoped that when Sam returned he would sleep a little more, and then he too might find some solace in physical activity.

He was back before the pub opened for the day. 'Hannah was sad,' he reported, 'but seemed resigned to it. She seems diminished, since the battle. As though she's aged. She's talking about leaving the Haven House. Without John Streeter using it as his base, she's getting less custom, tucked away down there. And all the bad memories it holds …'

'I wouldn't blame her,' Esther replied. 'You've done your duty by telling her. Now go and rest, please. Lie down again upstairs. I am all right here on my own.'

But Sam shook his head. 'I wouldn't sleep, at this time of day.

I'll go and chop that wood for you. Needed doing before I went away, didn't it? I can do it now.' He didn't wait for her to reply, and a few minutes later she heard the rhythmic thwack of the axe as he split a pile of logs.

In the late afternoon, as twilight fell, the door to the bar burst open. To Esther's surprise it was Hannah Sellars who came tumbling in. It was rare for her to visit any other pub. 'Esther! Oh, is Sam here? There's something … something terrible …'

'Mrs Sellars, come in, sit down, please.' Esther hurried out from behind the bar and ushered Hannah through to the kitchen. The few drinkers who were in the pub watched them curiously and she knew they'd all be listening to their conversation. Word of George's hanging had spread quickly around the town, and Esther suspected most men were drinking in other pubs so they could discuss it out of Sam's presence. 'Hannah, what is it?'

'Where's Sam?' the older woman asked again.

Esther opened the back door and gestured to Sam to come in from the yard. 'He's here now. What is it?'

Hannah just sat and stared at Sam for a moment. Her eyes were wide, her expression one of utmost horror. 'Oh, Sam,' she said at last. 'It's awful. They've brought him back. Brought him here, to the Haven.'

'Brought George?'

Hannah nodded. 'In a cage made of iron. And it's hanging from a gibbet they put up. Right outside my pub. Right there, in full view. As a warning to the rest of us.' She covered her face with her hands and wept.

'George hanging? He was hanged in Wapping, I was there!' Sam sat down heavily.

'And now he's hanging outside my pub, at the quay. What's left of him.' Hannah removed her hands from her face and took Sam's. 'It's awful. Horrible to see.'

'I must see.' Sam leaped to his feet, but Esther caught his arm. 'Don't go. At least, don't go on your own.'

Sam looked anguished. 'Blue, it's not for you. But I must … take him down. Give him a proper burial.'

Hannah nodded. 'Yes. We must do that for him. I will help.'

'Thank you.' Sam gave Hannah the ghost of a smile.

'I will help too. I will close the bar and we can go now.' Esther left the kitchen, and ran upstairs to tell Pa what was happening. Maybe Pa would rouse himself to come downstairs.

To her surprise, Pa was sitting up on the edge of his bed. 'I heard something, pet. I heard Hannah Sellars here. She wouldn't leave her pub at this time unless it was something important!'

Esther told him quickly about George's body being displayed at the quay. She and Sam had already told him about the hanging.

Pa pressed his mouth into a fine line and shook his head. 'That's not right. That boy deserves better.' He hauled himself to his feet, leaning on the post at the end of the bed. 'Help me dress, pet, and I'll come to help cut him down.'

'Pa, are you sure?' Esther was worried. Pa was grimacing with pain.

He nodded. 'Time I got moving about again.'

She fetched his clothes, helped him dress and tied his boots. Pa negotiated the stairs with difficulty, grunting with pain at every step. Sam raised his eyebrows to see Pa downstairs but said nothing. He'd already told the remaining customers to drink up and leave, and because they'd heard about George, they had not made a fuss about doing so.

'We'll take the cart, pet,' Pa said as they left the pub. 'To save me walking and to help transport poor George.'

She nodded, and she and Sam went to the yard to prepare Toby and the little cart. The poor pony was surprised at being disturbed but nevertheless he submitted to being strapped into his harness. Sam threw a few tools in the back, and Pa drove the cart while the others walked, a sad, solemn procession down the road.

The scene at Mudeford Quay was one Esther knew she would never forget for as long as she lived. There were only a few local folks there, gazing sadly upon the cage that hung from a hastily erected gibbet just yards from Hannah's pub. A couple were free traders Esther recognised from the beach.

'We've been guarding him,' one of the men said to Sam as he approached. 'We guessed you'd come down here.' The man had his cap pulled down low and a scarf wrapped around his face, but Esther recognised his voice. It was John Streeter. Seeing her eyes widen he gave her a little shake of his head, as if to say, *don't let on it's me.*

Sam stood regarding the cage, and Esther went to be with him, to hold his hand and lend him strength. The cage was made of iron, with a gate fastened with a chain and padlock. Inside, George's body was slumped to one side, the hangman's noose still around his neck and the end of the rope tied to the top of the cage so that his body remained upright. His skin was a horrific grey colour, his cheeks slumped and his jaw hanging slackly open. Although she knew it was George, there was so little there of the vibrant, happy man she'd known.

'Come on. Let's get him down,' Sam said at last, and the men including Streeter stepped forward to help. Esther was glad they were there – it took all of them, herself, Hannah and Pa included, to detach the cage from the gibbet and lay it down. With some difficulty Sam managed to break the lock and then they reverently lifted out George's body and laid it on a blanket Esther had brought from the pub. Hannah straightened his clothes and crossed his hands over his chest.

Sam knelt beside his brother's body, and then gently leaned over and kissed his cheek. 'This shouldn't have happened, George. But we will bury you somewhere quiet so you can rest in peace. It is all I can do for you now, brother.'

Everyone stood back while Sam paid his tribute, and then Pa stepped forward and put a hand on Sam's shoulder. 'We should go, son, before any Revenue men or militia come by.'

Sam nodded, and straightened up. With the help of the other

men they wrapped George's body in the blanket and loaded him onto the back of the cart. The evening was completely dark now, but a crescent moon provided a little light as they worked.

Sam turned to the other men. 'Thank you for your help. I appreciate it.'

'We'll stay here and clear away this gibbet and cage,' one man said. 'You make sure you do right by your brother.'

'Aye. Could have been any one of us,' another fellow put in, and the others grunted and nodded.

The men all doffed their caps and bowed as Pa mounted the cart and clicked his tongue to make Toby move on. Esther, Hannah and Sam followed behind, and Streeter joined them. 'You'll need help digging a grave,' he said to Esther, 'and you might need protection.'

'Are you sure it's safe for you?' she asked him.

'It's not, but it's no less than George deserves.' He shook his head sadly. 'Ah but this is a far cry from the way I like things to be. Back when I was just a schoolboy, being taught in the room upstairs in the Priory, we used to watch smuggled goods being landed in broad daylight over on Hengistbury Head. I always wanted to be a part of it, you know, bringing money into the town, employment for the men, good things at fair prices. I never wanted to bring death. This is wrong, all so wrong.'

Esther blinked back tears as the little procession made its way inland, away from the quay. 'Where will we take him?' she whispered to Sam.

'Somewhere no one will find him,' Sam replied. He spoke to Pa, who nodded to him, and they walked in silence save for the clip of Toby's hooves on the road, for an hour and a half to Sam's house in Burton and then beyond, into a patch of woodland beside a small stream. There, where the cart could go no further, Sam bade Pa stop. 'Here. It's a quiet spot.'

'Unconsecrated ground,' Hannah said, sounding uncertain.

'George was not a churchgoer,' Sam replied. He pulled a couple of spades from the cart and passed one of them to Streeter. They began to dig, while Esther held a lantern aloft and Hannah and Pa kept vigil.

When the hole was a suitable depth they lifted George in the blanket and laid him carefully in the grave. 'Sleep well, brother,' Sam said, as he began to shovel soil back into the grave.

Hannah let out a sob at this, and Esther moved to her side, comforting the older woman. 'No one can hurt him now, Mrs Sellars.'

Hannah leaned against Esther, seemingly unable to speak. The group stood in silence while Sam refilled the grave. When it was done, they spread dead leaves and vegetation over the top until there was no trace of the grave left. Sam took a small knife from his pocket and carved the initials GC in a nearby tree. 'There. The place is marked, but only to we few.'

'A good job,' Streeter said. 'I'll be away, now. You never saw me tonight.'

'Of course. And thank you.' Sam shook his hand and then Streeter melted away into the dark night.

'Mrs Sellars, Esther, hop on up to the cart. Old Toby can manage. You too, Sam,' Pa said.

But Sam shook his head. 'I'll sleep at my own place in Burton tonight. To be near him, and to check all is well in the morning. I'll come down to the Ship later.'

Esther kissed him, and climbed onto the cart with Hannah and Pa. As they left, Sam was still standing over his brother's grave, head bowed, cap in hand.

Chapter 29

Dan Bradshaw's quote arrived the day after he'd looked at the garden, and it was well within my budget, so I phoned him straight away and asked him to start whenever he could. As it turned out he'd just had a cancellation – a garden makeover that had been planned and scheduled in, was delayed due to the homeowner having to go into hospital. 'It's one reason I was able to give you such a reasonable quote,' he said. 'I'll be able to start tomorrow, and I'm happy to work Saturdays as well.'

I loved the idea of getting on with the work quickly so I agreed, and made arrangements to take Friday off so that I could be there for his first day. Thank goodness my job had been so flexible and accommodating.

Dan arrived at eight-thirty, and a mini-digger was delivered shortly after. 'Heavy work first,' he said, 'and be aware it'll all look a lot worse before it starts looking better. This is the scary bit when we start clearing and digging out.'

Before long he had the garden cleared of all unwanted shrubs and weeds, and was getting started on the excavation work. He'd marked the area to be dug out – the approximate route of the tunnel. He was carefully positioning the digger on solid ground off the tunnel route so there was no danger of it falling into the tunnel void or causing a further collapse.

I watched for a while and then went inside, where I had plenty to do unpacking and arranging my kitchen stuff into the new units. It was all coming together – both the house, and, I hoped, my personal life.

Dan stopped for a lunch break. I made him tea and took it out, and stood gazing into the deep hole he'd dug. He'd begun at the end of the garden, away from the dip, and it was clear we'd got the tunnel route right.

'There was about a metre and a half of soil and then I hit the wooden planking that lined the tunnel – see there.' Dan pointed and I could see the remains of rotted wood at the bottom of the trench. 'So now I can backfill that with the spoil already dug, and as I work my way along I'll transfer the spoil backwards. It should work.'

I laughed. 'As long as *you* know what you're doing!'

'Yep, I do.' He grinned.

Soon he resumed the excavation and before long reached the marsh end of the collapsed section. He scooped a couple of bucket-loads and then I spotted something.

'Dan, stop a moment,' I shouted, over the din of the digger's engine. 'There's something …'

'What is it?' He cut the engine and climbed down, looking where I was pointing.

'That white thing. And there's some fabric scraps.' I pointed.

'Something that was in the tunnel under the collapsed roof?'

I had a horrible feeling about this. I lay down on the ground, peering into the trench. I couldn't reach the bottom. Dan passed me a length of bamboo, which I used to prod at the things I'd seen. I managed to hook a piece of the fabric and it came up. There was a brass button attached to it.

'Didn't you say something about having found old clothing in your hidden cellar?' Dan asked.

'Yes. Maybe there was more in the tunnel.' Or maybe … I peered again at the white thing, and gave it an experimental prod. It shifted position in the earth, exposing more of itself. 'Dan, is that a …'

'Bone? Good God. Yes, I think it is.'

'An animal?'

'Maybe. Probably. I hope so. Look, I'll get down there and dig a little more, with a spade, until we know what we've got here.'

He went out to his van and came back wearing a hard hat and carrying a spade. He jumped down into the trench and cautiously began shifting the earth around where we'd found the bone and fabric. More bones rapidly appeared, and more shreds of fabric, under the remains of the wooden tunnel lining. I put a hand over my mouth. I knew what it was we were uncovering here.

Dan stopped digging and turned to me, looking white. 'I think we'd better get the police here. I reckon these are human remains.'

I nodded. That's what I'd thought but hadn't wanted to believe. I gave him a hand up as he climbed out, and then went inside to call the police. Someone must have been trapped in the tunnel when it collapsed. We had no way of knowing when that had happened. Those scraps of fabric and the button must have been part of the poor soul's clothing. Maybe they'd provide some sort of a clue.

The poor police operator was incredulous as I explained what we'd found.

'A smugglers' tunnel? Bones? Goodness me,' she said. 'Well, I'll get someone out to you straight away to take a look.'

We only had to wait about fifteen minutes before a police car turned up. I recognised DS Michaels from his last visit here, when he was investigating Tiffany Coles's murder. I took him through to the garden where Dan was still standing looking shocked beside the trench. We showed him what we'd found and explained how it had come about.

'The other end of the tunnel you found, when Tiffany Coles's body was discovered, is in my cellar. It had collapsed under my garden, and we were digging it out to make it safe and to landscape the garden.' I gestured at the bones. 'I'm wondering if some poor soul was buried there when it collapsed.'

'Hmm, looks that way, doesn't it?' DS Michaels said. 'Do you know roughly when the tunnel collapsed?'

'No. I only moved here a few months ago, and when I bought it there was no mention of the cellar or tunnel. I think it had been out of use for decades or more.'

He wanted to see it, of course – the cellar, the tunnel entrance, the old entrance in the fireplace. I gave him the grand tour and explained how it had all been found.

'Bloody fascinating, all this, isn't it, Mrs Galton?' His eyes were gleaming with excitement. 'I suspect your bones may be very old, centuries perhaps. We'll need to excavate them all and send them away for dating. It's possible, I suppose, that if they're more modern – if the tunnel collapsed in perhaps the last fifty years or so – they might be tied to a missing person case. But if they're a hundred years old or more then there'd be no one left who'd have known the person. In that instance it'll be up to you to dispose of the bones however you see fit, I'm afraid. We can advise. Probably cremation is your best bet, which we can arrange.'

'Oh. All right, so will you just take a bone away with you or how does this work?'

He smiled. 'I'll call in a forensic archaeology team. They'll need to excavate around that area until they're certain they've retrieved the entire skeleton. If indeed it is a whole one. I recall a case when we dug up only body parts.'

For some reason I felt that would be worse. 'And the fabric scraps – you'll want those too?'

He looked at the piece I'd pulled out of the hole, and then leaned close and peered at the button. 'Ah, that's interesting. Unless I am very much mistaken these remains are likely to be at least a couple of centuries old. There's a chap I know – I reckon he'd know what uniform this button is from. He's retired; mind if I give him a call?'

'Are you talking about Arthur Watts?' I asked.

'Yes, that's him! You know him? I know him from the local history society, and we spoke to him about the tunnel entrance in the pool. Expert on all things Christchurch, he is.'

I smiled. 'He certainly is. He's been here a couple of times, telling me about the history of this house and looking at the cellar and tunnel. He was as fascinated by it as you are. Yes, please do call him.'

DS Michaels turned away and made the phone call. 'He'll be here shortly,' he said. Frankly I don't think it'd be possible to keep him away. And the forensic archaeologist team are on their way too.'

The house and garden were full an hour later. A police tent was erected over the trench while a team dug away at the collapsed section, removing all bones. It was quickly confirmed to be a full skeleton, probably male, most likely to have been killed when the tunnel collapsed.

Arthur turned up soon after, looking yet more sprightly than usual. 'Oh, you are such a source of wonderful mysteries, Millie! I am so glad you moved in here and began doing the place up. It's kept me so entertained. Now, let's look at this button Peter Michaels says you found.'

I brought it to him, and he took a close look, pulling a magnifying glass out of a pocket. 'Hmm, yes. Well, this all ties in with your tunnel being used by smugglers.'

'Do you recognise it?' DS Michaels was standing over him, and even Dan had come inside to look. Before Arthur had a chance to answer, the doorbell rang again.

It was Nick. 'I was passing and saw the police vehicles. Millie, what on earth is going on?' He took me in his arms as though relieved to see me safe and well.

I explained quickly. Over his shoulder, across the road, I

could see Sharon standing on her doorstep looking over. She'd be desperate to know what was going on, I knew. But she could wait. She was not a priority. I closed the door behind Nick and went back through to the sitting room where Arthur and the others were.

'It's a button from a Revenue officer's uniform,' Arthur said. 'Dating from the late eighteenth century, unless I am very much mistaken. I shall have to check it, of course.'

'But you're never wrong,' DS Michaels put in, patting the old man's shoulder. 'That's just what I thought it was, on first glance. You've taught me well. If this clothing belonged to the body then the bones are most certainly not of interest to the police, although we will confirm that by carbon-dating them.'

'Oh, I love a bit of carbon-dating, me,' Arthur quipped, and we all laughed. 'You know, I seem to recall a bit of a mystery about a Revenue officer who went missing around the time of the Battle of Mudeford. It was thought he might have got on the wrong side of the smugglers and they'd done away with him. What was his name now … think, man …' He tapped his forehead and stared at the floor. 'Ah, yes. Walker. Thomas Walker. Maybe this is him. Perhaps he's been here all along. Though why he was in the smugglers' tunnel we'll never know.'

'He must have known about the tunnel. Maybe he was one of the officers who were on the take,' I suggested. 'Or maybe not, and they collapsed the tunnel on him on purpose.'

'They wouldn't have done that,' Arthur said. 'It would have been too useful to them. No, I suspect he was using the tunnel as a way to get in or out of the pub unseen. Perhaps to warn them of an imminent raid by less-friendly officers, or something like that. And then the poor bugger was just incredibly unlucky that it collapsed on him right when he was in the middle of it.' He shook his head sadly. 'We'll never know his full story.'

'No. But perhaps we can do something more dignified with his remains.' If they ended up being mine to deal with, I thought

I'd have them cremated and then perhaps scatter the ashes on Stanpit Marsh, around the pool, perhaps. Near where he died, but not somewhere people would walk over him.

'That would be nice,' Arthur said, and Nick put his arm around my waist and gave me a little squeeze. It was noticed by Dan, who grinned and winked at me.

'Well, thank goodness I took the day off and poor Dan didn't have to deal with all this by himself,' I said. 'Right then, cup of tea? How many of us are there?'

DS Michaels did a quick count up. 'Including everyone out there and in here – ten. Hope you've got a big enough pot!'

By the end of Saturday, the police forensic archaeologist team had completed removal of all human remains from my trench. DS Michaels told me he'd be in touch in a few days with news, and my garden – what was left of it – was my own again. Dan was due to come back on Monday to carry on with his work. Arthur had taken photographs of the button and promised to email me within a few days with any further details dating it.

The house felt too quiet on Sunday morning after all the activity. I was singing along to the radio as I made myself break-fast and drank a coffee on my patio with its wonderful view of a mound of earth, a mini-digger and an open trench.

The reason for my good mood was that Nick was due to call in the late morning, and take me out for lunch. A date, our first proper date since all the misunderstandings. The first of very many, I hoped. And for once I didn't feel nervous. It felt right, it felt like a natural progression of events and I was simply looking forward to spending time in his company. The good weather had held, and we had decided to head inland to a pub in the New Forest for lunch, rather than add to the crowds at the beach or quayside restaurants. Lunch, then a walk, was the plan. I'd dressed casually in shorts and a T-shirt and flat walking sandals. Somehow I felt so much more confident in our embryonic relationship that for once I hadn't fretted and dithered about what to wear.

Nick called at eleven-thirty, also wearing shorts and with a baseball cap on his head. He drove us to the pub, where we ate an early lunch of enormous club sandwiches and chips.

'Now we'll need a long walk to work off those calories!' I said, and he laughed.

'Do you realise we'd need to walk hundreds of miles to burn off that lot? Perhaps we'd better get started.'

We left the car at the pub and headed off along a track that took us through a mixture of deciduous woodland and open heath. The heather was in full August bloom, vibrant purple against the azure sky. I spotted a red kite flying high above in the thermals, and a family of rabbits scampered away as we approached.

It was only natural to hold hands, and even more natural to fall into Nick's arms in a secluded area of woodland where we kissed, long and deep.

'I missed you, Millie. I am so glad we have sorted everything out.' He pushed a strand of hair off my face and kissed me again.

'Mmm, I'm glad too.'

'It's been quite an eventful few months, hasn't it? Since that day I came round to give you a quote on the work in your house and helped rescue the kittens from the fireplace. Finding the tunnel and then the bones. The murder of Tiffany Coles. And you thought you'd moved to Mudeford for a quiet life.'

I laughed. 'I know. Maybe things will settle down now.'

'Yes, I expect they will. Actually, there's a piece of news I can tell you now. Remember I said Dad had plans to do something to help the community, after the Tiffany Coles murder?'

'Oh yes?'

'Well, he's got the go-ahead now. He's bought a piece of land and a derelict building over on the other side of Christchurch. He's going to turn it into a support centre for drug addicts or other people in need. There'll be rooms where the homeless can stay for a few nights, offices for counsellors to work from, and a kitchen and dining room. And a garden, laid out as a therapeutic space.'

'Oh my word, that sounds amazing! And is your father paying for all this?'

Nick nodded. 'He's funding the building and set-up costs. And he's establishing a charity that he hopes will bring in enough to finance the running costs. It'll help people from all over Dorset and Hampshire; anyone in need, referred by other institutions or charities. It'll take a good few months to get it all up and running – not least because he's employing my company to do the building work – but he's hoping to be able to open next spring.'

I was stunned. What a thing to do! 'What will the centre be called?' Even as I asked the question, I anticipated the answer.

'The Tiffany Centre.' Nick smiled. 'After both Tiffany Coles and Tiffany Marshall. What else? Will you be my guest at the opening?'

'Of course I will!' It was almost a year away, but I knew without a doubt we'd still be together.

Chapter 30

The winter felt long and hard after George's hanging. The days were cold and icy, and a freezing wind blew from the east for weeks. Sam sold his cottage in Burton and moved in with Esther and Pa permanently. Pa was up and about more now, not doing any heavy work but taking his turn behind the bar serving their customers. He was moving around a little more easily now, his back finally beginning to mend. He appreciated Sam's company and help, Esther realised.

'When you marry,' Pa said to her one day as she took a batch of pies out of the oven, 'you and Sam will take over this pub. I'll move into a little cottage somewhere nearby to give you two space to have a family.'

'Marry! Oh, but Pa, he hasn't asked!'

'But he will, he will,' Pa said, and there was a glint in his eye that made Esther blush, wondering if perhaps Sam had sought Pa's blessing already. She turned away to hide her grin of delight. With no sign of Thomas Walker for many months now they were beginning to feel secure that he was not coming back. Whatever had happened to him was irreversible, they had decided. Maybe he'd simply left the area. Or, a more sinister thought was that maybe he'd fallen foul of a gang of batmen who didn't know he was in the pay of the smugglers. Esther didn't want to dwell on it. He was gone, and she was sorry if he'd been hurt in any way, but his absence left herself and Sam with a chance to rebuild their lives together.

John Streeter's luck ran out a month or so later. He'd been dividing his time between Guernsey, where he felt safe from the authorities, and Christchurch, where he lay low and used disguises when he went out. It was Carter who brought the news to The Ship at Anchor.

'A Revenue cutter caught up with his ship, just off the coast. They demanded to board it, and found a load of tobacco. Streeter was trying to fob them off with some paperwork that said he'd paid customs, but there was something wrong with the dates or the quantities or something. That rogue had been using the same set of paperwork for every import. Anyway, they arrested him and are investigating all his business dealings, as well as his part in last summer's little skirmish.' Carter smacked his lips together. 'Mark my words, this is the end of our Mr Streeter. They'll have him, for this.'

To Sam and Esther's dismay, Carter was proved right. Streeter was imprisoned at Winchester gaol awaiting trial. Things did not look good for him. Smuggling activities in the area ceased completely without Streeter's organisation and finance behind it.

News came that William Arnold from the Board of Customs had widened his investigation into smuggling in Christchurch. Despite the fact that George Coombes had been hanged, John Streeter imprisoned, and the other wanted men such as the captains May and Parrott were nowhere to be found, Arnold was still working hard, gathering evidence. It was the fact that Streeter had been on such good terms with the local Revenue officers, among them Bursey and Walker, and of course their chief, Joshua Jeans, that was concerning him.

'Jeans won't say a word,' Sam told Esther. 'He's too deep in it himself. And he's too senior for Arnold to touch.'

'Unless they have evidence,' Esther replied. She was thinking of James Noyce, the one riding officer whom the free traders had never been able to corrupt.

As the year wore on and spring came again, it seemed that Arnold had indeed managed to gather sufficient evidence. Bursey and Jeans were charged with corruption and lost their jobs. New Revenue officers were brought in; all were men from out of town with no connections to anyone in Christchurch.

'They won't turn a blind eye like Jeans and his men did,' Sam said. 'It feels as though a golden era of free trading is over. Our lives will be very different now.' He turned to Esther, and then as though on a whim pulled her into a quiet corner of the bar. 'How about we change our lives even more, in another way? How about we wed? What do you say?'

Oblivious to the other people in the pub, Esther flung her arms around Sam and kissed him soundly. 'Oh, Sam. I thought you'd never ask!'

'Well? What's your answer?' he said, but his grin showed he anticipated a positive response.

'It's a yes, of course!'

As she said this, a cheer erupted behind them. Pa was behind the bar polishing some glasses and grinning broadly at them, and the other drinkers raised their glasses to toast the newly engaged couple.

'You were always my safe haven, my port in a storm,' Sam whispered to her. 'My storm girl.'

She smiled at the new nickname, and kissed him, long and deep, oblivious to the laughter and cheers from all around them.

A couple of weeks later, John Streeter's fortunes took a turn for the better. 'I suspect a sum of money changed hands,' Sam said, when he brought the news that Streeter had escaped from prison. 'Seems like the Winchester gaoler didn't see the point of prosecuting and imprisoning people for handling contraband, since so many people do it, and all those who don't still benefit from the cheaper goods. So Streeter was put in the least secure part of the prison, and left for periods with no watch. He's out, and the word is he's gone back to Guernsey.'

Esther smiled. Streeter might have broken the law countless times, but he was a good man on the whole, and his actions had brought wealth to many people in the town. She guessed he'd find a way to continue his activities, perhaps on a smaller scale, even from exile.

She was right. It wasn't long before the free traders were passing on news of another run. Sam helped with the unloading although Esther stayed at the pub and met Sam in the dead of night at the front entrance. From there they carried the goods inside and down to the secret cellar. It felt good to have a stock of fine spirits and tobacco down there once more.

'George would be pleased to see we're not giving up,' Sam said, as they stacked the last few kegs. 'I'm doing this for him. I'm sad he won't see us wed, though. He'd been on at me for ages to ask you to wed me, and do it properly. I was about to, when I heard about Thomas Walker's interest in you.'

'Well, that's all in the past now,' Esther said. 'And we will be married in just a few days.'

It was rumoured, although Esther didn't know whether it was true or not, that the Priory Church in Christchurch was the largest parish church in the entire country. Esther had grown up attending services there, although she didn't go every week. She'd dreamed of having her wedding there, and now her dreams were about to come true!

They married in mid-June, on a bright, cloudless day. Pa decorated the pony cart, including tying ribbons in Toby's mane, and proudly drove her into town. Esther was dressed in a new gown she'd had made in a pale yellow silk. Smuggled fabric, of course, and for all she knew it might have been one of the pieces Lovey Warne had wound around her midriff on that day a year before when James Noyce had so nearly caught her.

As she walked down the aisle on Pa's arm, towards a grinning Sam, Esther couldn't help but wonder how much contraband was stored in the tunnels that were rumoured to be beneath their feet.

The service passed in a blur of smiles and emotion, and then the Reverend Jackson was bidding Sam kiss his bride. They walked back down the aisle and out into the bright sunshine of the churchyard, where what seemed like half the people of town had gathered. Esther laughed as they were showered with rose petals. Standing a little back from the crowd was one rather large woman, with a heavy veil over her face. Esther caught the woman's eye and she winked through the veil.

'John Streeter's here,' Esther whispered to Sam, nodding towards the veiled woman.

But Sam's attention was taken by Hannah Sellars who'd pushed through the crowds to offer her congratulations, and Carter who stood nearby with a number of other free traders, clapping and grinning. Lovey Warne was also there, with her brothers, and it was she who caught the posy of flowers when Esther threw it. And Pa stood proudly to one side, leaning on a stick but getting stronger by the day.

As she watched Pa, a tall, bearded man in a sailor's uniform approached him, taking his cap off as he did so. For a moment Esther didn't recognise him, but then her Pa threw his arms around the man, weeping, and Esther realised who it was.

'Matthew!' she gasped, and Sam followed her gaze. 'It's Matthew, my own brother, back home again at last!' She ran to him and fell into his arms.

'Esther! I've arrived home just in time, I see. Who've you married? Not young Sam Coombes, is it? Took your time!' Matthew grinned as Sam clapped his shoulder.

'I got her to agree to wed me at last, Matthew,' Sam said. 'But it's been a bit of a long story. Are you home for good?'

Matthew shook his head. 'Just a week or two. I like the life at sea, and although I've done my time and could come home, I've now been offered a promotion. I'll go as an officer on the next voyage. I'm going to assume you'll be taking on the pub along with Esther when Pa gets too old?'

'They're taking it on right away,' Luke Harris said, and Matthew nodded.

'Good. Glad to hear it'll be in good hands. So, what's been happening here while I've been away? Anything exciting?'

'You could say that,' Sam replied. 'We'll catch up back at The Ship at Anchor.'

Esther held tight to her new husband's arm as the whole wedding party walked the familiar route from the Priory through town, over the bridge and across the marsh to Stanpit. She was grinning so much that her cheeks were beginning to ache as she looked around at these people, her friends, her family and her customers, her community. They'd lost George, but they had a future together with their friends around them to support and help them.

'All right, Mrs Coombes?' Sam turned to her, smiling.

'Very much all right,' she replied, as yet another handful of rose petals fluttered down over them.

Chapter 31

It was hard to believe it had been a year since I moved into my house on Stanpit. A year that started with much upheaval but that now had settled into a joyful, happy life. All work on the house and garden had been completed, and I was looking forward to a summer of watching the plants Dan had put in my garden establish themselves and flourish. My little pond was stocked with aquatic plants and I was delighted that it had already accommodated a generation of tadpoles, which I'd enjoyed monitoring as they developed limbs and eventually climbed out to make their own way in the world.

My house was fully furnished now, and I was really proud of the way it looked. The old, oversized fireplace was now a beautiful inglenook, with a large vase containing dried grasses and reeds standing in it. My huge squishy sofa stood on the replaced wooden floor, angled towards the patio doors looking across the garden. It faced west, and I'd watched some glorious sunsets from that spot throughout the year.

Arwen had been a frequent visitor, and Steve with his new girlfriend Amanda had also visited a couple of times. Arthur, too, came every fortnight for a cup of tea and slice of cake, and a chat about local history. He was Mir's favourite visitor, and whenever he came she would jump onto his lap for a cuddle at the first opportunity.

'I reckon she can smell Henry on you,' I said. Arthur had been overjoyed to home one of the kittens when I'd tentatively suggested it last September.

I didn't see much of Sharon. We always had a brief chat if we bumped into each other on the street, but that was as far as it went, although I'd babysat for her and Brian once or twice. Another kitten, now called Tigger, lived happily across the road with her, and Jasper and Tabitha had proved to be great cat-owners.

The third kitten, a female, I'd kept as company for Mir. I'd named her Sal, and she was a dozy, skittish little thing I'd grown to love dearly.

Nick spent most of his time at mine, these days. He hadn't actually moved in though. We'd talked about it, and decided that for now we wanted to still keep our own spaces – although for him, his own space was that suite of rooms at his dad's house. 'You've had so little time living on your own, Millie,' he'd said. 'You went straight from your parents' home to living with Steve. You should enjoy the freedom that comes with your own place for a little longer, before we make things permanent.' I'd agreed, but was thrilled at the assumption that we *would* make things permanent, in time. I'd fallen deeply in love with him, a grown-up, mature love, and I knew I wanted him in my life for ever.

The excitement of finding the tunnel and human remains buried in it all seemed so long ago now. The forensic archae-ologists had confirmed the bones were over two hundred years old, and therefore of no interest to the police. They'd had them cremated and returned the ashes to me. Arthur was convinced it was Thomas Walker who'd been buried in the tunnel, and he, Nick and I had held a little memorial service for him, just the three of us, as we scattered his ashes around the pool where Tiffany Coles's body had been found. I hoped he was at peace now.

He'd been a victim, in a way, of the smuggling trade, just as Nick's sister Tiffany had been.

I checked my watch, then wandered through to the kitchen to make myself a cup of coffee. Nick had not spent the night with me last night, as he'd wanted to be on hand to help Des prepare for the big day. I was dressed ready for the occasion, in a dress and jacket and a pair of medium heels. Nick was due to pick me up in twenty minutes. Just enough time to sit and admire my garden while drinking my coffee. Life was good.

Nick arrived on time, as he always did. He was holding a large, rectangular parcel wrapped in stylish gift paper.

'You got me a present?' I said, in surprise.

'No. This was on your doorstep. There's a card stuck to it, look.'

I pulled off the card and opened it first. To my astonishment it was from Sharon. 'Saw this, and thought of you. Call it a peace offering and apology. Hope to see you later, Sharon,' I read.

Nick raised his eyebrows. 'Open it, then. Feels like a framed picture or similar.'

I grimaced a little, imagining Sharon's taste in pictures would not coincide with mine at all. She went for bright coloured abstract art, which wouldn't work at all in my house. But when I tore off the wrapping paper I found something entirely different.

It was a woodcut print in black and white, in an antique frame. It showed a ship, that to my mind looked like a smugglers' ship, anchored just off a beach, on which men were stacking barrels. A half moon lit the scene, with clouds scudding across. The picture's title was printed beneath, on the mounting card: *The Ship at Anchor.*

'Oh my word,' I said, grinning. 'This is so perfect. It'll look just right above the fireplace, don't you think?'

'Absolutely. It's lovely. We'd better get going now, but I'll hang it for you as soon as we get back,' Nick said. I propped the picture up on my sofa and stood gazing at it for a moment, before Nick cleared his throat to remind me we needed to hurry.

There was a huge crowd gathered outside the Tiffany Centre. Des had organised lots of local businesses and charities to come and set up stalls to provide a village fair atmosphere. The gardens had been landscaped by Dan and the building itself renovated and extended by Nick's company. It was looking fantastic. Although today was the official opening, it had already helped several local people struggling with drug addiction begin their rehabilitation and one had agreed to make a speech today.

Nick pulled me forward, through the crowd. 'Let's be up at the front. In case Dad does something embarrassing like call me up to the platform.'

I followed him to the little stage that had been erected in front of the main door to the building. It all looked so smart. The building had been rendered and whitewashed, and plantation shutters installed in the windows. The door was made of oak, recycled from an older property that had been demolished. Nick had tried to reuse old materials where he could, 'mainly to keep Dad's costs down,' he'd told me.

Everyone was milling around drinking glasses of soft drinks. Des had decided on a no-alcohol policy, as some of the people the centre was designed to support were recovering alcoholics. I saw Dan and waved at him, and I also glimpsed Arthur too, chatting to the mayor, who'd be declaring the centre open after the speeches. I spotted Sharon in the crowd with her family, which surprised me. After all her prejudices against the Marshall family I had not expected her to attend this event, even though there'd been an open invitation to every household in town. Des had wanted it to be a community event.

Sharon made her way over to Nick and me. As she approached, Nick touched my elbow and muttered in my ear. 'Just going to see if Dad needs anything done, see you in a bit.' I nodded, and turned to greet Sharon.

'Sharon, thank you so much for that picture. It's simply perfect.'

'You like it? It's not my kind of thing but … it made me think of you and your house. Smugglers on the beach and all that.'

'Yes. I absolutely love it, Sharon, thank you.'

She blushed, and looked pleased that she'd got it right. 'Quite something, isn't it?' she said, nodding towards the Tiffany Centre.

'It certainly is.'

'He's done well, that Des Marshall, setting this up.'

'Definitely.'

Sharon put a hand on my arm and turned to face me. 'Millie, I do mean it. I was wrong about him, and about his son. I can't believe I tried to turn you against Nick, but at the time it seemed the right thing to do. The evidence seemed stacked against them and I didn't want you caught up in it all. I'm so sorry. Look at all the good Des Marshall has done here, look at all the money he's donated for the good of the community. I'm honestly … so sorry I ever doubted him. And you, with Nick – you're looking so relaxed and happy these days. He's obviously good for you and I am genuinely, honestly, happy for you. Do you believe me? Can you forgive me? It's what I meant on the note about the picture being a peace offering.'

I smiled at her. 'Of course I forgive you, Sharon. It's all right, really. There was no need for a peace offering but I'm glad you got me the picture, because I adore it.' I gave her a little hug, and she hugged me back.

'Oh good. I'm so glad we're friends.' She sounded a little emotional.

'And yes, I do think Nick's good for me, and you are right that Des has been amazing in setting this up,' I added. 'Oh, here we go. It's time for the speeches and the official opening.'

We let go of each other and turned towards the little platform, where Des had stepped up and was fiddling with the microphone stand. He was smartly turned out and looked very pleased with the way things were going. Nick, I noticed, was standing beside the stage. I caught his eye and he gave a little shrug and a glance at his father, so I guessed he was indeed expected to go up there at some point.

I stood with Sharon for the speeches, which were the usual mix of thanks to all who'd helped, pride in what had been achieved, and good wishes for the future. Nick was called up for a hearty handshake and then a hug from his father. 'He would only take payment at half his normal rates, this lad,' Des said. 'He'd have done it for even less but as he said, he had to pay his lads. Anyone needing a builder – keep Marshall Construction in mind and you won't go wrong.'

Des spoke for a while about Tiffany Coles, whose murder had inspired him to set up the centre. 'I'd like to think that anyone in her situation, who wants to be helped, can now be helped, here, in the community and by the community. I'd like to think she might have come here, if it had existed, and that could have saved her from her fate.' He looked down at his feet for a moment, and I guessed he was thinking of his own daughter Tiffany, who might also have found such a centre beneficial.

At last, with all the speeches over and several bouquets handed out Des passed a giant pair of scissors to the mayor and asked her to cut the ribbon that was tied across the main entrance. She did so, with the words, 'I now declare the Tiffany Centre open for business' and there was a huge cheer from the crowd.

Nick had come back to my side. 'Well, there we are, then. The centre's open, my dad's a hero and all's well with the world.'

I hugged him. 'You're a hero too, for your part in renovating this building at minimal cost.'

He smiled. 'Well, let's hope no one in the town ever feels the need to get involved in drug smuggling to feed their habit, from now on. This town's seen enough of smuggling over the years.'

'It certainly has. But what a history it's given the town. And now thanks to you and your dad you are helping the community have a bright future.'

He squeezed me closer. 'As do we, Millie, I hope.' And I leaned my head on his shoulder and felt happier than at any time in my life to date. A bright future indeed awaited us.

A Letter from Kathleen McGurl

Thank you so much for choosing to read *The Storm Girl*. I hope you enjoyed it! If you did and would like to be the first to know about my new releases, click below to sign up to my mailing list.

Sign up here: https://bit.ly/KathMcGurlSignUp

This was a fun book to research and write, as it was set in the area where I live. I could simply walk down the road to Mudeford Quay and gaze across the harbour to where the battle took place. I found myself walking around with half my head in the past, in my book. It's a lovely part of the world, and I am lucky to live there.

I hope you loved *The Storm Girl* and if you did, I would be so grateful if you would leave a review. I always love to hear what readers thought, and it helps new readers discover my books too.

Thanks,
Kathleen

Website: https://kathleenmcgurl.com/
Twitter: https://twitter.com/KathMcGurl
Facebook: https://www.facebook.com/KathleenMcGurl

Historical Note

I only realised the extent to which smuggling had been a way of life in Christchurch when I moved to Mudeford in December 2020. There's an information board at Mudeford Quay that gives an outline of the Battle of Mudeford of 1784. It wasn't long after moving here before I had the idea to write a novel based around those events. My local library, even during the pandemic lockdowns, was incredibly helpful searching out local history books that covered smuggling, and putting them aside for me. (Mudeford, by the way, is pronounced Muddy-fud, although the little river Mude is pronounced to rhyme with 'nude'.)

Smuggling was rife all along the south coast of England in the eighteenth century because of the ridiculously high duties payable on certain goods. For instance, excise duties on tea were set at 120 per cent. This was drastically reduced in 1784, which effectively ended the smugglers' trade in tea.

In 1799 income tax was introduced, and from then on customs duties were no longer the main source of government income. Between 1784 and 1789 rates of duty were halved – this all helped cause the trade to decline. However, smuggling in Christchurch continued until the mid-nineteenth century before finally petering out. At its height it is thought that well over half the inhabitants of the town were involved with smuggling one way or another.

All locations mentioned in the book are real and still exist, with the exception of The Ship at Anchor. This is a fictitious pub, which in my mind is situated more or less where the Girl Guide hut on Stanpit is now, beside Tutton's Well, backing onto the reed beds at the edge of Stanpit Marsh. The Tiffany Centre is also fictitious.

Almost all the historical characters are also real. The exceptions are the Harris family, Sam Coombes, Thomas Walker, and Carter. The others are real, and their part in the events around the Battle of Mudeford and its aftermath are derived from my research. I've used a novelist's licence here and there, which I hope any readers knowledgeable about the area and its history will forgive.

The lovely thing about using real people and places in a novel is that I'm able to tell you what became of them, after the time period in which the novel is set.

The Haven House Inn was taken over by the Revenue service in 1823 and used as a coastguard station – a wonderful example of 'poacher turned gamekeeper'. A new pub was built just beside it, also called Haven House Inn. The original building is now privately owned. The 'new' Haven House Inn still exists and is a fabulous place for summer evening drinks watching the sunset over the waters of the harbour.

Hannah Sellars moved out of the Haven House not long after the battle, and took over The Ship in Distress pub on Stanpit. This is just a short way further up the road from my fictitious pub. Hannah continued to be a friend to the smugglers. There's a channel through the marsh that bears the name 'Mother Sillar's Channel' (her name was variously spelt) and rumour has it that it once went all the way to the back of The Ship in Distress and was used to bring in contraband. This pub still exists and is my local.

John Streeter managed to continue running his smuggling operations from Guernsey, with his wife in Christchurch overseeing his legitimate businesses. He would occasionally visit to make sure all was well, often in disguise, and fathered a number of children on his sporadic visits. During the Napoleonic wars when Britain was at risk of invasion from France, there were no recorded acts of smuggling and in 1804 a general amnesty was offered to smugglers, with all outstanding arrest warrants quashed. At this point John Streeter returned openly to Christchurch to rebuild his life. He died in 1824 aged 74 in the house he owned next door to The Ship in Distress.

Joshua Jeans lost all respect in the town in the aftermath of the battle, and died a broken man in 1786 not long after his dismissal from the Revenue service. It's not known what became of his fellow officers including Bursey and Noyce.

It's also not known what happened to the captains May and Parrott. It's almost certain that May fired the fatal shot in the battle, but he managed to avoid capture for all the years that there was an outstanding warrant for his arrest.

William Arnold, the Revenue service collector based in Cowes on the Isle of Wight, remained in service until his death in 1801 aged 55. He was deeply respected by his employers, colleagues and even his enemies. He remained totally incorruptible.

The naval ship *Orestes* saw active service in various parts of the world, until 1799 when she was overwhelmed by a hurricane in the East Indies and sank with the loss of all hands. The Scout hut on Stanpit, beside the car park used by visitors to the Stanpit Marsh and nature reserve, is named after her.

Will Burden, whose testimony was so devastating for the Christchurch free traders and especially for George Coombes, was never seen again.

Some of the minor events from Chapter 4 took place at different periods – I've used a novelist's licence to include them in this book; for instance the part about Dr Quartley's abduction by the smugglers to treat one of their gang – this actually occurred in the nineteenth century. Quartley's house by the bridge in Christchurch still stands and is marked with a brass nameplate, and there's a memorial to him in the Priory Church. There's also a locally made craft beer named after him, which seems apt.

Lovey Warne's close shave when a Revenue man chatted her up and almost discovered the contraband silks wrapped around her middle also happened at another time, but it was too wonderful a story not to include here. The Eight Bells near the Priory where this event happened still stands, but is now a quirky little gift shop. Lovey's protective brothers forbade her ever taking such an active role again. She still played her part, however – walking on a hill in the New Forest wearing a bright red cape if Revenue men were in the area. If the free traders spotted her, they'd know to take their goods inland by a different route.

The George Inn is now known as Ye Olde George Inn. My son worked there for a while, and tells me despite the rumours he could find no evidence of secret tunnels leading from its cellars to the Priory Church. I suspect he simply didn't look hard enough.

The Red House Museum in Christchurch is well worth a visit, though there's not actually much about smuggling in it.

William Allen's grave can still be seen in the churchyard of St Mary's, in Cowes.

George Coombes's body was displayed at Mudeford Quay, taken down and reburied by his friends, as described in my novel. His final resting place is not known, but I hope it is somewhere peaceful.

The Girl from Bletchley Park

Will love lead her to a devastating choice?

1942. Three years into the war, Pam turns down her hard-won place at Oxford University to become a codebreaker at Bletchley Park. There, she meets two young men, both keen to impress her, and Pam finds herself falling hard for one of them. But as the country's future becomes more uncertain by the day, a tragic turn of events casts doubt on her choice – and Pam's loyalty is pushed to its limits...

Present day. Julia is struggling to juggle her career, two children and a husband increasingly jealous of her success. Her brother presents her with the perfect distraction: forgotten photos of their grandmother as a young woman at Bletchley Park. Why did her grandmother never speak of her time there? The search for answers leads Julia to an incredible tale of betrayal and bravery – one that inspires some huge decisions of her own...

Gripping historical fiction perfect for fans of *The Girl from Berlin*, *The Rose Code* and *When We Were Brave*.

The Forgotten Secret

Can she unlock the mysteries of the past?

A country at war

It's the summer of 1919 and Ellen O'Brien has her whole life
ahead of her. Young, in love and leaving home for her first job,
the future seems full of shining possibility. But war is brewing
and before long, Ellen and everyone around her are swept up
by it. As Ireland is torn apart by the turmoil, Ellen finds
herself facing the ultimate test of love and loyalty.

A long-buried secret

A hundred years later and Clare Farrell has inherited a
dilapidated old farmhouse in County Meath. Seizing the
chance to escape her unhappy marriage she strikes out on
her own for the first time, hoping the old building might also
provide clues to her family's shadowy history. As she sets out
to put the place – and herself – back to rights, she stumbles
across a long-forgotten hiding place, with a clue to a
secret that has lain buried for decades.

**For fans of Kate Morton and Gill Paul comes an
unforgettable novel about two women fighting for
independence.**

The Secret of the Château

Everything is about to change…

1789. Pierre and Catherine Aubert, the Comte and Comtesse de Verais, have fled the palace of Versailles for their château, deep in the French Alps. But as revolution spreads through the country, even hidden away the Auberts will not be safe forever. Soon they must make a terrible decision in order to protect themselves, and their children, from harm.

Present day. When Lu's mother dies leaving her heartbroken, the chance to move to a château in the south of France with her husband and best friends seems an opportunity for a new beginning. But Lu can't resist digging into their new home's history, and when she stumbles across the unexplained disappearance of Catherine Aubert, the château begins to reveal its secrets – and a mystery unsolved for centuries is uncovered…

Unlock the secret of the château today. Perfect for fans of Kate Morton, Fiona Valpy and *The Forgotten Village*!

Acknowledgements

For this book, I firstly need to thank someone I don't know – Mike Powell, author of the little booklet *1784: The Battle of Mudeford*. This book, which I managed to get hold of from our local library, was absolutely invaluable in helping me tell the tale of smuggling in Christchurch and the skirmish between the Revenue ships and smugglers. It's wonderfully researched from primary sources and puts the lead-up to the battle into context, as well as describing in detail the events of that night and their consequences. Thank you, Mike. Your book is out of print but if ever I come across a copy to buy, I will snap it up, even though I've read it cover to cover several times.

Secondly, I must thank the staff at Christchurch Library who dug out Mike's book as well as several others on local history and smuggling in Hampshire and Dorset, and put them aside for me to collect. This was during lockdown when the library was not open to the public. Many thanks to them, and all other librarians who kept the country supplied with books during a difficult period.

Huge thanks are due to my editor Abigail Fenton, whose insightful comments really helped make this book the best it could be. Thanks, Abi. I love working on books with you!

Thanks also to all the team at HQ – copy editors, proofreaders, cover designers and marketing team. All do a wonderful job. I still find it hard to believe I make my living from writing, but I do, and it's in no small way helped by the team at HQ. Thank you all.

As always my husband was immensely supportive throughout the writing process. I disappear into my writing cave and he just calls me out when dinner's ready. Thank you, Ignatius!

Our sons were living with us during the lockdown while I was writing this book, and I bounced several ideas off them while we went for many walks in the locations described in the novel. Thank you, Fionn and Connor. Special thanks to Connor who came up with the idea of a cat in a bricked-up fireplace; that was the starting point for the book.

Finally thank you to all my readers. It'd all be a bit pointless without you. Thanks for buying my books, and I hope you continue to enjoy them!

KATHLEEN MCGURL lives in Christchurch with her husband. She has two sons who have both now left home. She always wanted to write, and for many years was waiting until she had the time. Eventually she came to the bitter realisation that no one would pay her for a year off work to write a book, so she sat down and started to write one anyway. Since then she has published several novels with HQ and self-published another. She has also sold dozens of short stories to women's magazines, and written three How To books for writers. After a long career in the IT industry she became a full-time writer in 2019. When she's not writing, she's often out running, slowly.

Also by Kathleen McGurl

The Emerald Comb
The Pearl Locket
The Daughters of Red Hill Hall
The Girl from Ballymor
The Drowned Village
The Forgotten Secret
The Stationmaster's Daughter
The Secret of the Château
The Forgotten Gift
The Lost Sister
The Girl from Bletchley Park

Praise for Kathleen McGurl

A MUST READ in my book!!'

'Utterly perfect . . . A timeslip tale that leaves you wanting more . . . I loved it'

'I may have shed a tear or two! . . . A definite emotional roller coaster of a read that will make you both cry and smile'

'Oh my goodness . . . The pages turned increasingly quickly as my desperation to find out what happened steadily grew and grew'

'Very special . . . I loved every minute of it'

'Brilliant . . . Very highly recommended!!'

'Touched my heart! A real page-turner . . . The perfect read for cosying up. I can't recommend this gorgeous book enough'